ALSO BY M. THOMAS COOPER

42

Tongue, Tied and Other Short Plays

CRUSHED

M. THOMAS COOPER

EMPTY C PUBLISHING

Mcminnville, Oregon, USA

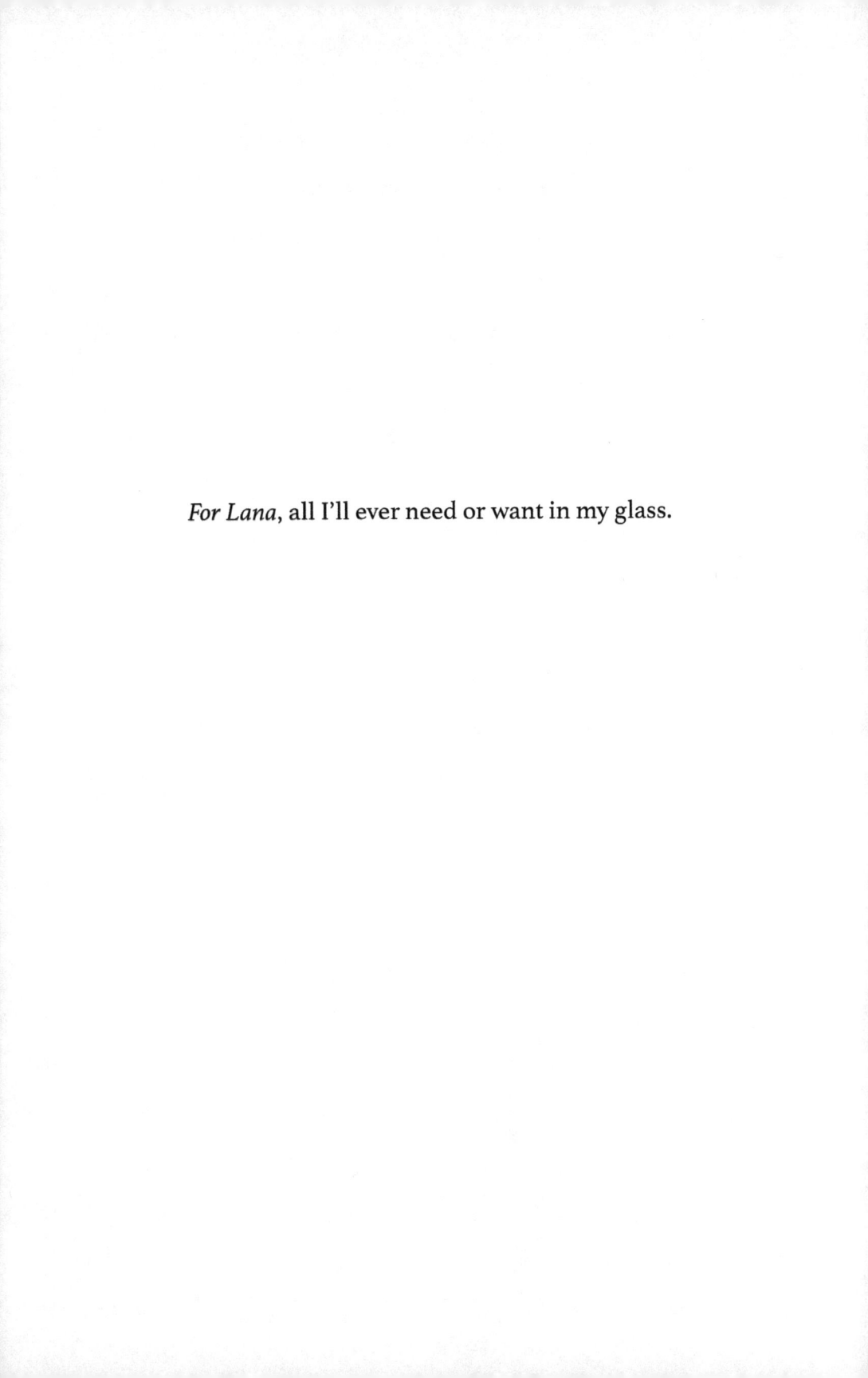

For Lana, all I'll ever need or want in my glass.

Chapter One
THE OASIS

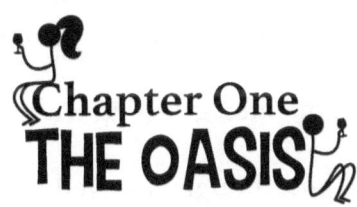

The angry, first chords of Blutnacht's thrash metal rendition of "Dani California" rumbled my earbuds when Claudette, nudging a shin, startled me.

"Hey, sweetheart," I greeted, slumping from beneath the wine-weighted, leather satchel, "how you doin'?"

The one-eyed, stray tabby gave another nudge. Oh, I knew what she wanted. She ever only wanted one thing. Nudge. Nudge.

"I love you, too, but you need to wait. Daddy's got work to do."

Pulling the four bottles from the satchel, I placed them along the back of the bench. Each was wrapped in a plastic grocery bag that, skin from a shedding snake, squirmed under my excited palms.

The bench was a sun-bleached green, cracked-wood thing. Gouged and tattooed with graffiti, it squatted behind a wall of rhododendrons in a shadowy corner of Parc Montsouris.

The bottles and bench were a comforting ritual, a secluded Parisian oasis for focusing, for attuning my palate before a competition. And if foul weather were the cast of the die, I'd sip disillusioned in Art's Wine Emporium, lamenting fate's fickleness.

Thankfully, as the old men had observed from their cafe chairs, it was *"un jour du genou"* and moon-pale knees, in plethora, had blossomed beneath newly freed, spring skirts.

Sitting, I admired Hakim's work. Years ago, when I'd explained to the thin-limbed, counter kid, "I want the bottles wrapped for anonymity's sake," his efforts had been flouncy as a babushka's bloomers. But now? They were tight and trim, a bodybuilder in a Savile Row suit.

As per usual, he'd replaced their original corks and stuffed the replacements in halfway. The lad had indeed earned the extra twenty.

The issue, however, with such trimness, based on the bottle's shape, it narrowed the scope of what it likely held. How practical was it to exchange frozen pizza boxes for the grocery bags? I'd ask. Maybe add a tenner to the twenty?

I rubbed my palms dry and, grinning with anticipation, pulled cork on the first bottle.

It gave a satisfying *pop*, though annoyed poor kitty.

Abandoning my ankles, she slunk from under the bench and extended a quivering paw toward the satchel.

"Yes, sweetheart," I assured her, popping the second, "everything's there. It's all planned."

She *meowed*, unconvinced.

Moving to number three, I countered her accusation. "You've never met Katrina. You don't know that. And just because she owns a dog doesn't make her evil." Pulling cork on the last bottle, I noted, "The dog is evil, not her."

And the dog, Vlad, was evil. Besides being a snotty, teacup Brussels griffon, Katrina, my soon-to-be fiancée, claimed he had half a million followers for his show, *Glad Vlad's Humpty Dumpty Circus*.

I, having a modicum of taste, had never succumbed to watching it.

The revenues garnered from the show were how she, while attending culinary school full-time, afforded the luxurious, top-floor, two-bedroom in the 8th. I wasn't so much jealous as annoyed.

Claudette pawed at the satchel.

"I told you, it's all there. Trust me. Okay?"

She—*meow*—remained unconvinced.

"Sweetheart, I went through it a dozen times last night. Twice this morning."

She, eye cast to the dubious shadows beneath the bench, raised an accusatory paw.

"Damn it." Lego in a sausage, I extracted Dr. Stanton Albright's hefty tome, *The Medieval Diet: A Pilgrimage of Plague and Plenty*.

Claudette perked up. She leaned and sniffed at the tome's yellowed pages.

Snatching the gold envelope paper clipped to the title page, I removed the enclosed evidence and brandished it about, "Tickets to Athens. Reservations for a seven-night stay at a caldera-view bungalow on Santorini. And the *pièce de résistance*?" I tapped the gilt embossed, mauve menu card, "Dinner at the most exclusive pop-up restaurant in Paris, Chez Shea."

Claudette, aloof and pragmatic kitty that she was, desired something more practical than love tokens—the *jambon beurre*. And the mention of Chez Shea had only aggravated her hunger.

She gave another plaintive *meow*.

"Chez Shea," I extolled. "Chez Shea."

Meow. Meow.

Resigned, I invited, "Fine. Get up here." I patted the gouged proclamation SP + MC = LUV and added, "I need something, too. Those three double espressos are broiling my belly."

The caffeine had compounded my morning's anxiety and had ushered me into making the first mistake of my day—abandoning Katrina at my derelict one-bedroom in the 16th.

Claudette hopped up and meowed more.

Envelope returned, I wrestled Dr. Albright's uncooperative tome back into the satchel and extracted the sandwich. The bag crackled sharply as I unsheathed a length. And she, a skinny, furry shark, circled, purring with anticipation.

Plucking a hefty lump of butter out, she scampered over and greedily sandpapered my fingers with her tongue.

Immediately, the nub was flicked off and *thunked* onto my lap.

"Son of a cosmonaut," I swore as she, before I could stop her or snatch the butter, dropped her head and licked ravenously at it.

I grimaced as her claws dug into my hip and thigh.

Familiar with her wrath, I knew removing her would be problematic. Besides, regarding the buttery stain, she was doing more good than harm. And her purring and biscuit-making, regardless my uninvited arousal, did great good for soothing my apprehension.

Blutnacht's thrashing transitioned to Dude Dingo's didgeridoo-laden "Summer Wine" and I placed the first bottle to my lips.

A bold uppercut of under ripe Bing cherry assaulted me. It, a heavyset Flamenco dancer in hobnailed jackboots, staggered around my mouth. The cherry tired, relinquished the stage to dark leather, dirty shale, and a powder keg of tannins. There were, after the initial brutal assault, a few more nuances to the tincture, but none that deserved assessing.

I spat the "wine" into the rhododendrons and received a startled *hiss* from Claudette.

"Yes, yes, I know. I know. But Hakim has created something distinctly—" I took another sip, properly slurped, and spat. Once the tart tang of green raspberries and burnt chocolate dissipated, I concluded, "Sinister."

Hakim had finally accepted my challenge: "Do what you will, though nothing illegal or lethal."

However, Crushed being Crushed, I hadn't disclosed the rationale for my request. There were, as the bylaws specifically stated, repercussions for "loose lips."

Speaking of blathering more than one should... On the other side of the obscuring rhododendron, a group of giggling girls had gathered and were inanely chattering about football, soccer, or whatever one called the ridiculous game.

Wanting to commend Hakim, particularly after years of waiting, I extracted my phone, paused Dude Dingo, and called him.

Annoyed by the girls, I jumped in as someone picked up. "Hakim, my friend, thank you for the elixir. It was a magnificently twisted mélange."

Before I rattled off the varietals and the other various ingredients, a cold hand of insight squeezed my heart. Perhaps one of his parents had taken over at the register? Burak and Tuba, each in their own right, were formidable accusers regarding me leading their son astray.

"Hakim?"

"Hello, infidel."

It was worse. It was the beautiful harpy, Beren, his sister.

Thankfully, though I didn't think coincidentally, my phone buzzed. I laughed at the ID, Dildo.

Claudette, suspending her work, raised her eye.

"Radcliffe," I explained, "that bloody reporter from *The Times*."

Avery Radcliffe, intrepid reporter extraordinaire, had been hounding me, Baskerville style, for the past week.

"My apologies, Beren—"

"Infidel, you know I have told you—"

"But I've another call."

"If you—"

Hakim's elixir had woken my "tasting persona" and, usually loath to offend, I did what must be done—I hung up and answered. I repeated the opening line I'd used the last three times he'd called. "What do you want?"

Radcliffe did the same. "Just a few questions regarding the five-year anniversary of *The Yank*."

My first and only novel, *The Yank*, had been greeted with lukewarm reviews and negligible fanfare. It was why I'd abandoned literature for comedy.

"Honestly, I don't think it deserves it." No one did. "Do you?"

"Wouldn't be doing a story on it if I didn't think it did."

"Really?"

"Really."

Rather than confront Radcliffe's lie or hang up, as I'd done before, I informed, "I need to talk with my agent."

"Perhaps I could give him a call?"

"Her." And, offended at such sexism, I hung up. "Men," I said, shaking my head in disgust.

Claudette, agreeing, returned to the butter, and I tucked bottle one under the bench for whoever was filling the Malongo coffee can with syringes.

I'd not spoken to my agent, Naomi Waters, in four years. I had, however, on Radcliffe's second call, texted her. She'd yet to reply, and I'd found myself missing her.

Desiring to drown the frolicking girls and their growing cacophony, I selected the "Get Shit Done" playlist. And, while Claudette licked and licked to The Black Keys' "Lonely Boy," I put the second bottle to my lips.

Chapter Two
OLD FASHIONED ASS WHOOPING

The second bottle, a placid and disappointing 2019 Nebbiolo from Roero, wasn't worth a second sip. Nor was it worth the 14.99 Hakim's market charged. And at that price, I may reconsider the twenty I'd been giving the skinny-limbed thief.

I tucked the bottle under the bench with the other and considered the remaining two.

Claudette, cued, left the slobbered expanse of my jeans, nudged past an elbow, and moved for a direct assault on the *jambon beurre*.

Plucking an earbud out, Nephew's *Va Fangool*! commencing, I held it to her notched left ear. "You, sweetheart, did not mention you were so sloppy. Look at this."

She turned her eye to me.

How could I blame her? Lacking such depth perception, of course she'd be sloppy. I'm surprised she hadn't bitten me.

With another *meow*, she made a half-hearted swat at the sandwich.

"Fine. Fine. One second."

Unsheathing more of the sandwich's length, I tore at it. I succeeded in decapitating a section. However, a buttery slice of ham flopped upon my damp lap.

"For the love of," I started but ended in a sharp *yelp* of pain as Claudette pounced and, pinning the slice, attacked and tore at the ham slice.

With a resigned sigh, I left her to her work and took a bite of my own.

A dagger shard of crust stabbed deep and painful into my gums. The tart copper of blood filled my mouth.

"Son of a clown," I spat, pressing a clump of butter with my tongue to the searing, throbbing wound.

Claudette's machinations had involuntarily aroused a reaction in my groin and added to my annoyance. For distraction, I reached for bottle three as a ball rolled into the trampled dirt expanse in front of the bench.

Lifting my eyes, I was startled to discover an incongruous tableau—three young, black novitiates, their sky-blue habits gathered and tied above their knees staring at me. Their rolled-down white socks made their legs seem all the longer, all the more fragile.

I smiled.

They gasped and two, crossing themselves, swore, "*Dios mio.*"

I ran my tongue over my bloodied, buttered gums and understood. Before I could calm them, an elderly, fire hydrant of a nun, in a black habit, burst into the clearing.

She squawked, "*Cuántas veces, señoras, les he dicho—*" and fell silent. Another five novitiates gathered behind her as she, frowning, studied the scene and danger her charges tottered on.

The novitiate with a bandage straddling a knee observed, jabbing an emphatic finger at me, "*Cuernos blancos.*"

With her own emphatic finger, the shortest added, "*Como la profecía.*"

I jumped to my feet, prepared to counter such absurd accusations. Claudette, still ravenous, still gnawing at the ham, clung desperately to me. Her claws dug deeper into my hips, and, screaming, I was unable to mount a rebuttal.

"*¡Silencio Diablo! ¡Silencio!*" the nun shouted as Claudette, swaying, bit at the ham in sharp, insistent punches. "*¡Silencio! ¡Silencio!*"

I slapped a palm across my mouth as Claudette, acquiring a firm grip on the ham, dropped to the ground and onto my phone, where it'd fallen. The clearing exploded in *Va Fangool!*

Knocking over the Malongo can and scattering syringes, Claudette scampered off with her ham slice.

The novitiates, the nun, watched her run away.

My groin had grown too stout for current company, and I attempted tapping, nudging it back into dormancy.

Claudette, the swift kitty, was quick, too quick. The nun and novitiates turned back sooner than expected. My hand stilled. They, however, gazed at the video playing on the phone.

To mimic a competition's environment as closely as possible, I'd use the band's video to listen to songs. Nephew's visual interpretation of their lyrics wasn't only curious, it was problematic.

The video, a black-and-white, computer-generated cartoon, depicted a bar scene. The scene included band members, Tony Soprano, a topless stripper, a pig, and a rat, and neared its climax. What had once been a chummy, innocuous gathering had escalated into a blood-splattered, decapitation-filled fight fest, accented in bright red flashes of gore. It culminated in the bartender committing suicide via a sawed-off shotgun.

We stared—they horrified, I slightly amused.

"*Dorogaya mat, ya nay*—" I started, but my morning with Katrina had strayed me into Russian.

Eyes blazing, they turned on me.

"Ladies, I'm sorry, but... Oh, right, Spanish." My Spanish had been gleaned on the high seas in the galleys of the *Oleander Princess*. There-fore, it was perfectly mediocre, though likely worse. "*Señoras*—" Under the gaze of such an angelic, bright-eyed jury, such a stern-faced judge, I fell silent. Regardless of my eloquence, should I discover it, I'd of course be found guilty. I knew it, and I understood it.

Thus beguiled, I was ignorant of the nun marching, in rapid strides, to me.

I did, however, take exceptional notice of the swift kick she planted between my legs and the pain exploding there.

Moaning, I crumpled to the trampled grass, curled tight and fetal.

The nun, having entered an ecstatic state, screamed jubilant and victorious, "¡*Morir Diablo*! ¡*Morir*!" And, calling the novitiates to her, she kicked me, over and over and over.

The one with the bandage—a vindictive, little piece of work—stomped on my phone, once then twice, and joined the others kicking me.

Rather than destroy the phone, she'd turned the volume up. The next song, DJ Shadow's "Nobody Speak," rose and reverberated through the clearing as if a concert were taking place.

Between bright shards of pain, the metronome of kicking legs, I glimpsed fleeting flashes of forbidden fruit—their underwear. I didn't desire such virginal delicacies. They only reminded me of something I'd forgotten long ago.

I crawled across the scuffed, black-and-white vinyl, checkerboard floor as a voice boomed through the classroom, shaking and shivering braces, bra straps, and the prepubescent from their sexual indifference, "Mr. Belltower, what are you doing?"

Stopping, staring past a scuffed, strawberry-hued knee, I replied to the cotton candy blue unicorn leaping over a rainbow and toward a mysteriously inviting cleft, "I dropped my pencil, sir."

"Mr. Belltower?"

I raised my eyes.

Over the ruffle of a red and yellow polka dot skirt, I found Trisha Andretti gazing at me. Besides a thin, black choker with a silver heart pendant, she wore a curious smile, a mischievous glint in her hazel-hued eyes.

Embarrassed, I looked away and found myself staring, again mesmerized, at the underwear-shrouded cleft.

"Mr. Belltower!"

"I'm looking for—"

Mr. Lexington, the tallest math teacher I'd ever know, gripped my collar and yanked me to my feet. He, as he frequently related, had played basketball for the University of Oregon. Thus, I found myself tottering on my toes, swaying about like an ill-guided puppet.

Being spring and recently freed from gym class, where for fifty minutes my classmates and I had hurled red rubber balls at one another, I was primed for arousal. And, like a mischievous cat, my erection swatted Trisha's travel mug of chamomile tea, knocking it into her lap.

Scalded, Trisha jumped from her desk, screaming and screaming, while Scott Stetson shouted, "Belltower's got a boner! Belltower's got a boner!"

The classroom erupted in laughter, as Mr. Lexington dropped me and awkwardly consoled Trisha.

Returned to my knees, I spotted the pencil and, crawling to it, knew, Q.E.D., from hence on nothing would be the same.

The novitiates had gradually lost their enthusiasm and, one by one, they'd drifted and disappeared around the rhododendron.

After a final flourish of kicks, the nun, whistling contentedly, followed.

Defeated and forlorn, I creaked an eye open. I glimpsed Salvation—bottle three. I reached for it. My arm was too short. The distance too far. The pain too much. My motivation inadequate.

Resigned, I wallowed deeper into my despair. I wouldn't make the competition. I'd owe Boonen more. And he, vindictive, but gracious, would charge me to "go play ugly with the Amsterdam Boys." And Katrina? She'd leave me for a caviar mogul named Dmitri.

I knew my future lay lost and abandoned like the syringes from the coffee can and my tears welled as footsteps neared.

A pair of shiny black shoes with white socks rolled down to the ankle and thin black legs trotted in. The traces of blood on the shoes were barely discernible, though upon the socks there was a red constellation I didn't know.

Regardless my ignorance, I knew my savior had arrived.

"*¿Por favor?*" I intoned, stretching a hand toward the bottle.

She, the chunkiest novitiate, picked up the ball.

"*¿Por favor?*"

She hesitated and turned.

"*¿Por favor?*"

She gripped the bottle by the neck.

"*Sí. Sí.*"

She cut me a sharp glance, tore the bag from the bottle, and pondered its label.

Someone, likely the *puta*, fire hydrant nun, shouted, "*Rápido, Sofía. Rápido.*"

I smiled.

Sofía, with a shrug, handed me the bottle.

"*Gracias, mi angel,*" I said, clamping a palm across the label.

"*De nada,*" her smile brightened as she added, "*Diablo.*"

She trotted off as DJ Shadow shifted to Miike Snow's The Rabbit.

I struggled to a sitting position, leaned against the bench, and took a sip. Confused, I punched the button. The Rabbit died, and I took another, though longer sip. Not because I needed it. I mean, I did, if for no other reason than to quell the throb and ache of my ribs, but because the wine was exceptional.

It was as good as anything I'd ever had. It was also unlike anything I'd ever had. Infused with dark, dried fruit, layered baking spices with persimmon and plum, and wet, Algerian shale.

I savored the moment until I swallowed, for this was too sublime to spit, particularly in such a desolate expanse at such a desolate time.

I pulled my hand away.

The label, to my confusion, claimed it to be a non-alcoholic *halal* wine from Syria. Being an upper mid-level Crusher, I knew what was in the bottle wasn't that.

I sipped again.

Where had Hakim acquired such a treasure? I knew the store's stock, too well. I'd suckled at that limited teat for years. It was why I loved his disguising this one.

I considered calling him. Demand he disclose his source. Mostly, I wanted to thank him, but there was Beren.

It was strange how much I owed and could blame on the skinny-limbed kid from Istanbul.

I sighed, took another sip, and gazed through the jumble of branches at a startling, azure, blue sky.

Hakim had been emphatic that first time. "*Pas ici. Pas ici.*"

I'd already twisted the cap off and held the bottle of mass-market Merlot to my lips, when the kid repeated, "Not here. Not here."

Lowering the bottle, I stepped back and to the left, the corner of the rack of bananas poking my butt. "*Ici?*" He glared. I adjusted a few more steps. Near the tomatoes, I repeated, "*Ici?*"

He sighed. "There's a bench in a nearby park."

I'd found it and had prepared for my first Parisian Crushed competition.

Ever since being cast as Dopey in Aloha Mountain Elementary School's rendition of *Snow White and the Seven Dwarfs*, I'd suffered from performance anxiety. Yes, portraying a mute dwarf placed an inordinate amount of pressure upon an eight-year-old. Having a mother who'd forsaken, not only her husband but her minor acting career for studies in psychology only compounded the issue.

"There are no small parts, only small actors," she'd asserted one afternoon, a glass of Cabernet in one hand, a Rorschach card in the other.

It would be freshman year, Aloha High, doing a scene from *Urine Town* when Professor Magaldi assured me Mother had quoted Konstantin Stanislavski. "Nor," the professor asserted, "is it meant to be literal." Hence, why I'd always performed on my toes and been voted in middle school as "The most likely to die of a head injury."

"Okay," Mother had asked, taking a sip and holding up the card, "what about this one?"

"Two pigs riding a dung beetle."

"And this one?"

"Two Santa bears playing Patty Cakes."

"And—"

As this was our third round in two days, I'd had the opportunity to prepare for this round's answers. Overexcited, on the next card, I replied prematurely, "Formal peacocks at a punchbowl."

Mother took a long sip and slurped. She swallowed. She took another sip, put the cards down, and stood. "If you're not going to take this seriously, why should I?"

I'd considered utilizing my father's patented reply to Mother's rhetorical questions, "Because there are moments I make you feel immortal." Instead, being eight and wiser than I am today, I'd said, "Because there is no one lovelier than you." In the uneasy silence that followed, I took the bottle and held it to my nose. The elixir smelled remotely of tart black cherry and violets but not displeasing and mildly arousing.

"Careful," Mother declared, "it's young, tannic, and overly oaked." She added, grimacing, "Rutherford Valley, I think."

I took a swallow and choked.

The wine gurgled up, spewed, and sputtered from my nose and mouth, staining my shirt, jeans, and the dull gray carpet I collapsed upon. Coughing, choking, I spewed mucous through wine-constricted nostrils.

Dying, a landed fish, I gasped for breath and realized Mother had been correct, the Cabernet was young, tannic, and overly oaked.

Mother slurped another sip. "And the reason you were cast as Dopey? It's called 'typecasting.' Accept it and move on." She didn't take the bottle nor declare, "Lesson learned." Instead, she said, "Write your answers down."

We glanced around. Though it was our fourth month in the third-floor, two-bedroom apartment on the well-manicured grounds of Mauna Loa Estates in Aloha, Oregon, most everything remained in boxes.

Surfing on the rising wave of her frustration, Mother spat, "Just write it on something. I'm curious what cleverness you think you've created," and left the room.

Blowing my nose, I listened to her shuffling through boxes, bottles *clinking*, as she mumbled an incantation, "*Dove sono gli Amaroni? Dove sono gli Amaroni?*"

I took another cautious, tentative sip. Behind the tannins and the oak, there lurked a nuanced hint of ripe plum, Cavendish tobacco, scuffed sandalwood, and a subtle smudge of Brazilian dark chocolate.

I swallowed and smiled. It was my first taste of love.

Chapter Three
SHAKESPEARE'S A SHITTY, LITTLE SHITE

In the low tide of my ass whooping, Sofía's soapy scent lingering, I sipped from bottle three and watched a school of pigeons flash across the azure sea of the sky. Needing such inspiration near, I reworked the cork back into the bottle and, fighting Dr. Albright's girthy tome again, tucked it back into the satchel.

I'd abandon the book under the bench with the syringes and bottles, but it, and shipping its 2.4 kilos from Kilkenny, had cost more than expected. It was Wesley Winston's, the renowned culinary historian and host of *Amazing Ancient Meals*, top, "all-time must-have" culinary book. And I felt it the lone token which, if Katrina had any reservations, would swing the pendulum in my favour.

Midnight Oil's *Beds are Burning* kicked in and, picking up the abused phone, I turned it off. Through the cracked, spider-webbed screen, I discerned I'd only lost ten minutes and found myself rallying and revisiting the necessity of having more than espresso, and now wine, in my belly.

Hoping fate couldn't be so cruel, but needing to test it, I turned to the *jambon beurre* lying innocent on the bench. Pulling it free of its paper sheath, I took a wary bite. I chewed, once, twice... Another shard of crust stabbed a gum.

Cursing, gums again buttered and bleeding, I chucked it, javelin style, toward the bush Claudette had disappeared in. I slammed bottle four to my lips and suckled, disappointed. It was Château Isolde, a cheap Bordeaux reliant for sales on the name and the impressive, though fictitious, manor house on the label. It was, as it'd always been, flat and tannic as an Egyptian mummy.

Under the bench, the bottle went.

I staggered to my feet and, swaying, slung the tome-weighted satchel over a shoulder. Not desiring another ass whooping, I clambered down a short, grassy incline and limped into the dog park.

I'd stepped in a pile of pooh and was dragging a heel as I searched for a taxi. The roadways, however, had grown thick with congestion. And the Metro? Its maw was clustered with commuters, heads bowed and buried in their phones, implying the worst—the authorities had been correct. They'd warned of strikes. Though most felt none would on such an auspicious day. The headline would read, *May the Fourth Strikes, Again.*

Thankfully, a competition rarely commenced on time. There was the signing-in and the subsequent banter and bluster between competitors.

I had about three kilometers to limp. If I could keep a steady pace, I'd be late, though not by much.

Turning onto a quiet, side street, I called Remy et Stakos Imports. Ania, the congenial office assistant, the one who'd promised and failed to provide insider info, didn't answer. Neither did Remy or Stakos.

I tried twice more. Each time Ania's melted butter voice droned, *"S'ils vous plaît, laissez un message. Merci beaucoup."*

To assuage my growing anxiety, I called Maurice at Bijou Bijou.

"Oui, oui," he assured, "the ring is here. And remains stunning."

"And you're open until nine?"

"Seven."

"Perfecto," I lied as my Spanish arrived, too late, *"y gracias."*

Ignoring the dog-shit brown footprints following me, I hung up and limped on.

The competition kicked off at noon with the first glasses placed at noon-thirty. It shouldn't run longer than a few hours. After a few congratulatory glasses, I'd dash off and grab the ring and a lone red rose from a corner florist.

Yes, the proposal swag and glitter, the ring, and Greece, Chez Shea, were above my budget. It's why I owed Boonen another twelve thousand. I'd been loath to ask him, but desperation and love can make one do stupid things.

Honestly, I'd hoped he'd have declined. However, "Boonen is fan of love. Yes, I grant this to you." Smiling Mephistopheles, he extracted his infamous little, black notebook from a pocket. After a moment, having found the page, he licked the tip of a well-used pencil and adjusted my tally from 18.7K to 30.7K. "You will initial here." The pencil tapped a spot where I jotted my initials.

He handed me the thin stack of crisp hundred-euro bills, and admitted, "Boonen thinks your Katrina is very lucky. You? Not so much." Walking away, he laughed and laughed.

Making the quarterfinals would pay off my credit cards. The semifinals would be enough to clear me of cards and most of Boonen. And if I sputtered out in an early round, a "*Niet*" from Katrina would be the least of my worries.

I, however, concentrated on the other side of the coin.

"Father," Katrina had once noted, "is a traditionalist. A man bound by his great love of food and drink. And his great loathing of Western Imperialism."

Her father, Oleg Vlasov, a St. Petersburg restaurateur, like the rest of her clan, I'd yet to meet. And, due to necessity, I was unconcerned with Russian nationalism, but whether Oleg would pay for the wedding, throw a few thousand rubles in as a dowry, and, perhaps, employ me in one of his restaurants. At this juncture, sommelier or "*plongeur*," I didn't care.

The day's competition, a "luncher," was utilizing a modified Rural Rothschild. Rather than a fifteen-minute seeding round of three wines, competitors would be randomly selected and placed in brackets. Then it was single elimination, *tête-à-tête* flash rounds of ten minutes and three wines until a lone Crusher remained.

The battle would be overseen by Isadora Cruz. Isadora, the illegitimate daughter of La Chica de las Pluseras de Oro, Maria Corbero, a Pamplonan Flamenco dancer, and Julen Herria, a Basque separatist, prided herself on innovation and intrigue.

I'd only competed in one competition which she'd overseen, Malta, 2010. She'd played a collection of Gregorian chants, *A Clockwork Orange* juxtaposed against the finals match from the 2008-09 Indian cricket championship, with burnt baklava befouling the air.

It'd been a disconcerting mélange, but I'd persevered and had made my first finals, where Arvi Und, an Icelandic wunderkind, had, thanks to a 2008 Omar Kayyam rosé, edged me, 23-21.

My phone "dildoed" and, rather than answer, I recalled one of Isadora's more provocative comments at the after party, "If ever I were cursed with a penis, I'd love to Super Tuscan a Neuf-du-Pape." Everyone, laughing, knew what she meant, some even provided visual aid.

Wobbling around a corner, I listened to Radcliffe's message. "Mr. Belltower," he bubbled, "I do think we should talk. Maybe get you, as they say, out in front of the situation? Call me."

Unsure of the "situation" he referenced, I was intrigued enough to consider meeting. Rather, I vowed to write a scathing email to Wesley Winston regarding Dr. Albright's "must have" tome and its adverse effects on one's posture.

Waddling along another tree-lined street, Naomi, finally, texted. It was a short string of emojis—A smiling pile of poop. Middle finger. Heart with an arrow through it—and a brief, blunt message, *FU will call soon.*

Such brevity was one reason I loved her. However, I needed to get into character. And the novitiates, Radcliffe, and Albright's tome, and now waiting for Naomi, was hampering that process.

No, I didn't enter a competition as myself. I was, I thought, a fairly nice person. And a nice person in a Crushed competition got thrown out into the street, naked and shattered with their panties stuffed down their throat.

It was why I hadn't cleaned myself after the ass whooping. Oh, no, I was keeping the beaten visage. I was keeping everything—split lip, black eye, torn, blood-stained shirt, dirt and grass-covered clothing. It would add authenticity to my Durden glare.

The glare, named for Tyler Durden, the main character in *Fight Club*, was a competition technique. True Crushers could sit opposite a wolf-mangled corpse as if it were high tea at the Ritz-Carlton. Hence, why embellishing with hyperbole was a recommended addition to the glare.

"Jumped by a squad of Spetsnaz. Killed all and ate most." And mustering a burp, especially if tainted with *époisses de Bourgogne*? Oh, no need to tally totals, send me to the next round, *muy pronto.*

Regardless of the nuances of the wine, the diplomas, and the accolades of the Crushers, competitions were little more than bouts of psychological warfare. Any Crusher could differentiate between a French or Chilean Malbec, or surmise which was an Austrian, German, or Croatian Spätlese, particularly at a cheese and cracker-infested reception with Bach playing lightly.

However, stick that little sipper in an underground bunker with Shonen Knife playing, the ox slaughtering scene from *Apocalypse Now* on a loop, and cat puke underfoot, they'd crumble like a sun-baked cracker under a tank's tread. That sommelier at that Michelin-starred restaurant, choking on fear, mortality, and their insignificance, mistook an Alsatian Riesling for a New Zealand Gewurztraminer. That article-writing, wine-rating pundit, out of the analgesic confines of the office, couldn't distinguish a Viognier from a Sauvignon Blanc.

In the Crushed trenches, when the lights dimmed and the music blared, and one was alone, staring into the glass, it didn't matter one shit who you thought you were, or who people claimed you were. If you couldn't tuck titties and balls and concentrate on those few ounces, well, you were another loser in a long line of losers. Loser! And after I'd won, I'd take the 50,000-euro purse and shove it in all their stupid, stupid faces!

Oh, yeah. There we go. The adrenaline was up, and the "Hyde" was crawling out. The growing growl of my stomach, however, undermined my conviction.

Yanking bottle three out, I stepped into the nearest *boulangerie* and took a long swallow.

Ignoring the stares and glares of the other two customers, they as gray-eyed and gray-haired as the proprietress, I ordered two *feuilleté au jambon*.

Accepting the bag, I tossed a tenner down and, with a wave and a *"Hasta mañana,"* exited.

The adrenaline surge, coupled with my nervous anxiety, had me limping faster and cursing Wesley Winston more.

I was on the second gooey, ham and cheese-filled pastry, only a few blocks from Remy et Stakos Imports when my phone interrupted.

Naomi's Bristolian accent basted my heart, "Dixon?"

"No," I replied, copping a posh barrister's tone, "it's the right honorable, Sir—"

"Listen, Dixon, you shite, now is not the time. Not. The. Time."

Her voice, the tone slapped me back those many years ago when, on our first and only "date," we'd attended *Hamlet* at The Globe.

"Shakespeare was a little shite," she'd declared during an intermission. "And nothing more than a glorified stenographer."

We were with the groundlings, and her statement treaded on blasphemy, particularly when declared in His cathedral.

"So, Zadie," I said, after confirming we weren't to be hanged, drawn and quartered, "jealous much?"

Her head snapped round from ogling Ophelia, who was miming picking flowers upstage, and glared me quiet.

At the time, I didn't know much about Naomi, except she was bright, beautiful, worked part-time for Upton Ink & Associates, looked remotely like the author Zadie Smith, and had, after a pint too many at the Drawbridge Pub open mic night, accepted an invitation from a struggling American novelist attempting to break into the hard knock life of British stand-up comedy.

"You know," she asked, with a last glance at the fair Ophelia, "how this ends, right?"

"Us or the play?"

"Yes this, if we want to be generous and call this pile of slag a play."

"Well, I'm hoping it ends in a jubilant song and dance number, with Hamlet confessing he's Harriet and eloping with Ophelia."

Aghast, she stared. "You saw, *Thumbelina in Hades*?"

Past a ghoulish smile, I confessed. "Found the Brighton and Cork performances. The Internet is such a magical place. I even found *Hoist High Your Hems*." She gasped. *Hems* was a convoluted amalgamation of *Pirates of Penzance* and the women's suffrage movement.

"Not my best creation," she admitted.

"Shakespeare," I said, hooking a thumb at the stage, "might say the same about this."

"Do not defend that shite." Before I could, she was dragging me through the appreciative crowd (everything is a performance at The Globe!) and out into the street.

Minutes later, tucked into a pub's dark booth, fresh pints in front of us, she confessed, after a long swallow, "I'm curious about cock."

"Well, who isn't?"

"No, I mean—"

"I'm curious about life after death, but I'm not committing suicide."

"You're equating—"

"From what I've heard from some women about how some men perform, yeah, it's reminiscent of dying."

Past her broad, beautiful smile, she asked, "Are you always attempting to be funny?"

"Yes but looks aren't everything."

"Particularly in your case."

Past the laughter, I *tinked* her glass with mine, and asked, "Then why'd you accept such an invitation from such a destitute comic?"

"I read your manuscript."

I was confused. Not because I'd ten manuscripts in progress, six finished, but because I was only querying one. "*The Yank*?"

She nodded.

"How?" And then... "Upton Ink & Associates?" She nodded. "Lionel Thames?"

"I'm his assistant. I took it home and read it."

With the condensation from the pint tickling my palm, I rubbed my chin, fearful, "And?"

"And it's brilliant."

"And that explains the curiosity about cock?"

She smiled, and I'd fetched two more pints.

"Dixon? Hello?"

Choking on a chunk of *jambon*, though keeping my hardnosed Crusher persona, I spat the gooey glob into a street corner flowerpot, admitted, "It's good to hear your voice."

Begrudging, but sincere, she replied, "Yes. The same to you."

"So about Radcliffe?"

"He, my idiot friend, might be the least of your worries."

I knew she didn't know about the debt to Boonen. Nor, like Katrina, did she know about my relapse into the nefarious underworld of Crushed. There were, however, other skeletons in other closets, so... "Go on."

And, to my dismay, she did.

Giving a quick CliffsNotes highlight of being a shitty client and a worse friend, for which I agreed and apologized, she moved on to, "And let's not mention your dalliances with Sabita and Beca while they were interns?"

"Okay, let's not mention them."

"How about I mention SloPony42?"

"Is that some Native American DJ?"

"It's a street artist."

"Tagging buffalo or something?"

She sighed and stabbed me with, "And then there's Kenan."

"What about him?"

"A bit of denial would've been... Doesn't matter. But there are the ramifications of pilfering his private life for profit. Particularly considering—"

"Well," I said, cutting her off before that skeleton escaped the closet, "I wouldn't say profit."

"Shut up."

"Yes, ma'am."

"So, are you SloPony42?"

"Why would it matter?"

"Well, there's the little matter of The Home Office charging you, sorry, SloPony42 with vandalism and various acts of terrorism."

"What?"

"You sound shocked."

"Because I am."

"Good."

"So, what did you tell them?"

"I told them I'd talk to you."

"Oh."

"Yeah 'oh.' Is it you? Are you SloPony42?"

For *The Yank*, I'd cobbled together the stories my Wickford Aldi's coworkers were telling and yelling. The main character, Christopher Angus Mountjoy, was an amalgam of those curious cranks. However, Chris's profession, a prostitute pleasing politicians and wealthy socialites with hand puppet hand jobs, was gleaned from one of my flatmates, Kenan. So Naomi mentioning "pilfering his personal life" rang too true. But isn't that what writers did? And, seriously, what profit?

Two coworkers, Bussy and Naria, were also street artists. One late night, early morning, after finishing our stocking shift and the last cans of Galahad lager, I was invited to "tag along." And one thing led to another and becoming SloPony42.

"Dixon? Hello?"

Limping around another corner, making my excuse, "Naomi, I wish—" I stopped and blinked in incomprehension.

What'd always been a quiet, bucolic, tree-lined street was engulfed in the flash-and-flare of a half-dozen squad cars' blue emergency lights. Not unexpectedly, all were angled toward the front of what had once been an old barn and stables, then an auto body shop, and now housed Remy et Stakos Imports.

Neighbors leaned out their flung open windows, while a few clumped in the street. Some, the most elderly, were in their faded nightwear. Small dogs on long leashes scampered around. Their barking and yapping exploded as a knuckled lump of gendarmes surged out of the import company's front doors. They struggled with a broad-shouldered, shaved-headed brute.

Under an undulating sea of fists, the brute momentarily submerged, though, like Poseidon, rose to his full height, six feet seven. The gendarmes fell away. Whirling, his falcon-sharp, gray eyes locked on mine. He smoothed the lapels on his 25,000£ Savile Row suit and smiled a blood-smeared smile. The nun's voice echoed in my ears "¡Diablo!" I, however, knew him as T. Thomas Boonen.

It was Singapore, late November 2008, and the heat and humidity still clung to the air like a bat to a cave's ceiling. I was on the second day of a three-day layover wending my way to Osaka for the world championships. Gripped by insomnia, I found myself wandering the infamous Geylang district, looking for distraction and the improbable—a wine bar.

Instead, I found a man, his height, demeanor, and suit stood out like a thumb in a jar of maraschino cherries. Smooth and deadly as a prowling panther, he slipped through the crowded sidewalk unconcerned with the stares and whispers following him.

After a few blocks, he turned into a narrow side street and spoke to a doorman with a grouchy mustache at one of the many entertainment parlors, aka brothels. The man cupped his right hand in the shape of the letter C and pounded his chest twice—the Crushed greeting gesture.

The doorman glanced around, nodded, and handed him a token. The man ducked into the parlor and I was left perplexed under the glow and glare of garish neon.

Four days later, in Osaka, during preliminary seeding, I discovered myself sitting across the table from him. For the entire fifteen minutes, as we sniffed and slurped, appraised, and scribbled assessments, he was silent as a statue.

The finish bell sounded, and he stood.

Towering, with an accent I'd later discover was Belgium, he swore, "One day I will kill you."

Days later, during the semifinals, he did, figuratively, 23-15.

The gendarmes regrouped and surged back.

Gradually, they overwhelmed him, though his eyes never left mine as they beat him into submission.

If I'd looked a quarter as ghoulish as he, the nun, the initiates, were justified to do what they'd done in quelling *el Diablo*.

"Those," Naomi asked, "are police sirens, yes?"

"Yes."

One of the houses with one of the closets with one of my skeletons was Remy et Stakos Imports. It wasn't just a Crushed venue, the mechanics' bays being ideal for *tête-à- tête* matches, but it also housed a blending operation, which I oversaw.

The counterfeiting of wine, besides being illegal, especially in France, could be quite lucrative. Blending cheap varietals and, if one was, like me, a philistine, utilizing other ingredients to mimic an expensive wine happened to be a forté of mine.

Our current catalog featured, as to be expected, offerings from Burgundy and Bordeaux, as well as a Poully-Fuissé I was rather proud of. There was also a smattering of reds from the Languedoc, Italy and Spain. Nothing too high-end, mid-range standards, where a buyer wouldn't be suspicious if the body and bouquet weren't exact. Remy explained, "Wine is a romantic creature and, like passion, fluctuates."

Besides Remy and Ania going round to hotels, we also worked with a network of restaurants, creating ultra-cheap house blends. Something they could glug into a carafe and be moderately proud of, though, more importantly, content with the profit.

We were, however, nearing the bottom of some barrels on several blends and were in the midst of creating new ones. This meant the blending room, a large basement built as a bomb shelter during World War II, was cluttered with an array of jugs, bottles, tinctures, spices, herbs, scales, beakers, et cetera.

Even to a novice, it would be apparent what we were doing.

"Dixon," Naomi queried, "why are there police sirens wailing in the background?"

"Naomi, now isn't a good time. How about I call you back?"

The gendarmes, fire ants swelling over a beetle, fought, shoved, and stuffed Boonen into a squad car. From the backseat, out the back window, eyes engulfed with flame, he glared as they sped off, sirens blaring.

Naomi pressed, "SloPony42, on rental signs, would paint an i shaped like a penis between *To Let*."

"Okay. So?"

"You don't sound surprised."

"I'm not. To let, add an i, *toilet*. Clever. But not surprising." The flashing police lights were assisting in playing it Bogart casual. "So? Go on."

"As it was related to me by Agent Anderson, the tags, or whatever you want to call them, were set in a series of letters. I-S-I-S with an exclamation point. ISIS!"

"No," I said, losing my casual, "that can't be."

Instead of mentioning it, she added, "Oh, and the period on the bottom of the exclamation point? It coincided with the eastern terminus of the Piccadilly line."

"Cockfosters," I confessed, confused.

"You've heard of it?"

"Of course. It's infamous amongst... A friend told me about it."

"Sure they did," she scoffed.

Before she demanded details, Remy, thin and angular, and Stakos, round and meaty, were escorted to a pair of squad cars. Both were handcuffed, sobbing and proclaiming their innocence to the beautiful, blue sky.

One could assume (their wailing apologies so sincere) they were repentant. However, having worked with them for the past two years, I knew the cold-blooded bastards they were.

"Dixon," Naomi, anticipating, cut in, "if you hang up again—"

Again? Oh, she referred to four years ago.

I'd been wallowing in a second tumbler of Jameson's and wondering if I should've added some onion pakoras to my order I'd just placed with Bangalore Gardens, when I'd inadvertently answered. It wasn't Manesh confirming my order, but Naomi pleading, "Dixon, you need to tell me why. I need to know."

I'd, again, missed a deadline for *The Jerk*, the sequel to *The Yank*. I'd pitched it in a morning delirium, after a cover reveal mixer and waking with two sweetly delusional interns, Sabita and Beca.

"Christopher continues administering hand puppet hand jobs. However, falling in love with a North African illegal immigrant, he begins blackmailing clients to ensure their future together."

"Rough draft in three months?" she'd asked.

I'd agreed but hadn't delivered.

Guilt, until Kenan, was something I'd never experienced. And I didn't like it.

"Dixon," Naomi had proclaimed, "if you hang up, I'm going to call Lidia and—"

I'd hung up.

Deluded, I'd believed I hated Lidia Newcomb, our Ganymede Press editor, more than the truth. That and *The Yank*'s lukewarm reception wasn't due to my unenthused and dower readings, but the public's incapacity to discern talent.

A few weeks later, out of Jameson's and sick of Bangalore Garden, I'd packed my squeaky wheeled suitcase, and, next to the *Doctor Who* TARDIS tea tin, left two months' rent and a short, stupid note—"No excuses. I suck. Dixon"—and vacated the shitty, little flat.

I'd wandered out into the usual gray morning filled with pissing rain and porridge-faced villagers. I'd caught the next train to London, where, staring at the station's departure-arrival board, I continued trying to understand Kenan's suicide. How could one seem so happy and light-hearted and yet be so miserable?

Thanks to Mother I knew the answer—overcompensation.

Doors slammed and the two squad cars drove off with Remy and Stakos screaming their innocence.

"Dixon?" my phone asked as I lowered it from my ear.

Sensing the excitement drifting into denouement, the spectators trudged home, their dogs yapping less and less until a precarious silence settled on the street.

Ania, deep in conversation with a plainclothes officer, exited. The officer and his goatee did and didn't look familiar.

They slipped into the last car and drove off.

"Dixon?" my phone asked from my hand, dangling at my hip. "Dixon?"

From a second-floor window, an old woman in a baggy, stained, blue bathrobe, a droopy, splotched breast flopped out, stared accusingly at me.

I waved and blew her a kiss.

She, with a practiced toss of the head and huff, clattered her window closed and smartly snapped the curtains shut.

Feigning I hadn't heard Naomi's last words—"I've missed you"—I hung up and limped off.

Chapter Four
THOU ART A SPONGY, SHEEP-BITING SCUT

A dozen blocks or so fled from Remy et Stakos Imports, my panicked limp had deteriorated to a sullen stagger. A cold sweat percolated my skin, as my heart and lungs, regardless of the diminished pace, raged like a rabid monkey in a cage.

I had had a plan. Perhaps not a good one, but I had had one. And I'd committed to it, fully. Professor Magaldi would've been proud, and surprised.

But now? Now a vast, churning chasm of the unknown broiled on the horizon. It aggravated my condition and angered the monkey more.

Of course, not being as delusional as I'd once been, I hadn't expected to win the competition. Regardless, the twenty thousand for third, even the ten for fourth, would've allotted me some respite from Boonen's clutches. Though with a few properly placed side bets, I may've managed another five, maybe ten thousand.

I slowed. Stopped. Waited for the monkey to escape.

Prison sentences in France for wine fraud were severe.

Remy would lose everything. And not just the business, as dubious as it was, but also Francesca, his wife, and his two daughters, Celine and Audrey.

Stakos would be forced back to Greece, where he'd return to working the family vineyard with his two homophobic brothers, Giorgos and Dinos, making "shit Retsina for overpriced tourist restaurants."

And what of Isadora and the competitors? Crushed was as illegal in France as everywhere else in the world. And my absence would be suspicious and would, partially, explain Boonen's hate-filled glare.

Then there was Katrina. Theoretically, I was in the west of the city, making sales calls to boutique hotels near Versailles. Perhaps, before being arrested, I should, confess my many lies? Prostrate my pathetic self before her, disclosing the skeletons and where they were housed, and ask for forgiveness? That, I knew, wasn't to be done over the phone. Maybe after dinner and the proposal? Of course, depending on her answer.

Achieving another block, Professor Magaldi's voice, accompanied by the rabid monkey, rang repeatedly in my ears, "The show must go on!" It was decided that Chez Shea, the stunning ring, the rose, the proposal, everything would be staged as it'd been rehearsed.

Throughout my childhood, Mother had repeated, "You won't get the lead, but you'll be cast." So, no matter my part—prisoner, fugitive, Amsterdam love slave—Katrina and I, stronger than ever, would persevere through this.

Mother had also, in a rare moment of lucidity, likened the difference between performance anxiety and a panic attack to "Being afraid of being hit by a car and being hit." She'd added, shoving me onstage for my first audition, "Just ask your father."

After another few blocks, hyperventilating as the tiring monkey grew desperate and erratic, my phone again "dildoed."

"What, Radcliffe, do you want?"

"Nothing more than I've asked for from the onset."

"An interview?"

"Exactly."

With my freedom dubious and suspect, and my apartment likely being redecorated in "modern gendarmian upheaval," perhaps I could squeeze a few quid from Radcliffe and his overlords to assist with my escape?

"Okay. When and where? And maybe—because a big bollocks on *The Yank*'s anniversary—you can give me some notion of what this is about?"

"How about now?" I hesitated. "This afternoon?" I hesitated. "Tonight?"

"No."

"Okay. Ten tomorrow morning?"

"And the where?" He hesitated. "Where?"

"*Deux Maggots*?" He sounded oddly excited, embarrassed as if a fantasy were nearing fulfilment.

Shaking my head at such a cliché, though appreciating the sentiment, I agreed. "Fine. But now, the real why." He hesitated. "Or I don't."

"Well, at the moment, this," he said, his voice infused with gleeful mystery, "would be why." In quick succession, two jpgs *pinged* my inbox.

His voice sounding thick as a noose, he repeated, "Tomorrow at ten," and hung up.

A nervous dread enveloped me as I, Pandora, opened the files.

Each was a photo of a morning television news broadcast. Under each the identical caption, at the bottom of the screen, declared, "*Not Terrorists, Just Genitals.*"

The first was of the Eiffel Tower. Its jutting, girded height had been transformed into a giant phallus. Huge, hairy, pink balls bulged at the base. A bulbous, pink, and billowing foreskin sprouted at its tip, and listed south in the morning breeze. There'd never existed a more bewilderingly beautiful phallus, ever.

The second was a split-screen view of another iconic Parisian monument, the Arc de Triomphe. It, also, had been ingeniously altered. The image on the left, from the Place de la Concord, showed traffic on the Champs-Élysées at a standstill. Bystanders, curious and confused, had wandered into the street and stared transfixed at the Arc. The image on the right, a close-up from its base, showed it magnificently transformed into a giant, hairy vagina.

Having a good idea of how it'd been accomplished, and by whom, I swore, "Well, fuck me," as salvation's door swung open.

A bright-faced, young man, carrying a box stuffed with bottles, smiled and replied, "Name the time and place. *Por favor.* Though you will need to clean whatever this is." Fingers from a hand under the box waggled at my beaten visage.

I smiled back, "Sancho, you know you're too hot and too much for me."

"*Sí.* But that doesn't mean—"

"And you know I prefer colder climes."

"Katrina *y las mujeres. Sí.*"

"So is Art in?"

"When is he not?" Sancho Miguel Alejandro Ortega, besides the name, had the smoldering good looks of a Spanish bullfighter. We'd been friends since he and Art had started their hyphenated relationship—lovers-partners-confidants-friends-soul mates, et cetera.

Leaning against the shop door, Sancho added with a wink, "Tell Katrina she can join us."

"I'll keep it in mind."

"No, you won't."

"You're right. I won't."

"Well," he sighed, jiggling the box, bottles laughing crisply, and killing the awkward silence, "deliveries."

He slipped out, "*Hasta mañana*, my friend," while I slipped in, "Yep. Yep. *Hasta*."

Art's Wine Emporium, an oasis to the most venerable of liquids, was a trailer park of wine boxes and crates after the tornado had hit. They were strewn and scattered in random disorder. Walls, floor to ceiling with shelves and racks, were stuffed with bottles.

It was, should it exist, like entering heaven, though without the necessity of dying or talking to a doorman.

Three steps in, the bell finished tickling the silence, and the bald man at the counter, the yellow stub of pencil working furiously upon a section of a newspaper, looked up. Over his wire-rimmed reading glasses, he asked, "Five-letter word for tragic loser?"

"Dixon," I replied, glancing around for someplace to throw the satchel.

Straightening, he shrugged, "I'll accept it." He tucked glasses in a pocket, the pencil behind an ear, and asked, "Three letters for what your breath smells like?"

"Ass."

Walking around the counter, an enthusiastic smile washing over his stern features, he asked, sincerely, "How are you, Dixon?"

Arthur Aldous Sinclair, if I wasn't me, would be the cranky curmudgeon I'd want to be. And not because he was a three-time Crushed world champion. The trophies—golden Bordeaux wine glasses with a pair of golden brass knuckles incorporated in the stem and engraved with the year and city of the event—sat atop the top shelf behind the register, embalmed in dust and neglect.

He extended a hand and, like being pulled into a life raft, I took it.

However, he declared, "You, my friend, are in trouble," and I thought, maybe, I should've remained in the water with the sharks.

"And you've got an *art* for stating the obvious."

Rightfully ignoring my pathetic pun, he slipped past, turned the sign from *Ouvert* to *Fermé*, and locked the door.

Once the bolt's sharp, metallic shout faded, I, with a satisfying *thud*, dropped the tome-laden satchel at my feet and asked the obvious, "That serious?"

Being a true Crusher, he kept his eyes locked on mine. "Pull up a chair, Little Killer."

Always gently pushing, and prodding, Art claimed, "If you can't take shit from those who love you, then you'll be eating it from those who hate you."

Hence, "Little Killer," his sarcastic nod to my failed comedy "career."

Returning to the counter, he called over his shoulder, "Start making your excuses, I've dozens more questions for you," and glided around a black felt curtain, disappearing into the back of the shop.

A portion of the shop, behind the smoked glass front window, was dedicated to tastings and contained three old bistro tables, each surrounded by rickety, wicker chairs.

Dragging, in lurches, the weighted satchel, I selected the farthest chair in the farthest corner and promptly collapsed into it.

Chapter Five
OEDIPUS'S COURAGE

Waiting for Art's return, rather than popping a cork on a nearby bottle, I texted Naomi: "I beg forgiveness. Help." Smiley face. "I am" pile of poop. "Help me. Please." Prayer hands. Prayer hands. Prayer hands. Smiley face.

In the unnerving silence, I scrolled through news reports regarding the chaos at the Eiffel penis, the Triumphal vagina.

I wanted to believe it coincidence, but the fact the night I'd chosen to propose to Katrina was the day the Parisian monuments were transformed and Remy et Stakos Imports was raided, at least to me, verged on conspiracy.

Panic welled and flooded me.

I stood and did a few laps around the table. Beginning to dizzy, I stuffed the phone into the satchel and plucked an issue of *La Revue du Vin de France* off a nearby chair, sat to read.

It was an old issue. One I'd read before and on which, the cover particularly, disgusted me. Annoyingly, a too attractive, too contented couple, wearing cream and gold gown and tux, champagne glasses raised, smarmed smiles from a balcony overlooking vine-covered hills. The rosé-colored heading oozed, *Vin? Il a un goût d'Amour, n'est-ce pas?*

"No," I replied, throwing the magazine back into the chair, "love tastes like betrayal."

Slipping backward past the curtain, carrying a tray of half-empty tasting glasses, Art declared, "You know, after today, many will want to have Oedipus's courage."

It was another baffling and incongruous statement from the man; something he'd been doing since I'd met him.

Oslo, 2008, The Stormy Seas Showdown, quarterfinals, I was the budding novice, he the old dog fighting to keep his bone and relevance.

He, as we waited for the wines to be placed, played it full Bogart, filling in a Sunday edition of *The New York Times* crossword. I gently bobbed my head to the guttural, metal music screaming into the sardine can fetid air, while *Sesame Street* played silently on a flat screen overhead.

I'd narrowed the band to either Eichen Frau or Blauer Nerv, when, the glasses placed, he'd raised his clear green eyes and, past a soft, friendly smile, said, "I'd want to fuck that pouty, little mouth of yours, but it reminds me, too much, of your father's butthole."

At the time, I sported a goatee, so, disturbingly, I understood the observation. It, as one might expect, affected my performance. I'd lost handily, 21-12.

Rather than comment on Art's Oedipus comment, I moved a chair out of his way.

"What were you thinking about?" he asked, putting the tray down and sitting.

"Nothing."

"You're as transparent as plastic wrap. Mochi would've gutted you."

Mochi, Mio Cho Musashi, was the newest "heir to the throne" to hit the circuit. She was also the love child of Ichiro Shibashi, the founder of the Kodoku nani Ronin sake empire, and Yuki Musashi, a hostess at the Pretty Kitty Club in Sapporo. She'd also been slated to compete in the day's competition. Like the other competitors, she'd be suspicious of my absence and would be plotting revenge.

"No answer," Art declared, pulling the glasses from my reach. "No taste."

"Thirty-seven," I confessed, tacking on a question, "And how do you know about Mochi?"

"It's a classic," he admitted, sliding the glasses back within reach.

Thirty-seven—"Father's Butthole"—was one of the two hundred or so opening lines Art, now retired, had employed during competitions. Over the years he'd begrudgingly divulged fifty-five to me. I'd been able to glean another twelve from other competitors.

I'd used thirty-seven twice, handily winning each round. Having a few more years under my expanded belt, I stayed on topic, "So, about Oedipus?"

Nodding toward the crumpled magazine, Art countered, "Still carrying that holy iron grudge, are you?"

Art, unable to answer a question, insinuated my "grudge" wasn't with the lady but the lord, the handsome, millionaire husband, Roland St. Fer.

Before I stumbled down the rabbit hole of reflection, Art tapped my tasting glass with a nail. "You know I ravaged your sister."

"I don't have a sister."

"That's because I killed her. Then ravaged her." He lifted his glass and sniffed. "Ninety-one. You're welcome."

How did such a nice man come up with such vileness?

Shaking my head, I joined him in tasting. "You said I was in trouble?"

"You're correct. I did say that."

"How bad?"

"You've heard of 12M?"

Rather than lie directly, I shook my head and downed the first glass. "Walla Walla. Bordeaux blend. 14.2? 14.3? Probably 2018 or 2019." This wasn't a competition, so I left it ambiguous.

And yet Art said, "Don't lie to me."

"No. That is—"

"I read your book, you know."

"*The Yank*? Really?"

He nodded, tossed back his glass, and added, "The British government has classified them as a terrorist organization."

"Seems extreme. Washington winemakers aren't—"

Art glared.

I fell silent and fiddled with the second glass, another deep, dark monstrosity.

"Safe to assume you don't want to talk about your new tossed salad look?"

"Very safe." Foregoing a sniff, a preliminary sip, I gulped it down, an Australian Cabernet.

With an uncharacteristic squint of concern, he asked, "You've heard about the ruckus at the monuments this morning?"

"I have."

He grunted softly, did the same as I had, tossed the wine down, and picked up the magazine. With a bemused smile, he commented, "They've started a sister winery. Somewhere in the U.S. Sonoma, I think." He placed the magazine face down. Rather than mention how much happier the ex looked without me, he said, "The Monkeys are claiming credit for the 'installations.'" Once done with the air quotes he sipped the third wine. "Thoughts?"

Twelve Monkeys, aka 12M, was the moniker for a brash group of street artists committing thought-provoking social commentary on the bland walls of the lurid streets of London. And, regardless of the movie featuring Brad Pitt and Bruce Willis, and the use of them in *The Yank*, they were a fictitious group. The disturbing fact a group was inspired to do the same deeds outlined in *The Yank*, well, that was just coincidence, right?

To gauge if it sounded as stupid as it did in my head, I said, "12M doesn't exist. And if they did commit today's 'installations,' the UK, and France, would be justified placing them on any list they wanted."

His silence was answer enough. Though Bussy would have plenty to say; it was, after all, his idea.

Lighter than the first two, I twiddled with the third glass and considered the possibilities.

I sipped and speculated, more for misdirection than an answer, "Maybe it has something to do with the raid this morning?" I knew it was unlikely, but I disliked the silence more than being wrong.

"What raid?"

"Remy's," I said, confused at Art's confusion. "I thought you knew. You mentioned Mochi."

"I mentioned her because I thought you'd been smart enough not to go. Hence, being here and not at that vile den of dung."

Art, like me, also lugged some spite for his ex, Stakos.

I shook my head, "Not so smart." And, because Art was the lone person I could confide in, I told him everything, beginning with the debt to Boonen and the necessity of the day's competition, and the raid.

"It would've been rigged. You know that."

"I thought I could—"

"Oh, my sweet Dixon, you're good, but not that good."

He, of course, was right.

So, with a sigh, I moved on, expounded on the devil's *jambon beurre*, Claudette, my awkward chubby, and the novitiates.

"Ah, so you didn't cut yourself shaving?"

We found our glasses empty when I blurted, "And I'm proposing to Katrina tonight."

A look of astonishment flashed across his face.

"What?" I asked.

"Nothing," he lied. "Go on."

"That's it." He looked dubious. "Really."

He stood, stepped to a shelf, and ran a finger over the bottles. "Even if you didn't call the gendarmes—"

"I didn't."

"Boonen is going to kill you."

"Yes, I know." The little apprehension and panic I'd lost returned, twofold. "So what should I do?"

Art pulled out a bottle and flashed me the label. I nodded. It was a well-balanced Malbec from just outside Puy-l'Eveque, a little village on the Lot River in France.

Pulling a wine key from a pocket, he, opening the bottle, asked, "Can you change the dates for Greece?"

Reservations were for the first of July, a week after her classes ended. "Probably. For a fee. Why?"

Pouring, well past the half-empty mark, he stated wistfully, "There's nothing like escaping to a Greek island. And if you're like me—" It was a story I'd longed to hear, but the front door rattled as someone attempted to enter.

Sancho, with a curse, tried again.

"One second, sweetheart. One second." Art, filling another glass and taking it, went to unlock the door.

Loath to leave such succor but needing more than gooey pastries in my belly, I stood and hoisted the tome-weighted bag.

Unlocking the door, Art gave Sancho the glass and a kiss.

I hoped Katrina and I could find something similar. Perhaps, maybe, in time, we would—if we were lucky and I wasn't languishing in a French penal colony.

They turned and, past mischievous smiles, in unison, asked, "Where do you think you're going?"

Chapter Six
THE APOCALYPSE GARNISHED
WITH PEANUT BUTTER AND PAIN

Katrina had a break, a few hours, between lunch service and dinner prep. "Just enough time," she'd disclosed, "to bandage cuts on fingers and soul. Cry a little. Eat something. Change underwear. And cry a bit more."

Her confession had broken my heart. It was the major rationale for slinking back into the dirty depths of the Crushed circuit.

Though, because of our dinner at Chez Shea, she'd taken the night off.

My plan, mildly modified, was to still sweep her off her feet over an amazing meal, though, with a glass or two too many, I'd convince her jetting off to Greece the following afternoon was the most romantic and practical thing we could do.

Katrina, however, despised surprises. Hoping it warning enough, I'd texted, "No fear. I am near. And bringing cheer, my dear."

I'd promised Art I'd "collect it before the apocalypse" and had replaced Albright's tome with a bottle of moderately priced, French bubbly (for Katrina), a spicy, full-bodied, Australian Shiraz (for me), and, because I'd need a drink for preparation, an inexpensive but reputable Rioja sporting a twist top.

The sidewalks surrounding Katrina's apartment building, a venerable Haussmann a stone's throw from the Triumphal vagina, were teaming with the curious.

Thanks to an impromptu rehearsal with Sancho regarding Katrina's possible protestations, my limp had transitioned to a confident, though staggered, swagger.

I'd remembered Hakim's mystery bottle three and, after ordering a pair of pizzas, had plunked the bottle down and challenged, "Either of you dirty Crushers think you can name this?"

They couldn't and Art, annoyed, had returned to his beloved crossword. Sancho and I, less competitive and more romantic, had delved into preemptive answers should Katrina protest our escape.

"No. No. No," Sancho had corrected with an assertive, wagging finger. "You're eloping. Eloping to a magical and romantic land. A land called Greece."

Spontaneously, we'd slipped into character—me Katrina, he me.

"What about passports?" I asked with a quaint Russian accent.

Sancho leaned back, spread his legs, and, copping a rugged American drawl with a palm across his crotch, answered, "Greece, sweetheart, is part of the EU. We'll be fine." He took a beat and added, "Trust me."

"And my schooling?" I blinked coquettishly.

He adjusted his crotch. "What more authentic place than Greece to explore—"

I repeated, verbatim, what Katrina had declared when enlightening me, "Community cooking inspired by ancient traditions, particularly perpetual stews."

"Exactly right. That. And Greece, my sweet lady," Sancho winked, "is the perfect place for such exploration."

Hopefully, I could say it with a straight face, because he couldn't.

"The real issue," I sighed, pouring off the last bit of bottle three into my glass, "will be Vlad."

Sancho leaned forward, Art glanced up. Each smiled, each asked, "Vlad? Who's Vlad?"

"Her dog."

Disappointed, Art returned to his crossword, Sancho picked up another slice and shrugged, and I swirled my glass, watched the wine go round and round.

We'd considered a few ideas, but, except for the most nefarious, all involved taking the creature.

Making the building's wooden carriage door, I took a last glance at my phone. She'd yet to reply.

Rubbing a palm over the Rioja's lump, a gentle creaking growing behind me, I pressed Katrina's button on the call box.

An elderly woman and her rickety grocery cart, loaded to the brim, clattered to a stop alongside me.

Widow Shriver was an aged Englishwoman who'd talked me blind riding the building's cantankerous elevator one of the infrequent times I'd visited Katrina.

Begrudging the spring weather, she sported a full-length, camel-hued Mackintosh, a yellow and green head scarf double knotted under her chin, dark sunglasses, and, incongruously, black, Nike, high-top basketball shoes.

"Good afternoon, Madame Shriver," I intoned, "and how are you today?"

"I'm fine," she snapped, though added mysteriously, "except for those damn gnomes."

"Gnomes?" I asked, confused.

"I despise them. Dirty bastards they are."

"Yes, ma'am." She shot a sharp glare. I affirmed, "Right you are, ma'am, dirty bastards gnomes are."

With one last press of Katrina's buzzer, I followed the widow into the building.

Katrina's apartment, which she shared with an elusive roommate named Kelsey, who I'd neither met nor seen, was one of the four jewels crowning the building.

When first she'd told me her roommate's name, I'd attempted some "cleverness." "Instead of the brothers, it's the Ladies K, eh?" She'd stared, perplexed. There were times I questioned the state of the Russian education system. I'd clarified, "Dostoevsky? Maybe David James Duncan?"

"I wonder if your cleverness," she countered, "isn't a deep-seated masking of your desire for your mother."

And there were times when the Russian education system was too annoying for its good.

Widow Shriver trundled toward the ancient, cantankerous elevator. It, its dark metal girders and cage, Eiffel-phallic, a crooked middle finger to gravity, was planted against the back wall of the marbled foyer.

I veered toward the stairs.

The widow stated, "You know, the gnomes took the stairs."

Thus obligated to prove I was no gnome sympathizer, I accompanied her.

Rising slowly, slowly, I was again regaled with tales of her husband's death by "the dark, foul hand of rectal cancer" and her daughter's "liberating hysterectomy."

"And that's how," Widow Shriver concluded, "Margery knew she wanted to be an accountant."

She, and the elevator, wheezed, clattered, and shook to a stop. The elevator considered collapsing, but, as there were only the two of us, it didn't.

Widow Shriver, kissing the small, silver crucifix chained around her wrist, warned, "Be wary the gnomes. They're a vindictive lot."

"Yes, ma'am," I agreed, pulling the metal accordion door aside, "thank you. I shall be wary."

"Americans," she observed, creaking off, "smell of wine and stupidity."

To her bowed back, I raised my hand in agreement. "Guilty as charged, milady."

The rickety contraption shuddered to a nervous stop, and, with more effort than before, I yanked the door aside. I leaped to freedom, though came to an immediate halt. Not, as the widow had, to give thanks, but because Katrina's door was wide open.

I imagined it a coy invitation to amorous adventures, hence, why she'd not texted back. However, a strange, smoky, 1930s Hong Kong, opium den aura emanated from it.

The Ladies K's apartment, as were the other three, was a renovated stretch of servant's quarters transformed into a spacious two-bedroom. Since our collision in the Edinburgh Monkey Barrel comedy club, I'd only entered the hallowed apartment a few times.

In the aftermath of the Monkey Barrel collision, the hotel room strewn with wreckage, we untangled our naked, sweat-laden limbs.

"Perhaps," I'd asked, tugging on boxers, "after breakfast, I might escort you to your door?"

"It's rather far south of here."

"Is it?"

"Paris actually."

"Hey, me too."

"Paris?"

"I've accepted," I explained, my ribs still sore from Thander and Svorg's invitation, "a position with an import company there."

Her face, a bug in amber, was trapped in a vague, flat smile. Confusion? Yes. And something I interpreted as joy. "Why? What's wrong with Paris?"

"I," she answered, tugging on the little black dress, "live there."

Over a hefty, full Scottish breakfast, we'd agreed—neither of us believed in fate.

Splitting the check and with a quick, dismissive kiss on the cheek, we'd separated in the cold October rain. It wasn't a great last goodbye, but an adequate one.

However, being on the same flight, it was only practical to share a cab. And my AirBnB being near a kebab shop and having an exquisite view of the Jardin du Luxembourg mere coincidence, as was the multi-spray, massage shower, and the king-sized bed.

I crept to the door and peeked in.

"Katrina? Hello? Katrina?" My voice, a ghost in a mist-shrouded moor, was lost down the long hallway, its beguiling parquet floor.

I pulled the Rioja out. Twisted cap, sipped into a legitimate swig, recapped, and tucked it back in.

The red settled and I found myself, even having been cleaned and coifed by Sancho ("You don't want to look like you've been raped by goats before you get to Greece."), regaining my Durden. I massaged my Dr. Albright-stiff hip and, after another swig, slunk in.

Aligned along the wall, next to the antique coat rack, under the gold framed mirror, were six pairs of children's shoes. Katrina, like me, disliked children. And given so many, the apartment was quiet, too quiet. Perhaps it was nap time? Though, somewhere, a low thump, thump, thumping droned.

Recalling Widow Shriver's gnome comments, I hesitated. "Katrina? Hello? Katrina?"

Again, silence replied.

The door opened onto a *petit foyer* at the confluence of two hallways. The shortest, on the right, led to an expansive bathroom with an en suite shower and Katrina's bedroom beyond. The longer led to a spacious galley kitchen, the dining-slash-living room, a WC, and, at the far end, Kelsey's bedroom. I'd never seen her door open before, nor had I met the illusive lady. Perplexingly, a moody, inviting glow seeped and sparkled onto the parquet floor.

"Katrina? Hello?"

Fondling the Rioja, I gave the shoes a final frown and slunk across the hallway into the dining-slash-living room. The shutters on all the windows overlooking rue Washington were shuttered three-quarters and cast the room in a nuanced gloom.

Slipping from beneath the wine-weighted satchel, I squinted around.

Katrina, a fully-fledged organizational zealot, had decorated in hardcore Ikea. And though she constantly chanted the mantras of *mis en place* and *feng shui*, the room was awash in party clutter and an array of empty bottles.

Candy and potato chip wrappers were strewn across the four-seat, red, Söderhamn sofa and the three orange Ekerö chairs. Bottles were dumped into the Rågkorn planters and their ferns. The Fugelsang glass coffee table was covered in pills, rolled-up bills, and traces of illicit narcotics.

This wasn't a conservative Russian woman's altar to practicality, but a Rolling Stones' hotel suite, vintage 1973.

Unsure if I was disgusted or envious, I noted all the bottles were Champagne, no, Prosecco, no... I picked one up and sniffed. There were hints of tainted apple, medicinal lemon, and sweet ammonia. It wasn't a Crémant or Cava or something just as vile from someplace just as beautiful.

The label, rather than the name or image of a chateau or vineyard, was dominated by a flute playing satyr. The flute was his curved, swollen phallus. He was stomping grapes in a vat and the juice flowed out and over three dancing maidens, each with a breast flopped from her toga. Around the border Cyrillic lettering repeatedly declared, "Alexi's Boubles Vine Fine Wine."

There was nothing regarding country of origin, vintage, brut or sec, or alcohol content. There was, however, an exceptionally long phone number.

Rather than make the call, I tilted the remnants into my mouth. I was reminded, immediately, how I despised bubbles, or boubles, and anything reminiscent of cat urine.

"What do you mean we need to take Tabitha to the vet?" Mother had asked, slinging two five-liter boxes of wine, a Merlot and a Cabernet, up onto the kitchen countertop.

"You know that Pinot Gris," I explained, "the one you left for me to assess?"

Mother burst into bright laughter and nearly dropped one of the bottles she'd pulled from the recycling bin.

"Yeah. That one," I admitted. "Well, besides being mostly a New Zealand Viognier with some flat, Napa, sparkling shit, there was also—"

It took minutes for her to quell her laughter. Wiping tears away, she asked, "You smelled it, didn't you?"

"I did."

"Then for shit's sake, Dixon, why'd you drink it?"

"I was curious if it was what I thought it was."

"Oh," she said, blowing her nose, and placing a few more bottles in the sink. "And?"

"It was. And Tabitha may have leukemia."

"Oh, bullshit," Mother spat, attempting the math, ten liters divided by 750 milliliters.

I answered, "Thirteen point three-three-three repeating." She, with a disgruntled grunt, pulled more bottles from the bin as I asked, "What are you doing?"

"Tonight's *Sex and the City*."

"And?"

"And I'm not wasting good wine on those witches and bitches I call friends."

"And Tabitha?"

"I'll take her in tomorrow. Now start rinsing and mixing."

Stepping around and over the minefield of pizza boxes, a few with greasy slices left cold in them, I slipped past the broad, derelict, white-washed fireplace, the busts of Rimsky-Korsakov and Tchaikovsky eyeing me contemptuously from the mantel to the second pair of sliding double doors.

Putting the boubles bottle down, I delicately separated the doors and leaned into the hallway, "Hello? Katrina? Katrina?"

Encouraged by such silence, could I flee to Greece, alone? Forego the lying and obfuscating to Katrina? The debt to Boonen? I'd learn how to make tourist Retsina, feta and baklava. At night, staring bewildered under the unforgiving stars, I'd speculate on where Katrina was and what Kelsey's room contained.

Like the Tabitha-infused elixir, my compulsion for knowledge outweighed my rationale for ignorance and I slipped into the hall only to find more of Alexi's boubles bottles.

Bottles of Alexi's boubles littered the hallway and, like bread-crumbs, led to Kelsey's door.

Nearing the alluring golden glow, the soft, underwater *thump*, *thump*, *thump*, somewhere behind me I heard a door explode open.

I spun as the soft thudding of feet pounded the hallway.

Slipping, sliding around the corner, through the gloom of the hall-way was... Widow Shriver's gnome?

I squinted in disbelief as the figure, its white-socked feet finally gripping the floor, trundled toward me.

The golden glow from Kelsey's room illuminated not a classic gnome, but something more hideous.

Though the short man was painted cotton candy blue and wore a yellow beanie, after that everything took a hard turn into fascism—greased, raven black hair, a Hitler mustache, assless, black leather chaps and bicep tassels with a red-and-black swastika emblazoned on his chest. Girded about his loins was a monstrous, glistening, pink-and-purple swirled strap-on. It, an excited dog's tail, wagged about, slapping him, to his glee, in the face.

Too frightened, too confused, frozen, I stared.

Pressing myself to the wall, he passed without a "Hello" or "Howdy-do." He skidded to a stop in the glow of Kelsey's door and, gathering himself, socks slipping on the parquet, he, in a rich, Germanic accent, shouted, "*Eins! Svei! Drei!* Geronimo!" and shot into the room.

Tabitha curious, I took a few hurried steps and peeked in.

Too confused and frozen, I stared.

Thanks to the Crushed circuit, I'd had the misfortune to witness several lude and lurid acts. Though, fearing the necessity for greater psychological intervention than I already needed, I'd never felt compelled to partake.

Also, as one might imagine, it undermined one's competitive edge. There were Art's false, though jarring, insinuations regarding one's father or sister. Then there was the truth, "I hear you enjoy a golden shower while gargling man seed dressed as Dorothy."

And one, so I'd heard, did not readily wish to confront such observation over a meager tasting of Sancerre and Chenin Blanc.

Regardless of how prepared I believed Crushed had made me, I'd never seen anything so deprived as what stewed within Kelsey's bedroom.

Across the giant, heart-shaped, pink latex bed, glistening with bodily fluids, oils and lubricants, a woman wearing a garish, turquoise-blood red tiger luchador mask was splayed. Her gold flaxen hair pulled through the back into a firm ponytail. Godiva chocolate wrappers clung to the nipples of her firm breasts, while a pair of ruby red, knee-high, latex boots with six-inch stiletto heels sparkled her long, toned legs.

In each hand, she stroked a mini-Nazi's psychedelic strap-on, while another had theirs in her tiger's maw. All three, inexplicably, were doing the Chicken Dance, while the one which had trundled past was backing, with a tart grimace, onto a lube-dripping heel. And, finally, something furry excitedly wriggled between the woman's legs.

Rubbing my eyes, I realized it was a greedy little dog licking away.

"Vlad?" I gasped, not envious but appalled and sickened.

The dog raised its stupid, teacup, Brussels griffon head. Its muzzle dripped with goopy, gooey peanut butter. Ears at attention, he glanced around. Peanut butter splattered about. After a few sloppy, wet smacks and slurps, he yapped, once, twice, and buried his head back between the woman's legs.

The room, except for Vlad's lapping, fell quiet. Even Geronimo Nazi, nudging onto the stiletto, had stopped his gentle grunting to turn to me.

Spitting the strap-on from her mouth, the woman exclaimed, "Dixon?"

The cameras, one in each corner of the ceiling, red transmission lights blinking, rotated toward me.

I was now more committed to fleeing for Greece, though would forgo previous plans to join a remote mountain monastery.

An anguished moan roiled the air, as the woman, quite probably Katrina, extricated Geronimo Nazi from her heel. She slipped in a wet *sploosh* from the bed and swayed atop the stilettos as Geronimo Nazi staggered away in pain.

"Dixon," Katrina demanded, stomping a stiletto, "you do not leave. You stay here. You stay."

Geronimo Nazi, moaning, bent over, sprayed brown bile across a wall.

Horrified, I, like the others, turned away as he collapsed into his filth and wheezed, "Geronimo. Geronimo."

The room filled with a putrid stench as he writhed in pain, and I fled.

"Dixon! Stay!" was followed by the awkward *cack-cackling* of stilettos on parquet and Vlad's *yap-yapping*.

Kicking bottles out of the way, I stomped for the door, and Greece.

Katrina called out again, her voice a twisted amalgam of Midwestern American and Russian. Regardless, she sounded frantic, desperate, "Dixon wait! Dixon!"

I spun, and screamed, "What?"

She, backlit by the golden glow, stuttered to a stop and Vlad scampered to her ankles and yapped more. Peanut butter dribbled across the floor in shapes I knew well—formal peacocks at a punchbowl.

The mini-Nazis gathered and grumbled behind her as she claimed, "Dixon, I can explain."

A Godiva wrapper slipped from a nipple and drifted to the floor. Vlad sniffed it.

"Bullshit." I snatched my satchel. Its uncooperative weight nearly tugged me to my knees, but I kept my feet and found the front door.

"Dixon, wait!" Katrina yelled over the peanut butter-muffled yapping.

Clenching the door's handle, I spun and glared as something I'd thought I'd buried deep and dark exploded.

"What do you mean the Azores?" I'd asked Liza's forlorn eyes and packed suitcase.

We were in Bruges, lodged in the Relais Bourgondisch Cruyce, a quaint historic inn. I'd returned from the last round of the Battle in Bruges competition having been pummeled by Gunnar Skarsgård, an annoyingly jovial Swede.

Liza and I, so I'd thought, had planned on a candlelit dinner and a stroll around the village.

Instead of a bit of beautifully romantic, I'd entered something all too tragic.

Liza remained silent, so I continued, "And who is this twat?" I, with a sharp, disgruntled thumb, indicated the dashing, self-assured gentleman in his debonair ensemble of black Amiri jeans, Versace boots, a pearl white, Loro Piana quarter-zip sweater, and Kiton Blue Vicuna overcoat.

He, infuriatingly, remained silent, though gave his muscled companions a twitch of a smile, which required me to ask, "And who are those two puckered assholes?"

The concrete bricks in dark suits smiled and, not surprisingly, said nothing.

The gentleman twat gave Liza a gentle nudge, whispered in her ear. "Liza?"

"I," she said, biting her lip, "wanted more than to be with just a Crusher."

"What? Why would... Just a Crusher?" For comfort, I squeezed the fourth-place winnings lumped in my pocket and bit back explaining the nuance of *what* one was wasn't *who* one was. Or was it vice versa?

Regardless, she observed, "I thought you were a writer," and, grown comfortable with the dagger's hilt, continued, "I thought... It doesn't matter. Not anymore. I'm sorry, but we're finished."

My anger and I, and the bottle of 20-year tawny I'd planned on having for a nightcap, with difficulty, squeezed past the bricks.

Now she and that pompous twat, Roland St. Fer, were starting a sister winery, while I got kicked around by novitiates, went deeper in debt to a wrathful Belgium, and my almost fiancée, buggering a mini-Nazi with a heel, was getting... by Vlad. Fuck. Fuck. Fuck.

"Dixon—"

Stomping out, I slammed the door with every ounce of frustration and anger exploding from me. Fuck!

Instead of the satisfying crisp explosion of wood screaming in agony, there was only a muffled *thunk*.

Katrina, attempting to stop me, had to have the last word, but, goddamn, not today. Not today.

I slammed it again.

I ignored the shouting, the screaming, the scraping, the scrambling of fingernails.

I slammed the door over and over and over.

I slammed it until the wood screamed closed and the world collapsed into graveyard silence.

Righteously indignant, I settled the satchel over a shoulder and... something rolled past.

Moderately round with two dark, glassy things and two floppy things, it, disconcertingly, trailed blood in Rorschach spurts.

I leaned and stared. Momentarily, I caught my reflection in the object's dead, dark eyes before it tumbled over the first step.

"Vlad?" I asked, disbelieving at such a sick and gruesome hoax.

Prepared to denounce such wickedness, I shouldered the door open. Vlad's body, pushed by the door, slid across the parquet, bounced off bottles, and made a wriggly red trail to Katrina and the mini-Nazis, where it skidded to a stop, oozed blood.

Katrina, horrified, screamed, "Vlad!" and swept up two bottles. She slammed them against the wall. Shards of glass and boubles sprayed everywhere.

Screaming, "Death to tyrants!" she charged, as the mini-Nazis, also frenzied, swept up bottles, broke them, and followed.

Katrina's heels, designed for debauchery, were not nonslip. She, across the blood-splattered parquet, skated and slid through Vlad's red smear, flailing the broken bottles chaotically through the air as she bounced off the walls toward me.

The mini-Nazis, diligent heroes at her hips, attempted to guide her. They, however, were cut and sliced as they did so.

Blood and boubles slathered the floor, as a tentative truce between Katrina and gravity seemed to have been reached when both stilettos shot from under her.

Regardless of the mini-Nazis, she slammed to the floor in a solid, skull-cracking *thunk*.

The mini-Nazis, just as my fellow dwarves had done in our Aloha Mountain production when Sleeping Beauty was woken by the prince, made a great gasp.

A foreboding rose of blood bloomed from behind her luchador mask. Horrified, we knew no prince could wake her now.

Aghast at her grotesque twitching, my breath and heart stuttering, I turned away in disbelief and dismay.

Hoping for understanding, I found only the rage-filled faces of the mini-Nazis.

They, in another bright explosion of glass and boubles, shattered more bottles across the walls and, screaming like she, "Death to tyrants!" charged.

Forgoing grieving, engulfed in self-preservation and panic, I slammed the door shut and ran.

Scrambling down the stairs, one hand on the railing, the other quested for the Rioja.

Making the next landing, extracting the bottle, I stopped and stared.

Between gasps, I raised, lowered, raised the bottle, took quick sips, and pondered the bewildering scene.

Vegetables—a stalk of celery, four red potatoes, an eggplant, and a red bell pepper with a large carrot straddled by two Portobello mushrooms—and four tins of sardines were a tangled trail to the Widow Shriver.

Katrina style, a snow angel, she lay splayed on her back, stared toward the ceiling with a fistful of letters crumpled at her waist and Vlad's head at her feet.

She didn't seem to be breathing. And her dark glasses hid her eyes. I could take them off, maybe press fingers to a wrist or..."Madame Shriver?" I asked, nudging her with a toe. "Hello? Madame Shriver?"

Overhead, angry shouts exploded as the mini-Nazis burst from the apartment and clambered into the elevator. It creaked in complaint.

"Sorry, Madame Shriver," I explained, "it's those damn, dirty gnomes. Gotta go." And, with a final sip, I turned and tucked the bottle in.

Across the way, on the opposite landing, an elderly Japanese man in a traditional, men's black-and-white kimono, stood staring.

I waved.

He waved back, and I, dodging two oranges and a carton of shattered eggs, set off.

Making the final landing before the foyer, an ear-splitting, tortured banshee screeched and flayed the air.

A raging Armageddon meteor, the elevator, aflame, spewing sparks and acrid smoke, plummeted past. The screaming mini-Nazis shook the cage and attempted escape.

I spun from the railing as it slammed into the foyer's marbled floor, shuddering the building in a great, resounding *boom*!

Smoke, a poisonous army, dark and toxic, bloomed and billowed, and invaded the building.

Descending, coughing, choking, through the thickening gloom, I stumbled for the front door.

Halfway, the front door opened, and a beam of light sliced through the smoke and shadows. I turned toward the crumpled, smoking carcass of the elevator.

A figure, slapping at its flaming, melting strap-on, stumbled from the elevator's crumpled mass when it exploded in a great, fiery ball.

The hot fist of the explosion punched me to the cracked, marble floor, as the mini-Nazi's smoking body shot past, and slammed into the person standing in the doorway.

Fueled by adrenaline and panic, ears ringing like tambourines in an echo chamber, I struggled to my feet and swayed as warm liquid ran down my legs, spread out across the floor, red and bubbling.

Engulfed in panic and fear, I searched for the gaping, shrapnel wound. Attempted recalling arterial pressure points, but realized... Disgusted with such loss, even for the Champagne, I dragged the wine-oozing satchel behind me.

Prostrated across the door's threshold lay a mail carrier, a trickle of blood running from her nose as she blinked and smiled awkwardly.

"*Merde. Qu'est-ce que c'était?*"

"A mini-Nazi," I answered, as we turned to the charred, smoking body and watched her mail cart wobble away.

Dragging the satchel, I trundled out and considered giving chase. The streets, however, were consumed by confusion and chaos, the screaming, and blaring of car alarms.

I chose stillness instead.

The cart, pushed by the spring breeze, wobbled faster and faster toward a street corner where a lanky, dreadlocked, fire stick busker performed.

I raised an ineffectual warning hand as, from my pocket, a plaintive animal chirped.

Turning from the inevitable, I answered.

They said something.

Unsure, because I'd not heard their voice for nearly five years, I asked, "Mother?"

She, because she'd traded the therapist's chair for a real estate license, a convertible Mercedes, wine coolers, and Christ, said, "Dixon, I'm sorry, but your father's bought the farm."

"Farm? What farm?" I asked, as flaming letters fluttered and drifted up into the air, down the street.

"The Big One. The one in the sky."

"You mean he's dead?" I asked, as emergency vehicles arrived, as flames engulfed the building, the trees, and what lay beyond—the hairy, giant vagina.

"Yes. I suppose that's another way to put it. Your father's dead."

Off in the distance, another explosion thundered. More car alarms erupted as a small mushroom cloud rose into the pristine azure sky.

I watched the cloud rise and rise.

Something tapped my shoulder.
I turned and discovered greasy-green pigeon poop.

Chapter Seven
PLACES BETTER THAN HOME

Through a hazy, cotton candy cloud of antidepressants, I stared at a face I was supposed to know but didn't.

More than once, as I floated on the ethereal blue, someone claimed, "That's your father."

Regardless of what the angelic, wavy faces declared, the man, bright gray-green eyes over an aquiline nose and friendly smile, all secured beneath a thin, though firm ridge of nut-brown hair submerged under waves of gray, was a stranger.

Before I belted out "Cat's in the Cradle," another someone nudged an elbow, offered a glass of wine, and advised, "Smile. Just keep smiling. And don't drink this."

Accepting it, I sniffed and replied, "Screw you, do you know how long it's been since I've had a decent Meritage?"

"Mr. Belltower," the someone said, reaching for the glass, "it's been advised—"

Deftly I dodged, *tinked* their glass with mine, and observed, "You'd take such hope from me at such a dark time?"

Before she replied, another someone joined us. "Mr. Belltower? Jackson Tate of *The Oregonian*. I was hoping we could—"

"Mr. Tate, I'm sorry," the first someone, insinuating between us, said, "but Mr. Belltower has been advised not to answer any questions."

"And who are you?" Tate asked, unsheathing a pen and notepad.

"Officer Alicia F. Tilden," I chimed, "State Department liaison officer out of Washington, DC." Her look of surprise suggested I may've been wrong. "Aren't you?"

"Are you?" Tate asked, smiling.

Officer Tilden, happy to match Tate's unsheathing, declared, "Actually, I'm the person you need to explain how you got in here without an invitation." She took his elbow and guided him toward a bulky shadow by a door.

Happy to quest for more Meritage, I glided off into the dark, coral-crowded shoals of the room.

The room, however, was larger than the initial cotton candy cloud had implied. I became disoriented, lost, and drifted aimless.

Thankfully, there were those willing to fill my sagging sails.

"Just a topper."

"This is from Alexander Valley."

"Screw Sonoma. Try this."

And there were the assholes, the anchors.

"I'm terribly sorry."

"You have our condolences."

And, of course, there were the curious.

Over a Penfolds Shiraz, I replied, "Life's a shit pie, which I'm happy to eat." Beat. "With enough whipped cream." Out of the light laughter, I extended my glass, "Now, someone, cream me." More laughter and a question. "Briefly. Yes." Another question. "Pubic Enemy Number One." And another. "The importance and power of small things and how even a pubic hair can affect change or cause catastrophe."

Returning to my elbow, Officer Tilden, the cold undercurrent of intoxication having swept me from the shoals to much deeper, darker waters, found me sitting at a silver prep table Durdening a woman.

"Mr. Belltower, didn't I ask—"

I put a firm finger up, "Not now, Tilden."

The woman, a Sara something with brown hair and brown eyes like a tired squirrel, was good, but local good. She was a medium fish in a small pond. I, however, was a big fish in an inconceivably vast ocean.

"Mr. Belltower, I can't sanction this." Officer Tilden glanced at those crowding the small banquet kitchen. She'd hoped for help or understanding or... Instead, she discovered the ravenous visages of fanatics.

We'd shooed the sniveling little caterers out and had organized a TOD, a Taste-Off Duel. I'd offended someone by declaring, "Pinot Noir is as delicate as a baboon in a tutu. Yeah, it can dance, but you still wouldn't want to screw her." Beat. "Or him." Beat. "Though maybe you would."

The offended someone had whispered in an ear and, eventually, Sara Something was tapping my shoulder.

Officer Tilden sighed. "Make it quick."

"She sounds," I declared, keeping my Durden, though adding a slight smile, a nod, "like all my girlfriends." Beat. "And your husband."

Over the gentle laughter, Officer Tilden and Sara wanted to raise objections. However, a round, terrier of a woman, flanked by a taller, younger replica and a gangly, familiar-looking youth, in ill-fitting tuxedos *sans* jackets, marched in looking for a fight.

Everyone turned as the woman demanded of the youth, "Jeremy, who called you a sniveling, little twat?"

Jeremy raised his arm and pointed a trembling finger at me.

Her eyes ricocheted off my bulletproof Durden to another mark, a depressed Owen Wilson-looking gentleman. "What the hell is this, Daniel?"

Daniel and a few others mumbled excuses.

The woman wasn't buying what they were selling—bullshit. "No, Daniel, it isn't. It's a damn Crushed competition. How many—Theodore, Margery, Nathan—how many times have I explained—" Officer Tilden stood. "No, sweetheart. No."

"Excuse me? Do you know who—"

"Do you know I could lose my license? Do you know the temple could be shut down? Do you? No, I didn't think so." Discovering a renewed sense of authority in the spectators' anguished complaints, she commanded, "So, Anna, take Jeremy here and start breaking down the bars. Now." She glowered around and, as her cohorts exited, called over her shoulder, "And tell Norris we're done."

The woman, with a final blistering stare, stomped out.

Officer Tilden took my arm. "All right, Mr. Belltower, we should go."

I did not.

Something in me, the vision of the mini-Nazis amassing behind the tiger-masked Katrina, made me believe I was responsible for her... the D-word. And beating Sara would make amends, for some of it, somehow.

Turning from the stack of bills on the countertop held down by a tray of mangled mini-quiches, I asked Officer Tilden, "Do you have four hundred dollars on you?" It was a meager wager, as I'd seen thousands bet on a lone glass, but the winnings (assuming I won) would be a start to what I owed Boonen.

"I do not," she admitted.

"But the U.S. government does, doesn't it?"

"Well, I should hope so."

"Excellent." I clapped. And, excitedly rubbing palms together, I called out, "S-R. Three minutes. D-O-N."

Those who knew their rule book gasped.

Those who didn't whispered sharp inquiry to those who did.

And those that knew excitedly enlightened.

For emphasis, to prove I wasn't a Rosé amongst Cabernets, I curled my right hand in the form of a C and solidly pounded it against my chest, echoing each thump with, "Crushed. Crushed. Crushed."

Once all were in the know—Speed round. Two minutes. Double or nothing—everyone swiveled their attention to Sara Something, who, cautiously, though not convincingly, replied, "I can accept that."

Sara Something's tired squirrel eyes flashed around, and found an unassuming gentleman a few bodies back, off-center to her right. Perfectly aligned for when she held the glass and assessed.

Secret codes were nothing new in the Crushed world. Pay a few back-of-house pourers to get the Intel on the wines and stick a plant in the audience. A few flashed signs and a mediocre taster became a dégustateur exemplaire.

If that was the case, I needed to stick a curly hair in her salad, so I asked, "International World Championship rules?"

Sara's eyes filled with panic. The squirrel knew her tree had caught fire and there wasn't time to scramble to another.

"You know, don't you," Elizabeth ("Call me Liza") Anne Pillsbury ("No relation to the dough empire") had once observed, "the competition changes you?"

We were in Innsbruck for the Christmas holiday, the snow and fondue. We walked arm in arm down a quiet, cobbled street, snow drifting in tiny flakes through the street lanterns' light.

Even though she was one of the worst whites, a Moseler, I planned to leave the circuit for her. And though I was the worst of the reds, a Malbecian, I felt she'd agree to be with me. I only needed a few more competitions to acquire funds for a sommelier training program in Bordeaux and, maybe, self-publish a memoir regarding my trials and tribulations competing as a mid-level Crusher.

If everything worked to plan (after Porto, Manila, Stockholm, Berlin, and Bruges) Luxembourg would be the last.

"I know it's not possible," I replied, pinching nipples and gyrating hips, "but it makes me sexier, right?"

She smiled and shook her head. "No. A strange glow suffuses you, consumes you. And you become hyper-focused and animalistic."

"Still," I replied, pinching and gyrating, "that's sexier than I usually am."

"So," she asked past her laugh, "where are we going?"

Opening the restaurant's door, a bell dully tinkling, I announced, "Here. For the fondue. And..." With a shiver I added, "...and a glass of Chasselas or Grüner Veltliner."

Two months later, the initial butterflies of infatuation drowned in reality, she'd been more succinct, "You transform into a prick. That's what."

We were in Manila, and I wanted to blame heat and humidity, but I knew she had a valid point. And having taken second and being another competition closer to Bordeaux and becoming a sommelier, and maybe an author, I hadn't heard the truth to her words.

"Mr. Belltower," Sara squeaked, "we don't have the resources for an International."

In shark mode, smelling blood and needing to feed, I reinforced Liza's observation, "Only need a few phones and the Internet."

Sara, surprised, glanced around.

People nodded, pulled phones out, waved them. It seemed Sara might have enemies here.

I grinned, "International?"

She nodded.

"And, Madame, maybe you could advise Fingers there to keep his hands in his pockets?"

"What?" the man mumbled, feigning offense at my finger pointing at him. "Why?"

"Because I don't want you flashing signs to Squirrel Eyes here."

"You little—" The man, halfheartedly, lunged for me. He flailed, but was held back by a few spectators.

"Such exaggeration," I noted, "only proves my point."

After a nod from Sara, he calmed.

"And you're cheating will be useless if Bowling Ball returns."

"Shasta?" Sara answered.

"Whoever. If she returns, we'll... Her name is Shasta?" Officer Tilden shrugged, while everyone nodded. "Okay, well, I, and the U.S. government will deal with Shasta...if it becomes necessary."

"Well, then," Officer Tilden advised, "you best hurry."

"Okay, people," Daniel ordered, "boot 'em up."

Heads bowed, faces glowed as everyone logged into the Crushed competition website, a repository of officially approved and sanctioned music and videos.

Daniel scribbled an access code on a scrap of paper and passed it around.

I was impressed and surprised at their efficiency. Perhaps Sara Something wasn't such a damsel in distress?

Sweet, guttural, German death metal, either *Der Himmel wird brennen* or *Schwarzer Engel*, crawled from silence's grave and attacked our ears.

Sara bit her lip, and I, hungry shark, pressed on. "What about—"

The lone component of an International the website couldn't replicate was...

Daniel, spooning pink goo from a Sterno canister atop the mini-quiches, declared, "Got it covered." Finished, he lit them with a wavering flame from a red handled wand.

The flaming quiches filled the air with a pungent, burnt egg and broccoli stench.

I closed my eyes and inhaled. Perfection.

With the stench thickening, everyone encircled us and settled into place.

Officer Tilden, uncertain and unsure, slipped from the ring and drifted to a defensive corner position.

Having fully accepted the mantel of overseer, Daniel asked, "Mr. Belltower, since you called for the International, Sara is granted first and third selection. Agreed?"

"Agreed."

Handing us a scorecard and pen, Daniel noted, "We've eleven wines to choose from. So, Sara, whenever you're ready."

Each wine would've randomly received a number, one through eleven, and we'd... "Seven," Sara declared.

"Seven," Daniel called out.

From the far end of the kitchen, someone echoed, "Copy. Seven."

"Nine," I stated, while Sara, regaining some composure, immediately added. "Two."

Daniel called out and received an echo. "Copy. Nine and two."

A moment later, the glasses, each with a paper skirt and a number—7, 9, 2—written on it, were placed before us by a young caterer.

Seven shimmered like an over-oaked Californian Chardonnay, 9, a deep garnet, could be any of what I'd had throughout the night, while 2 was likely a local Pinot.

"Thanks, Kris," Daniel acknowledged.

"Welcome-welcome," Kris replied, walking away and flashing a peace sign over her shoulder.

"You're ready?" Daniel asked.

Continuing to Durden Sara, I adjusted my seat, and replied, "I am Crushed."

"Water?" someone asked, offering a bottle of sparkling.

Not knowing if it were to cleanse or poison the palate, I tightened the Durden. "Baby's piss. No, thank you." In the surprised, but appreciative silence, I added, "Kill the lights. Turn that shit up. And let's Mouton this hell hole. I am Crushed." Again thumping my chest with my cupped hand—thump, thump—I repeated, "I am Crushed."

The lights dimmed and the kitchen collapsed into a wavering twilight. The quiche fires glittered in the darkened windows, and the phones cast a milky pallor.

Daniel confirmed, "Two minutes?"

"I'd say one," I replied, adding some Dopey to my Durden, "but that Pinotage will be tricky."

My statement was greeted with a smattering of confused whispers. It forced Daniel, wearing the overseer cap, to reiterate, "Silence is the only thing I will tolerate. Understood?" A few replied. "Silence," Daniel barked. "Silence. Understood?" He was answered with what he wanted, what he expected—silence.

None of the wines, of course, were a Pinotage or South African. It was more mind games, which Squirrel Eyes seemed unprepared to counter.

And two minutes for three wines wasn't much, but that was the point—compress the time and compress the stress. Some thrived, some died.

Legend claimed the ill-fated Vincenzo Pozzovivo had assessed seven in three minutes to win, with an outlandish score of 34, the 1963 Moscow Hammer and Sickle Wine War. Due to the political climate and lack of substantiated evidence, poor Vincenzo's only championship would never be recognized by ICCA, the International Crushed Competition Association. He would die seven years later, impoverished in a rundown tenement in Naples.

"If you're ready, Sara?" I, being Crushed, didn't hear Squirrel Eyes' reply. "Mr. Belltower?"

"I am Crushed," I repeated and, playing more games, stage whispered to the glasses, "Now, little ones, do as Daddy likes, and bring on the pain. Bring on the pain."

Daniel, fighting an amused smile, counted down, "In three. Two. One. Taste."

The gathered, as was tradition for a TOD, intoned, "We are Crushed."

German death metal rose and phones, playing the identical video, a wake of vultures ravenously feeding on a bloated hippo carcass along the banks of a river, were turned on us.

Due to the time limitations, I forego any pleasantries. No sniffs or swirls, just a mouthful and slurp, keeping a bit in the glass lest I need a second taste.

Slurping away on the ridiculous Chardonnay, I fill out the scorecard.

Moving to the second, I found it meatier, more tannic and robust than anything I'd tasted all night. It was also something I hadn't had for some time and took longer than I'd like.

I was halfway through its assessment when Daniel shouted, "One minute." After chewing past the black plum, cacao, and balsamic, something clicks and I scribble.

On the third, I took a quick second and gathered myself as the music shifted to Chet Faker's "Gold" and the video from a black-and-white clip of people water skiing to a scene from *The Creature from the Black Lagoon.*

Daniel called out, "Thirty seconds."

I tossed the third down and filled in the blanks as I slurped. Satisfied and pleased, I slammed the pen down, "I am Crushed."

Daniel counted down the last five seconds and called out, "Time."

Everyone killed the feed on their phones. The underwater image of a scaly monster staring back faded and the world returned to a pensive silence.

Through the smoky quiche haze, Sara asked, a slight quiver in her voice, "Can we turn the lights back on?"

The lights flickered on, and we blinked in the brightness.

Sara, her hand shaking, reached for the first glass.

I glanced at her scorecard—it was blank.

Daniel, about to claim her forfeit, fell silent as she cried.

Her failed accomplice, screamed, "You bastard!" and lunged at me. Again, he was held back by a few alert spectators. Still, he made a few inept swings for me.

Sara wiped at her tear-stained cheeks, reached out, and, hand on his arm, said, "Nathan, please. Please stop."

Cursing, he struggled free, helped her to her feet, and, whispering in her ear, escorted her from the kitchen.

In the sudden denouement, the smoldering tray of quiche was placed in the sink, where they hissed under the faucet. A window was opened and the cold, night air rushed in.

Needing new entertainment, a few spectators offered "Congratulations" then wandered away.

Accepting the wad of winnings, etiquette dictating I count it elsewhere, I tipped the overseer. "Thank you, Daniel. Well done." And, due to the adrenaline, the added wine, I'd drifted further out into the undulating sea and wasn't just more nauseous but sincere.

"Of course. So," he smiled, tucking the bills away, "are you curious how you faired?"

"Am I?"

"Thirteen. And a savvy get on that Tinto Alentejo."

I was curious how it got here, but Officer Tilden had made her way through the thinned crowd.

"Are you ready now?" she asked, not impressed, just a different form of annoyed.

I thanked Daniel again and offered my arm to Officer Tilden. She declined and gently pushed me out.

The vaulted, color-glassed room swirled with activity as the caterers, to the confusion and consternation of the attendees, broke down the food and beverage stations.

With the resounding, echoing clatter of tables and glassware, the nausea rose higher and higher. The sea's undulations grew and grew. Something dark and dank boiled up from my bowels. I burped and a foul stench billowed from me.

Someone called my name and handed me something.

Automatically, I accepted it.

The item had a lid; thus, they knew what I was about to do.

Thankful, I thanked them, "Thank you."

Their reply was lost under an explosion of broken glass and cursing.

Losing the battle to constrain the inevitable, I hunched over, yanked the lid off, and held the cool, smooth thing to my mouth. Bile, hot and molten, rose out of me and spewed into the container.

A foul dust flew up and coated my mouth and nostrils in a thick layer of damp ash. Coughing, choking, I doubled over and vomited more.

Between agonizing wretches, I glimpsed thick, muddy gravy in a dark gloom. Before it flooded over and the foul slurry stained my shoes, the floor, and the world, someone snatched the container from me.

Without the buoy, I sank to the sea floor. Silt drifted up as I, primordial, curled in upon myself and waited for evolution's answer.

Eons later, on a second bottle of water (baby's piss my arse, this was the nectar of the gods), I chiseled a question from the stone of my throat, "What was in that thing?"

Finishing her glass of Merlot and glancing around for more, Officer Tilden confessed, "Your father."

Chapter Eight
A PRIMORDIAL NEW LIFE IN HELL

Under the soft weight of old quilts, I woke on a king-size, four-poster bed in a damp,mildew scented room. Syrupy-yellow light suffused the expansive room and highlighted the water stains in the outlines of murder victims that populated the ceiling.

Sitting up, I glanced around for a clue to where I was, besides the master suite of an old farmhouse.

Muffled voices, sad sea creatures, rose through the old, cold building, the ancient shag carpet. Rather than stagnate listening to such melancholy, I, the first being escaping the primordial ooze, crawled from bed.

Wobbling and swaying, a dormant nausea returned and I considered being sick, again.

Defeating the urge, I discovered I remained in the dark mourning suit with shoes still on, though laces untied. More perplexing, my mouth was minty fresh.

Running my tongue around my slippery smooth teeth, I staggered to the nearest glowing shade and pulled it aside.

A condensation-covered window greeted me.

My palm hovered as I considered wiping it.

Fearing the view would be no better for the effort, I turned to the eight black, military-grade plastic crates stacked along a wall. Each had an invoice taped across its lid and a gold lock hung in their hasps.

Were they the mini-Nazis' coffins? Or something more grotesque?

Bewildered, I squeezed the wad of winnings crowding the jacket pocket, just under a thousand crumpled there. I, a cat making biscuits, was comforted and continued.

Did Greece remain an option? Or something outside the EU? Maybe... A crisp knock startled me and was followed by an unfamiliar voice, "Mr. Belltower, are you awake? I'd like to speak with you."

"And," my minty fresh, though cat-scratched voice rasped, "who are you?"

"Jeffrey Malcolm Saunders. Regional affairs officer. U.S. State Department."

Opening the door, I discovered a tall, broad-shouldered man with wavy, chestnut brown hair and stern blue eyes looming in the cold, darkened hallway. A newly born porpoise, he glistened with hair gel and aftershave and wore a dark blue suit with a red tie. A silver briefcase, its black strap slung over a shoulder, glowered at his hip.

"May I?" he asked, with an insistent nod.

"What? Yeah. Come in." I stepped aside and he, and his aftershave, entered.

He marched to a far corner where, worn and sun-bleached, two antique, button-cushioned, puffy chairs and their matching settee lurked.

Settling on the settee, snapping the briefcase open, he, to my glance at the black crates, explained, "Your personal effects."

"From my apartment?"

"Correct."

I'd disliked that apartment and had planned for Katrina and me to transition to something... "Please, Mr. Belltower," a well-manicured hand indicated a chair. "I'm somewhat pressed for time."

"Aren't we all?"

Too sarcastic, too philosophic, he shot me an aggrieved stare.

Eschewing his invitation, I wandered to a pair of French doors, also choked with condensation. I ran a palm over the glass and peered out.

From the second floor, past a wraparound balcony, through a world shrouded by thick fog, could be glimpsed a series of grape vines running off into the gray distance.

Saunders, reiterating his annoyance, coughed, and ruffled some papers. "Shall we?"

With a resigned sigh, I sat and wiped my palm on the chair's scratchy arm. "So, where are we?"

Placing a stack of papers on the ornately carved, Mahogany coffee table between us, he declared, "Dundee. Now what I have here is—"

"Scotland?" Father had claimed family there.

"No. Oregon." My confusion lingered. He added, "Your father's vineyard."

"Oh." From a dull gold tray, I picked up a green crystal decanter where it sat with its red counterpart and three aperitif glasses. Pulling the stopper, I sniffed. "I didn't know he had one." To Saunders' stare, I answered, "Cognac. Likely—" I sniffed again, "Hennessy. Though perhaps Martell. Distinctly an XO." I smiled weakly at his growing glare. "Would you care for a glass?"

"No."

Pouring, I explained with a mangled Scottish brogue, "Just a wee bit of the hair of the dog, aye?"

Saunders, as I sipped, pressed sheet after sheet across the table. Each sheet was accompanied by a clipped explanation. Eventually, the pile lay before me.

Lastly, he, villain in a melodrama, placed a gold key on the table.

On my third glass and glowing, I was more confused than when he'd begun.

"So, Officer Tilden is for my protection?"

"Well, as I said, there have been threats."

"Threats?"

"Various factions have called for... I believe one, the—" He brought his phone out and scrolled. "The International Lovers of Bubbles—"

"I know them. And don't confuse them with LOBI. Lovers of Boys International. They don't appreciate it. At all." I sipped. Saunders glared. "Bubble lovers, what a bunch of pretentious twats. Right?" I'd met I-LOB's president, Hanson Smythe, and knew he was what I'd claimed.

"Regardless, they've released a statement, and I quote, 'decapitate him and use his head as a *cochonnet*.' Which, I'm told, has something to do with *pétanque*?"

"It's the little fob you throw the *boules* at."

"Okay, whatever. Just know Officer Tilden isn't going to take a bullet for you. She's here to facilitate you being left alone. The media away. And you, hopefully, not doing anything more stupid."

If I'd taken such advice, I'd never have met Katrina.

Nursing a pint at the end of the Monkey Barrel's bar, pondering Paris's potential, she'd sidled onto the next stool. "That was nice set."

"As are yours." I'd kept eye contact. It helped I'd gazed on her earlier. How could I not? Low-cut LBD that buttoned up the front with calf-high Dr. Martens, a black choker with a yellow smiley face pendant, and Arctic blue eyes which made me believe hypothermia wouldn't be such a bad way to go. And her accent was the cherry.

She laughed and I asked, "What's your take on whipped cream? Pro or con?"

She smiled and replied, "*Da.*"

A blood-hued butterfly's wing fluttered from a tiger's skull, eclipsed the memory, and I was dropped back into purgatory—the present.

Pouring another glass, I asked, "How long do the powers believe I should be 'left alone'?"

"Mr. Belltower, we're sorry, and you've our heartfelt condolences regarding your loss, but—" I picked up the top sheet. Its header read, *Week One Schedule*. As I scanned it, Saunders continued, "It's liable to take a few weeks to assess the situation and get the French to, well, as one embassy member had put it, 'calm the fuck down.'"

There was only one item scheduled. It was one I heartily disagreed with: Thursday, 11 a.m., Dr. M. Montgomery, therapist. "And if I refuse?"

"Mr. Belltower, I'm afraid you don't understand. I'm not here to negotiate. I'm here to tell you how it is. And how it's going to be. Unless—" He put a stern forefinger up, killed my complaint. "Unless you'd like to return to France?" He pulled one of the pens lined up like missiles in the briefcase and extended it to me.

France, I loved that place, but what remained there for me?

I picked up the key and accepted the pen.

Initialing the pages, and signing the final page, I set the pen down and Saunders said, "And you may want to consider how your actions affect Officer Tilden. She, too, is on thin ice."

"I don't like you."

"No one does," he declared past a wolfish grin, snatching the pen and tucking the papers into the briefcase. He snapped it shut and stood. "Oh, and you've got some schmutz." He considered a spot, but, recalibrating, waved his hand in the general direction of my face. "Well, everywhere."

Laughing, he exited, leaving the door open. A cold, insipid draft eked in and took up residence.

Chapter Nine
MONSTER UNMASKED

Staring in the bathroom mirror, I discovered someone I didn't recognize, myself. The "schmutz" Saunders referenced was a grotesque, clumped and caked mask of... The toilet was right there. It took no effort. I collapsed and hugged it like an old, dear friend.

Between intermittent dry heaves, another round of melancholy sea creature conversation sifted through the cold, damp house.

Stomach empty, and back in place, I rolled over. The chill of the tiles seeped through the suit, deep into me, my bones. What I'd hoped would be a moment of introspection was one of cold annoyance.

Downstairs, a door slammed. The old, thin windows, like shivering crickets, rattled. Someone strode across gravel. *Crunch. Crunch. Crunch.* A car door opened. A car door slammed shut. An engine revved and they sped off. The spraying gravel, chickens tap dancing, clattered against something thin and metallic.

The complaining tires drifted off into the distance and the world waded into an awkward silence.

Struggling to my feet and, averting my eyes from the monster, I pulled the mirror aside and exposed the medicine cabinet behind. Except for an old, used tube of Preparation H and an empty bottle of Nyquil, the shelves were bare.

To de-monster myself, I'd have to do it the hard way, manually, and venture into the claw-footed tub, where, like a noose, a large, round showerhead dangled.

I undressed and, pulling the faded aquamarine shower curtain back, discovered two dead mice, mummified atop the cracked rubber stopper.

Rather than sort through the crates, I crawled back into the soiled suit. Stepping to the mirror, a middle finger hiding most of the important parts of the monster, I turned the hot water on and waited. And waited. And waited.

Under a weak stream of cold water, I, with a cracked and yellowed chunk of something smelling of lilac and urine, washed my face and nothing else.

Invigorated by accomplishment, I strolled out of the bedroom and down the carpeted main staircase. The aged and yellowed plastic runner shod down the middle cracked and crackled, brittle bones, with every step.

At the foot of the stairs sat a large, foyer with whitewashed, slatted wood walls, benches, and coat racks on either side of the wide front door.

Functionality over pomp was something I appreciated.

On the left, a large living room with brown, well-loved leather furniture and a river rock fireplace sprawled in shadows. Upon the mantel sat a harbinger of doom and gloom, my father's urn.

To the right, an inviting glow wavered at the end of a hallway.

Stumbling into the light, I discovered more than the kitchen, but also a woman. She was hunched at the breakfast nook kitchen table staring into a mug of cold coffee.

Nearly positive she'd heard me, she hadn't glanced up.

Ringlets of hair, dark, tangled and curled, hung off to one side of her face, a mesmerizing mélange of Maya Rudolph and Halle Berry.

Shafts of morning sun slanted through the ebbing mist, the corn silk-hued drapes, and a modern-day Vermeer, gave her and the array of to-go menus strewn at her elbow an ethereal quality.

Struck by such beauty, I was enlightened, "Officer Tilden, good morning." I'd striven for enthusiasm, though feared, as usual, I'd achieved sarcasm.

"Is it?" she said into her mug, "I hadn't noticed."

"Well, what about the chickens?"

"What?"

Waggling a forefinger around, I indicated the clock, knobs on the cupboards, drapes, the timer, and framed cross stitchings cluttering the walls, all reinforcing a singular theme.

"Oh. Yeah. Chickens."

Plucking a dangling mug from a hook under a cupboard, I clucked, "Agreed. Too early for such profundity."

Emblazoned on the mug, a perplexed chick with a sunny-side-up egg draped over its head declared, "The Yolks on You."

I glanced around for the coffee pot.

Incongruously, before I asked, Officer Tilden said, "No one delivers here."

Perhaps it was cold-brewed? Gripping the silver-levered handle on the old, red refrigerator, I tugged.

Too late, she warned, "I wouldn't," when a dense, putrid stench punched me in the nose, "do that."

My scratched and clawed throat couldn't accept such rot. Coughing, I staggered back and exchanged my mug for hers.

It wasn't coffee. It was insipid, artificially sweet, and, like water from the shallow end of a clean swamp, filled with fatigued carbonation.

I lurched to the sink, spat, and coughed. Coughed and spat. A few chunks from yesterday's urn incident came loose as a dark, oily liquid stained the white porcelain and oozed, serpentine, toward the drain.

After sucking off the faucet's cold stream, swishing and spitting, I lifted my head. Through puffy eyes, I squinted out the window, across the short gravel drive to wine trellises lost in the morning mist.

Glancing up the drive, it curling around the corner of the house and up the ridge where... An apparition, thin limbs undulating akimbo, scampered awkwardly down the slick grass skirting the drive. Its skin, pale gray, was caked and dried like the monster's face. Torn shards of fabric were wrapped all about it, trailing like kite tails.

"What the hell is that?" I blinked and rubbed my eyes, as the apparition twirled and twisted off into the mist-shrouded vines.

"Diet Dr. Pepper," Officer Tilden said, picking up the can and scrutinizing it.

"What? No. No. There was something—"

"I was desperate and... You saw something? Someone?" Scrambling to my side, she jabbed a shard of elbow into my ribs.

"What the hell, Tilden?" I stepped back, as she and her 9mm surveyed the mist.

"Tell me what you saw. Tell me." Saunders had mentioned death threats, but her overreaction ... "What'd you see?"

In great detail, to her annoyance, I described the apparition, including some spot-on renditions of its undulating akimbo limbs.

She stared, unconvinced.

Limbs stilling, picking up a delivery coupon for a sub shop and "out of this world deals," I offered, "Maybe something to do with this UFO festival this weekend?"

"We're outside their delivery zone."

"Regardless, is it me, or is that Saunders a real wanker?"

At the sink, pouring out the mug and can of dead soda, Officer Tilden with a smile observed, "I can't call him such. Though, if you were to add 'weasel-faced prick,' I couldn't stop you."

"There's nothing here," I declared, opening another empty cupboard, adding, "And that Saunders is a weasel-faced prick."

Officer Tilden laughed, picked up a dark blue jacket, the US State Department's insignia on the left lapel, and moved toward the front door. "You're welcome to join. If you want."

"Ten minutes too long? I can do five. Though I'd like to put my dancing shoes on and redo my mascara."

"It'll take more than mascara to fix that."

"You doubt me?"

"Yes, I goddamn doubt you."

"You know—"

She pulled her phone out and fiddled with it.

"What are you—"

"Three. Two. One." Her forefinger touched the screen. "Go."

I was sliding around the corner, up the thickly carpeted stairs, yelling over my shoulder, the cracking of plastic bones, "You have a potty mouth for a federal agent."

Stumbling into the bedroom, I heard her muffled, sea creature reply, "I'm not an agent. I'm a goddamn officer."

Chapter Ten
SMOTHERED IN JAM AND CATSUP

Officer Tilden, while we waited for the hostess's return, searched on her phone and mumbled, "Back home there's a Waffle House on every corner. But, no, not here."

Our third "restaurant," like the previous two, was a glorified high-end country store with a handful of tables scattered throughout the overstocked shelves clogged with overpriced jars and cans of shit no one ate.

Like the previous two establishments, it too was filled with a slew of pretentious Sallys and Steves.

I knew more than hunger hurtled her finger, as, like with me, a barrel of residual adrenaline coursed her veins.

I'd made the mistake of being clever and had taken the back stairs down from the balcony, circled and slipped unnoticed into the green-blue, blue-green sedan.

Massaging my shoulder and ribs, I considered myself lucky Officer Tilden hadn't used the 9mm on me.

"I'm sorry," I repeated for the sixteenth time, "I scared you."

Her finger hesitated and resumed. "And," a smile nudged her lips, "I'm sorry for punching you. So hard. So many times."

Mother, over her textbook, *Practical Jungian Theory in Private Practice*, and a glass of midrange Tempranillo she'd purchased on sale, had asked, "What do you mean he apologized?"

I, too, had been confused. It was accepted behavior at Mahalo Middle School if one felt slighted, regardless how slight the slight, one needed to throw down or go home like a little, whimpering baby. Baby-baby-baby!

Matthew Holmes, however, instead of calling me out for calling him out for cutting in line and snagging the last chocolate milk, had had the audacity to apologize.

"No. No. No," Mother declared closing the book and standing, where she finished the glass in a gulp. "That is such a classic ploy."

I crumpled to the couch as she poured another glass and continued, "That's exactly what that bastard... What's his name?"

"Matthew Holmes."

"Right. Let me guess, gray-green eyes, aquiline nose, dagger spy smile with a firm outcropping of nut-brown hair?"

"Sandy blond. Steel blue. Very Steve McQueen or—"

"Jesus, not more Turner Classics with Grandma Bubba?" Grandma Bubba, aka Josiah Hubbard, was an octogenarian screenwriter who would watch me when necessary, and whom Mother claimed, "Could only rape you in his mind." Before I conceded it was one of the few pleasures I had (not the raping but the classic movies), she'd moved on. "Matthew Holmes is a sly, little shit, isn't he?"

"I only have him in English, so I can't say. He does like Hemingway and Irving though."

Mother gained steam as she shoveled coal, or at least Tempranillo, into her. "I'm sure he's a regular Iago, Machiavelli, Atreus piece of work. Oh, yeah. I know his type. Nice like a burly eight inches, until he pulls a goddamn Brutus on you."

She sipped and I kept my feet out of her deepening path.

She came to a full, sudden, stop. She turned and considered me.

Weakly, and rather fearfully, I smiled back.

"Before I tell you exactly what you're going to do to that little shit, Mathew 'The Back Stabber' Holmes..." She poured off the bottle into another glass, held it out to me. "...I want you to taste this."

I accepted the sparse few ounces of salvation and drank.

Mother's smile grew, as did my fear, as she added, "But first, a few questions regarding production, *terroir*, and vintage."

"Was it me," I asked, as Tilden remained searching on her phone, "or did you sound spiteful, as if directing each blow at a specific someone?"

"That was you."

"So, you declaring, 'Take that you motherfucking piece of shit, take that,' was just—"

"Yes. Exactly. Training kicking in."

Having told so many, I knew a lie when I heard one. I would've called her on it, but the dark-haired Barbie returned and asked, "May I have a name?"

"Why," I replied, "don't you have one?"

"No, it's for—"

"Weren't yougoing to find out how long for a table?" Tilden cut in.

"Oh, forty minutes, or so. It's hard to say."

"No, what's hard to say," I said, "is *Liebfraumillch, sex, Drogen, und Eine kleine Nachtmusik das ist der Senn der Lebens.*"

Barbie stared.

"Unless, of course, you're German."

Tilden, patience on empty, stated, "We'd likely be eating if we'd stayed at that first place."

"The one crowded with the bourgeoisie and serving fifteen-dollar porridge?"

"Oh, my god," Barbie confessed, "Norman's is so, so good."

"Okay," Tilden said, doing the math, "forty minutes to sit. Five, at best, to get the order in. Another fifteen to twenty for cooking—"

"I need a name if you're going to—"

"Yeah, I'll give you a name, you—"

Officer Tilden, gripping my arm like a bald eagle did a fish, dragged me out, proclaiming, "I'll clean the frig if you cook something."

"Oh, I can cook, and I'm gonna make that damn Viking my bitch."

Tilden shoved me in the sedan, clambered in, and, turning the key, warned, "Hold on." She slammed her foot down and the sedan, tires squealing, leaped forward, my head shot back, as she explained, "My father was a military man. Everything—brushing teeth, eating, cleaning my room—was time-based."

"Okay," I said, struggling with my seatbelt, as she maneuvered the sedan through traffic. "I understand that, but if we die in a fiery crash—"

"There's no benefit to having left if we're not eating in less time than if we'd stayed." She blew through a yellow light. "Agreed?" I did, and she asked, "So, why are you so hot for Vikings?"

Minutes later, a few miles farther East on 99W, finishing my diatribe on the benefits of a flattop grill, we were fishtailing into the Newberg Fred Meyer's parking lot.

Over the clatter of the cart's epileptic wheel, we cobbled together a shopping list. It was standard breakfast fair (at least in the U.S.)—eggs, hash browns, bacon, orange juice, the basics—until she curdled the conversation with "And catsup."

"'Tis an abomination to say it like that," I declared, as we pondered the expansiveness of the "one-stop" shopping center.

"Catsup?"

"Ketchup."

"Catsup."

"Condiments. Aisle 24," answered a harried, middle-aged woman wearing short, dark hair, a red and white vest, and a nametag declaring her Assistant Manager Cindy.

Marching for Aisle 24, "And," I added, "a greater abomination to use such filth."

"Nonnegotiable." Tilden shook the car keys and, with a smart-ass smile, tucked them into a hip pocket. "I'll need hot sauce too."

"Oh, I don't doubt that."

"And a coffee maker."

An espresso machine seemed impractical, so I conceded, "Fine. Coffee maker. With one caveat."

"What?"

"I want—and don't take this the wrong way, but I want dark roast."

Tilden slowed and drifted closer.

We'd sped through pastries, bagging a few ooey-gooeys. Losing Cindy around a corner, we drifted into the jellies and jams, an aisle short of 24.

Tilden's proximity was disconcerting, and arousing, like getting an erection by a one-eyed cat licking butter from your crotch.

"Go on," she said, smiling, "you want dark roast, do you?"

There were flecks of gold sprinkling her deep brown eyes. A subtle, Milky Way band of freckles spanned her nose, cheek to cheek. And, somehow, she smelled of the lamb kebab with extra sauce Algerian I'd once enjoyed in Istanbul. It aroused me more.

I hadn't forgotten the principle precept to my high school's improv troupe, The Yes Squad. And, sidling up to her, I welcomed yes into my life.

"Yes, I want, need, desire dark roast," I declared in my best butter-smooth, radio voice. "I want beans that are unafraid of leather or lace. And I want those beans firmly ground into a submissive powder so fine, so soft, so delicate, it causes angels to weep."

She took a deep breath, sighed, and said, "I'll comment on that later, but... Is it me and my black paranoia, or are people staring?"

Shoppers had indeed stopped and were staring.

Tapping my chubby down with one hand, I shooed them away with the other. "No, Agent Tilden, I'm sorry, but it's your black paranoia. Not to discount it or imply it doesn't exist. Well, not your paranoia, but—"

Placing jars in the cart, I stammered about Mark Twain and seeing *Roots* at an inappropriately early age.

Tilden placed a hand on my wrist. "If you can—"

"They're jars," I said, waggling the two I held.

"Can it." She took them and placed them back on the shelf. "Please, be quiet and choose something besides blackberry. Okay?"

"Oh," I said to the eight jars of various forms of blackberry preserves, "okay."

"Maybe honey or peach?" she winked, adding, "And calm that beast. I don't want spunk in my eggs."

"But you're going to use catsup, you won't even notice."

She gave me a quick peck on the cheek, admitted, "No, but you will," and walked toward the breakfast meats.

Making a final chubby adjustment and heading for Aisle 24 and its catsup and hot sauce, I declared, "Fine, but I'm in charge of the coffee."

An hour later, having taught the Viking a lesson or three, we were satiated at the kitchen table, a trove of condiments between us and our empty, yolk and ketchup-stained plates.

"Wow," Tilden said with a satisfied sigh, "was that as good for you as it was for me?"

"Possibly better, as mine didn't have spunk in it." Past my laughter, I snatched the plates and took them to the sink. "I'm kidding. It was in your coffee."

"I don't use that much cream, do I?"

I shrugged, refilled our mugs, and, sitting as she added cream, said, "So, that Saunders, what a weasel-faced prick, right?"

She fought back a smile and observed, ominously, "Well, I'm sure you'll have a few more adjectives for him in a few minutes."

With the last bag of groceries, from the trunk, she'd also lugged in an identical-looking suitcase to the one Saunders had had. Through the meal it'd sat, a wary gargoyle, next to her.

After a furtive sip and glance, she popped it open and pulled out a thick manila envelope.

I knew my past would catch me, though I'd hoped to be much older and much less sober.

She tapped the envelope, "Maybe we should take a minute or two?

"Two? You mean, like drop a deuce?"

She stared, disappointed, "Humor as a coping mechanism to alleviate internal tension in a perceived threatening situation?"

I frowned at the too-accurate diagnosis. "No. Maybe. Yes."

"Well. Okay. Whatever works for you." I started to comment... "Don't." Reluctantly, I didn't.

"First," she continued, "thank you."

"For what?"

"Just thank you. Can we leave it at that?"

"I suppose, though—" We stared. "Okay. It's been left at that. You're welcome."

"And, secondly," she said, sounding sad, "I'm sorry."

"Sorry? I suppose you'll not say for what?"

"For what." I smiled.

"For taking off the Alicia hat..." She mimed taking a hat off and putting another on, "...and putting the Officer Tilden helm back on."

"Hat to helm? That serious?"

"Yes," she said, pulling a few other items from the briefcase.

Biting back my standard nervous commentary, I, in agonizing silence, watched her set up a small tripod, a light ring, and her phone. All directed, ominously, at me.

Pulling a packet of papers from the envelope, a state department ballpoint pen from a jacket pocket, she asked, "Are you ready?"

"You know I'm not. But I never am. So let's do this."

After the standard declaration of time, date, location, persons in attendance et cetera, including a sincere condolence for my losses, Officer Tilden began, "Okay, Mr. Belltower, let's start with Kelsey Anne Conrad of Billings—"

"Who?"

"Kelsey Anne Conrad?"

I shook my head, but then... "Oh, wait. Kelsey? That's the roommate, right?"

"You may've known her as," Officer Tilden ran a finger down the page, "Katarina von Klit?"

"You're kidding, right?"

"I am not."

"Seriously?"

"Yes, seriously."

"Katarina von Klit? Who in the—" Oh, the mini-Nazis, Vlad, the cameras, the peanut butter, the stilettos....

"So you," Officer Tilden, cutting in on my reflection, asked, "don't know Kelsey Anne Conrad as Katarina von Klit?"

"No. No, I don't." I stood and rummaged again through the cupboards, searching.

"Recording paused."

"Did we not get anything to drink?"

"Coffee and orange juice, though—"

"Right back," I shot, shuffling out and up, and returning with the two decanters.

Having topped up my coffee, Tilden continued, "Okay. So, do you know, did you know a Katrina Vlasova?"

I took a long sip, "Yes."

"But not as Kelsey Anne Conrad?"

"No. Nor as Madame von Klit." Tilden scribbled. I sipped. "And who are Kelsey and Madame Klit?"

"Katrina and Madame von Klit are two of Kelsey's aliases."

"And she's the one from Billings?" I asked, ignoring the looming cliff.

"She is. Yes."

Officer Tilden, her pen unsure, hesitated.

I sipped and, like a blind man unknowingly led to the gallows, said, "You've got it all there, right? Go on. I mean, it can't be that bad, can it?"

And it wasn't. It was much, much, oh, so much worse.

"Kelsey," Officer Tilden explained, "was a cash mule. Instead of drugs, she worked as an online adult fetish hostess."

"Katarina von Klit?"

Officer Tilden raised a glossy headshot of Katarina in her luchador, tiger mask, blue eyes, sapphire daggers, stabbing. "She funneled funds to two bank accounts here in the U.S."

"Charities, right? Agencies benefitting orphans and stray kittens? Right? Right?"

Officer Tilden consulted a page. "A right-wing gun advocacy group in Idaho, Bullets for Believers, and a South Carolina knitting club, Lynching Knots. Each affiliated with The Power Initiative, a white supremacist group." With a slight, forgiving smile, she added, "We are, of course, unsure what, as Ms. Vlasova, she was doing with you."

Finishing off the green decanter and abstaining from the comedic response, "Reveling in my c-o-c-k." I grasped for a straw. "At least tell me the dog was named Vlad?"

She, with a quick, sad nod informed, "He was owned by McLickerson Unlimited, LLC. Also located in Billings. And his full, legal name was Vlad Licky McLickerson-Conrad."

"McLickerson-Conrad?"

"It's hyphenated," Agent Tilden said, unconvincingly hiding her smile.

"Hyphenated?"

"They were married in a private ceremony five years ago in Las Vegas."

"Thursday," I sighed, pouring more from the green decanter, "can't get here soon enough."

"Thursday?" Tilden asked, "That's your appointment with Dr. Montgomery?"

"I'm hoping he prescribes something as delectable as what I had the other night." I reconsidered. "Oh, wait. Shit. That was last night." I sipped, unsure. "Wasn't it?"

"Yes, your father's memorial was last night."

Distracting from the heartbreak, the betrayal, the overwhelming confusion, I asked, after another sip, "So what about Remy and the gang?"

"Who?"

"Remy Demare and Nikos Stakos, my employers."

Ignoring my slipped confession, she consulted her papers. After a moment, clicking her pen a few times, she declared, "All remain in French custody."

I, honestly, only cared about one, the one I owed 30.7K, T. Thomas Boonen.

"The gang, as you call them, were remarkably tight-lipped with the French authorities." So maybe I hadn't been implicated. "Except one."

My mug—the coffee pot too—was empty. I pulled the stopper off the red decanter and considered my options.

"Mr. Boonen doesn't like you much. He went into great detail about what he hopes to do to you."

Reinterpreting my most celebrated role, Dopey, I stared, blankly.

"It's all quite gruesome. Perhaps you'd like to explain why?"

"Mr. Boonen? Sorry. Not sure who that is."

"Thomas Thomas Boonen?"

"Wait. He has... His first and middle names are the same?"

"They are. So nothing to do with the thirty thousand he claims you owe him?"

"Well, maybe."

"And Kelsey wasn't working for you?"

"You mean as von Klit?"

"Yes."

"No."

"Not assisting you in repaying your debts?"

"No. And I'm offended and outraged you'd suggest such a reprehensible relationship." Proving my point, I took a slug off the decanter. "You know, I was about to propose to her?"

Making a note, she replied, "I didn't. But that doesn't prove your point."

"It doesn't?"

"No."

"Oh."

"Which brings us to those proposing to do you injury."

"Like I-LOB?"

"The bubble lovers, actually, have walked back their initial threats."

"Smythe must've had a flute too many to do that."

"More that Alexi's Boubles isn't champagne, cava, prosecco, or, and I quote here, 'piss from a passing Aussie ferry.'"

I laughed, "The pretentious bastard isn't far off."

"Oh? How so?"

"It's Czechoslovakian semi-dry Riesling and Spūrt."

"I'm sorry, what?"

"Spūrt, their equivalent of Squirt. Likely an eight-to-three ration with a bit of diethylene glycol and—" I, not needing to incriminate myself more, trailed off.

"Regardless, they stopped calling for your decapitation. They've downgraded to..." She consulted a page. "'...kick him in the balls anytime anyone sees him.'"

"Well, Saunders said you'd take a bullet for me. That goes for kicks to the balls, too? Right?"

She shook her head and pulled another report out. This one, sheathed between plastic covers also had an official government logo and stamp splayed across the title page.

It was in French and was likely my initial statement and interview with the French authorities.

"*Vous parlez Français*?" I asked, failing to hide my surprise.

"*Oui. Mais pour le moment* we need to speak English. It helps the folks back in Washington."

"And some of those conspiracy nutbags don't even comprehend English." I delivered a fake laugh. "Hahahaha," which she, turning a few pages, ignored.

A perplexed wrinkle ruffled the fabric of her brow, "I'm going to need a minute. Okay? It's more convoluted than I'd imagined."

"True that, sister."

She fired a glare at my raised high-five palm.

"Sorry. I'm nervous. And—"

"Give me a moment. I've the basic data, but not the situational logistics."

"Yes, ma'am."

Tilden read, turned a page, and bit a lip. "The French claim—" She turned back a page, leveled her bright eyes on me, "They claim you claimed 'mini-Nazis' were involved?"

I nodded. "Correct. I did."

"The claim or the mini-Nazis?"

"Yes. Both."

"Nazis? Mini-Nazis? And..." She read, dubious. "...Geronimo Nazi?"

First, I explained the title was in no way derogatory toward the Native American shaman, but simply as a term to differentiate that mini-Nazi from the others, who, to this point, remained anonymous.

Afterward, I described the man and his strap-on. "And when he ran it slapped him in the face." I slapped my cheeks with my palms. Alicia laughed, and I admonished, "It's not funny. I think he hurt himself when he pulled himself off her heel."

"Wait. What?" she asked, flipping pages, searching.

I stood, mimed erotically wiggling on and desperately off a long stiletto. And, slumping to the floor, I wheezed, "Geronimo. Geronimo."

Tilden's laughter renewed as I stood and repeated, "It's not funny. I'm sure he injured himself."

"And Vlad," she observed past a broad, bright smile, "lost his head over it?"

"Well, the little shit deserved it."

"Did he?" She dropped her head, read, and burst into laughter.

"I'll never be able to have peanut butter ever again. It's not funny."

Fighting her laughter, she agreed, "I know. I know. It's not. It's just—" She took a deep, composing breath and sighed, "But there has to be something lost or at least," she tapped the report with the pen, "exaggerated in the translation?"

"No. I told Officer Dujardin—"

She flipped to the last page, and tapped a signature, "The interviewing officer."

"Yes. And I, to his disbelief and disgust, confessed the ugly unblemished truth."

She returned to the report, bit her lip, and clicked the pen. "So then?" The bite deepened, and the clicking increased. "Then after Geronimo and Vlad and—" She took another deep breath and exhaled. "The elevator collapsed?"

"Yes. Was Geronimo on it?"

"If he was Constantine Yaman then no, he wasn't."

Tilden, reading the report in halting breaths, continued, "And a survivor tumbled out and was subsequently hurled... causing *le vagin de l'Arc de Triomphe s'enflamme*?"

"Yes," I admitted, "it sounds impossible, but the vagina Arc de Triomphe burst into flames."

She announced, "Recording paused," and, pulling the phone from the light ring, added, "Bullshit."

She fiddled with her phone, and I explained, "There was an art installation that set off a protest regarding the vagina being masculine." She shot me a glance. "You know, *le* instead *la*."

She erupted in laughter as a man's voice shouted from her phone, "*Mon dieu, l'horreur. L'horreur.*"

Standing, laughing, waving a hand, she admitted, "I can't. I can't," and escaped down the hallway to the living room.

I peeked at her phone. A video showed a great conflagration—the hairy, vagina Arc de Triomphe going up in flames.

Mesmerized by the monstrous, burning genital, I called over my shoulder and her laughter, "I'm liable to go to prison for this." It caused her to laugh more.

Many minutes later, wiping the last tears from her eyes, she returned, in a different pair of jeans.

Prudently, I mentioned nothing.

Resettled, coffee reheated, we returned to recording and her reading the report.

"There was," she bit her lip, "also an Eiffel penis? And a Louvre anus?" She glanced at me. My confusion only aggravated her amusement. "Recording stopped."

Standing, laughing, she returned to the living room.

I called out on her exit, "It's not funny. I'm going to prison. The UK is placing me on a terrorist list. Then there's Vlad. And poor..." Tilden laughed and laughed, and I sighed. "...Katrina." She returned, in the same pair of jeans, and I asked, "By the way, what anus?"

"The Louvre's."

"I know," I grinned, "it's got the Mona Lisa, but I know nothing of its anus."

"Okay." She took a deep breath, another sip. "You're prepared to answer questions about that anus?"

"Any anus you've a question for I've an answer for."

Determined, Tilden sat and repeated the recording protocol. After another sip, she asked, "So, what do you know about the Louvre anus?"

"I know many things about many anuses, particularly mine, but nothing about the Louvre's."

Past a firm stare, she announced, "Recording paused,"

In a stiff silence, she showed me the overhead drone shot, the words, the blue lettering, E. Pluribus Anus, discernible in the pink fabric highlighting the Louvre's glass pyramid, its anus.

Like the Eiffel and the Arc, the Louvre was likely the work of 12M, though the group was fictitious. Or so I'd thought.

We were on another episode of *Community*, tripping balls, and gobbling pizza after a spray fest through the bucolic, brick-bound jungle of Wickford, when Bussy, handing me the cherished dragon bong Smaug, had asked, "How about an ass in Paris?"

"Thank you very much," I commented, "but I like it just fine here." I took a big hit and handed Smaug to Naria, who explained, "Bussy's feeling inadequate."

"Insignificant."

"And he wants to do something great and grand."

"Profound."

"Like?" I asked, exhaling a cloud to the ceiling.

Bussy held up the magazine he was reading, a copy of *The Artist Magazine*. The article was titled, "Banksy's All Smiles at the Louvre." There was an overhead shot of the glass pyramid. In the atrium below, a shadowy figure stood with a distinct yellow smiley face head whose artificially long arm snaked out. The spray paint can the figure held was a can of Cream of Tomato Soup.

Knowing how much Bussy despised Banksy (we'd heard many a nuanced rant about why), and the magazine explaining nothing, Naria and I just shrugged.

Hitting pause, Bussy declared, pointing to the dubiously acquired flat screen, "Louvre anus."

The episode nearly over, Dean Pelton marched past a flaming Winnebago and planted the newly instituted Greendale flag, on a blue field a pink circle with six arrows pointing outward from a central spot. Encircling the pink, in white, was written E. Pluribus Anus.

"Well," I said, unsure of Bussy's exact intent, but always happy to take "yes" too far, "if you're going to do the Louvre, you might as well do the Eiffel and the Arc."

Tossing the magazine into a corner, Bussy's smile grew as he encouraged, "Go on, Belltower. I'm listening."

And I, until Smaug's bowl was sucked dead and dry, did.

Naria, cupping her petite breasts through the thick, black sweater, had then queried, "Aren't we forgetting boobs?"

"So," Tilden, having reset everything, asked, "you know nothing about the Paris penis, vagina or anus?"

"No," I declared, shaking my head and swallowing the urge to riff, "No, I don't."

She stared.

I, Dopey, stared back.

She nodded curtly, "Terminating interview. Now." She, with an exaggerated sigh of relief, another sip, leaned back, and eyeballed me.

"There's something else," I said, "isn't there?"

"Well, Mr. Belltower, yes, yes, there is."

"Thus," I nodded to the phone, the darkened halo, "this being off the record?"

"I'm, and I quote—"

"Saunders?"

"Not so oddly, I'm not at liberty to say."

With a courtly tumbling of the hand, I invited her to do so. "Okay then, please, do quote the anonymous one."

Using air quotes, she did, "'Prod him and see how loyal he is.'"

"You've been prodding me, have you?" She smiled and I continued, "Odd. I've not felt anything. You're a gentle prodder."

"It's a forté of mine. It seems few enjoy hard prodding."

With her Mata Hari confession, I reconsidered our chemistry, the jam aisle, and asked, not too spiteful, "So, if I'm 'loyal,' what do they want?"

"I'm under the impression it'd involve working for us."

"The U.S. Government?"

"Yes."

"In what capacity?"

"That wasn't disclosed to me. Though I was instructed to reiterate the possibility of you being returned to France should you decline."

"Nothing like a bit of blackmail, or is it extortion?"

"I think it's coercing someone to realize a patriotic duty."

"More soft nudging?"

"No. Maybe."

"Well, it's like getting your tasting fee 'waved' if you purchase a case."

"And that's a poor example."

"What? No. That was spot on."

"Only if you've been wine tasting."

Aghast, I stuttered, "What do you mean? You've never been wine tasting?"

"Hey, don't judge me. Judge Georgia."

In my best Southern drawl, feigning hammering a gavel, I pronounced, "I, Judge Georgia, do declare, you darn, damn scallywag to be guilty, guilty, guilty."

She, smiling, giving an appreciative golf clap, said, "You, besides your looks, are rather funny."

"Thank you. But really, you've never been wine tasting?" I hadn't meant to sound so incredulous, but, "Seriously, never?"

"I'm sorry, but regardless of what that is..." She waved an accusatory finger at me, the disbelieving shaking of my head. "...have you ever..." She eyeballed me, mercilessly, settled on. "...ever seen Wanda Sykes perform?"

"I assume you're referring to the African American female comic and not the Filipino transsexual trumpet player on East 71st?" Tilden's glare wavered. I admitted with a smile, "I like hard nudging."

She laughed, shook her head, and, pulling a small, white box from the briefcase, threatened, "A present."

Chapter Eleven
A VIRGIN NO MORE

It wasn't a present, but a tracking device some called a phone. Of course, it was the newest, slickest model, and also, of course, it was silver.

Tilden tucked the receipt I'd initialed into the briefcase. "You don't like it?"

"Like it? I love it." I was greeted with justifiable skepticism. "I'm sorry. Sarcasm is my voice's natural default tone. You'll get used to it."

"If not, I'll just shoot you."

"Hahaha," I laughed overly dramatically at her sternness.

"No, Dixon, I'm serious."

She did seem so. Maybe Tilden was a gun junky? Got off on shooting shit?

Before I recalibrated how far I could flee on the wrinkled wad of winnings, she'd laughed and I'd offered, "Well, to prove my love, I'll escort you to the nearest winery."

"You assume I want to go?"

"I assume nothing." She looked dubious. Regardless, I continued, "Though I speculate, you being an intelligent woman and, having observed your exuberant use of hot sauce and catsup, you enjoy pushing your boundaries."

"I can't help it. I know what I like."

"And," I paraphrased, "if you don't go beyond your boundaries you learn nothing but how to reinforce your limitations." I bowed and informed, "The Yes Squad."

"The Yes Squad?"

"Yes, The Yes Squad."

"Who are they? White suburbia's equivalent to The Mod Squad?"

I laughed, golf clapped, "That's funny."

"Thank you."

"They're my high school's improv troupe."

"You were a thespian?"

"No."

"But you said—"

"Once a thespian," I proclaimed, bowing and rolling a regal hand, "always a thespian."

She smiled, "That does explain some things."

"And I'm offended."

She raised eyebrows and sighed. "What now?"

"Why," I asked, waggling the phone, "does this infernal spy contraption need to know my height, weight, and date of birth?"

"Fine" she sighed begrudgingly, closing and locking the briefcase, tucking it under the breakfast table.

"Tasting?"

"Yes. Let's go." Rather than her jacket, she swept up an oversized, green and black plaid, flannel shirt with silver buttons.

Marching for the front door, she called, "Are you coming?"

"Not even close, though I am following."

With an animated hourglass spinning on the phone's screen, I locked the front door and headed for the sedan.

Tilden, however, was powering up the ridge, taking a sharp left and disappearing into a thin stand of pines.

"Hey," I called, "where are you going?"

The murky, muddy path meandered, after a few languid turns, across a creek and up and out into a sun-drenched vineyard.

At the end of the long length of vines sat a squat, cement, whitewashed building. Its red, corrugated metal roof had been baked dull by the sun and time. Under an overhang four large, silver, fermentation tanks stood like blind idols, while nearby sat a crusher destemmer. To the left of the building, where the pavement ended was a dusty parking lot with a half-dozen cars.

In the background, a mile up the hill, a glittering glass monstrosity lurked.

Catching her, I repeated, "Where are we going?" Before she answered, I, with an emphatic finger, pointed to the monstrosity, "You cannot take us there. No."

"It's one of the most prestigious estates around."

"No. Not for your first time. No."

Rather than argue, she pulled her phone out and scrolled.

"I don't care how many stars, or bottles, or whatever it has. Or if Robert Parker claimed, 'The *terroir* is rich and bountiful, but...'" I glanced at the monstrosity. "'...Vane and Vacuous Vineyard's true beauty is in the glass.'"

"Whoa, that's a mouthful."

"That's what she said."

"So, she wasn't with you for your humor?"

"She? You mean Katrina?"

"Kelsey."

Tilden's apology was cut off by my spinning away and, to my surprise, the phone ringing.

She'd explained earlier, "The techies have arranged to keep your old number active."

I was impressed, though not surprised they'd also had the thoughtfulness to keep my original caller IDs.

Marching off for the whitewashed building, hoping it contained what I needed, I answered, prepared to give Dildo a few choice sentences.

Instead, an automated voice droned contentedly, "Waiting for authorization. Your patience is appreciated. Thank you." And the line went dead.

"So," Tilden asked, sidling alongside, reworking her apology, "who's Robert Parker?"

Appalled, I made a blatant spectacle of gazing upon her and her ignorance.

The last time I'd been around such a vine virgin was with Mother's friends. And those witches and bitches were hysterical.

"Okay," Tina had said, "I do think Charlotte is the most attractive."

The witches and bitches had groaned and I, having become one over the season of *Sex and the City*, joined in.

"Going lez" was a frequent topic for Tina, particularly on her third glass, "What do you call this, Dixon?"

But they knew. It was Wrong Way Red. We even had a marketing slogan: Wrong Way Red—get lost in a glass.

It'd been during Episode 13, "Games People Play," of Season 2, when Carrie starts therapy and Mother's blending secret was discovered. As junior partner, I was blamed for the entire operation. However, I also received their praise and had been invited to join their semi-secret society.

"Tina," Shannon interrupted, "we know your Charlotte crush. Let's hear who Dixon lusts for." She held a hand up as I'd disclosed three episodes before my complete devotion to Carrie. Shannon, however, had a more diabolical idea, "Amongst us."

Shannon, to the delight of the others, turned her green eyes on me, "So, Dixon, do tell." And her open, upturned palm invited me to behold the other five ladies.

It was a foregone conclusion, it'd been settled on the Season One finale, amongst the group Lydia was number one, for everyone. But Lydia, the flight attendant, had been called up on a last-minute overnight to San Francisco and was missing and missed.

Confused, I turned to Mother.

"I better not be your number one, you sicko," she declared, adding, "Hell, I shouldn't even be up for consideration."

"Fine," Shannon said with a disappointed sigh, "Claire, you're not on the list."

The ladies, each unbuttoning a button or two, raising a hem or cuff, blinked coquettishly, promised various erotic delights if I chose them.

Occasionally after an episode, I'd return to my room and please myself fantasizing about one or a few of them. This though? Indignant, I stood, "Thank you, no, this is just too weird, even for me."

"Where," Michelle asked, dropping her skirt back to her knees, "does he get such prudishness?"

"He has," Mother explained, "a limited male social group, and without a father figure much of his masculinity is derived from the theatre."

This statement had sent them clucking and me marching down the hall to my room, though not before snatching a bottle of Wrong Way.

There'd been no pretense or posturing with the witches and bitches. Wine was nothing more than a lovely elixir to transport one to a space of joyful acceptance. And I loved them for that.

Tilden, like those lovely ladies, had yet to become contaminated by the presumptuous pricks congregating the wine world. It made her all the more alluring. And, I feared, that introducing her to it would corrupt her.

The phone rang. I answered as Tilden commented, "You're a hell of a chaperone," and continued down the vines.

"It could be important."

"Could it?" she asked, as the automated woman informed, "Authorization and activation completed. Have a superlative day." After the curious use of "superlative," the voice added, "You have seven new messages."

I scrolled through the IDs. There was one from Naomi and Art, two from Dildo, and three from a blocked number. All, except one from Dildo, were on the day of the Parisian apocalypse.

It was easy speculation on what they'd likely said.

Naomi: You're a right regular wanker. Talk to you never again.

Art: That damn cooking book is cursed. Return immediately and take it away.

Dildo: I want to interview you. Please? Pretty please?

The blocked number, however, was the one I was least prepared to listen to.

Katrina, as much as I'd explained my annoyance, had kept her number blocked.

"Why?"

"You don't find it exciting to not know whose calling?"

"No, I don't."

"Would you're Yes Squad," she'd asked, blue eyes glittering with knowledge, "agree with such fear of the unknown?"

"Hey, brandy boy?" Tilden enthused, a Napoli pizza parlor owner to a young cook—*Più velocemente. Più velocemente*—slapping her palm with the back of a hand. S*mack-smack*. "Time to rally. Let's go. Let's go." *Smack-smack. Smack-smack.*

With a sigh, staying perfectly in the present, I deleted everything and tucked the phone into a pocket.

She must've spotted me, a Sopwith Camel riddled with fatigue, sorrow, and the enormity of time and existence, smoking, spiraling toward a vacant, muddy field.

Marching back down the row, she sauntered to my side and nudged me playfully toward the whitewashed building, "You know, for my first time, I'd like you to at least hold my hand. Okay?"

Taking her hand, joining her in sauntering for the promise of the whitewashed building, I agreed, "Okay."

After only a few steps, the sudden, awkward intimacy repelled our palms.

Continuing, our hands bumped, once, twice, before she asked, "So, tell me, why do you love wine so? And why does someone like you compete in Crushed? And, lastly, who is this Robert Parker guy?"

She, it seemed, needed distraction as much as me.

"First," I said, "it should be obvious. Secondly, I don't know what Crushed is. And, finally, what do you mean by 'someone like me'?"

"You're ignoring Robert Parker."

"Yes, as much as I can. So, someone like me?"

"I'm liable to disclose that after a third glass."

"And when will that be?"

"Sooner than you might think," she said smiling at a hand-painted, wooden sign proclaiming Sheppard's Woods Winery, a wooden silhouette of a hand pointing the way.

We walked up a short flight of steps to a cement landing dominated by equipment and fermenting tanks.

Looking out over the undulating hillsides, Sheppard's was a good sixty acres of vines at the end of a road running a half-mile from the highway, which my father's gravel drive turned off of.

Stepping through the sturdy metal door, its rusted hinges creaking with the effort, we were greeted with a medieval church's vast, comforting, cool stillness.

A good portion of the facility was carved and tucked into the hillside and housed, along with a few hundred barrels neatly stacked in rows, eight more large fermenting tanks.

The door clattered shut, and I explained, "I like wine because it forces me to be aware of small things—the undulating cobwebs, the Oregon Beavers calendar on the wall, the galoshes and squeegee in the corner. To appreciate them as they are. And it makes me appreciate what's in the glass rather than what's on the label. Exactly like with people, judge on who they are not what they are."

Tilden gazed intently at me.

Rather than do something stupid, like kiss a federal officer (she was armed after all), I pointed to the elevator lift. "They're on a gravity flow system."

She shrugged. "So?"

"So I'm impressing you with my knowledge of the winemaking process."

"Are you?"

"You can't tell?"

"I can. I'm just wondering why?"

"Well, that makes two of us." She frowned at my smile. I shrugged and, extending a palm toward another sign, Tasting, suggested, "Shall we?"

The tasting room was a bright, airy expanse with windows overlooking the other half of the vineyard.

A long, weathered plank of varnished wood placed atop seven stained wine barrels operated as the tasting counter. A half-dozen laminated tasting sheets, with the requisite information on each offering, were scattered across it. At each end, with another in the middle, was a black plastic, spit bucket. Behind the counter were racks of glasses, cardboard cases of wine, a few with their tops ripped away, and a small, silver dishwasher, which drained, from a green hose, directly into a drain in the cement floor.

The crowd was a typical, mid-week, mid-afternoon crowd—a half-dozen locals with twice that in smart tourists hitting the wine trail before the summer tasting season raises its hideous head. One, a man about my age, clean-shaven with hazel eyes under a head of well-coiffed amber hair, looked perplexingly familiar.

Before I tugged at a few memory strings, discovered if the ball unravelled into recognition, a bright, cheery, sandy-haired woman in a denim shirt called out from behind the counter and waved us over.

"Hi, my name's Cecilia," she chirped, placing two tasting glasses on the counter, "and welcome to Sheppard's Woods Winery. Your first time here?"

Tilden turned to me.

I confessed, "Cecilia, it is. But most importantly..." I turned to Tilden. "...this is this lass's first time wine tasting. Ever."

"No way," Cecilia gasped in mock shock. She winked. "Well, I'm happy you've chosen us, me, to be your first." Selecting a bottle from the half-dozen huddled at her elbow, she pulled the cork, and enquired, "You, sir, however, are..." She trailed off, unsure how to define what my bruised and abused visage confessed.

Tilden happily did. "You're correct. He's nothing near virginal."

"Regarding wine," I admitted, "I'm as slutty as any. Otherwise, you're making assumptions I'll not corroborate or refute."

"You forget," Tilden said, "who I work for."

She had a point. She may know more about me than I did myself.

Not so coincidentally, the phone vibrated my pocket. I pulled it out, swore, "Goddamn, Dildo."

"Who?" Tilden asked as Cecilia shrugged.

"One second, asshole," I answered and, pulling two crumpled twenties, smoothing them out on the edge of the countertop, admitted, "I hate this asshole, but I'm going to take it."

"Dildo?" Tilden asked, biting back a laugh, "You're going to take the dildo?"

Ignoring their smirks, I Crushed on, "So, Cecilia, please be gentle, yet firm with her. I think she appreciates that." Each, like I, was surprised by such audacity, but, keeping with the bravado, I declared, placing the twenties down, "Teach her all you can. And if I can get a glass of the Red Hills Cuvee that would be wonderful." And to Tilden, I added, "Sorry."

"No, you're not."

"But I could be."

"Maybe."

Cecilia slid the glass of cuvee my way and I reminded, "Firm but gentle. And..." I lifted the glass in salute. "...thank you."

Turning to Tilden, Cecilia explained to my elation, "We'll start soft and fruity and gradually transition to some stiff, firm tannins. Okay?"

Having slipped around a few other tasters, I didn't hear Tilden's reply. Disappointed, I arrived at the end of the counter and asked, "What now, Radcliffe?"

"Mr. Belltower, good news. I've been authorized to offer ten thousand for an exclusive."

It was twenty short to get free of Boonen, but it was a start. Maybe I could squeeze more from them? If nothing else, it should minimize the number of bones Thander and Svorg broke.

Radcliffe, attempting to make the sale, droned on about the article, "The seductive allure of the Crushed world on a young, naïve American." And blah, blah, blah.

Once he'd stopped, I asked, "I thought this was about *The Yank*'s anniversary?"

"My apologies, Mr. Belltower, but mere pretense. Regardless, I can assure you, the article will be very positive. You as the victim."

"Of Crushed?"

"Exactly. And the dark forces lurking within and billowing beneath. Exciting right? People want, nay, need to hear your story, Mr. Belltower."

"Get me thirty, and you can paint me any way you want. But not as a mini-Nazi."

"What?"

"Is there a deadline?"

"Nothing definitive."

"Right. Talk to your people. Get me thirty."

"Mr. Belltower, that's—"

"Got another call. *Ciao*." I'd not lied. There was another, from a blocked caller.

Taking a robust sip of the cuvee, an earthy, well-balanced Pinot Noir, I answered.

I was greeted with heavy breathing, which, to my consternation, didn't disprove it wasn't Katrina from the beyond,

"Hello," I asked, "who is this?" They continued. I took another sip and returned to the first rule of improv—yes. Emboldened by another sip, pressing the glass to a nipple, rubbing it, I encouraged, "Oh, yeah, that's what daddy likes. Make it huskier." They complied. "Yeah. Oh, yeah. Like Kermit with a cold."

Their breathing quickened and grew excited.

I was tempted to join, but recalled... Turning, slowly, beyond the aghast tasters, Alicia and Cecilia smiled.

"Let's do this again, soon," I suggested and hung up. Tucking the phone away, I sauntered back to the ladies. "So, do disclose, do you like stiff, firm tannins?"

"Not seemingly as much as you." Alicia added in a stage whisper, "You need to adjust yourself."

Before I explained that she couldn't dictate my behavior and that I'd never sacrifice comedy for anything, she, with a nod, indicated something well below my integrity. "Adjust yourself."

"Oh, you mean?" Yes, the monster had awoken and was again wandering and frightening the villagers. "Right." Once adjusted, I apologized with the usual, "Mind of its own, you know? So, which do you like?"

If she said rosé I'd walk out. She'd have to return alone and fend off the wolves and extraterrestrials herself.

"We've yet to get to the stiff tannins, but this single-bloc Pinot is rather nice." She lifted her glass. "Floral but with that structured earthiness I gravitate toward." I stared, "Never said I didn't know something about wine. I've just never been tasting."

Before Cecilia poured the next in line an elderly gentleman, a thin, white-haired Tom Selleck with a horseshoe mustache, sidled from around a fermentation tank and sauntered over.

In one hand he carried three big-bellied Bordeaux glasses upside down by their feet and in the other an opened bottle by its neck. Its label, unlike the other Sheppard's Woods bottles, which sported a watercolor stand of pine trees, simply sported a white label with black lettering claiming it to be Paradox 101.

The man whispered something to Cecilia and poured some of the Paradox into a tasting glass, which, after a brief nod of thanks, she took with her as she gave her goodbyes and walked away.

"Afternoon," the man said, arranging the Bordeaux glasses on the counter and pouring a healthy amount in each.

I sighed. I'd hoped not to offend anyone. It being wine, that was nearly impossible. And another offended cellar master, me not partaking of their personally selected offerings, was par for the course.

"This," the gentleman began, "is a proprietary blend of—"

Not waiting, I punched him in the nose first. "Yes. A blend of..." After a quick swirl, sniff and slurp, I declared, "Predominately Pinot Noir, but..." I went through the swirl, sniff and slurp again, and concluded, "Cab Franc, Nebbiolo, and Merlot.

He smiled.

I asked, "How long in the French oak?"

"You tell me."

"Ten, maybe twelve months."

With an odd scratch of his chest, hand curled in a recognizable C, and behind a mischievous smile, he said, "I'll wager you can't get the percentages."

"The standard plus or minus three?" I asked, again swirling and sniffing.

"The standard works for me."

"The wager?" I asked after a glance at Alicia and her amused smirk. "Pride?"

"As I've little, pride it is." After another sip and slurp, I pronounced, "Seventy, fifteen, ten, and five."

The man extended a weathered hand. "Theo Sheppard. I saw you coming up from the Belltower's place, through the woods."

"Yes, sir. Attempting to get the lay of the land. I happen to be Dixon Belltower."

"Thought ya might be. Don't open these..." He tapped the bottle of Paradox. "...for just anyone."

"And thank you for doing so. It's delicious." I introduced Alicia, though didn't disclose her affiliation with the U.S. government.

They shook hands as my phone vibrated.

"Dildo again?" Alicia asked as Sheppard nearly choked on his sip.

"One second." I shot into the phone. "Mr. Sheppard, Alicia is..." I, regardless of the consequences, plowed on. "...something of a vine virgin."

"There are so few anymore," Sheppard said, smiling, doffing an invisible cap, added, "Ma'am."

With a deferential nod, she replied, "Good, sir."

A screech of frustration stabbed from my phone. I shot, "Keep your panties on," while to Alicia, "Would you explain Dildo to him?"

"Or," Sheppard replied, as I returned to my spot at the end of the bar, "if you'd prefer, anything else."

"Sorry, about that. So what's up?"

Over the general clatter of bar conversation and a band playing something Celtic or Irish or Gaelic, Naomi slurred, "Mate, you were trending."

"I was what?"

"Trending. You know. Briefly. But still."

A deep, male voice, accused from the background, "Back on the phone already?"

A flash of annoyance enflamed me and I, just as outraged, also accused, "You're with that wanker, Basil, aren't you?"

Basil Alastair Gurney was a posh wanker banker, whose family, also wankers, had both legs knee-deep in the UK publishing world. I could never tell if Naomi was using him, or if she genuinely liked being around wankers, which would explain why she was my agent.

"Naomi?"

She didn't answer and, thanks to the classic hand over the receiver, the bar and band went silent.

My annoyance was distracted by a dark, delicate creature descending gently down from the rafters on an invisible thread. The spider lithely landed on soft, pearl white sand, and scurried into a shadowed crevice. Curiously, the sand was Moroccan satin, and the crevice button lined.

"Hey, asshole?" a woman with rich brown hair and light, acorn-hued eyes glared at me. "My eyes are up here."

"Not sure where else they'd be, but, yes, you're correct. Well done." I gave a brief golf clap and returned the phone to my ear, where Naomi, returned, droned something about some publisher.

Before I could ask her to repeat her drunken assertion some publisher was inclined to print something of mine, Acorn Eyes, deploying from the upturned wine barrel she and her friend tasted at, stuttered, "What? Oh. No. No No. You don't get a free pass. Not with that attitude."

"Naomi," I replied, ramming a "once second forefinger" into the air, "I'll call you back. Got a matzo playing the kebab card."

"What are you talking about?" Naomi asked, "You cannot—"

Giving Acorn eyes a hard Durden, I explained, "Gotta run, Annie Acorn is about to go hissy." I hung up and Naomi's long wail of frustration, "Nooooooo!" was severed.

Before Annie spouted accusations, I threw an explanation, "I thought I saw—"

"Yes, I know, I'm not wearing—"

"A spider."

"A bra."

"It was rather large. You may—"

"I've been told, by many, that my nipples are quite normal."

"I'm not arguing. I'm just saying—"

"Hey," the familiar-looking man said, "maybe you should leave the lady alone?"

"Troy, don't."

Troy was the well-coiffed one, who, if for no other reason than his hair, I despised, regardless of how familiar he seemed.

"I'm not bothering," I attempted to explain, "I'm attempting to—"

"You want me to make you?"

"Oh, please, Straw Girl McGregor, as if you could."

"Or is," Acorn Eyes kicked in, "'rather large' some innuendo about your dick?"

"Megan," Troy admonished, "I've got this."

Megan, raising a placating hand to Troy, declared "No," and was seized by sudden paralysis.

"Megan?"

Her eyes exploded in horror and, screaming and screaming, she raged about, franticly slapping, tugging at her blouse.

"See," I said, raising a sarcastic palm, "I told her."

"That's it," Troy swore, launching himself at me, "you fucker."

I dodged most of Troy's swing. A few knuckles caught my lip, exploded pain, dug a cut, and introduced blood to my tongue.

Megan, terrified, after a few screaming three-sixties, had stumbled back our way. Troy's blind, misguided fist plowed into her nose.

A great gasp exploded from the other patrons as blood sprayed from Megan's broken nose. Adrenaline keeping her on her feet, she wobbled about, screaming and tearing at her blouse.

And, yes, from the brief glimpses I caught as she flailed, it seemed she'd told the truth—her nipples were quite normal.

Megan collided with a barrel and another.

As she screamed and flailed, the other tasters, their glasses and bottles crashing, shattering to the blood-slickened floor, panicked. Those attempting to flee, deer on ice, slid headlong into one another. Slipping to the floor, they lay splayed, moaning and groaning.

Unsatisfied with the cut to my lip, Troy charged me. Blind with anger, he tripped over a wriggling taster and flew headlong into me.

Joining the blood-covered tasters, we sprawled and gyrated across the floor.

Twisting, turning, nearing something erotic, I kicked him away and took a defensive position under the tasting counter.

Alicia at the opposite end, raised her glass and, past a superlative smile, mouthed, "Thank you."

Chapter Twelve
A LITTLE INVITATION TO A LITTLE FRIENDLY

A City of McMinnville squad car and an ambulance were the last vehicles in Sheppard's oil-stained, gravel parking lot.

The barely injured, though exceptionally annoyed, all with hateful glares and a middle finger directed at me, had, after being attended to, their statements taken, left for calmer, quieter climes.

I pulled the blue ice pack from my swollen lip as Sheppard, after shaking hands with a parting EMT, walked over and sat beside me on the cement landing's steps.

"Mr. Sheppard, you've my heartfelt apologies. I can only hope she killed that damn spider."

"Ah, hell, son," he chuckled, pulling from a back pocket a dented, silver flask with a gold eagle punched on it, "don't worry about it. Most fun I've had around here in a long time."

"It can't be that boring here, can it?"

"Oh, you'd be surprised." He took a long draw off the flask and added, "Besides, I've got a nice little offer on the table to sell the place." He shrugged and stared out across the vines toward the setting sun.

With an awkward nod, Alicia, from the tall, blond, blue-eyed, square-jawed linebacker of a police officer, accepted a business card and disengaged herself from the squad car's rear bumper. Running the card back and forth across the tips of her fingers, she walked to Sheppard and me.

"Well?" I asked, returning the ice pack to my lip.

"Seems no one's pressing charges."

"Yet," Sheppard piped up.

"Exactly. Though Officer Ferguson there..." Alicia noted him with his card. "...did have a few questions about Crushed."

"Oh, Ferguson," Sheppard sighed, "the man's always going on about one white whale or another."

"Crushed is illegal in Oregon. Maybe he has reason to?"

"Whale hunting is also illegal. Though they did blow one up on the coast a while back." Sheppard stood and added, "Well, I best go. See if Cecilia needs a hand cleaning up. Nice meeting you two."

Alicia and I returned the sentiment.

At the door, Sheppard hesitated, "You know, Belltower, you should swing by tomorrow night. Around eight."

"Okay. Why?"

"We're having a little friendly." He smiled at Alicia and explained, "Just a tasting."

"On a weekday?" I asked with mock surprise.

"Nothing aggressive," he assured, "Just a small gathering of friends tasting. You'd be welcome to join."

"And not me?" Alicia asked with a distinct tone of accusation.

"Only," Sheppard said, straight-faced as an executioner, "if you can tell me the color of God's underwear."

I laughed. Alicia wanted to be offended but was too confused to be.

Around my laughter, Sheppard added, "Bring a couple of bottles. Appropriately masked."

Needing to know, I asked, "Would you prefer a Sauvignon Blanc or a Liebfraumilch? Something from the Mosel? Bubbles perhaps?"

"You bring any of that shit near here and I will fuck you up. Fuck. You. Up. Is that understood?"

"Yes, sir. Clear and concise. My apologies."

Softening the killer's glare, he added, "Your dad said you weren't funny. But you're hysterical. Don't forget, eight. I'll see ya then." And, just before the door squeaked shut behind him, he added with a bow, "And, ma'am, it was a pleasure meeting you."

Alicia, tucking the card into a pocket, turned on me. "Okay. What's going on?"

"What do you mean?"

"No, Dixon, do not play coy with me."

"I hate those fish," I admitted, standing past the soreness and stiffness of my beaten body, nodding toward the departing squad car, "but did Jenkins offer you a ride?"

"You're jealous?"

"Never. Just lazy. Thought we could've caught a ride."

"Oh, shit. Good idea." She, hand raised, set off after the EMT, "Hey, Alejandro, *un momento por favor!*"

Briefly, they conversed.

Then, again, slapping the back of her hand into a palm—*smack, smack*—she called, "Let's go. *Venga, venga.*"

"Nice guys," Alicia admitted as we crackled across the sharp gravel to the front door.

I agreed as Alejandro and Dominic, with a squelch of the sirens, drove off.

The house, cool and quiet, was, after such a turbulent afternoon, a damp oasis.

Alicia placed the ambulance service's card, with Alejandro's number scrawled on the back, on the kitchen table with the menus.

"So," I asked, "does he deliver?"

"I'll not be ordering. He's a chocolate chaser."

"Not heard that one before. That's funny."

The quiet of the old farmhouse, suddenly, overwhelmed and forebode a long, grueling night of introspection. I opened a cupboard and stared into the shadows.

"You okay?" Tilden asked, concerned.

"What?" I replied, knowing the painkillers Dominic had given me were a poor replacement for last night's antidepressants.

"You get—" She opened a cupboard and stared. Closed it. Opened it. Stared.

I smiled and opened another.

"I imagine," she admitted, closing her cupboard, "it's difficult?"

"Only," I replied, closing mine, "if you think about it."

An awkward melancholy eddied through the kitchen.

Had I been less sober, I may've had the audacity to inquire about a hug. Maybe a lie about how it'd be all okay. However, given the basic parameters of our relationship, it seemed socially untenable.

Therefore, keeping things acceptably bland, I asked, "So, what about dinner?"

"There are some frozen pizzas."

"Are there?"

"Yes."

I'd not partaken of frozen pizza or practically frozen anything for years. Not even in Wickford had I succumbed to such barbarity. My stomach, after the adrenaline rush of the scuffle, shouted for sustenance more than painkillers and Pinot.

"Hey?"

"What?"

"Stop."

I was opening another cupboard. Like the others it was empty.

"Oh, I'd like to, but we've nothing to drink and the painkillers will wear off. So?" Defeated, I shrugged. Wasn't our plight self-evident? Why need I to express such obviousness?

Perhaps because I was so stupid, I noted as Alicia answered, "Well, there is the cellar in the basement."

"Basement? What basement?"

"The one beneath the house." Adding dumb to my stupid, she added, "That basement."

"But you called it a cellar?"

"I did. Yes."

"A wine cellar?"

"Yes."

"You, sweet lass," I declared, a sudden strike of inspiration bolting through my brain, igniting the dark, gray matter clumped within, "please, fetch us a bottle. Nay. Hold. Make it two."

"Not a problem."

She'd replied too quickly, too confident. I needed to add complexity to her quest.

"They must be red."

She hesitated, "All right."

She opened an innocuous door hidden by chicken-covered aprons on a hook and flicked a switch. Fluorescent lighting stuttered and pushed itself into the kitchen.

"And," I added, "the older the better."

Again she hesitated.

And I insisted, "Please, goeth and fetcheth yon elixirs." And, having witnessed a professional, I slapped the back of a hand into a palm—*whack-whack*—and proclaimed, "*Venga. Venga.*"

"And what, oh, prince," she asked, smiling, "will you be doing?"

With a regal bow, I replied, "Besides being giddy with anticipation, I shall baketh pizzas. And selecteth a movie for thy enjoyment." She smiled. Maybe now I should kiss her? Instead, I, *whack-whack*ing more, proclaimed, "Now, *muy pronto. Venga. Venga.*"

With a nod, she spun and disappeared into the light, shouting, "But no war movies."

"What?"

"I hate war movies."

"You mate with Tories?" I asked, as her footsteps receded into silence. Katrina and Liza also hated war.

Katrina had claimed, "Because of stupid author and his stupid, big book."

"Tolstoy?"

"*Da.*"

Liza's issues were inherent with what I'd learned to love, Crushed.

Settling at a dueling table, I'd asked the strawberry blonde woman, cheeks flushed with too much sun and not enough malice, "So, what's a princess like you doing in a dungeon like this?"

It'd been spring, 2016, Mallorca, with the Crushed circuit underway. And we were in a literal dungeon, with *The Ruling Class* filling the video screens and Ravi Shankar playing hypnotically.

"Princess," she admitted, patting her vacant tresses, "needs a new tiara. And you?"

"Isn't it obvious?" I grinned, "To beat the pants off you."

And I had, figuratively, 20-12.

Two weeks later, Alexandria's Antony and Cleopatra's Clash, second round, her cheeks had evened out, joined the rest of her in a honey-hued tan. She still, however, lacked the basic maliciousness to be competitive.

"It's you, again."

"Right back at you."

We stared and waited for the glasses.

A crash exploded in the background and the small, 13th century chapel filled with shouting and cursing, I asked, "So, tell me about your first round?"

"No." It was firm and final. She'd found a coach, a competent one.

"Okay." Her shoulders, taught under a dark blue muslin blouse, relaxed. "I'll tell you about mine." Her eyes flashed and I knew they'd never be more beautiful than then.

I'd still beaten her, though, due to an Israeli, dry, Gewurztraminer and Sauvignon Blanc blend, it was much closer, 20-17. Regardless, as she stood, I'd said, "We should go out."

"Like on a date?"

I shrugged. "Or, if you'd prefer, an intimate tutoring session with the possibility of romantic entanglement."

"Yes. Okay."

"What?" Her response was quick and sincere. I was disoriented. "What?"

"Yes, to romantic entanglement, particularly if there's restraint to said entanglement."

"Um."

She pulled me to my feet. We kissed. Our mouths remained redolent from the last wine, a deep, dark Sciacarello from Corsica. She pressed me away. "And, yes, the comment about restraint referred to bondage. Mind you, light. Okay?"

Confused, my mind continued reeling, while my mouth, limbered up, agreed, "Yeah. Okay."

"I'm in room 328 of the Steigenberger. We'll have room service and watch something. After that?" She shrugged, turned, and added over her shoulder, "Maybe nothing. And, maybe," she slapped her butt, "everything."

In the next round, by a spindle-limbed South African woman named Victoria Froome, I was thoroughly thrashed, 22-11. I didn't care. The loss meant Liza and mine entanglement could commence.

To the few that'd wagered on me, I attempted, unconvincingly, to assure them I hadn't purposefully thrown the round.

The scent of frozen pizza baking wafted down the hall and found me and my growling stomach pondering the chest-high, faux wood cabinet's library of ancient VHS videos.

Most, as Alicia had noticed, were war movies.

I extracted *Blazing Saddles* and *High Anxiety* from between *Fort Apache* and *The Bridge on the River Kwai* and added them to a small, non-war movie pile.

Alicia, gliding from the pantry, called out, "Where are you?"

"Living room, m'lady. Attempting to solicit thy entertainment."

Pulling my eyes from *Hell in the Pacific*, I found a most alluring silhouette, Alicia backlit by kitchen lights. She gripped the necks of two bottles, while another smaller one, bulged a back pocket. "I was offended by your Tory comment."

"No, you weren't."

"Correct. From you, it was a compliment." She spun and returned to the light.

I knew my excuses, pills and fatigue, brandy, wine and woe, but what were hers? More calculated, gentle prodding? Or something more nefarious?

My finger had fallen on Steve Martin's underappreciated classic, *Dead Men Don't Wear Plaid*. It was lodged between *Kelly's Heroes* and *Apocalypse Now*.

I pulled it out, jammed it in the obsolete VCR, cued it up, and headed for the kitchen, curious what Alicia had acquired.

Hunched at the corner breakfast table, struggling with a bottle and its cork, she commanded, "Go away. I've got this."

"But I can help."

"No. Go away." Putting the bottle down, spinning, and keeping herself between it and my curiosity, she ushered me out. "You've selected the princess's entertainment?"

"Yes."

"Is it ready to go?"

Yes."

"Oh, well, have you considered getting out of this..." With a disgusted finger she indicated the stained mourning suit. "...and into something—"

"More comfortable?"

The innuendo, like the oncoming evening, tantalized.

Gazing into her bright, beautiful eyes, I knew I needed to forget Katrina-Kelsey-Madame von Klit or at least put the malevolent bitches in a locked box and drop it into the deepest section of the deepest sea. I needed something quick and frivolous, something supernova brilliant and bright, something so hot it seared the past from me.

Though what did Alicia want, if anything? And did I dare ask? Or did I step to her, and after the collision of our lips we'd stumble, tearing at our clothes, collapse upon the couch, claiming we couldn't, but knowing we could and would?

Something, a startled bird, screeched and screeched from the kitchen.

"My phone," she admitted, I think disappointed.

I nodded and she, with a sigh, abandoning a possibility, flew to the kitchen.

Long minutes later, wearing her jacket, briefcase slung over a shoulder, though carrying two glasses of rich red burgundy, Alicia strolled into the living room.

"Bad news?" I asked, from the video cabinet and reading the synopsis on the back of *Seven Samurai*.

Placing the glasses on the lacquered, tree-slice, coffee table, she rambled an explanation. It had to do with "an initial limited assessment window," "the fluidity of the situation," and "a recalibration of desired results."

Hoping for a more favorable reinterpretation, I asked, "Which means what?"

"Me," she said, smiling a frown, "lodging at a different location."

That I understood, though still asked, "And not here?"

"No," she said, shaking her head, "not here."

With odd, vacant smiles we stared. Before either said something stupid, we turned to the coffee table, the glasses of wine.

"Why two glasses?"

She sighed then shrugged. "The pizzas are done, though a bit burnt."

"Yeah, the Viking runs hot."

"Well, they're cooling on the butcher block."

She moved toward the front door, collecting items as she went, putting them on or tucking them in.

"So, you'll be taking that bullet for me from DC?"

"Not that far. A little bed and breakfast down the road."

Distracting from an awkward goodbye, an ill-advised attempt at a kiss, she glanced over my shoulder at the unrealized possibilities.

The television was frozen in a black-and-white image of an old-timey Universal Pictures logo as it circled a glitzy, star-studded globe, the two glasses of red stood expectant, while the fireplace, logs, stacked and ready to assist with mood lighting, pleaded for flame. And the urn stared, accusing.

"Well, as they say, don't be a stranger."

"Maybe another time?"

I had nothing else to do but agree, "Yeah. Another time."

Alicia, with a quick nod, turned and walked out of the house and into the newly darkened night, puffs of breath, ethereal ghosts, drifted over her shoulder and disappeared.

Realizing I could've been more enthusiastic, I, with a sense of trepidation, waved half-heartedly and watched Alicia drive off, the headlights briefly illuminating an expanse of vines.

The sharp crunch of gravel died, I was then able to hear the light tapping of panic from my heart, as if it were trying to escape. Before it did, I closed the door.

Chapter Thirteen
GLASSES AND SKIES FILLED WITH WONDER

The old farmhouse, a giant, empty and vacant urn, loomed around me. Adding to my apprehension, I'd realized I'd never been so alone, ever. Whether down the hall, through a wall, or on the adjacent bunk, there had always been someone nearby. But surrounded by over forty acres... Was such isolation a luxury or a curse?

Regardless, I knew discerning the answer wasn't advisable in such a state, sober.

Grabbing a glass, ignoring the thing on the mantel, I headed up-stairs to shed the vomit-hued, sadness-stenched mourning suit.

Over the crackling of the stairs' plastic runner a long, cold howl shuddered through the night.

I slowed. Was that why Alicia had left? Was she a werewolf?

I gave a soft howl, recognized my ridiculousness, and continued to my room. Gripping the doorknob's cold handle, another baleful howl clawed the night.

My glass and I marched to the French doors and continued onto the balcony where a sincere blanket of crisp, cold air wrapped itself around me. My breath hovered, as I stared out into the darkness, waiting.

Above the ridgeline, defined by a dark, jagged expanse of pines, a bucket of stars had been spilled.

Finding Cassiopeia, another howl erupted. It seemed to originate up the hill, at the rectangular building, where the apparition had likely run from.

Mother emboldened by another sip of something deep and red, had declared, "Your father left after I'd again attacked him with a Ginsu." Another quick sip. "She was a cocktail server at that Japanese restaurant, Seppuku." She, Atlas shrugging the world from his shoulders, sighed and pointed to the object she'd, upon barging in, had plunked down in the middle of my room, "That's your second present."

The first was her theoretical confession regarding my father's exit.

"It's an Orion X-16," she stated, fluttering the owner's manual about, "with spotter scope and... and stuff."

Obviously it was a telescope; she'd unboxed it.

Regardless, I knew what she attempted to convey. She loved me. And it confused me. And being only four months before graduation it seemed late, and, if I wished to use her nomenclature, manipulative.

The X-16, infuriatingly, was exactly what I'd wanted, three years ago.

"'You don't understand,'" I decried, brandishing my best Brando, "'I could've had class. I could've been a contender. I could've been somebody.'"

"You don't like it?"

She sounded disappointed.

I'd been memorizing lines for tomorrow's audition for my final high school production, *Hedwig and the Angry Inch*. The lines, not from the play, but a self-penned piece, "Alas, Poor Josiah," had been gnawing me existentially, so my tone was blunter than intended. "They're rather specific on what I can and cannot bring aboard. Though I imagine, for a small dinghy, it'd make an admirable anchor."

Mother threw what remained in her glass, a cheap Chilean Malbec, into my face, swore, "I hope you go down like the Titanic," and dragged the cumbersome telescope out and down the hall, to the balcony, and over the railing into a robust rhododendron.

Another howl split the night.

Filled with sudden understanding, I gripped the wood railing and, with every atom of my being, joined the creature, wailing into the great, magnificent night.

Expunged, I closed the doors, pondered the black boxes and which likely held... A hint of sweet sandalwood and dried, dark cherry wafted through the air.

I knew it wasn't me or the burned pizza seeping up from the kitchen.

I sniffed. A deep, seductive mélange of spices and herbs tickled my nose. There was also a hint of Tunisian dark plum and something musky and ethereal.

Still holding my lifeline, the glass Alicia had poured, I turned to it. My hand, quivering, raised it to me.

I took the gentlest of sips and lightly slurped.

Lest I collapse and spill such magnificence, I sat on a scratchy, parlor chair.

How had such exquisiteness fallen into my hands? How?

The miracle, less revelatory a second time, still deserved the ritual of sniff, sip, and slurp.

I marveled at the nuanced layers of dark fruit, the subtle play of earthiness and leather, accented by a melancholy hint of ripe cherry. A notion of decadent plum. And though it could've benefitted from a decanting, it was glorious.

Perplexed by how such glory could be in a glass not just in Dundee, Oregon, but more specifically, my father's house, I declared, reverently, "Chăteau Lafleur. 1950."

Disbelieving, I took a healthier sip and let it drain into me, slowly.

How could Alicia, knowing what she'd poured, have left? Had that been the anger, the frustration in her eyes and voice?

Saddened, I sipped, stood, and grumbled down the stairs to crumple on the couch.

As the wine's perfection (or my perception of it) ebbed, I poured Alicia's glass into mine.

Something this exalted deserved more than what my self-pitying self was offering. It should've been with a beautiful woman watching a ridiculous comedy before a sultry, little fire, while the urn reminded us life was short, celebrate.

Rather than rejoice, a hook of fear caught me. She'd poured two glasses, could she have also opened the others?

Hurrying into the kitchen, greeted by a bewildering trinity, I skidded to a stop.

There'd been many thousands of moments I should've remembered, held on to, but hadn't. Only a handful of times had I told myself to remember the moment, swore to myself never to forget.

First, Trisha's cotton panties and their unicorn and rainbow.

Second, the way Shannon's ponytail bobbed in the moonlight as she, as a "going away present," a week before I'd left for my cruise ship job, gifted me with a blowjob.

Third, Liza's contented cat smile as she slept in the sea of white satin sheets after our first night in Alexandria, the orange morning light glowing upon her and our future.

Fourth, the entire sequence from Geronimo Nazi to the tree-lined boulevard caught in a deluge of flaming mail. Though, honestly, that would require more effort to forget than remember.

It was odd, but little besides that tragedy about Katrina stood out. Yes, there were wonderful moments. But we were like photos of a battlefield. Not those taken on the ground, intimate and specific, but aerial, surveillance photographs from 30,000 feet, distant and rational. Or, perhaps, as a survival mechanism, I'd purged all the good we'd had?

And, fifth, what rested there on the table.

Oh, to be a painter, Vermeer or Velazquez, to have such capacity to set such beauty upon canvas. The way the early moonlight slipped through the drapes' yellow, ephemeral fabric, angled across the labels, exposing half, while the other portion remained lost in shadow. How the grains of wood were static waves on a glistening, brown, and tan sea. The crumpled cap of foil, a tiny, tin man's heart.

But no, I could only encourage myself, "Never forget this. Never forget this."

Alicia's second selected bottle, of all things, was a 1945 Chateau Petrus. It stood, at least for me, precariously close to the table's edge. She'd thankfully not opened it and the possibility of catastrophe enhanced the vision.

Masked by the larger bottles' shadows, the third, the one Alicia had tucked in a back pocket, was a demi with a stained and faded ivory label filled with a golden yellow elixir. But—oh, the horror!—the wine key was halfway into the cork of the 1975 Chăteau d'Yquem.

I stared and sipped.

Being remotely familiar with wine pricing, I knew, if sold, a good portion of my debt to Boonen rested there. Was there enough in the cellar to be free of the Belgian bastard?

The innocuous door, hidden by the chicken aprons, opened into a gloomy pantry. The walls were lined with shelves and held only a few cans of beans, corn, peas, and a single tin of sardines.

Set in the back wall was another door of unfinished wood with a dull gold handle.

The Lafleur's beauty was gently dissipating, dying in the glass and the opened bottle. The only way, ironically, to save it from a futile death was to kill it, to drink it. The mystery of the cellar could wait; the wine could not.

I retreated to the kitchen, collected a plate of semi-burnt pizza and the bottle of Lafleur, and drifted back to the living room, the couch, the thing on the mantle.

I knew what I was supposed to feel—sadness, sorrow, grief—but I had nothing. And coupled with Paris, I was too confused, too overwhelmed to feel anything. Besides my father was an enigma. The urn only deepened and complicated the perspective. And Mother's propaganda, even with her theoretical confession, was difficult to ignore. Over the years she'd made many an outlandish claim regarding his "syphilitic exodus."

"He ran away with a squadron of YMCA boys."

"He joined a cult worshipping a two-headed lizard called Caligula."

"He became a sadomasochistic love slave in a Japanese Go-Go brothel."

The lone memory I have of my father was of him making pancakes in the shapes of animals. They'd be served with butter-flavored syrup, sausage links, and orange juice. However, after "The walrus anus founded a camel dairy in Abu Dhabi," we'd shifted to frozen waffles, maple syrup, sausage patties, and tomato juice.

So whatever was contained in the urn was more myth and, to a lesser extent, lies.

Standing, removing it from its perch, I discovered it was heavier than I remembered.

The memory of when I held it last was muddled, though a sickening vision explained why the contents sloshed some.

Twisting, nudging, back and forth, I lifted the lid off.

A deeply soured and fecund stench greeted me and confirmed my fear, my memory.

"Sorry, Dad," I whispered with a slight smile. "Can't make it any worse, can I?"

I poured nearly all into my glass and Alicia's, and the last bit, the final dregs of sediment into the urn.

Once capped and returned to the mantle, I lit a fire and resettled on the couch.

Slowly, steadily, I drank and watched the fire burn itself out, promising, that tomorrow, maybe, I'd get myself out of the stupid, stinky suit.

Chapter Fourteen
BOTTLES AND BOTTLES AND A LUNATIC BANSHEE

Morning, too early, the sun still slumbering beneath the horizon, found me curled on the couch, the Lafleur finished, the fire cold and the urn's accusing transitioned to disappointed.

Taking the plate and its single slice with a single bite taken from it, I wandered into the kitchen.

The Petrus remained precariously close to the table's edge. The horror also remained—the wine key halfway into the Yquem.

Like the urn, gazing on such sacrilege so early was unacceptable.

Gripping the wine key, an old and well-used Laguiole, I pondered the last few turns, the steady, gentle pull as the cork eased from the bottle. To hold its sweet mustiness to my nose, to pour a glass and taste such perfection would be the way to begin the day.

I sighed and twisted the key from the cork.

I've been fortunate to have had many magnificent wines. And I've had the pleasure of enjoying most of my "bucket list wines."

Two, however, have remained elusive.

First was an old, austere Yquem, like the one I held. Though partaking of it now, like this, would be a hollow victory. Not to mention lonely. It deserved, like most wines, to be shared.

The second missing wine I'd named MR2000. It was a mysterious red which, one evening, had sent Mother into a lurid and lunatic fury.

"By all the demons haunting the haunted lands," she'd screamed, "I curse thee! I curse thee!"

She'd poured a bottle down the drain and smashed it on the countertop, the label, ripped, torn, and stained, was unrecognizable.

"You mention this," she threatened, gripping the neck of the bottle, indicating the destruction, "and I'll castrate you and shove your hair nuggets down your throat. Understood?"

Considering the bottle's jagged edge and its chaotic wavering, I'd agreed. However, my interpretation of the promise, as I didn't view it as anything more, didn't discount me from searching for it, which I'd done, diligently, since that night.

If the cellar held such treasures as the Lafleur, the Petrus, and the Yquem, could it hold MR2000?

Dourly dressed and despicable as I was, I was ill-prepared to be disappointed.

"If one is to play a part," Professor Magaldi had proclaimed, "one must dress the part."

Thus, I found myself desperate enough to use Saunders' key.

After a frantic scrub with a cold, wet cloth, I tugged on worn jeans and a *Star Wars* T-shirt depicting the yin and yang symbol with an X-wing and TIE fighter, light and dark respectively. To finish the ensemble, I snuggled into my beloved, black cardigan and a pair of thick wool socks.

Knowing it was unwise to venture so on an empty stomach, I, unenthused and uninspired, flogged myself with pizza and coffee.

Once hunger had been quelled and my mug refilled, I marched to slay curiosity.

The unpainted, wooden door inside the pantry opened onto a flight of sturdy, black metal steps. At the bottom, a small landing sat before a cement wall reminiscent of a World War II bunker.

Set into the middle of the wall was a decorative wrought iron gate, replete with a prancing, flute-playing satyr. Rather than his phallus, it was a flute. He was encircled by a sinuous vine laden with grape clusters. Behind the gate was a large mahogany door. The door had the same satyr carved upon it, though where the eyes would've been a dark metal plate glared.

I almost expected a thick-necked, bull-eyed, flat-nosed bastard to pull it back and, with a mob-thickened voice, demand, "What d'ya want?"

A digital display, on the right at eye level, claimed the temperature, 56 degrees, and relative humidity of 60 percent.

Art had once stated, "I would prefer to know what's in one's cellar than what's in one's heart." Thirty minutes later, on another glass of Barolo, he'd said, "To know what's in another's heart, look inside their cellar."

It was enough to give me pause and reflect on more of Mother's propaganda, "That hyena testicle sold your twin brother to a pharmaceutical company to finance a puppet troupe performing Punch and Judy shows for rebels in the Yucatan."

There were times I wished some of her bullshit were true.

Opening the door, ignoring my fear and excitement, I stepped inside.

Beguiled by the shadowy shapes of barrels, the stacked boxes, crates, and racks filled with bottles and bottles, I clawed around until I found a row of switches and flicked a few.

The first ignited a series of can lights in the ceiling, two sets of five illuminated two aisles running the room's length, a large rectangle, the size of the house's foundation.

The second powered string lighting that ran above the filled, floor-to-ceiling wine racks. There were, at minimum, a few thousand bottles. Even Art's shop couldn't compete with such volume or variety.

And the third, in a far corner, illuminated two, felt green, dome lights over a dark, teak table surrounded by a red leather banquette.

The lights' golden glow also illuminated the ceiling—a *trompe l'œil* representation of the most idyllic summer sky, azure with wispy clouds here and there.

The icy sheen of the sealed cement floor reflected the world in muted-gray shadows.

Six Ibérico hams hung in the nearest corner, on the right, which was also crowded with an array of international condiments, snacks, tins, and foodstuffs. It was more a testament to enjoying the apocalypse than surviving it.

Unlike the movie cabinet, this was a more intimate glimpse of my father.

The magnums of champagne implied he didn't drink it himself, though, if he did, it'd be during a gathering, a celebration.

The five barrels of whisky (two Irish, and three Scottish, one each from the Lowlands, Highlands, and Speyside), besides the mystery of how they got here, spoke of a certain philosophical introspection.

The cases and bottles of port, practically all vintage, suggested someone somber, contemplative, who likely wrote poetry.

Wandering the shelves, pondering the labels, the scope of vintages and varietals, the eclectic array of Jeroboams, beer, and chocolate bars, a niggling question buzzed my brain—how had he amassed such a collection?

Under the staggering realization of what it was worth, millions, my confusion and incomprehension overwhelmed me, and I collapsed upon the cold leather of the banquette.

Who, exactly, was my father? And where in here was MR2000? If it were anywhere, I knew it was here.

I'd be methodical in my search. I'd be... The snarl and growl of gravel churning through the cellar startled me. It pushed me, reluctantly, from the banquette and upstairs.

Scrambling into the kitchen, ignoring my excitement at Alicia's return, a pair of headlights ignited the kitchen. Unexpectedly, another pair cast the first car in silhouette. It wasn't Alicia's sedan, but a limousine.

I ducked as the two limos drove past and up the short hill to the rectangular building I assumed had something to do with the vineyard.

Crouching, I shuffled to the back door, pulled the drapes, covered in dancing and fiddling chickens, aside, and peered out into the pre-dawn gloom.

On the other side of the door was a cement landing with green plastic trash bins and an oil drum barbecue with a crumpled bag of briquettes beneath it.

Up the hill the limos parked.

In the eerie red glow of exhaust lit by taillights, from each, clowns from circus cars, spilled silhouetted apparitions.

The groups merged and, rather than shake hands, they bowed in greeting.

I'd, of course, feared associates of the mini-Nazis, but with such salutations, I knew who these assholes were—the yakuza. They'd be seeking blood vengeance on the son of the man who'd dishonored their boss and stolen his sake and whisky collection, which the *gaijin* had stowed in his cellar's southeast corner.

Granted, I could be paranoid. Though as Mother had often said, again unlocking the door and letting one of the witches and bitches in, "I'd prefer to be perceived as an asshole than have my asshole raped out by a rapist."

Mother had had a point, and the ladies had been reluctant to argue against it.

I called Alicia.

Greeted with a recording, I left a brief, moderately panic-stricken message.

Peeking back through the back door's chicken-tainted drapes, I discovered the horde of yakuza, even the two swarthy drivers, had disappeared.

This time, using the ancient, faded pea green, rotary phone on the wall by the frig, pacing the kitchen at the end of its two-mile, curled chord, I called Alicia again.

The phone's line had either been cut or was no longer in service, but it was dead like I was soon to be.

Channeling my inner Jason Bourne, I searched for firearms or items to MacGyver into guns, bombs, or anything deadly.

Having found nothing, I was back on the cell phone, this time more urgent, more desperate, I added more flair to the "situational dynamics."

For distraction, I shuffled through the to-go menus Alicia had cursed the other morning. Wait, yesterday? No. Yes. But... Time was transforming, becoming elastic and disconcertingly malleable.

I didn't like it.

I snatched Alejandro's card from the pile and rushed for the cellar.

Behind the speakeasy's locked door, I searched the cellar's wares for a suitable beverage to be murdered with when Alicia called, "Did you say something about yakuza?"

"No. Maybe. Yes."

"What's going on?"

Keeping most of the fear from my voice, I explained, "Two limos filled with yakuza unloaded up at the building on the hill. I'm sure their murdering me has something to do with my father."

"Really?"

"You've been in the cellar," I noted, "what do you think?"

With an exasperated sigh, she agreed, "Okay. I'll be right over."

Halfway through my second can of sake, Kikusui's Funaguchi Kunkou Black, I heard the sweet crackle of gravel.

Sliding from the banquette, I shuffled into the faded, tan Carhartt jacket I'd pilfered from a peg in the foyer, tucked two more cans into its pockets, and headed upstairs to my savior.

Making the front door, I finished off the can, threw it toward the fireplace, and stepped out to Alicia sauntering (too casually for my liking) toward me.

She raised her palms and shrugged in the universal "What's-the-deal-dude-where's-the fire-because-I-sure-as-shit-don't-see-anything-to-cause-your-little-girl-panic." Yes, she was verbose in my mind, though not more attractive, that was impossible.

Nearing, she asked, "What's the sit rep, Jittery Jane?"

"What took you so long?"

"I was in the middle of something called sleep. Besides—"

"Aren't you supposed to be—"

"I'm not at your beck and call."

"Protecting me?" She spun and stomped for the sedan. "Hey, where are you going?"

"I'm leaving. I'm not your—"

Oh, shit, she'd nearly thrown down the s-word. Surely not the n-word?

Either way, we were offended, though likely for different reasons.

We both knew the situation could go sideways into a dumpster fire inferno. If one of us... A deep, resounding *ba-bum-bum* exploded out across the vines. After a second, or two, it was followed by an echo, *ba-bum-bum*.

"What the hell was that?"

"Alicia, goddamn, I'm sorry. In no way, nor would I ever—" Again, the *ba-bum-bum* resounded. The echo chased it, *ba-bum-bum*.

She slipped past, declared, "We've shit to talk about."

I considered mentioning her proclivity for swearing but, considering the situation, didn't.

Instead, I scurried after her.

Dodging around a minefield of molehills littering the dew-dampened strip of grass running along the drive, I gave her the sit rep. "There are two, stretch, Lexus limos. Tinted blackout windows. One driver each. Loop antennas on both. Otherwise, I'm unsure how many perps, possibly as many as two dozen. Assuming each is armed with—"

A cold razor sliced down my spine, as I realized I was alone.

A sniper had taken her out and... I spun and found Alicia staring at me, shaking her head with a tight smile, biting the fat of a forefinger.

Hunched and hugging the morning shadows, I retreated to her, looking, as I neared, for bullet wounds.

"Are you okay? Did you get hit?"

My questions caused her more pain.

Placing a hand on her shoulder, I said with more confidence than I felt, "Let me see," and realized she was laughing. "It's not funny."

She, fighting the laughter, made a flurried series of hand gestures about keeping quiet, keeping eyes peeled, and silently making our way to the back of the building.

"Alicia, my concern was genuine. I—" The deep, guttural *ba-bum-bum* cut me off and, since she'd already set off, I had no choice but to follow.

Skirting the limos, another round of *ba-bum-bum* thundered the quiet. Rather than a frontal assault, Alicia circled to the back of the windowless building.

The back, unlike the front's broad, double-wide front door and the expansive rolltop garage door, had only a lone, windowless door stamped into its corrugated metal side.

Crowding the requisite cement slab was a glistening, new, green John Deere tractor and, for sullen company, stacks of blue plastic, harvest crates.

Overhead there was likely an apartment, as a balcony with potted plants could be glimpsed.

We moved toward the door, the tempo of *ba-bum-bum* increasing, becoming furious, frantic.

The door burst open.

From its dark maw, a chalky white, skeletal specter wailing in agony shot out. Torn lengths of burlap, tales on kites, were tied and taught around its limbs.

It was the apparition!

It flew maniacally, screaming, toward us.

We backpedaled; Alicia fumbled for her gun.

Behind the wailing apparition, a group of elderly tourists, most sporting Grand Canyon sweatshirts proclaiming, "Mind the Gap," flowed from the doorway.

Alicia and I stepped aside as the apparition shot past, limbs flailing akimbo, eyes rolled back, screaming and moaning and wailing.

The tourists followed and formed a semicircle as the apparition dramatically collided upon a large, granite thumb of rock situated between the cement slab and the vines.

For five minutes, she twisted and curled, wrapped and crawled, in agonizing beauty around the rock. Her movements were haunting and mesmerizing as thin shafts of sunlight stabbed at it through the pines.

After a final attempt at mounting the edifice, a defeated wave, she slumped to the ground, panting. Her breathing slowed, slowed, slowed. Stopped. And, after a long unsettling shutter, a last exhale, she stilled, dead.

The tourists erupted into applause.

Alicia and I were compelled to join.

The woman lightly jumped to her feet and bowed, regally.

I gasped in recognition, "Aori?"

An odd look of fearful surprise morphed her face as she too recognized me. The tourists turned as she asked, "You Dixon-san? *Hai*?"

Her voice, though it'd been many years since we'd spoken, was heavily accented.

Over the past year, in preparation for when next I sat across the dueling table from Mochi, one of my on the circuit, I'd been studying Japanese. So, with an appropriately deferential bow, I, sincerely, respectfully, hopefully, said in Japanese, "*It is a great pleasure, after so many years, to be reunited.*"

Overwhelmed, Aori charged me and threw herself around me. Her spindly limbs, thin tentacles, wrapped around me, squeezed me, tight and tighter.

Awkwardly, I accepted her weight.

In English and unaccented, she whispered, "You tell anyone, and I will gut you." She wriggled, threw her head back, laughed with sweet, sharp joy, and returned to my ear. "Gut you, stem to stern, like a dirty, fucking fish."

In smooth, boa constrictor fashion, she uncoiled from me.

Briefly, sweaty, her bone-knuckled back pressed against me, she danced around me, a dumb thumb of rock.

She sighed and slipped to the ground, dying.

After a moment, leaping to her feet laughing, she bowed, flailed her arms and, screaming insanely, disappeared inside the building.

The covey of excited, appreciative tourists followed.

"So," Alicia asked, releasing her grip on the 9mm as the door slammed shut, "that's your stepmother, is it?"

Chapter Fifteen
REMORSE-STAINED APOLOGIES

Pulling the cans of Funaguchi from my pockets, I handed one to Alicia, opened mine and sipped. The taiko drums resounded from the building and, as much to myself as her, I explained, "I think that was *butoh*."

"Whatever," she spun and marched back toward the house.

Following, I spotted a trampled brochure. It was for Go There, Stay Here Adventures. It proclaimed, "All the adventure without the headache or hassle." Besides the Japanese Culture Package, they also had Scottish Highlands Escape and Himalayan-Everest Ascent packages.

Chasing after Alicia, I read, "Lady Wabi-Sabi performs *Ookina Sekai, Chisana Jinsei* (Big World, Little Life) as part of the Japanese Culture Package." I sped up to catch up. "It also includes a tour of the Japanese Gardens and a tasting at the Saké One brewery."

"What are you implying?"

"And lunch is... Implying? What?"

"What is this?" Next to the sedan, Alicia, an animal's dark heart, held the sake can at me.

"Well," rather than stumble-mumble over stating the convoluted obvious, Kikusui's Funaguchi Kunkou Black, I said, "It's a can of sake."

She pressed it into my chest, "You have issues."

"Well," I admitted, accepting the can, "I know that. I mean, who doesn't, right?"

She flung the sedan's door open and climbed in. After a curse-laden struggle with the key, the sedan started. "Oh, and next time you're life's in danger—"

"Don't call you?"

"Exactly. Don't call me." Grabbing the door's handle, she added, "Oh, and have fun with your racist friends tonight." She slammed the door. I stepped back. And she sped off.

Shaking my head, I declared to the can, "And I'm the one with issues?"

After a long sip, as I considered calling her, my phone rang, "Alicia?"

"No. Who's Alicia? Doesn't matter."

"Naomi?"

"Do not hang up," she swore. "If you do, I will come over there and kill you."

"You hate flying."

"I'm beginning to hate you more."

She, like Alicia, sounded sincere.

Trudging toward the vines, I sipped, "Okay. I understand that. But can we make an appointment or something? Because—"

"Because you're so busy?"

"Well, I could be," I said, stepping from the gravel onto the cold, damp grass bordering the vines,

"Unlikely considering your circumstances."

I rambled off a few excuses, dead girlfriend-slash-fiancée and deceased father at the fore. Finishing confidently with, "And my crazy ass stepmother is living here."

"Where'd you expect her to be?" Naomi asked, ignoring my plight.

"Well, I don't know. I thought maybe... Well, I don't know."

The first time, last time, only time, I'd met Aori was my high school graduation. Having accepted my diploma from Principal Ferguson, her handshake remarkably firm, though disconcertingly moist, I marched across the last length of the stage waving blindly to the vague sea of attendees.

Trundling down the creaking metal steps, I found Tina fighting through the hugging families. Yanking me aside, she proclaimed, "Your mother's beating the shit out of Aori. Come quick."

I was confused, not by my arousal, but by her statement and who Aori was.

Tina, her tanned, pert, angular body pressed into the summer, watermelon print, bias cut sundress, grabbed my hand and exponentially increased my arousal.

Considering Shannon's "gift" three days prior, I happily followed.

Tina's frenzied yanking, however, was overly dramatic for foreplay. It could, prematurely, go to waste should she continue with such insistence.

Turning the corner past the formaldehyde-stenched biology lab, we collided with the other witches and bitches, all dressed in slinky, summer, sun dresses.

Rather than, as hoped, an erotic entanglement, they clasped a young, Asian woman against a wall. Mother belted the pour woman, rhythmically, over and over, in the stomach, chanting, "Take that you *butoh* dancing bitch. Take that. Take that."

At the time, I'd thought *butoh* a racial slur. One of the many reasons I'd not gone to the court hearing and had submitted a signed statement.

In hindsight, regardless of the accusation's accuracy, Mother's actions remained unforgivable, particularly with the assistance of the witches and bitches. Throw down Crushed style, *mano a mano*, or not at all.

"Dixon, listen," Naomi continued, "I've spoken with Lidia at Ganymede. We think we can pivot the situation to our advantage."

At the vineyard's southwest corner, I turned left and started on the southern border.

A head high hedge, filled with flitting, chirping sparrows, separated the vineyard from a thin stand of pines. Beyond droned the traffic hum from the highway, 99W.

"Naomi, I don't think—"

"Just listen. Okay? Please?"

"Okay. Fine. What've you got?"

"She'd like *The Jerk* on her desk in three months. Twenty thousand advance."

"Nothing more?"

"Is that not enough?" She sounded, because she was (rightly), incredulous. "Dixon? Hello?"

Had I not read this script before? Attempted this role before?

"I'll send everything in an email."

I felt the anxiety rising. People's expectations of who I was, what I needed to do, to be.

"Dixon, it's going to be okay. Okay?"

Oh, I loved Naomi, even when she lied.

"Oh, my god," she'd observed, as we swayed naked and drunk in her East End apartment, "why would anyone want one of those inside them?"

"At least you can see what you're getting with this." I indicated my erection and continued, "But with that mystery cave?" I shook my head, "We've got to trust there are no creatures lurking within." To her quivering smile, I added, "Mind you," I ran a palm up and down the afore-mentioned erection, "this is much less disgusting than most."

To my confusion and dismay, she started crying.

"It's ugly," I admitted, foregoing underwear and tugging on jeans, "but not that ugly. Right?"

She continued crying.

After tucking her in polar bear pajamas, we curled up on her futon, pulled the comforter over us, and snuggled.

Moments before collapsing unconscious, I'd whispered in her ear, "One day, I promise, I will fuck the shit out of you."

"And when you do," she observed, "you're cleaning it up." She kissed my cheek, closed her eyes, and drifted off to sleep.

As an only child, you always wonder about having a sibling, some-one to share the agony and frustration of having such annoying parents. A sister like Naomi? She'd be ideal. Though we wouldn't have cuddled like that, my erection had been rather indelicately pressed against her butt when I too had fallen asleep.

"There's one caveat," Naomi confessed, as I found the southeasterly corner, which, not surprisingly, was reminiscent of the southwestern corner.

"There always are. And one isn't bad. Right?" My optimism had tak-en her by surprise and kept her silent. "Well, go on."

"They want you to help Home Office clear yourself of the terrorist charges being filed against you here and in France."

"But isn't that notoriety why Ganymede wants *The Jerk*?"

Through the thin band of pines defining the eastern edge, the som-nolent hum of heavy equipment, bulldozers and dump trucks, droned as they reconfigured a hillside into cul-de-sacs for tract housing.

"Just take scrupulous notes and we'll spin it into a memoir." She had a point, a good one. It was annoying, particularly after she added, "It could help your stand-up."

"Maybe. Not sure I feel like doing comedy anymore."

"Well, you're alive, aren't you?"

"Physical comedy doesn't count."

"Regardless, keep notes. And I'll include the Home Office info in the email."

"Sounds good."

My reply had been hollow, unenthused, so she, the sweetheart, en-couraged, "Dixon, it's going to be okay."

"Everything is—"

"There you go."

"In the short term," I admitted and hung up.

Knowing who I needed to talk to regarding the Paris "installations," I made the call. "Hey, Split, can I talk to Bussy?"

"About what?"

"About Paris."

"Who's dis?"

On my first restocking shift at the Wickford Aldi's, Stanley, the grave-yard shift supervisor, a middle-aged man with fatigue filling his placid gray eyes and two-day bearded cheeks, waggled an unenthusiastic fin-ger toward four silhouettes under the docking bay's fluorescent lights. "You'll be working with those grunters there. Go say hello or some-thing." He turned and trundled back into the shadow-shrouded store.

Ambling for the silhouettes—"Dicks in whose tower?"—I pon-dered an alias.

A muscular, lanky bloke with a lithe, mean swagger glided my way.

"Bussy," it said, extending a hand, "what's yours?"

Taking it, trying not to get caught up in the politics of the shake, or how he looked like the improbable love child of Elvis Presley and David Bowie, I answered, "Just call me DJ." No one called me DJ, ever. I needed a new start, and a new name was a start to that start.

"You a DJ?"

"What? No, it's—"

"What ya spin, mate? No judgments here amongst the cages." He rattled one of the portable, metal stocking shelves. "We're all slaving for king and country, yeah? So, what do ya spin? Techno? Trance? Elec-tro? Dubstep? No, no, don't tell—Afro-Beat, yeah?" Over his shoulder, he called out, "Ubu?"

"Yeah?" the bigger, broader of the three remaining silhouettes called out.

"Bloke here's gonna take yer gig at Bananas."

"Bussy, what're ya yammerin' 'bout?"

"Yer mother's arse."

The two had some forth and back before they turned to me, and I explained, "Sorry. Misunderstanding. Name's Dixon."

"That's a wanker's name. End of shift we'll have something better for ya."

"Not gonna wait," Split declared, "for ya to pull yer prick out. Who's dis?"

"It's Yank."

Split laughed, but realizing I'd told the truth he went cold and distant. "Don't know no one by that name. And if I did—"

"Split, come on. Let me talk to Bussy."

"And if I did, I heard she's well dead."

"Split."

"Gang raped by a bunch of ring-tailed lemurs."

"A troop."

"Whatever. Seems she liked it right well."

"That's because the Yank's a whore."

He laughed past his usual spite, "Yeah, wanker, what about the Paris thing?"

"So you admit there was a Paris thing?"

The line went dead, and I declared to the annoying twittering sparrows, "I believe that answers that question."

The limos growled down the drive, the gravel cackling nervously over the vines.

A wide swath of grass, rutted with tractor treads, separated the lower half of the property from the upper, which sloped gradually uphill. This was also where the rows altered orientation, from east-west to north-south. At the end of the swath sat the house. From this perspective, with the full brunt of the morning sun, it glowed as if on fire. The bright yellow glare pushed me up the slope, toward the northeastern corner.

My left hip, a residual effect of Troy and the nuns, flared with the effort. I slowed and, unbuttoning the jacket, stepped into a stray sunbeam shooting through the pines.

The Willamette Valley, a broad, luxurious, patchwork of greens, muted tans and browns, vineyards, farms, and forest, stretched off in the distance. Blue-gray whorls of smoke from clearing fires rose into the sky, giving a layered depth to the scene.

Before colliding headfirst into introspection, my phone rang.

The limos, dark sharks late for a feeding frenzy, flashed down the highway, and I answered, "Radcliffe, what do you want?"

"Besides your story?"

"Yes. Besides that."

"An apology for not making it to *Deux Maggots*."

"Not my fault."

"Extenuating circumstances?"

"Exactly." A brief silence lingered as I suspected he knew what'd happened.

"Maybe you'd like to tell me about it?"

"Maybe."

"Speaking of, I can offer another five thousand."

"Radcliffe, sorry, I'm just too busy."

"Maybe you can tell me what you're busy with? Say, next week sometime?"

"Sorry? What?"

"Yeah, I'm flying out your way."

"Why?" Did he know I was in Oregon? If so, how? "I thought I said I was busy?"

"I've a curious theory that what occurred in Paris may've had something to do with your book."

"*The Yank*?"

"Which may have something to do with an illegal international wine tasting competition. And, get this, the world championships this year are in Portland. Coincidence?" Even in the spring-warmed air, my skin went cold. "So, I may be repeating myself, but what do you know about Crushed?"

"Nothing." I hung up, which only reinforced the fact I was lying.

Why hadn't I known the championships were here? Easy. I was in Paris, had quit the circuit, and, regardless of what Boonen may've had planned for me, I wasn't going to compete in the championships.

The ache in the hip had dissipated to a dull throb and, with a resigned sigh, I continued up the hill.

The northwest corner spent most the day drowsed in shade and, therefore, hadn't been planted, but had become a wayward space dominated by a dozen or so felled, moss-covered trees, a decrepit, red tractor, a pile of rusted barrel straps, and a large mound of tires, oily rings of water inside them reflected the softly clouded sky.

Again, my phone broke the tranquility. Blocked caller. After the incident at Sheppard's, I wasn't sure I should chat with Heavy Breather. However, it could be nice to have some distraction, someone to confess to.

"Hello?"

"Let it go, mate," a voice growled, heavy with Cockney.

"Bussy?"

"Let it go." And he hung up.

Succinct as usual, though the desperation and the threat were new.

I kicked at a stone. It loosened, exposing a wet divot of earth, a few small, thin worms wriggled, like me, annoyed.

After all the stories, tales, and legends I'd heard over the years, I didn't completely understand why Crushed was illegal or outlawed, or exactly what the difference was.

The leading theory involved big gambling houses wanting in on the action. They wanted to regulate it, require licenses, and standardize everything from glass size to what wines were permissible, even music and videos. And, to a certain extent, that was what the website had done. However, as the website stated, it was for making ease of access and making "pop-up" competitions, like the one with Sara and me, a viable option.

There was even the notion, amongst a coterie of competitors, to televise competitions on "an independent cable network."

Radcliffe implying my novel was connected with Crushed was, of course, preposterous. The closest thing to wine mentioned in that insolent tome was blackberry brandy. He was suckling on the conspiracy theory teat.

I moved on to Aori's lair, the crushing facility.

Though not prepared to be gutted like a fish, I was ready to apologize for interrupting her performance, and my mother beating the shit out of her.

Chapter Sixteen
INNOCENCE PISSED AWAY

The pleasing, deep, earthy rankness enveloping the crushing facility's rear door greeted me with open arms.

At the mud-stained, back tire of the John Deere, I stopped, glanced around, confused. The stacks of crates and fermenting tanks spoke of activity and yet of all the bottles crowding the cellar, I hadn't seen a single bottle from Oregon.

Granted, I'd glanced through the racks and was pleased at his preference for reds. Regardless, there was only a narrow section representing the West Coast, almost exclusively California with a smattering of big, bold reds from Washington.

It didn't make any sense. Oregon had world-class Pinots. Then there were the niche blends and vintners from the Rogue Valley or the Columbia Gorge.

And, assuming you weren't throwing away your harvest, where were the bottles from your land? It didn't make sense unless he sold the grapes and was a glorified farmer.

Frustrated and annoyed, why apologize? Maybe I'd tell Aori it was her fault my parents divorced? It wasn't, but I could always lay blame. And I'd ask her how long she planned on staying here, though that likely depended on the will. Then there was her threat. And there was the awkward goodbye with Alicia. Did she believe I was racist? I'd have explained (if Crushed wasn't Crushed) it had everything to do with Crushed. But the first rule of Crushed, well, you didn't talk about it. Oh, shit, now I was pissed off.

I yanked the metal door open and stepped into a black velvet blackout curtain. Untangling myself from its soft clutches, I twisted and staggered into the facility.

The space had the distinctive warm musty scent of a winery and yet it wasn't. Yes, there was a section dedicated to bottling, corking, labeling, and packing, though not an automated system, but hands-on, slow, and meticulous work. However, there were no bottles, corks, labels, or boxes. And once, based on the severed bolts in the floor, there'd been eight fermenting tanks, with the two nearest the front remaining.

Most of the interior acted as a theatre space. Forty or fifty gray folding chairs were set up before a small stage, maybe thirty by fifteen feet, and two feet off the floor. A rudimentary lighting system of a few dozen canned stage lights, like fat bats, hung overhead.

The most interesting aspect of the stage was the scenery or lack of it. There was only a bare tree limb with a noose. They were inverted as if defying gravity. The limb sprouted from downstage left, undulated to center stage, though never more than a few inches off it. The noose, shoulder high, dark, and burgundy-discolored, shot erect from the limb.

Adding to the arresting presentation, the stage, like the cellar, had been painted *trompe l'oiel*, and continued the inversion theme. The gnarled limb ran to an old, venerable oak. Its bare limbs were speckled with dark-eyed crows. Overhead, more of the murder circled against a sunset-stained sky.

I'd performed on stages much smaller and in venues much less accommodating but on nothing nearly so dramatic or beautiful.

A seductive melancholy coiled around me and joined the underlying sorrow.

Sinking, sitting on the edge of the stage, I realized, once again, I'd failed.

The crowd, to my hunched retreating, had hissed and booed. Most had thrown their complimentary pretzels and peanuts. Some, after chugging their drink, threw the plastic cup.

Stumbling past Rodrigo, the stage manager, Kris and Kirk, the "juggling joke couple," trotted on stage, and I found a trashcan and dumped my stomach's luggage into it.

I'd recently been promoted from Treasure Chest Saloon's barback to Ahoy Deck night bartender. Malcolm Arterberry, the *Oleander Princess*'s smarmy entertainment director, thought making drunks laugh about chicken-legged, old men playing shuffleboard and chain-smoking, old women hunched at the slots transferred to stand-up.

So when Doctor Laughter, a prop-heavy comic, again failed his sobriety test, I was thrown to the wolves.

My "act," hasty scribbles on a few dozen stained bev naps, may've worked, if the audience hadn't been those same chicken-legged men, smoking-wheezing old women.

Lifting my head from the can, a middle-aged man with crystal blue-gray eyes and a thick head of pristinely coiffed silver hair, tapped me with a bottle of water and jutted his chin toward the audience, "They're a tough crowd. The toughest. Forget about it, kid."

Accepting and chugging the sweet water, I glanced back at the octogenarian crowd. They were an enraged town searching for the monster, and instead of pitchforks and scythes, they, crazed, shook crutches and canes.

"Name's Arne Ronk," the man stated, offering a hand.

Shaking it, I asked, "Your accent? Where are you from?"

"Iceland."

He lied, but it didn't matter, because he said, "I don't think comedy is your thing."

I'd prove him wrong, someday, but, curious, I asked, "Okay. So what is?"

"Have you," he answered with a question, a mischievous smile, "heard of the Vine Suite?"

Had I? Every hand on the *Oleander Princess* had. Usually in hushed and reverent tones as someone added another layer of mystery to its aura.

Santiago, stirring lobster and black truffle risotto, had claimed, "*Sí, amigo*, black cat sacrifices and Baphomet. It's a devil's den of debauchery."

While Maria, pulling toilet paper rolls from her cart, confessed, "A portal to another dimension. Why do you ask?"

Later that night, after I'd repacked my stomach with a burger and fries, Arne manipulated me into a blindfold, promising "a peek behind the curtain."

Five others, also blinking confused into the light, were scattered around the expansive double suite's oblong, white marble dining table.

We were surrounded by a shadowy, giddy crowd gambling and drinking as if it were Casablanca entrenched in the midst of World War II. The air, thick with cigar smoke and cognac, was tainted with something more sinister than money, privilege and gunpowder.

The crowd grew quiet as the room filled with the guttural, bleeding howl of angst-riddled German speed metal.

My skin crawled with fear and something unexpected—exhilaration.

Wearing a deep garnet-hued suit, with a white carnation on the lapel, a tall, angular, dark-haired, dark-eyed man with a dark scar slicing his right cheek slipped from the shadowy gloom.

The crowd buzzed with excitement.

A glass of wine was placed before each us, and he explained, "I will ask questions. You will answer on the piece of paper before you." In front of each of us was the standard *Oleander Princess* pad and pen, each emblazoned with the mermaid wrapped around a trident logo. "You will fold the paper in half and hand it to the person behind you." Six hooded figures stepped forward from the gloom, took guard behind us. Scarface continued, "Those who answer incorrectly are removed. Is this understood?"

Too confused to question, we mumbled ambiguous affirmations.

"What," Scarface asked, raising his voice to match the music's escalation, "is the varietal?"

We, in a Spaghetti Western, glanced around from one to the other.

"You may taste."

We tasted.

The woman to my left, maybe the Poseidon dining room's sommelier, assessed, "Pale gold. Hints of tropical fruit and—"

Glaring, Scarface declared, "Those who speak are removed."

"Just a moment, this is—" The woman fell silent as the figure behind her placed a hand on her shoulder.

"Write your answer," Scarface instructed. "Fold the paper in half. Hand the paper to the person behind you."

We did as instructed.

Silently the figures read our slips.

The figure behind the man I'd realized was the day manager at the Parrot Café shook his head.

A buzz of chatter fluttered the crowd.

The figure tapped the manager's shoulder and placed a hand on the back of his chair.

He, a tight, stern grimace roped to his lips, stood, slipped through the crowd, and disappeared into the darkness.

The glasses were gathered and another placed before us as a sharp, brittle shout rang out.

Startled and confused, we glanced around while a flurry of betting erupted.

Scarface, unflinching and unmoved, as we were pressed back into our chairs, stated, "You may taste."

The woman to my left, fueled by fear, again spoke, "Wait one moment. Was that a gunshot?"

Scarface nodded. The person behind the woman tapped her shoulder and placed a hand on the back of her chair.

"No, I will not. I doubt the captain knows about this. But when he does—"

A commanding voice bellowed from the shadows, "Oh, but he does." All knew the accent, the voice, the baritone. It was Captain Augustine Mondova. "Now take her away."

Two hooded figures, shaped like Panzer tanks, though slightly larger, stepped forward. They, in a precise fluid motion, picked her chair up.

She wriggled, outraged. "No. No. No. You cannot do this."

They marched through the crowd. It parted like the proverbial sea. Another shot rang.

"What," Scarface demanded, "is the varietal, the country, the region?"

"Wait. Wait. Hold on," the rotund man wearing a garish orange and turquoise Hawaiian print shirt stuttered, "how can you expect us to know that?"

The Panzers returned. After a brief struggle, each gripping an arm, he was escorted off into the darkness.

After a muffled shout, scuffling, and screaming, another shot hammered the air.

"Please," Scarface insisted, "the varietal. The country. The region."

The remaining three of us, heads buried in the glass, sniffing fervently, praying to any god that'd listen, tasted, slurped and slurped, and answered.

Behind the bird-like man on my right, the hooded figure waved Scarface over.

Briefly, they whispered, and then Scarface announced, "No. I'm sorry. It is incorrect."

The man, verging on arguing, reached inside his blue dinner jacket.

The crowd, like I, expecting a gun, gasped and stepped back.

Instead, he extracted a dented, green, metal flask.

Relieved, the crowd sighed and surged back.

Standing, he swore, "*In vino veritas*," took a long suckle from the flask and, resigned, walked out toward where the Panzers awaited.

On the shot's dying echo another flurry of betting erupted.

Another glass, with a deep, dark burgundy liquid, dragon's blood, was placed before me and my remaining competitor, an auburn-haired woman of indiscriminate age with a sad glare like a circus lion.

"This is a blend," Scarface informed. "Write the varietals and their corresponding percentages. You may taste."

The previous wines, being a single varietal, were relatively simple to assess. This one was not.

Leaning toward a classic Bordeaux blend, preparing for a second sip, the woman, glaring scalding fire into me, slammed her pen down and spat, "Eat that tuna face. Eat. That."

The crowd tittered in subdued jubilation.

I blinked in confusion and Scarface declared, "You have one minute,"

Panicked, I drank. I slurped.

It wasn't Bordeaux but where? There were plenty and too many vintners around the globe making subtle and complex reds with balanced tannins, soft, chewy dark fruit, and an earthy hint of mint. New World. South America or Australia?

"Thirty seconds."

Right, shit, I didn't need to know country or region, just the varietals. I slurped.

I scribbled.

"Ten seconds."

Oh, shit, shit, and the percentages.

I sucked at the last vestiges in the glass.

I scribbled.

"Time."

The slip of paper was tugged from my tight, reluctant fingers.

The woman, perfecting her circus lion glare, licked her lips, and mouthed a repetition, "Tuna face."

I had nothing, not a flask or reasonably intelligent quote. Nothing.

Lifting me from my chair, the Panzers escorted me through the shadowy, ghostly faces of the crowd. Exiting past the last few disappointed faces, we stepped into a gunpowder-stenched cloud.

The Panzer on my right, the one I assumed with the gun, because he reached into a pocket, loosened his grip.

Filled with fear and flight, I, peeing myself, shook loose and ran headlong for freedom.

Three strides from a door flanked by an ornate gold and teak wet bar and a double door humidor, at a well-lit corner table loaded with sumptuous tapas, my fellow competitors loitered. Rather than bullet holes embellishing hearts and foreheads, they, all wearing light blue infirmary pants, were smiling and laughing, drinking and eating.

They waved.

Waving back, I stumbled to a stop and turned to the Panzers.

Tanner and Lars, personal trainers at the Hercules gym on the Mermaid deck, had pulled their cowls back and laughed and laughed, verged on peeing themselves.

Tanner tossed me a gym towel, Lars a pair of infirmary pants, and said the best four words I've ever heard, in any order, "Welcome to the club."

It was a Debutants Duel. Gather a few newbies, pit them against one another, and let the gambling and hilarity ensue.

Arne, handing me a small clump of cash, clapping me on the shoulder, added, "Great fun, particularly if you enjoy watching people pee and poop themselves."

My little indiscretion had, besides Arne, made two other bettors ten thousand richer. It'd also sparked seven offers to do the same, though in the privacy of their cabins.

Two days later, docking in Helsinki, I hadn't renewed my contract. Instead, I clambered aboard a passenger ferry for Stockholm and my first Crushed competition, The Syndrome Throwdown.

During the preliminary seeding round, Arne had dropped his Icelandic for a West Country drawl and introduced himself as Arthur Aldous Sinclair. And, as the lights dimmed and In Flames' Take This Life swelled, he clapped my shoulder, said, "See ya around sometime, kid," and disappeared into the pickled herring stenched shadows.

Standing, I stared at the inverted noose, the circling murder, the empty chairs.

An understandable panic rose in me.

In a futile attempt to outpace the rising tide, the creatures—peanut butter slathering dog, the smoking mini-Nazi, the naked, masked tiger vixen—crawling from my memory, I paced across the stage, from one end of the sunset to the other.

Back and forth.

Back and forth.

As quickly as I'd begun, I was slowing.

A rhythmic sighing, like practicing CPR on a rubbing-alcohol-flavored dummy and its rheumy response, wheezed somewhere.

There was a breathy groan and moan.

Stepping from the stage, I slipped toward where the sound emanated, a cluttered storage alcove near the front door.

I peeked around the corner.

Aori, propped atop a wine barrel, remained in her dance outfit. Lengths of the caked mud makeup had been clawed from her arms and belly. Her skin glistened bright as moonlight. Head tilted back, eyes closed, she grimaced, not in pain but pleasure.

The one at work, head pressed deep into her loins, had their arms curled around Aori's hips, hands gripping her, caressing her. The arms, tanned and svelte, were a woman's. Tattoos were wrapped around each wrist. The left was a tangle of thorn-covered vines with a series of varied colored flowers blooming from it. The right had three or four bands of script encircling it.

Due to the angle, and Aori's leg, I couldn't see the woman's face. Her brown, silver-streaked ponytail, held tight with a red scrunchy, rhythmically bobbed to Aori's mounting pleasure.

Before I knew what I was doing, I'd shoved a hand down my jeans.

Aori placed a hand on the back of the woman's head and pulled her closer, the other, tugged a swath of burlap aside and squeezed the dark nipple. It justly, accusingly, stared.

The woman's ponytail, reminiscent of Shannon's, bobbed faster, and Aori neared climax.

I'd soon, too, but a crackling growl of gravel scratched the passion-charged air.

Oh, Alicia and your sedan, how you needed to work on your timing.

"No, no," Aori whispered breathlessly as the woman's head rose, "don't stop. Don't stop."

Disappointed and envious, I pulled my hand free and ducked back around the corner, shuffled, a bowlegged cowboy, for the front door and out of the facility.

Making the strip of grass running along the drive, my erection continued fighting my attempts at de-escalating it, when I heard voices.

I turned, curious about who joined Aori in pursuit. Another shout had me realizing they were ahead and not behind.

Spinning back, I plowed a foot into one of the boulders bordering the drive.

Yelping, I flew face-first down the grassy embankment.

Sliding down the wet lawn, bumping and humping over the dark lumps of the molehills, my breath lurched from me in gasps, "Uh. Uh. Uh."

My speed increased, as did my arousal, and I found myself being overwhelmed by the sensationally pleasing sensation.

Wet, covered in grass and mud, I came to a stuttering stop atop a molehill. Its soft loam enveloped my crotch. Fighting would only elongate the experience and increase the probability of discovery.

Acquiescing, quivering with pleasure, I ejaculated as a voice, not Alicia's and much huskier, called from the front of the house, "Mr. Belltower?"

With a contented smile, from the hole, the cluster of prepubescent dandelions, I raised my head. An elderly man, reminiscent of Max von Sydow, stared from the walkway. A taller, gaunter, younger version peaked over his shoulder. "Mr. Belltower?"

Groin gooey and sticky, I wobbled unsteadily to my feet. Waddling for the back door, I pointed to the front and instructed, "I'll meet you inside."

I made the stairs as they arrived.

Lumbering up, each step at a time, warm lengths of goo escaped and oozed down my thighs. The plastic runner cackled gleefully, and I shouted over a shoulder, "Whoever you are, make yourselves at home."

Chapter Seventeen
THE WIZARD BEHIND THE CURTAIN

I'd shed the goo-soiled clothes and, after a harried splash and scrub, having seen the suits the two gentlemen wore, felt obligated to mimic. Therefore, with much grimacing, I crawled back into the filthy, mourning suit.

Thanks to my release on the molehill, I felt calm and at ease. Regardless of who they were, I was comfortable playing the character I'd been cast—myself.

After the formalities of introductions, and they succeeding in not inquiring about my bestial visage, I'd discovered Mr. Jonathan Enright and his son, Malcolm, with great expertise, had done as instructed—made themselves at home.

Home, based on the bountiful spread laid across the living room's table, was a Jewish deli.

The elder, to my confusion, explained with a toast dry voice, "Whenever we'd visit, your father insisted we bring this."

A pale, crooked finger indicated the array of white ramekins. All stuffed with a deli item, cream cheese, locks, cornichons, sliced red onion, liver pate, et cetera, et cetera. A silver teaspoon stuck in each.

The Enrights had even, atop the movie cabinet, created a Bloody Mary station Markella in the Nautilus Lounge would've been proud of.

I was unclear why such wares were here.

Ignoring the urn, fearing my hunch, I hesitated. Catching a whiff of the suit, however, I was emboldened, "Okay, but you're not Jewish, are you?"

"No. We're not. Your father was—"

The elder Enright held up a hand, and the younger held his tongue. The elder said, "Let's say your father was eclectic."

"Okay, let's say that. Eclectic." And, because I didn't despise being myself as much as I'd thought, I added, "But a rose by some other name might be bigot or racist?"

The younger, ignoring the accusation, annoying me more than obfuscating the truth, smarmed, "We thought we'd stick with convention."

On my second Mary, infused with extra Tabasco, horseradish, and vodka, to my annoyance, I had agreed—convention had its merits.

I'd also lost all guilt regarding not sharing with the urn.

"Besides convention," I asked around the straw, "why are you here?"

The younger removed a sheaf of papers from a black satchel sitting at his ankles and squeezed it onto the table.

The elder droned, "Your mother and Aori have already signed these."

The younger tapped the papers. "You, Mr. Belltower, only need to do the same."

Setting down my last scrawl and pen, I, dubious and dumbfounded, shook the cramp from my hand. Mary Three's straw jitterbugged around my lips, as I asked, "And the rest is going to me?"

The Enrights nodded.

The rest, excluding undisclosed cash payouts to Mother and Aori, was everything.

I clamped down on the straw and repeated past it, "All of it? To me?"

"Yes, Mr. Belltower," the younger replied, tucking the pages back in the satchel. "Yes."

He, to my confusion, sounded as annoyed as I.

They'd each had a bagel and Mary prepared when first I lumbered into the room, but neither had partaken of either. It made me suspicious.

"Why?" I asked.

"Because," the younger admitted as if he knew too well, "it's one of the only benefits of being an only child."

"None to contest," the elder added, as if it were planned.

"None to contest," the younger agreed, dismantling the spread into a large, wheeled, red cooler.

I drained the last vestiges of Mary three, made to make another before they destroyed the station.

Turning from the disappointed urn, I asked, indicating the new sheaf of papers sprouted upon the table, "And what's all that?"

"These," the old, savvy bastard confessed, "are the offers on the property," and arranged the papers in a pleasingly symmetrical array on the newly cleared table.

Once satisfied with their arrangement, he asked, "That's assuming you're interested?"

"Was I?" I asked Mary four.

The younger Enright interpreted my retort as an invitation and presented the nine offers. Seven of which had been made since my father's passing.

Past a mild frown, I inquired, "Could he have been murdered?"

"No," the elder declared with a smirk of surety.

"So how did he," I glanced at the urn, back to the elder's watery eyes, "you know, go?"

"An accident." Rather than explain the nuances of how assassins operate, I listened and eyed the stapled clump he pressed toward me. "RoEl Unlimited's offer, at least in our estimation, is the most advantageous."

The propaganda papers proclaimed, besides being pronounced "royal," RoEl Unlimited was "an international conglomerate specializing in transforming dreams into reality."

Something nagged me. And it was more than the cloying statement, their insipid logo (a gold crown of fleur-de-lis and heart-shaped rubies), or the younger's renewed smirk.

I scanned the offer sheet. The caveats and contingencies were distilled into a $10.5 million offer. At each clause, the RoEl Unlimited representative's initials, GC, glared.

The nag, after a few dozen chews on the straw, clicked.

Jumping to my feet, I swore with a frigid forefinger, "*J'accuse!*"

The Enrights feigned confusion.

I and the Mary decried, "Roland St. fucking Fer."

To their lying faces, I tapped the initials and enlightened, "GC. *Gran Crus*. General classification. The tall turd's obsession with pretentious wines and cycling?"

With less conviction, they continued feigning ignorance.

My outrage, fueled by more than mere Marys, grew. "Doesn't ring a bell? Ding dong? Ding dong? No? Really?"

Stalking the shag, I searched for something appropriate to punch.

The elder, with a resigned sigh, admitted, "Yes, Mr. Belltower, we were made aware of your relationship with Mr. St. Fer. And his wife. And—"

He faltered and the younger took over, "And we don't believe inter-personal relationships should jeopardize the transaction. Particularly one so—"

"Lucrative?" I offered, with a knowing smirk. "Like a little *quid pro quo*?"

"Advantageous to all parties," the younger smirked in return.

"Precisely," the elder declared. "As Mister St. Fer mentioned he'd like to start—" He stuttered to a stop. A brief silence lingered, awkward, until, resigned, he added, "He'd like to start right after harvest."

"Start? Start what?"

"The vines," the younger observed, "are elderly and well past their prime. The land is worth more developed and requires no reinvestment." He shrugged, picked up his lox and cream cheese smothered bagel, and took a bite.

The vision of the bulldozers, the reconfigured hillside, and the tract housing cul-de-sacs made me shiver. And was Sheppard's offer from RoEl also?

Staggering to the Mary station, I contemplated another and what I could do with 10.5 million, even if it was gleaned from that asshole St. Fer. A whitewashed house on a Greek isle? Or a Tiki hut in the South Pacific?

Placing the glass down, I paced beyond the fireplace to the double pair of heavily draped, French doors.

Requiring some spectacle to underline and accentuate my conviction, I channeled Eva Perón, her operatic version, and, yanking them back, I proclaimed, "No."

Searing sunlight, mercilessly, punched me in the eyes with a bright, blinding fist.

Groaning, gripping the drapes, I spun and staggered back, retreating.

My scalded retinas only had eyes for a pulsating orange orb and were blind to the cowhide footstool. Falling to the shag, entangled in the drapes, their rod was yanked from the wall and clattered over me.

Hip and shoulder flared in familiar meteor showers of pain, and I groaned in greeting.

"Mr. Belltower," the elder asked, unmoving and without notion of a helping hand, "are you all right?"

Peaking from under the drapes, tossing the rod aside, I assured, "No, but I'll be fine."

They, loitering in their indecision, glanced at one another, unsure.

"Really," I insisted, waving a dismissive hand and crawling to the couch, yanking a cushion off, "I'll be fine."

"And the offer?" the younger insisted.

I lied. "I'll consider it." I snuggled a little deeper into the drapes. "Well, gentlemen, I believe it advisable you take the Mary station with you." The younger considered commenting, but, shaking my head, I sighed. "Regardless of convention."

They nodded and, with a modicum of whispering, packed up the Mary station.

"Thank you, gentlemen," I said, idly waving them on their way. "And, please, have a superlative day."

The Enrights and their cooler clattered off.

The front door *thumped* shut.

I wrapped the drapes tighter, and the sun's warmth seeped through the fabric and into me. It took only a moment before I knew I wanted to remain like this forever.

Chapter Eighteen
A GLASS FROM THE PAST

Clutching the "Give it a Roost!" tote bag where the two bottles for the friendly nested, I maneuvered along the same route Alicia and I had taken... Yesterday? Earlier. Whenever. The pines, in the cooling breeze, swayed and whispered like drowsy crickets, and I realized I should've worn a jacket.

I'd been indecisive in selecting the bottles and was ten minutes late. By then, the last enlightening rays of sunset had disappeared.

Walking the shadowed row, I discovered I was looking forward to a friendly night of tasting. More than a furious fling, it was likely what I needed.

Nearing the halogen-lit landing, soft jazz, early Miles Davis, trickled from somewhere.

Climbing the steps, a silhouette slipped from the shadows.

Startled, I stepped back, keeping the bag between myself and my assailant.

Backlit by the docking bay's light, Sheppard, a vengeful god, loomed over me.

"You're late, Belltower."

Even to such a deity as he, I felt no compulsion to explain the wave of ennui that had swept me swiftly into unconsciousness that afternoon cocooned in drapes,

"Yes, sir," I stammered and continued, "Sorry, sir. Overwhelmed by selection and wanting to bring something appropriate. Something—"

He burst out laughing. "Damn, son, relax. Pull your panties up, and let's go."

I hesitated. If my father had been "eclectic," perhaps they were too? Maybe, which would be unfortunate, Alicia was right?

Heading for the door, he placed an arm in my way, "Don't be presumptuous, boy. What's the color of God's underwear?"

In the halogen's glare, we stared.

Sheppard, regardless his name, and the soft, suppleness of Paradox 101, was a hardened asshole.

Because I was Crushed, I had the identical asshole, and answered, "That, my idiot friend, is a stupid, fucking question."

Any question anyone posed to enter a competition, a tasting, or a friendly, was exactly that—a stupid fucking question. The key wasn't in the question, or a theoretically correct response. No, it was in simply responding, "That, my idiot friend, is a stupid, fucking question."

Clapping my shoulder, Sheppard replied, "Welcome, brother, you've been long missed."

The second piece of the puzzle was the reply. If it were anything else it was a trap and advisable to run, run fast and far.

Early on, such subterfuge wasn't necessary. However, as the prestige and purses grew, the possibility of being abducted for the competition's secrets grew. After the Josephine Sagan incident (Budapest, 1977), things changed, swiftly.

Sheppard, mistaking my hesitation for fear, added the reassurance phrase, "All have gone and all will go, so know you are not alone."

That's what I loved about Crushed—the camaraderie and the community. Yes, we were competitors, desperate and occasionally dastardly, though in the end we were a family of misfits that, more than anything, revered the vine and its master, Time.

Through the darkened facility we glided to a back wall where a discrete door was hidden by a metal shelving unit on castors. Down a short flight of steps, an expansive rectangular room had been carved into the hillside.

To the right, embedded in the stone was an ensemble of kitchen appliances, and on the left were three small alcoves with seating around rock-hewn tables.

The domed ceiling was lit with a warm, yellow glow from recessed lights, while against the back wall hunched a cherry-red metal fireplace with glass doors. Its smoke drained, mesmerizingly, up through a glass chimney.

And floating in the background was the Miles that'd drifted across the vines.

The conversation between the four elderly gentlemen in the corner stopped as we entered.

Sheppard advised, "Anything those scoundrels say tonight, ignore it." With an elbow, he nudged me toward a counter where an outcropping of bottles wrapped in the requisite frozen pizza boxes and duct tape sat. "You can put those over there."

"Okay."

"And pour yourself something."

"Okay."

"And stop sounding like a damn greenhorn. You ain't convincing."

"Yes, sir. Sorry, sir."

"Such an asshole," he chuckled, walking away to join the others, "now I know why he left you."

Though harsh, given the Crushed context, it was a fair comment.

Placing my bottles at the end of the row, I scanned the boxes on offer. There were another ten lined up. Two per head was the bare minimum for a friendly.

Crushed "founder," Eugenio Mendoza, so lore and legend went, was a Brooklyn caterer. Working a wedding anniversary dinner party on the Upper East Side, he'd become disillusioned. Not only because his beloved Jackie Robinson had been traded to the despicable N.Y. Giants, but because he'd been cutting the bottles with Tennessee jug wine. The "connoisseurs" throughout the festivities had continued blathering about bouquet and body and bullshit.

After Eugenio, having been partaking of the jug himself, made an ill-advised remark to the wine pundits—"You couldn't differentiate Sangiovese from a cat's butthole."—the situation escalated to a taste off.

Enraged, not with Eugenio's use of jug wine or frozen pizza for appetizers, but his audacity to challenge such a scion of society as himself, the host, Edward Tottenham, wagered Eugenio his new convertible Corvette.

A nameless tax accountant designed a rudimentary scoring system on the spot, and, like today's scoring, it was based on the "facts" of each wine. Initially, there were only three, vintage, varietal, and country of origin. Alcohol content and region were added after the infamous, 1981, Murder in Manila four-way semi-final fiasco.

Neighbors attending the party, their excitement reaching a crescendo, fetched bottles, and three were randomly selected by a bleary-eyed, six-year-old named Norman Neusbaum who'd been woken expressly for the task. Hence the rhetorical question among Crushers, "Hey, did Norman select that?"

Ensuring neutrality, Norman was instructed, with promises of German chocolate cake, to wrap the bottles utilizing discarded pizza boxes and duct tape, a technique used to this day.

The wrinkled silver tape dully reflected the candlelight, and I selected a double cheese and meat combo.

Turning, I walked directly into the stares of the five curmudgeons. A few bills were exchanged between them as I sniffed at my glass and its promise of something exceptional.

"Finally," said a chubby Bob Barker looking man with a thick, well-groomed mustache, "do you keep all your choir boys waiting so long?"

"Only when they're as ugly as you."

He chuckled and extended a hand. "Name's Ogden. And before you ask—" The others chimed in, "I'm not from Utah or a goddamned Mormon."

"Okay," I said, shaking his hand, "but do you write poetry?" He, like the others, stared blankly. This time they weren't acting. "Ogden Nash?"

"Johnny Cash's evil cousin?"

"American poet." They shook their heads, and I recited "A Flea And A Fly In A Flue."

"Not poetry."

"That's bullshit."

"Sounds like e. e. cummings."

"That's what she said. He... he... he's cummings."

They laughed, and I, amongst heathens, shook my head, disappointed and disillusioned.

Sheppard, patting a burgundy-hued cushion next to him, introduced the other three men, "Wheeler, Fulton, and Bennett." Each was a wrinkled variant of the other. "And you know this codger—"

Ogden reinforced he wasn't the poet, "So, what'd you bring, Pumpkin Butt?"

I asked Sheppard, "I thought you said this was a casual, little friendly?"

He shrugged, "Who says it isn't?"

Pumpkin Butt, in the Crushed world, was akin to any of the derogatory slurs used upon populaces considered "lesser." None know why, but great speculation abounds. Even Lincoln James, the grand taster and two-time world champion, had written in the 1990s a treatise, *Don't Call Me PB*, on why. Though short, the brevity and insight made it all the more compelling. I'd had a single criticism of the work—he'd not discovered a definitive answer. Though he favored the implications of the 17th century, Salem, Massachusetts, joke, "How many black cats can fit in a pumpkin? Twenty. But just their butts."

"Come on, Pumpkin Butt," Ogden pressed, "what'd you bring?"

With a firm Durden, I sniffed and countered, "Something much nicer than this 2006 Tuscan swill." I gulped the entire glass and, past the exquisite and supple layers of the nuanced dark fruit and barbecued meats, declared, "I brought a 2022 New Zealand Pinot Blanc, you mustard face."

Ogden, and his gold accessories, launched themselves across the table at me.

The others saved their glasses, while Ogden, crazed, tumbled from the table, scrambled to his feet, and threw punches.

They were ineffectual blows and reminiscent of a Taiwanese masseuse, Mai-Li, whom I'd, years ago, received a hand job from.

"Easy there, Midas, I think you've lost your touch."

He swore, "Touch this, PB," and slammed his knee into my groin.

With my balls clogging my throat, I collapsed to my knees, leaned to be sick, but the old asshole again brought his knee up, smashed my nose.

Groaning, spewing blood, I collapsed to my side and vomited the three slices of burnt pizza I'd shoveled in before tiptoeing over.

The vomit merged with the growing puddle of blood. It was a nihilist's wet dream.

Ogden, unrelenting, stepped around the filth and, to the merriment of the others, kicked and kicked.

His feet, thanks to the brown leather, boat shoes, were as light as his fists, and once my vomiting and bleeding transitioned to laughter, they pulled him away.

Over the cleaning, the bandaging, and a few more glasses, we apologized and he thanked me, "Damn, Belltower, I haven't felt that energized in years. Maybe you need a bodyguard?"

"Thank you, but I have one. And she's much prettier than you."

Sheppard, hand over the heart, the other in the air, admitted, "That I can attest to."

"Hell," Wheeler observed, "the way I hear it, one or two won't be enough."

"Yeah," Fulton added, "pretty boy here has a few admirers wanting his head for a trophy."

The next fifteen minutes were spent on them explaining what they'd do if they were as young as I.

Ogden, maybe noticing my befuddled gaze, repeated, "So, what did you bring?"

Keeping the paper towel-wrapped ice cube to my lip, I limped over, poured a glass from the thin-crust pepperoni, and presented it. "You tell me, Crusher."

Holding it up, blood splattered on his wrinkled, age-splotched forearm, he said, "First, I'm sure this isn't a New Zealand Pinot Blanc. Of any vintage." After a brief chuckle, he went through the tried and true, the sniff, sip, and slurp.

He slumped, did what I'd just done, cried from pain.

Past unrelenting tears, he explained to our confusion, "It was 1975. I'd met my wife. That fall. After Saigon. September. At the jazz festival. Monterey. Dizzy Gillespie."

Ogden fell silent, dropped his head, stared into his glass.

Wheeler leaned over, "Margaret passed. Three months ago. Cancer."

I retrieved the thin-crust pepperoni and set it before him. "I'm sorry."

"Well," he smiled, "you sure look it." After the laughter, he lifted the box and instructed, "Finish what you got, Crushers."

We did and he poured the bottle out into our empty glasses.

We settled in and after a few long moments of silence, of appreciating time, and the frail and frivolous nature of existence, we raised our glasses and drank.

I destroyed the silence with, "So, who knew my father? And what can you tell me about him?"

"Besides him being an asshole?" Sheppard replied, jokingly, I assumed.

Over their laughter, I quipped, "Yeah, besides that."

"You're serious?"

"Yeah."

"Oh."

"Well, nothing."

"He was an asshole."

"A rather big one."

"Okay," I sighed over their renewed laughter, "how about something about how he died?"

They grew silent, guarded.

I'd asked the right question, but did I want the answer, the insight?

Sheppard, without a word, stood and walked away. Rather than fetch another bottle, or pour more for himself, he exited through the cave's lone door.

The other codgers stared at their glasses, hungry dogs at empty bowls.

Fulton, like Sheppard, without a word, stood and placed a few more logs on the fire. With a nod to Wheeler, he set off in one direction putting out candles. Wheeler, in the opposite, did the same.

Fulton chose a quick lick of thumb and forefinger, a firm, quick press of the wick, while Wheeler, with an aperitif glass, placed it over the flame and waited for it to die.

Each technique, gruesome in its own way, foreshadowed my fate. I considered escape routes, but there was only one—through them.

I stood, but the door creaked open and Sheppard, carrying a golden tray with a glass of light ruby-colored wine on it, returned.

Fulton and Wheeler took their seats as Sheppard placed the tray on the table and, keeping silent, sat.

The glass, obviously, particularly with the codgers staring so, was for me.

Taking the glass, I sniffed.

The tart, green strawberry and rhubarb bouquet punched my nose and knocked me into the past.

Mother, while cleaning the bottle's murder scene, continued cursing, "Curse thee! Curse thee!" Once finished, she stalked out of the apartment and down the hall, "Curse thee! Curse thee!"

I'd no idea where she was headed; I rarely did, but a rose-hued ring stubbornly remained, clung to the rim of the drain.

Curling forefinger around and into it, I dipped and wetted the digit, garnering as much of the liquid as possible.

After a quick sniff, tapping, tickling the tip of the digit to my tongue, I stuck the entire length in.

Greedily, I sucked it.

It was tainted with fluoridated tap water, a hint of dinner's spaghetti sauce, and, under the ripe rust of the drain, was the wine.

Mother, having cursed herself into silence, marched back in and demanded, "What are you doing?"

Around the green berries and Spanish plum, I mumbled, "Practicing," and poked my cheek and feigned giving a blowjob.

"Well, okay. But," she advised, demonstrating, "don't forget your other hand. It can always do some poking and prodding. Give a tug or two."

To the codgers' shock and delight, I dropped a forefinger up to the hilt into the glass.

Closing my eyes, I shoved the dripping digit in and, like so long ago, I sucked it.

"Damn," Fulton joked, "it's like he's done it before."

"Well," Sheppard replied past a laugh, "you'd be the one to know."

It was, for there were few as bad, MR2000. It had the identical tart, green fruits, as well as the rusted drain earthiness.

Reeling from the realization of finding such an elusive white whale, I sat up, adjusted myself, and dug my cheeks firmly into the cushion.

They continued their sophomoric banter about blowjobs, while I, a hardened Crusher and intermittent optimist, extracted the Laguiole wine key from a pocket.

Playing it casual and acquiescing to tradition, I took the glass in one hand and unfurled the Laguiole with the other. The foil knife slipped along my thumb as the screw extended and poked my hip.

I tossed the glass's entirety in and swallowed. Returning the glass to the tray, I demanded, "Where in high Hades did you get something so infernal and foul?"

Guilt, deeper than time, was etched on their faces, and they glanced at one another. Thus distracted, I threw an arm around Ogden's thin shoulders, pressed the wine key to the old bastard's throat, and demanded, "Seriously, where'd you get that vile vinegar? Or do you want me to open this asshole's throat?"

My Durden, deadly and dastardly like never before, glared. Already covered in blood, what would a little more matter?

Ogden squirmed.

Pressing the key deeper, though yet to draw blood, I advised, "Don't."

The others scooted away.

Realizing they'd retreated without their glasses, we reached a tentative detente, and I asked, "Now, who would make such shit? Who?"

Hands over hearts and in the air, they swore, "Your father."

Chapter Nineteen
ANGRY, ANGRY BEES

The morning light, a rusty pitchfork, stabbed my eyes, deep into the gooey gray mush of my woozy-woozy brain. I turned from the vindictive brightness and tumbled off the couch, thudded to the floor.

Cursing cruel fate, I curled fetal and pulled the drapes tighter around me.

A vague, wine-themed nightmare had been replaced with specific recollections of my father from elderly, drunk bastards.

"He was a badger's butthole that had once berated a waiter for bringing him half-and-half and not heavy cream."

"Who puts heavy cream in coffee?"

"Apparently badger's buttholes."

"And what's the difference between half-and-half and heavy cream? Aren't they the same thing?"

After Bennett explained the nuanced differences, Wheeler reflected, "He was a racist asshole."

I turned to Sheppard, who, with a heavy nod, added, "Afraid so."

They stared into their glasses, twidled with the stems.

Surely Mother's vitriolic accusations couldn't be accurate. I suggested, "I'd heard he was an extensive reader. Loved literature."

"Well, if he did read a book, which I doubt, it would've been *Mein Kampf.*"

"Or *How to Build a Pipe Bomb.*"

"*A Thousand and One Ways to Kill Your Neighbor and Not Get Caught.*"

They laughed.

I brooded, drank, and sank. All the dreams and the hero fables I'd constructed of my father were lies and should be erased and forgotten for eternity.

By the end, with dawn cracked the shell of the horizon, the pizza boxes were empty, and we'd deteriorated to the usual Crushed drinking game, "I Bet You Can't."

Fulton, in a corner, puked into a potted mandarin orange tree. His fist choked the trunk and shivered leaves from the poor thing, as Bennett placed another glass in front of me. "I bet you can't."

He tottered off, and I stared at the shot's dark, murky liquid.

Sheppard explained the fault with MR2000. "Someone spiked the barrels with turpentine."

I smiled.

"No. Not me. Nor any of these assholes."

"Okay. So, do you know who did?"

He shook his head. "No. Not that we put much effort into looking."

Before Sheppard expounded, Wheeler, with a devil's grin, placed a shot in front of him. "I bet you can't."

Melding with the cold shag, I recalled (assuming the day was the day I thought it to be) that day was my appointment with Dr. Montgomery. Maybe, besides the antidepressants, he had something for a hangover?

Lamenting the loss of the Enrights' Bloody Mary station, I heard voices at the front door. Though muffled, I discerned it was Spanish.

Standing, I wobbled to the door.

Hearing "*pistola*" and "*cuchillo de desollar*," I staggered *rapido* for my phone.

My racist father had pissed off the local cartel, and they were seeking revenge.

Alicia answered, "What did I say about calling me to save your life?"

The answer, as I'd been nearly sober, was remembered, "Not to?"

"Exactly."

I stared at the phone—Call Terminated.

I called back.

"What?"

"How do you know I'm calling to ask you to save me?"

"What other reason could there be?"

"Maybe about a date?"

She scoffed, "Are you?" I hesitated. "And at this hour?"

"Well, it's not that early." Again, the phone declared Call Terminated.

The doorbell died attempting to ring and, subsequently, the front door shuttered with knocking.

"Please stop calling or—"

"Just listen," I hissed, holding the phone to the door.

My *Oleander Princess* gleaned Spanish sucked *huevos*, but I knew these *vaqueros* weren't discussing "*más cervezas*" or "*donde están los baños*." It helped, for whatever reason, they'd switched to English and I caught unnerving snippets.

"Use a sniper rifle" and "No. Toss a few coins to the sheriff."

Peeking through one of the side windows framing the front door, I glimpsed two angular silhouettes, bulges dangling at their hips.

The one on the right mimed pulling a six-shooter from his hip and rapid firing, and instructed, "Just go into the cantina and drop him."

"Why," the other asked, "do you always shoot first?"

I backed away, "See, I told you. I... Goddamn it." I called her back, again.

"If this is another *butoh* performance," she threatened, "I'm going to beat you like those drums."

"No. No. I swear. I swear."

The pair moved off around the house.

I paralleled, down the hall, through the kitchen as they lurked for the back door.

It was odd, but each had the same gate, the same physique, the same... They turned. I gasped. A beam of sunlight flashed across their faces.

I pressed my back against the door.

"They're identical. Identical."

"Like twins?"

"Or clones."

"What?"

"You do the killing while your clone's out creating an alibi."

The brief silence implied she'd thought about it, though declared, "Bullshit."

"I swear, Alicia. I swear on all I hold sacred and holy."

"Didn't you mention you were an atheist?"

"How's that pertinent?" Maybe the adrenaline, the fear, the residual wine, the loss of Katrina and the little world I thought I understood in Paris, helped with sounding sad and pathetic, "Please. Just get here."

The clones neared. One, with a hollow knock on the barbecue barrel, said something. The other laughed.

Alicia sighed, "Ten to fifteen," and, again, hung up.

"No hurry," I admitted, "I'll be dead in five."

Egan and Julio—the twin Carapaz brothers—were from Ecuador. To tell them apart, their father, Ignacio, had given them the same scar, a razor cut, but on different eyebrows.

My father, so they claimed, had hired them for the past six seasons from spring through the harvest. He'd also provided room and board, though at a price which he'd deduct from their pay.

I'd not asked their fee, or what he'd charged, or what they "banked" at the end of the season. I feared the answers, as the situation rang of exploitation.

They'd apologized for missing the memorial and were explaining the nuances of *Red Dead Redemption Online.*

I had to agree, there were times I would have liked to "double barrel a bastard," but guns were not so readily available in the more civilized parts of the world, i.e. everywhere outside the U.S.

We were around the corner from the front door, preparing to inspect the vines, when the squeal of tires and the angry crunch of gravel stilled our feet.

"That'll be her," I said, stepping back and to the side, putting them between me and her wrath.

The sedan skidded to a stop, a small, gray cloud of dust rising into the air.

Alicia leaped from the sedan.

I waved, though she was glancing at the brothers' old El Camino and heading for the front door with speed and conviction.

She hurdled an outcropping of daffodils and, in elegant strides, sprinted up the walkway.

"*Dios mío*," Julio observed, "that *mamacita's* got moves."

"And," Egan smarmed, "I know what I'd like her to move onto."

"Mi *amigos*," I said as she, nearing the front door, pulled the 9mm, "*por favor*, keep it clean. That's my wife."

"Bullshit," the two swore, as Alicia spun and fired twice.

The first bullet exploded through a grayish-white mass protruding from under the corner of the balcony. The second burped a dark puff of Irish wool from an expanse of the cardigan at my right shoulder.

Having, over the last few days, become quite familiar with pain, I knew I'd not been hit. However, thanks to my improv training, I collapsed to the grass in a dying, mortal moan.

Alicia shrieked.

I regretted my choice, but having made it I played it to the end.

Egan and Julio, hands held high, backed away.

Alicia, holstering her weapon, sprinted to my supine body.

Leaping to my feet, I laughed and waggled a forefinger through the bullet hole, "Just a sweater wound."

The brothers, as I waggled my finger more, made exaggerated motions of wiping their brows.

My finger stilled as Alicia stared. Where was the cursing, the well-deserved condemnation? To compound my confusion, she threw her arms around me and hugged me.

The brothers gave thumbs ups and, miming us, hugged one another.

An angry, rusty blender buzzed the air and distracted us from our embrace.

The grayish-white mass, masked by a thick swarm, broke free and smashed to the porch in a loud *thunk*. A mushroom cloud of bees exploded from the crumpled mass.

"Run!" Egan screamed as the infuriated horde descended upon us.

After our first frantic collisions, slapping at the bees, ourselves, we decided on the front door, the safety of the house.

Slamming the door shut and stumbling into the living room, we fought off the last few dozen with cushions, magazines, VHS tapes, a length of kindling, and a fire poker.

"Damn," I rasped, as we caught our breaths, "those little shits are angry."

"Reminds me of my nephews," Alicia admitted, inspecting her arm and the two swelling stings.

I looked at her and smiled. It was the first bit of personal information I'd gotten since she'd confessed to never having gone wine tasting.

"So, you've nephews?"

"I do," she admitted, reluctantly.

"How—" Two succinct *thuds*, Egan and Julio collapsing to the floor, interrupted.

Alicia bolted to their sides and explained, "Anaphylactic shock. Do you have—"

Julio tugged at her sleeve. She leaned and he wheezed something in her ear.

"EpiPens. In their car," Alicia insisted as a set of keys smacked my chest and clattered to the carpet. "In the glove box." I looked down at the keys and back to her. "Go get them! Now!"

Snatching the keys, I sprinted out the door into the cloud of enraged bees. Maniacally, head bowed, running, I blindly swatted at the bee-infested air.

Angling across the yard, the overgrown grass dappled with alluring molehills, I was reminded... Motherfucker. The back of my neck ignited with a sting. Motherfucker. And another. Motherfucker.

I swatted frantically about.

They targeted my back and butt.

Motherfucker. Motherfucker. Motherfucker.

Hands waving, head bowed, the bright stings distracting me, I plowed into the side of the El Camino. My momentum carried me into the bed, where, with my legs shooting up into the air, my face slammed into a bag of fertilizer.

Spitting the tart, sour fertilizer from my lips and rubbing an eye, which only made the stinging worse, I scrambled to the driver's side door.

Eventually—motherfucker—I jammed the key in the lock. I turned it and tugged the handle. It had been open, and I'd locked it! Motherfucker. Motherfucker. I turned the key again, opened the door, and dove in, slamming the door shut behind me.

A handful of the dirty bastards followed me. The relative silence of the car's lemon-scented interior was comforting, but not enough to forget the brothers' need or to not get stung again. Motherfucker.

Keeping one hand waving around, I yanked the glove box open. Besides a dog-eared Spanish copy of Vonnegut's *Cat's Cradle (Cuna de Gato)*, two crumpled Carl's Jr. burger wrappers, and a bottle of hand sanitizer, there was a cardboard box.

Pulling the box out, I tore it open. It was filled with Epipens.

Exiting through the passenger side, cradling the box, I ran for the house, colliding with a few stingers. Motherfucker. Motherfucker.

Eyes streaming with tears, I floundered at the front door, where the milling mass of the swarm remained. A few more—motherfucker motherfucker—used me for target practice; I stumbled in, slammed the door shut.

Staggering into the living room, I waved the box toward a blurry object between two other blurry objects, "Here."

The first object snatched the box, dumped the contents, and tore at the packaging housing an EpiPen.

I smacked one and another—motherfucker motherfucker.

Across the back of my hand, a miniature, furry astronaut on a soft and fragile planet lumbered. I yanked it off. It left something behind, embedded in the soil of my skin. "Alicia? Uh, Alicia?"

"What?" she asked, driving a pen into Egan's, no, maybe Julio's. No... "What?"

"Can I have one?" I asked, as she did the same for the other brother.

"What?" she repeated, as I toppled onto the couch, bounced off and onto the sweet, sweet shag.

Two hours later, Alicia, brooding, was driving me to Dr. Montgomery's office in downtown McMinnville, a mere ten minutes from the vineyard.

I was, as suggested by Dominic, the EMT, rehydrating. Because of the minimart's sale, I was doing so with a 64-ounce Arctic blue sports drink.

Alicia didn't want to talk about the odd coincidence of the same EMTs, Alejandro and Dominic, responding to the call, nor how I got the black eye and swollen lip from "my racist friends," nor Egan and Julio's true appreciation for her heroics, nor about my anonymous friend, Heavy Breather.

Gripping the steering wheel like a lifeline, she remained steadfast, focused on one subject, "You don't understand. I have to file a report. I could've killed you. I almost did."

"Yes. But you didn't."

She was shaken. Understandably, but regardless of how I attempted to spin it, she didn't want to hear it.

"And you didn't even hit me. Sure, the sweater has seen better days, as has that beehive, but... But you saved them."

She snorted at my interpretation. "Had I not pulled my weapon and fired—"

"Yes, but I called you, right? So, theoretically—"

"Why," she asked, glaring, "is everything a joke to you?"

I turned, stared down the road, and looked for the monster she stared into.

Untangling from the knot of middle school classmates disgorged from the bus, I, like everyone, heard the blaring television. Only in the stairwell, a floor below, had I suspected it came from our apartment.

On our dirty tan, coconut fiber, stenciled, "So Freud Up With It" and a smoking cigar welcome mat, sat my Spider-Man overnight bag with a note, "Grandma Bubba's 2? 3? nights. Heart M." A twenty-dollar bill was stapled to a shoulder strap.

Over a bowl of mint chocolate chip, after *Some Like It Hot*, I asked Josiah, "So, what is it this time?"

"What? Oh, your grandfather died." Past a mouthful, he asked, "How about some Marx Brothers?"

Taking another bite, newly tainted with sorrow, I said, "Abbot and Costello, please."

He smiled and nodded. "We love those guys. *Mummy* or *Frankenstein*?"

Perhaps that's why Mother was so relentless toward my father for leaving? Father had chosen to.

Something smacked gooey in the corner of the windshield, an iridescent wing fluttering in the aftermath.

I considered explaining I didn't believe the incident was a joke, but that life in itself was absurd, which, by default, made everything funny, in a sick sort of way. I knew the nuances of the observation were above my rhetorical skills, so the last five minutes curling around McMinnville's Mayberry streets were spent in silence.

"Don't worry," I said, exiting and sounding snottier than intended, "I'll get my own ride back."

"I know you will."

I closed the door, and she sped away.

Chapter Twenty
CRAZY IS AS CRAZY DOES

Dr. Montgomery's office was on the third floor of The McCallister, a six-floor, sandy-hued brick building sitting on the corner of SE Third and W. Main.

Under a black awning supported by gold poles, I found the smoked glass entry door. From the list of instructions, I punched in the security code.

The door, with a soft *click*, sighed open.

The doctor's waiting room had all the requisite trappings to define it as such. There were two pairs of adequately comfortable chairs, a coffee table strewn with magazines, all pop culture, *Sunset*, *People*, *O*, *Cosmopolitan*, *Wine Enthusiast*, and nothing relating to psychology or news. On the walls, rather than inspirational clinging kittens or exuberant mountain climbers, there were comforting black-and-white photos of vineyards and vines. And a water cooler with a gray waste basket sat in a corner.

Instruction Number 4—Make yourself comfortable—I felt impossible and may've been meant as irony. Though if it helped get me those pills, I'd play along. If I wasn't depressed about Katrina and my father, or the bees, or the ass-whooping Ogden had given, I was about Alicia's guilt.

Number 5, less ironic than 4, was straightforward. "Wait for the chime..." (Pavlov, that asshole, again.) "...the office door will open and you may enter."

Number 6, though mundane, was the most ironic and improbable—"Have a Great Session!"

I, as anyone would, had an issue with the term "great." Most appalling was the gratuitous and presumptive use of the exclamation point. Who did he think he was to wield an exclamation point so arbitrarily?

Had the note been handwritten rather than printed I might know.

Regardless, of "great" and the exclamation, I harkened back to the subtext of 4 and 5, "make yourself comfortable" and "wait for the chime."

One could not wait and remain comfortable. They were polar opposites; any idiot such as I knew that.

Scooping up the latest issue of *Oregon Wine Press*, I turned and hesitated. Which chair was "appropriate" to wait and be comfortable in?

Walking into our apartment, softly singing the lyrics to The Fairest of All, I found a red velvet rope stretched across the entry hall.

On the tall, gold, reception table under the gold-framed mirror were a pile of 3x5 index cards. Taped to the mirror was another index card on which in black marker was an arrow pointing to the pile and a command, "Take One."

Shaking my head, I swore to the floor, "Not again."

Mother, working on her thesis, *The Dilemma of an Only Child*, had, every week or so, devised another ill-conceived experiment for me to partake in.

In the Paramour Vegetable Paradox, I was tasked to organize an array of vegetables on "allure, sensuality and attractiveness." In the Stained Sock Supposition, I needed to separate a mound of socks, differentiating between the ones I'd ejaculated in and their imposters.

"Hey, Kid Indecision," Mother called from the kitchen, "do as instructed—select a card."

I sighed and did as instructed.

The card read: *You are Sebastian Santiago, a 47-year-old bus driver, originally from Costa Rica, and living in Boca Raton, Florida. A year ago, your wife's secret, female lover killed your wife and daughter and herself. Choose a meal, a beverage, and a place to sit. And, yes, there is only one correct answer. Suck it up. Deal with it.*

Gazing into the mirror, I queried, "Who is the fairest in the land?" I, angry and annoyed, declared, "You are. You are."

Setting my Iron Man book bag down, I pulled the rope aside and, ignoring my trepidation, stepped into the living room.

Everything—chairs, tables, couch—had been pushed to the corners, against the walls. On the dining table were strewn more index cards, each with a description of a meal. Porterhouse steak, medium, with garlic mashed potatoes, and broccolini. Fried chicken, creamed corn and bacon-brazed Brussels sprouts.

The coffee table was drinks. Manhattan on the rocks. Cuba libre. A large milk. Diet soda. Hot chocolate.

Taped to the chairs and the couch's cushions were descriptions of the "chairs." Louis XVI Regal Salon. Wicker rocking. Electric.

Overwhelmed by the multitude of variants and variations, I discovered myself in the middle of the room, Kid Indecisive, again.

Mother's voice, a syrupy ghost, oozed from the darkened kitchen, "Go on. Choose. Choose."

A chime sounded.

Closing the magazine, I felt the chair in the corner, under the photo of the grape-filled harvest crates, a setting sun in the background, was likely the correct option.

There was a second chime, and smiling I gave a soft *woof*.

Returning the magazine to the table, I stepped to the door, which, as promised, had sighed open, slightly.

The door was pulled fully open by the good doctor.

I extended my hand to shake his, but he was a she. And, even with two black eyes and a bandaged broken nose, I recognized her.

Past my newly acquired injuries, she too recognized me.

Ugly mirror to the other, we stared in stunned incomprehension.

I glanced at the business card stapled to the instruction's upper left corner. "Dr. M? Megan?"

My eyes exploded in agony.

Screaming and flailing, I backpedaled into the waiting room as another blast of mace fisted my face.

The door, and two locks, slammed shut. Pictures rattled against the wall. One fell, broke across the floor.

Screaming and screaming, I flailed at the flaming napalm scorching my eyes. As I blindly quested for the water cooler's salvation the magazine-laden coffee table chewed into the back of my knees.

I toppled backward, screaming more as my hip and shoulder broke my fall, fed pain to the inferno.

The table collapsed. I tumbled off and collided with the water cooler. It fell to the floor and rolled away as another picture shattered on the floor.

Crawling, I curbed my screaming and concentrated on the *glug, glug, glugging* of my dying savior.

Shredding magazines, a palm in the glass, I scrambled to the large plastic bottle and raised it overhead to douse the inferno's flames. It slipped from my grip, plowed into my groin, and emptied its last vestiges there.

Defeated, I curled fetal and, to hide the tears as I cried, I splashed water into my eyes.

Handcuffed to a soggy chair (a random one haphazardly placed in the middle of the wreckage), head held back, I balanced the ice pack across my puffy, swollen eyes.

Someone crunched across glass and called, "Hey, Doc Montgomery?"

"Yes, Anthony?" the mace-wielding, fear-intoxicated doctor replied from the lair of her office.

"What would you like me to do with him?"

I peeked from under the bleached blue ice pack. It sounded as if, besides letting me go, there were other more nefarious options. One or two, as it was Officer Jenkins, the blond, blue-eyed, square-jawed linebacker from Sheppard's, likely entailed handing me a shovel and commanding I dig.

"You can uncuff me for starters," I observed, shaking my wrist, the cuffs clacking like dull bones.

"What? Oh. Yes, Anthony," the doctor agreed, "he can stay."

Jenkins turned and called over his shoulder, "You sure?" She didn't reply. He grinned. "Doc?"

"Yes. That's fine. Uncuff him."

I smirked.

He lowered himself until his Axe body spray enveloped me.

I abandoned the smirk.

He uncuffed me and Boonened, "You hurt her and I'll hunt you down." Exiting he added, though not to me, "You take care and get better."

"Yes. Thanks, Anthony," the doctor called out.

Steph, the red-headed EMT with Clark Kent glasses, tore a copy of the patient care report from her silver metal clipboard and handed it to me.

"Ah, excellent," I said, folding and tucking it into a sodden pocket, "another for my collection."

She and her companion, Travis, packed their equipment up and followed Jenkins.

Doctor Montgomery, unenthused, invited, "Mr. Belltower, if you'd join me?"

"You're coming apart too?"

"Please, Mr. Belltower," she said, less unenthused than before, "whenever you're ready, we can start."

Standing, water ran down my legs and overflowed from my full shoes, soaking the carpet more. I shook a leg, then the other, and squished into her office.

As much as I may've wanted to leak across the Turkish throw rug and soak an armchair or the couch, I stood and dripped in the doorway.

A folder rested on her small, utilitarian desk hunched in a corner, next to a tall window covered with a thin, muslin drape.

"I will admit," Dr. M., Megan, Montgomery said, tapping the folder, "I was intrigued by your file." She pulled a few sheets out and added, "Particularly looking at these."

She held up a heavily redacted page, and another, and another.

The first had everything redacted except for the phrases "claimed mini-Nazis," "The mini-Nazi gave chase," and "a smoldering mini-Nazi nestled in the mail carrier's crotch."

I wanted to mention creative license for dramatic effect, but she was already presenting the second page. It had a single phrase "his fiancée Katarina von Klit," while the third and final page, "Eiffel penis, Arc de Triomphe vagina, and Louvre glass pyramid anus."

She lowered the pages, and our bloodshot eyes met. We smiled, awkward, insincere.

"Unfortunately, as intrigued as I am," she said, returning the pages to the folder, "I believe, given our history, there's a conflict of interest—"

"You can say that again."

She didn't, but finished her sentence, "And you'd be better served seeing someone else."

"Is there someone else?" Rubbing the back of my neck, I wondered why Steph hadn't offered me painkillers. Alejandro and Dominic would've.

The doctor shrugged. "Not necessarily here in McMinnville. No."

"Doctor, regardless our," I air quoted, "'conflict of interest.' I agree with you." Her brow wrinkled a question. "And, honestly, I'm currently not concerned with bettering my mental health index."

"Okay. And what are you concerned with?"

"Getting through this trying and difficult time." She looked dubious. "Yes, that sounded cliché. But it's the truth." Regardless of how ridiculous that sounded, I pushed on. "The prescription for the antidepressants is likely more a liability issue for the government rather than concern for me."

She flicked the folder open, scanned a page, and another. "I don't see anything here about you taking antidepressants."

"That's because I'm not."

"But you believe you should be?"

I took a slow, deep breath as she reached into her pocket.

We'd just finished dinner and Mother, pouring us another glass of Côtes du Rhône, had, again, thrust a stack of cards at me and demanded her standard, "Pick one."

"Mother, I've things I need to do."

"Oh, and I don't? Pick one."

I, a good, trained dog, did.

"Now," she said, sipping, "go rehearse. And on your return, be convincing. I'm tired of you half-assing."

Senior year and I should've been planning for college, for auditions to acting schools, for the future. But Mother had somehow got her license, and I was playing another round of "Be My Client."

I sulked into my room, flopped onto the bed, gave a glance to the Blue Aegir Cruise Lines' employment brochure I'd acquired at career day that morning, and read Tristan O'Malley's personality profile: *Tristan is a left-handed narcoleptic and kleptomaniac suffering from arachnophobia complicated by an addiction to painkillers, antidepressants, and 30 Rock with a deep seeded lust for baseball players, particularly second basemen and catchers.*

"And you've taken them before?" the doctor asked, calling me back from the edge of Tristan.

I nodded and, recalling how cathartic the late-night howling session had been, added, "I think they'd be beneficial. Just in case." She made a note on a small pad. I continued, "And I'm not bringing charges against the guy that hit me." I smiled and added, "Or you."

"You mean, Mr. Andretti?"

"Right. Mister—" Something clicked, a shard of skull or a memory? And McMinnville wasn't so far from Aloha. "Does he, Mr. Andretti, have a sister? Trisha?"

An answer flashed in the doctor's eyes, though she redirected, "Let's try and stay on topic. Okay?"

"And I'm the topic?"

"You know you are."

"I do. Yes. So what would you like to know?"

"Well," she said like the clever witch I was discovering she was, "I thought I might let you decide that."

"Now?"

"I've canceled all my afternoon appointments. So, yes, now."

I could see how she'd make an excellent therapist, straightforward, kind, and concerned, though firm. A bit, I had to admit, like Mai-Li.

And not since the *Oleander Princess* with Dr. Portis had I genuinely confided in someone, which likely explained the Titanic and Hindenburg success of my relationships. My disclosures to Dr. Portis, however, were fraught with inaccuracies and lies, as I'd been, like now, more interested in acquiring medicated solace than doing the work.

"Where would you like me to sit?" I asked as the water stain (Rodney Dangerfield on a three-legged camel) spread out around me.

"I've plenty of towels. So, please..." With a nod she indicated Mr. Dangerfield and his camel. "And don't worry about that. Wherever you'd like." Ah, yes, that old ploy. "Unless, of course, you'd prefer to stand?"

Oh, she was a clever witch.

"Anywhere you'd like," she repeated, pulling out a small notepad and pen, and spinning around in her black, ergonomic chair.

Sitting on the other window's sill, forcing her to swivel more (point for me), I took a long, shallow breath and got into character.

The window, being at the other end of the room, forced me to relate my great and sorrowful tale in a tone much louder than I liked.

The added tragic events of Paris and Dundee, regardless of how poorly played I may've conveyed, had enhanced the believability of my need.

Throughout, the good doctor had jotted notes down, regularly and consistently. After each flurry of her pen, her eyes flared. It was moderately disconcerting, though oddly reassuring, and fundamentally arousing.

"If I my ask, how did your father pass?"

Somehow, after that angst-driven confession, I'd thought she would've wanted to hear about my enemies. Isn't that why I was playing a hint, subtle though diagnosable, of the paranoid schizophrenic?

I asked, "You don't want to hear about my enemies?"

"Perhaps later." She jotted something down, "You seem disappointed?

"No."

"I'm sure your enemies are," she dug through the papers, "very interesting and—"

"Real and psychotic?"

Her hand slipped back into her pocket.

I hesitated but would not be deterred and expounded on the factions organizing themselves against me.

Vlad had the most rabid of fans. They were concentrated in Florida, Texas, and the Carolinas, north and south. The "clubs," Vlad's Varmints, Vlad's Vicious Vixens, etc., were howling for my fatal mauling. Those in mourning, as a sign of devotion, smeared their upper lips with peanut butter.

The mini-Nazis, according to DrJuggles who'd commented on an article in *Le Monde*, were members of a performance coalition. DrJuggles also claimed their performance comrades had hired "a shady someone" from the shadowy organization known as ICAS, the International Circus Assassination Squad, which "metered out swift justice to the deserving."

Kelsey's family, clan Conrad of Billings, Montana, ran a 40,000-acre private hunting reserve, The Bigger Horn Bullet Range. It was touted for its "Wild West Experiences." Hank Conrad, the eldest of the six brothers, had been quoted in the *Billings Gazette*, "I sure do hope to mount his head up on a wall one day."

Kelsey's Madam von Klit also had a hundred thousand "admirers" and stalkers. They, since the site she'd streamed on had removed her video library, were also clamoring for my demise. Ted6969 had put it succinctly, "If we are incapable as a community from removing the negative influences which deteriorate the foundations of that community it is inevitable we will collapse and return to being beasts."

Lastly, I-LOB had updated their "tactical treatment of the anti-bubble bastard Dixon James Belltower." Due to the liability issues, they no longer advocated swift kicks between the legs or any physical contact. However, "any verbal abuse one would wish to foment upon him is appreciated."

Tragically, ironically, and not amusingly, I realized I needed those damn pills.

The doctor, losing a battle with a yawn, asked from behind a hand, "I'm sorry, but can we circle back to your father's passing?"

Thanks to Mother, I understood the doctor's father fixation but wasn't sure it warranted the exclusion of the other issues.

"If we must."

We stared.

"So," she asked, again, "how did he pass?"

It was a simple question. One I'd asked Sheppard and the codgers the other night. Though they'd not answered, I was sure it had a simple answer. Yet I had none.

"I honestly don't know."

The doctor made another note, unlocked her desk drawer, and pulled a prescription pad out. "You don't seem particularly affected. Am I mistaken?"

Her pen, a vengeful angel, hovered over the pad.

I, unexpectedly unconcerned with the consequences, told her the truth. And a little more.

Chapter Twenty-One
FROM THE ASHES, UNICORNS AND RAINBOWS

Late afternoon sunlight seeped through the thin veil of curtains, casting the bedroom in an insipid yellow glow. I was, thanks to a second glass of a Vacqueyras and a Doc Montgomery pill, back amongst the black boxes, searching for a flash drive.

If memory served, I'd stored *The Jerk,* the skeleton of the sequel to *The Yank, on it.*

In my quest, I'd dumped the boxes out into a magnificent pile.

Having found only disappointment and the reality of being relocated, I was eyeballing the two Clive Cusslers, *Plague Ship* and *The Jungle*, on the little bookcase in the corner when the doorbell gargled its death rattle.

Happy for the distraction, I called, "One second, I'll be right down."

Gripping the door's handle, not considering who lurked beyond (blame wine, pills, and Alicia), I opened the door.

The asshole that'd punched me at Sheppard's stood there. Not Ogden, but the other—Troy.

Instead of a sawed-off shotgun, or a Walther PPK with a suppressor, he held grocery bags, one in each hand.

"What," I asked, wishing I had some mace, "are you doing here?"

"Oh, my god," he said, eyes wide with horror and shock, "I'm so sorry. I didn't think I hit you that hard."

"You didn't. You did enough, but—" I shrugged at the absurdity of explaining Ogden's knee, the bees, the doctor's mace.

"Then how?"

"Why are you here?"

"Right. Why am I here?" He took a deep breath and exhaled an explanation. "My grandmother, Carlotta Maria Andretti, always said, 'The only way to ensure someone forgives is to fill their stomach.'"

"She meant food and not lead, right?" He smiled, nodded, and raised the bags. Regardless, I needed vocal confirmation. "Right?"

"Well, depending on the slight—"

"Wait. Wait. Wait. You said Andretti?"

"I did. Yes."

"Like Trisha Andretti?"

"Yeah," he admitted, biting his lip, "you could say that. I'm Troy."

Recalling Dr. M's semi-confession regarding his sibling, I enthused, "So, Troy, why are you standing out there? Get in here and tell me what you've got in those bags."

I stepped aside, and he stepped in, asking, "Kitchen?"

Confused at the plastic containers Troy pulled from the grocery bags and placed on the chopping block island, I asked, "What's all this?"

"Well," he said, glancing around, "I'm making you dinner."

"You know," I noted, examining one of the containers, "there's another option."

"Another option?" He asked, gently taking the container from me, briefly reorganizing them. "Oh, besides lead in the gut?"

"Right," I confirmed, as he returned to the bags and unpacking.

"Like?"

"Like," I said, remembering the classics *Hamlet*, *Arsenic and Old Lace*, and *The Court Jester*, "poison?"

"Nope, no poison," he admitted, a sagging green bag in a hand, "just horse laxative."

Past a laugh, I asked, "And what's in the bag?"

"Wine," he declared, pulling a bottle out, adding, "I assume you've an opener? And a little less paranoia?"

"Yes, to the opener." I pointed at it, an executioner's axe laid before the condemned, the Petrus, the Yquem, on the table where I'd returned it from the other eve.

He hesitated. "I assume you know what these are?"

"I do."

"And what they're likely worth?"

"As glorious as they are," I said, as he worked the bottle's cork, "I know they're not worth the trials I've gone through to acquire them." He gave a questioning glance, and I added, "Maybe after a few glasses."

He nodded, and I found, as the cork *popped*, a handwritten note on a yellow, chicken-shaped sticky note taped to the refrigerator: *Egan and I have gone to brother's home to recover. Back Monday? Tuesday? —Julio.*

In a slightly different scrawl, I assumed Egan's, *Maybe never* ☺, had been added.

Unless they had a private jet and flew to Ecuador, their brother lived close.

"Is it possible," Troy asked, "to get the kitchen to myself?"

"Why?" My paranoia returned and trebled at spotting the bottle he'd brought, a Chianti Classico Reserva. "You don't, perhaps, have any fava beans in there, do you?"

"Fava beans?"

If he did, he wouldn't admit it and they'd be incognito in a plastic container, like everything he'd pulled from the bags.

"Oh," he asked, organizing the containers, "you mean Hannibal Lecter style?"

"'I ate,'" I recited in my best rendition, "'his kidney with a glass of Chianti.'"

"I don't. I gave up cannibalism for Lent." I laughed, and he added, "I just work best alone. Give me thirty minutes or so? Okay?"

"And you'll tell me about your sister?" I asked, hoping she too was in town and could join us for a glass. Or two.

With a hesitant smile, he nodded and, reluctantly, I left him.

Plating a third slice of the deep dish, Chicago-style, Troy topping off my glass with the perfectly paired Chianti, I asked, "And you made this?"

"I did," he admitted with a distinct smile of satisfaction.

While I nibbled at the slice, he sipped and explained owning and operating a chain of pizza restaurants, "Peter's Pan Pizza, from San Francisco to Seattle."

"So, what are you doing here?"

"McMinnville?"

"Yeah. There. Here. Wherever."

"Megan, Doctor Montgomery's my therapist."

Not wanting to get into the sticky thicket of why a therapist went wine tasting with a client, I redirected, "Well, this is delicious. It's too bad you're not... Or I'm not... or—"

Troy gazed into his glass.

I did the same, considered which sounded worse, or better, or... "Too bad you're not a woman/I'm not gay," finishing with the proverbial, "otherwise I'd marry you."

"So," he asked, after a sip, "what were you going to say?"

"Something quite stupid."

"Like?"

"Like marrying you, it's so delicious."

"Funny you should say that." His tone contradicted his statement, particularly with such a haunting and tragic look in his eyes.

"Care to explain?" I asked, unsure what I wanted for an answer.

"No."

"Not even after another glass?"

"The bottle's empty."

I smiled, "Stay right there."

He'd ignored me and, returning with another Chianti Classico Reserva, though a 2015, I found him tucking the leftover slices into a plastic container. Before I could overstep and ask if he could leave a slice or two, he'd popped it in the refrigerator.

After agreeing the 2015 was more nuanced than what he'd brought, I asked, "And what's your sister up to?"

"Trisha?"

The way he said it, it sounded like he may've had others. "Yeah. Does she work with you at Peter's?"

He stifled a laugh and redirected with answering with a question, "What took you to see Dr. Montgomery? I assume it wasn't to get maced?"

"She's my drug dealer." To his confusion, I explained the contorted series of events, like a Rube Goldberg machine, that returned me to Oregon.

"Jesus," he said, shaking his head.

"I'm pretty sure he had nothing to do with it. And if he did, well, all the more reason to hate him." I raised my glass. "My apologies if I offended."

"You don't mean that, do you?"

"Which? The apology or—"

"Doesn't matter."

We found ourselves in a pensive silence, unsure where to go. I wanted, again, to ask about Trisha, but it was fairly apparent, even to me, that he didn't wish to talk about her.

What little regard for etiquette I'd gleaned on the *Oleander Princess*, I'd lost years ago. Pouring us another glass, prepared to get an answer and not another question, my phone buzzed. I, with a reticent smile, answered.

"So did you find it?"

"And hello to you too."

"Dixon, did you—"

"Naomi, I thought I told you I'd look?"

"And have you?"

"Well, yes, actually I have. But—" Hadn't she asked that just the other day, or was that yesterday or this morning? "What day is it?"

"What do you mean what day is it?"

Conveying to Troy five minutes, I headed down the hall to the living room.

"Naomi, I'm sorry, but I'm with someone."

"So soon after Katrina? No, sorry, Kelsey? I'm sorry, but, seriously, Dixon, you're disgusting."

"First, thank you for your honesty. Second, it's just dinner. And it's a guy, so—"

"Finally, Dixon. Good for you. I always knew, but felt—"

"Wait. What do you mean? You thought I was gay?"

"No. No. Bi. Definitely bi."

"Naomi, what do you want? Besides me, *The Jerk*?"

"Anderson at Home Office wants your signature on some documents. And," she sighed, "I'd like you to pretend I matter enough for you to take this seriously."

"Naomi?"

"What?"

"It's going to be okay."

Leaning against the movie cabinet, ignoring the gargoyle on the mantel, I glanced at Troy. The man had something chewing inside him.

"You mean it?" Naomi asked.

"No, but I trust it."

"Fine. I'll take that."

"Good." Getting serious, I said, "And send me whatever Anderson wants signed. I'll sign everything. And I'll find that flash drive. And if I can't—" Fear rose, a needle of panic poked my balloon heart as I recalled the deadline. "Did you say three months?"

"I did." Naomi, concerned again, reiterated, "Dixon, it's going to be okay. Okay?"

"Okay."

"Good. So I'll send everything tomorrow. And we'll talk in a day or two."

"Okay."

"Now," she said, a sarcastic meringue suffusing her voice, "go give that guy of yours a big kiss for me." Laughing, she hung up.

Turning from the dark, dead thing in my palm, I caught Troy staring at me. He smiled, nervous.

Apologizing and pouring more, I declared, "Oh, my God, women, right?"

"Yeah. Women," he admitted, though sounded as if he disagreed.

Another uncomfortable silence surged in.

"Why don't we—" Go someplace more comfortable, was fraught with innuendo. And the living room had the gargoyle. Annoyed, I asked, "So, what's going on?"

"What? What do you mean?"

"Well, it seems you've had something to say," I patted my stomach, "besides your apology, since you've arrived."

"Oh." He looked again into his glass.

Being familiar with the solace and understanding there, I asked, "So, what is it?"

After a quick sip, he tilted the bottle and checked its level.

"Don't worry, there's plenty around. So? You didn't poison me, did you?"

"What? No."

"Not even with horse laxative? Because..." I patted my stomach again. "...I could lose a few pounds."

"No. It's—"

"Is that," I asked the chicken clock on the wall, "the right time?"

"I think so. Why?"

"Because... Wait for it."

"Wait for—" Right on schedule the baleful howl split the cold, clear night and the clock clucked and clucked.

"Cathartic, right?" I asked, as we caught our post-howl breaths, they, fragile ghosts, surged into the cold night air and disappeared.

"Very. Yes."

Heavy breathing and sipping, we considered the stars, and he asked, "So who is it?"

"What do you mean?"

"I mean, who's howling?" He noted my confusion. "You thought it was a wolf?"

"Or something. Yes."

"But—"

"I grew up in the city. The most time I've spent in the countryside was yesterday, walking the perimeter of the property."

"Okay. Sorry."

"So, that was someone howling?" Troy nodded. "Curious."

"Any idea who?"

Rather than get entangled in that cold, noodle salad regarding my stepmother, I lied, "No."

"Okay."

He didn't believe me, and I didn't care. Rather than fall into another uncomfortable silence, I admitted, "I'd hoped it was a werewolf."

"Why? Do you believe in them?"

"No. I think the monotony of existence without the fantastical gives people an excuse to be assholes. Or something like that."

Taking a quick sip, he blurted, "It's about Trisha."

The quarterfinals of the 2012 Milan Maelstrom, found Art and I tied at 14 with two wines left.

"I've something to disclose," Art declared over Blutnacht's *Wut die Wut* and added more swirl to his glass. The deep, rich ruby wine climbed to the lip of the glass, fell back, and climbed.

"That's great," I admitted, matching his swirl, "I've something also."

We stared, swirled our wines, and listened to sweet, angry, German thrash metal.

"Please," I prompted, thrusting nose in and out, in and out, sniffing, "you first."

He took a long, languid mouthful. With overt innuendo, he slurped, and, swallowing, confessed, "I'm gay."

I drank the glass down, filled the scorecard out, waggled my pen at his hesitation, and encouraged, "I'm so happy to hear it. Me too."

To his doubt, I mimed Mother's blow job antics. His smile blossomed like a sunflower under a supernova.

"Hurry up," I encouraged, "we can go to my room, and you can bury yourself in me." Speechless, he stared and I added, "Your choice of hole."

I beat him, 22-18.

The semis found me in hysterics and unable to concentrate. I was soundly beaten by Mochi for the first time, 22-12.

I found Art in the bar, lounging and spinning his room key on a forefinger.

The first rounds were on me, as I consoled him on losing the match and my holes.

"Trisha?" I asked, preparing for my own disappointment

Troy, saddened, acknowledged, "Yes, my sister."

The way my world was being butchered at a back county abattoir, it could only be one thing—"She's dead?"

An amused smile flitted across his lips. "Sort of."

Stepping back, I reconsidered him in the sallow light seeping through the yellowed, faux Victorian lace curtains. He'd of course have her eyes and nose, lips too.

Grinning as if it hurt, he nodded and pleaded, "Please don't hit me. Or hate me. Or... Please?"

"No. No. No," I said, tears filling my eyes as I threw my arms around him, "No. No. No. I'm just glad you're alive."

Chapter Twenty-Two
BETRAYED BY BUDDHA

The early morning sky, like the bruises beneath my eyes, was blue and dark. I was again listening to the urn chat with the house and vineyard spirits, while the garden gnomes inquired about "entering the big house" and "security measures."

I'd forsaken the couch and drapes—entering Heaven was none of my business or care—and had returned to the cold, damp room. As romantic and fantastical as spirits and gnomes were, I knew it the brothers commencing their morning libations.

Nearly back asleep, I realized the brothers were at their brother's.

Bolting upright, I grabbed the closest weapon-like object—an empty bottle of Petrus?

I frowned and the night's end, a dream remembered days later, returned.

Hugging Troy, past my tears of relief, I'd attempted to explain something my heart knew, but my head didn't.

Troy, a stiffness tapping my hip, had broken free and fled into the house.

I'd chased and as he threw the front door open, I'd yelled from the top of the stairs, "Petrus! Petrus! Petrus!"

Before completing his escape, he turned, curious. "What?"

Descending, the plastic runner cackling, I repeated, "Petrus. "Petrus. Petrus."

"You're going to make me ask again, aren't you?"

"No." He flinched as I curled my arm around him, closed the door, and gently nudged him back inside.

"Then?"

"Then you're my excuse for opening the Petrus."

He stared, disbelieving and suspicious.

With a knowing smile, I explained, "You're not the first to get an erection in my presence. Nor are you the only one to get one at an inconvenient and embarrassing time." Walking down the hall into the kitchen, I called over my shoulder, "And be warned, one of my tales deals with a nun and novitiates."

"Young nuns?" he asked, following.

"Indeed, good sir. Indeed."

"They're my favorite kind."

Laughing, gripping the Petrus, I instructed, "Now, follow me."

I slipped into the pantry, down the stairs, and into the cellar.

Behind, tottering at the top of the stairs, he hesitated, "Where are you taking me?"

From "Where Now?," the penultimate song in *Beauty Sleeps!,* I sang, cracked and creaky, "To the top of the mountains, where you can see forever and forever. And forever and beyond."

Unconvinced, he remained perched and tottering.

Extending the Petrus, the bottle sparkling in the light, I declared, "Angels have fallen much farther for much less." The truth of my words lingered and I, with a final, gentle waggling of the bottle, slipped back inside. I'd have it with or without him.

At the cellar's doorway, he, like I'd done, gazed, enchanted and amazed.

"I know," I admitted, "It's heaven in a hole, isn't it?"

Entranced, he passed and I, cackling maniacally, revisited my Hannibal, "This is where I keep my fava beans and trophies."

A self-defense instructor in a midnight infomercial, he spun and, lightning quick, bolted a foot into my groin.

Grunting a moan, I spat an apology and collapsed to my bruised and battered knees. They exploded in something I was becoming comfortable with—pain.

Twisting, keeping the Petrus from crashing to the floor, I sprawled, face first, across it.

Nestling a mixed bag of frozen peas and carrots between my legs, Troy and I were settled into the banquette, uneasily eyeing the nearly empty decanter the Petrus had died in.

After my initial laughter and gratitude for him saving the bottle, I'd regaled him with my recent tales of woe.

He, more tragically, explained his many years of misunderstanding.

"All starting with my boner?" I asked, smiling.

"It did. Not to mention—"

I poured the last of the Petrus, each knowing we were not just at the end of the glorious wine, but also the evening.

"Go on," I nudged with a nod of my glass.

And he did. Explaining how Lexington, on the way to the nurse's office to care for the tea burns, had attempted slipping a hand down his pant, only to discover something unexpected—a penis.

"Well," I observed, "that explains Lexington's abrupt departure."

"It does. Yes."

After the confession, the insight, his business completed and our glasses empty, he'd made a quick and awkward exit.

Tightening my grip on the bottle, unready for battle, I lumbered from the bed.

Staggering downstairs, I searched for the cleaver-wielding, peanut butter mustached, mini-Nazis.

The house was empty and, instead of sweet revenge, I started a pot of coffee.

Pouring a second cup, the soft chugging of an engine and the clatter of tires across gravel fractured my reverie.

Pulling the drapes back, I watched an old, though well-kept, split-window, VW van, painted like a reclining Buddha, chug up the hill.

I followed to the back door and peeked out.

A woman verging on the middle of middle age with shoulder-length brown hair streaked with gray hopped out of the van. She wore a sleeveless, knee-length, dark green summer dress. Under it was a yellow, long-sleeve exercise top, special loops hooked around her thumbs, and black leggings. Her sandals' leather straps were wrapped around her ankles, up her calves.

The woman, who I was nearly ninety percent sure was my mother, gave a cursory glance around and fell into a series of yoga stretches.

My surety dropped a full ten points.

I set off, barefoot, to investigate. Maybe say hello. Or, if it were the daemon, attempt to kill it.

She, in the quintessential gesture, Namaste-ed the recently risen sun, and I took another five points off.

I'd settled on the comment—"Buddha-ful paint job must have cost a Dali Lama or two"—when a figure, Aori, slipped from the crushing facility.

Rather than wearing Lady Wabi-Sabi's cakey butoh make-up, she'd showered and was dressed in a flowing, white robe. Her hair, free of the brown, muddy bands, glimmered like a raven's wing. She, an ethereal ghost, glided through a series of bands of shadow and sunlight created by the scattered pines, the sun.

The effect was mesmerizing.

This time, without the witches and bitches to hold her, Aori would kick Mother's ass, thrice.

Anticipating a Quentin Tarantino-esque bloodbath, I slowed and awaited the katana and the killing.

They lunged at one another and, to my startled surprise, hugged and kissed.

The kiss wasn't a French *faire la bise*. There were no cheeks involved but plenty of tongue. Plenty.

Recalling Mother's instructions regarding Matthew Holmes and *il bacio della morte*, my panic wasn't quite quelled.

The lunch bell had clanged its woeful wail and, unlike the other prepubescent, starving Mahalo Middle School teens, I'd slipped into a bathroom to slip into character, Don Corleone.

Transitioning from mild-mannered Dixon Belltower to mob boss, I stared in the mirror, slicked back my hair with petroleum jelly, and practiced my Pacino, "'After all I've done for you? This is how you treat me?'"

Marching to the cafeteria, the stench of macaroni and cheese and Thousand Island dressing suffocating the hallways, I monologued, "It was the second Tuesday of March, a day of infamy and ill omen, a day Matthew Holmes would remember as his last, for Mr. Holmes had crossed me. And by crossing me, he'd crossed *mi famigilia*. The only solution for such a scoundrel, for someone who crossed me and *mi famiglia*, was death."

Sauntering past the burger munching, chocolate milk suckling plebes, I intoned, "Pedestrians on a pathetic path to an anonymous grave in an unknown cemetery."

One, Colin Snyder, called, "Dixon, hey, scene buddy, don't forget today's rehearsal."

Though mere seventh graders, we'd overstepped ourselves with *Glengarry Glen Ross*.

The kid had moxie, but I still shot back, "If I were you, Snyder, I'd worry about making a goddamn sale before you worry about me forgetting my goddamn lines."

"Bring that focus, Dixon," Colin shouted to my back, "bring that."

I found the snitch, Matthew "Turncoat" Holmes, chatting to another snitch, Scott Stetson, who'd recently been anointed with the nickname Harry Palms.

I pulled Holmes aside and glared dead into his eyes. "'You know I trusted you, yeah? Treated you like *mi famiglia*.'"

"Dixon," the backstabber stuttered, "what are you talking about?"

Like Pacino in *The Godfather II*, I held his face in my hands and declared, "'And once family, always family. Until death.'" And I kissed him. Gave him *il bacio della morte*.

Unlike Fredo in the movie, who'd struggled, Matthew fell into it, kissed me back, and slithered some tongue in.

Once finished, with much less conviction than I'd rehearsed, I mumbled, "I know it was you, Matthew. I know it was you."

Before I could get my next line out, he was kissing me and stealing it, "Because you broke my heart, Dixon. You broke my heart."

We fell apart, wiped our lips on the back of our hands, and turned to the shocked, confused faces of the prepubescent masses.

They stared, sheep recognizing the herding dogs were wolves. Harry Palms backed away, as Matt and I laughed and laughed, and Snyder shouted, "Bring that, Dixon! Bring that!"

The van's side door, as Aori pulled it open, hissed hollowly. She pulled a wicker picnic basket from the shadows and handed it to Mother.

Mother, smiling and looking happier than I could ever recall, stepped to me, said, "Dixon, we've things to discuss," and, with a peck on the cheek, continued to the house, adding, "There's an ice chest in Halen. Fetch it, please."

Following, Aori whispered as she passed something more frightening than another threat of gutting me, "Thank you, son."

Chapter Twenty-Three
OH, OEDIPUS, THY NAME IS MINE

Mother, setting a bamboo tray of curious confections on the living room's coffee table, stated, "Home brewed, homemade, it makes all the difference."

Aori nodded, while I continued floundering in confusion. Mother didn't brew or bake. She concocted misguided psychological tests and neglected leftover delivery food until it grew green and hairy.

To disprove my point, she then presented the vegan, almond butter tea biscuits, while claiming the cloudy liquid in our glasses, sitting murky before us, was "Iced chamomile and green tea kombucha infused with rose hips and organic honey."

I frowned, unsure how honey couldn't be organic.

The entire spread, even the roasted, biodynamic chickpeas, was a cruel mockery of what the Enrights had brought. Yesterday? No. Day before? Regardless, I was disappointed by the uncompromisingly pretentious and healthy fair.

"Now, I've something to tell you," she admitted, setting her glass down, "and I know it will sound strange."

I added puzzled to my confusion, as Mother looked as if she were about to cry.

Given the circumstances, her ex-husband's death, perhaps she'd be expected to show some emotion. Though she'd promised, randomly a multitude of times growing up, "The day he dies I'm throwing a big ass party." I didn't believe this meager fair constituted such and was surprised she wasn't dancing on his grave. I turned to the urn and realized he didn't have one.

Aori took Mother's hand and placed it between hers. It was a sweet, endearing gesture.

Puzzled and confused, I stared.

They lounged on the leather sofa, while, after much struggling, I'd maneuvered the rotund, black leather recliner from its corner into the middle of the room, where it'd ground to a halt in the shag.

The glow of the morning sun streamed through the drape-less windows and cast a bright ocean of light between us.

Thanks to a Dr. M pill, which I'd administered while they'd puttered in the kitchen, I felt comfortably distanced and rather unconcerned about anything.

We'd forgone a fire, as neither condoned the pollution nor, as Aori had put it, "The visceral sound of once proud wooden creatures screaming in flame."

Mother, with a firm nod, pulled her hand from Aori's. Unhooking the yellow garment from her thumbs, she pushed it to her elbows and declared, "We've decided to get married."

I choked on the kombucha puss, not from the statement, but from her arms. They were firm and tanned with tattoos wrapping each wrist—a vine with multi-colored flowers and dark script.

Aori whispered something to Mother, who kissed her cheek in reply.

Resolved, Mother turned to me, "Dixon, we're in love. And you can either—"

I waved a hand, coughing, "No. No. I just... Just something in my throat." Catching my breath, I asked, "You have tattoos?"

She rotated her wrists, smiled at them, and turned to Aori. "I do. Yes."

"Are they part of a cult? Can you buy them online?"

They stared, confused.

"Do others have them? The same, identical tattoos?"

"No," Mother beamed, "they're our design." She extended the wrist with the script, quoted, "'I am a single, perfect and brilliant teardrop falling through a turbulent expanse into a deep, dark sea of eternity.'" Mother added, pecking the guilty woman's cheek, "Aori wrote it."

Downing down the last of my glass, I tried forgetting the other afternoon and Aori propped on the barrel and... "It's lovely," I replied. And, knowing I'd need a referral from Dr. M regardless, I asked, "So, you're getting married?"

"Summer solstice," Aori declared, pulling the flaying knife through my gut. "June 21. Kauai."

Mother provided clarification, "We've purchased a little piece of land. We're creating a yoga-artist retreat."

And there was my excuse. "Well, this calls for a celebratory glass or three. There are some lovely bottles downstairs. I think maybe... What?"

Mother, eyes downcast, was shaking her head. "I don't drink anymore."

"What?" Did the Pope convert to Islam, and did bears learn to use toilets? "What?"

"I've changed, Dixon. And much for the better." She gave Aori another peck. "And I'm sure you have to."

I stood and paced. "No, I've not changed. I'm just able to cope with my neuroses better. Thanks to my best friend, wine."

"Dixon, drinking sometimes is—"

"No. And after all the shit I've been through?" I waved my hand in front of my swollen, enflamed, bruised, bee-stung, and bloodshot-eyed face. "After everything that's happened, I think I'm allowed, nay, deserve a bit of the drinky drink." The pacing, the ranting, had taken my breath. I stopped and fought to catch it before I collapsed.

With a smirk, Mother clarified, "I was going to say—sometimes it's the only thing to do."

They were so damn happy, it was annoying. I may've been more annoyed about them than any of the other shit fouling my life's shoe.

I had so many questions. And if I were a stronger, more emotionally adept individual, I'd ask them. As it was, I only cared about the answer to one. "Because no one seems to want to, maybe you can tell me how he died?"

They shared an understanding smile, their hands reunited, and, after a soft squeeze from Mother, Aori said, "Well, that's a funny story."

Senior year, as there were but three episodes left in *Sex*, I'd been granted the opportunity to tweak the living room. Rather than the chaos of tradition, I'd instilled a staggered row and aisle configuration for optimal viewing, drink, and snack access. It should, in theory, have cut down on Tina's complaining about "butts being in the way."

"So," I asked, handing Mother a glass of Wanderers Red, the newly rebranded Wrong Way, "what do you think?"

Mother, still in her therapist uniform—a cream and indigo pants suit—stared at the scene and declared, "Life is a pile of shit and I wish I could afford an assassin to murder whoever keeps pooping it." She took a quick, angry sip and shot a surprised glance at me. She took another. "What'd you do?"

Not getting entangled in the technical aspects, I elucidated on the transformative properties of Harissa, ketchup, whole black peppercorns, maraschino cherries, rusty nails, and vigorous shaking ("what's called 'aeration' in the industry"), which elevated the crappy Cabernet-Merlot blend into something nearing a sturdy Argentinian Malbec.

On her second glass, splayed across the couch, Mother confessed, "They're not coming."

"Who?" I asked, exchanging the remote for my glass.

"Everyone," she said, snatching the remote.

In the middle of our second bottle, I made the mistake of continuing the interrogation, "Why?"

"Well, that," she said, pressing mute as Carrie walked away from Miranda at Lexi's funeral, "that's a funny story."

It was funny if the prescriptions you were writing for your friends were necessary and your co-conspirator, the pharmacist, hadn't, as part of a plea deal, sold you out to the authorities and the Oregon Board of Psychology hadn't revoked your license.

"Well," she'd claimed, "if I can sell those witches and bitches sugar pills as Valium, I can sell Californians on living the Napa lifestyle in Hood River." She tried laughing, but couldn't, and took another sip.

"No," Mother reinforced, as Aori nodded, "it is an amusing story. Though maybe not for your father."

They giggled and I asked, annoyed, "Then maybe you should tell me all about it?"

"Only," Mother said, fighting back her laughter, "only after a bowl. Or two."

"You're smoking pot now?"

"Marijuana has many beneficial aspects."

Halfway down the hall, headed for the cellar, I shouted back, "You witches and bitches bowl up; I'm fetching some friends for this fecund fiasco."

"Fiasco?" she yelled back, "Fiasco? What are you talking about? This is the beginning of that big ass party!"

Ten minutes later, Mother and Aori, two played-out kittens, were entwined and contented on the couch. A thick, blue cloud, like an industrial city from the 1880s, hazed the room.

I'd gobbled another pill and was midway through a third glass of Macedonia red, and the world, everything, was fine, fine, fine.

They'd each finished a tug on the green pipe, Bean, and I, because everything was fine, fine, fine, asked again, "So, his death? It's a funny story?"

They giggled into one another's necks, exchanged a few kisses.

"Tell you what," I said, losing my chill, my fine, "I'll tell you my funny story if you tell me yours."

Transitioning to something nearing vertical, Mother said, "We'll go first, shall we?"

Father, for no apparent reason, so the pharmacological findings indicated, had ingested approximately 800 micrograms of LSD, three erection pills, and ten grams of psychedelic mushrooms. After wearing out a local trollop named Vivian, he was found attached to a transfer hose at Peterson's wine co-op.

"Attached?"

"Shrunken and shriveled," Mother admitted, "though, I'm told, with the most angelic smile on his face."

After such disclosure the conversation petered out and Mother, standing, stretching, plucked the urn from the mantel and announced, "Oh, we're taking your father with us."

"To Kauai?" If you couldn't dance on his grave, you could, at minimum, go down on his ex in front of his urn. "Why?"

"Because we're going to Kauai."

"To get married?"

"Yes." She was firm, expected a fight, and likely wanted one.

Instead, "Is he part of it? The ceremony?"

"Are you kidding me?" Aori laughed. "Wow, your mother must've seriously fucked you up."

They laughed, kissed, and laughed more.

"And," I asked, needing to confirm my suspicions, "you're taking him?"

"Unless you want him?" Mother dared.

"No. No. Just keep it sealed." I explained the liquid additions to the urn.

"You did not. No one's that stupid." Mother appraised. "You're simply trying to be comedic." She opened it, gasped and, spilling some muck across her skirt, stumbled back from the stench onto Aori's lap.

Laughing, I handed her a napkin and observed, "Who's the comic now?" Before she replied, I asked, "And you're leaving tomorrow?"

Dabbing at the muck with the newly kombucha wetted napkin they sucked on Bean and blew blue smoke to alleviate the stench.

After another round of huffs and puffs, Mother admitted, "A town car. At the crack of dawn. Off to PDX."

"And love island," Aori giggled.

They laughed, kissed, laughed more.

Again annoyed, I noted, "Didn't you say summer solstice?"

Not that I'd particularly wanted to reconnect with Mother, but of all the versions of herself she'd conspired to be I preferred this one. Oh, the irony.

"We've an intimacy intensive this weekend. Then some bank stuff and such."

"Always one for details, weren't you?"

"Your green-eyed monster, Mister, should stay in its hole."

Had she seen something? Did she know about me and the molehill, and before?

Rather than press, I withdrew. "Is there anything I can help with?"

"There isn't. Although..." She pulled a piece of paper from a pocket. "...there is this."

The paper was a detailed chronology of the next month or so. It outlined when Halen would be collected for long-term storage and when a shipment of personal items from her Hood River home would be delivered, etc., etc.

"Detailed enough for you?" Mother asked.

I poured another glass and admitted, "Like a mime at a convention for the blind."

"You know, Dixon," she admitted past her confusion, "you're a weird one, but I'm so glad you're my son." She headed for the back door, my father, the urn, an odd, cancerous protrusion on her hip.

Aori whispered, "I am too," and followed.

The door clattered shut and having had the rare foresight to bring a second bottle of Greek red with the first, I knew what I was doing with my night.

Chapter Twenty-Four
BEAUTIFUL, BEAUTIFUL BRUTUS

The tranquility of the afternoon and evening after Mother and Aori's departure had been unexpected. There'd been no calls, no texts, nor probable or actual yakuza or drug cartel assassins. Though, because of their absence, there'd been no Alicia. Nor was there any particular rationale to call her. There were pretenses to be exploited—cardigan sweater shopping, a trip to a shooting range—but I didn't want to sell her something she wasn't shopping for.

The night had been howling free and I'd taken my disappointment into the bedroom. Defending myself against introspection, I quested for the flash drive. That, however, was an abbreviated lesson in futility. And I'd quickly found myself at the kitchen table scribbling notes from the vagaries of my memory regarding *The Jerk*'s primordial manuscript.

The morning, except for what lingered in my brain, was fog free and my notes read all the worse in the clear light of sobriety.

Finishing my mug of coffee I realized, somewhere, somehow, I'd pissed off the God of Gravel, for the grinding *crunch* of the accursed gray rock groaned the air.

The chicken clock declared it nearly nine and the town car had already whisked the ladies off to PDX.

Perhaps, I hoped, it was an excuse to call Alicia?

A high-pitched *beep, beep, beep* of a vehicle backing up filled the house.

I peeked past the curtains.

A moving van maneuvered in the drive, while from behind sprung a magnificently beautiful apparition, an angel.

I knew her, though had never seen her armored so severely. Her hair was pulled back into a tight bun. Her black slacks and dress shirt, sleeves rolled to the elbow, bristled under a bulletproof vest. A badge, on a chain around her neck, swayed side to side as she, clipboard clutched, marched for the front door.

If I called, would she protect me from herself?

Opening the front door, she slowed as I lifted a welcoming hand. "Alicia, a pleasant surprise, although—" The moving van, turning to parallel the front lawn, exposed a weasel-faced prick leaning against the sedan. "Why are you here?"

The question seemed to cause her pain. The van sighed to an anguished stop.

"Mr. Belltower—"

"Don't Mr. Belltower me. What's this about? I mean, based on your moody scowl, the badge, the vest, the van, and that prick Saunders, this isn't a social call, is it?" I hadn't thought much of the situation, the ramifications of who was here and why, until I'd said what I had. My annoyance transitioned into apprehension, and I asked, "So, why are you here?"

A black, windowless, transporter van sped in and skidded to a stop. A cadre of ICE agents, mirrored sunglasses and skeleton scarves pulled over their noses, spewed into the gray dust cloud. Puppies to their mother's teats, they scurried to Saunders.

"I may've made a few disparaging comments regarding this fine country," I observed, "but nothing so severe to be deported, right?"

Alicia, with a sigh, explained, "They're here for Egan and Julio."

"You filed that report, didn't you?"

"Are they here?"

"I don't think so."

"Their car is."

The El Camino did loiter where they'd parked it.

"Not sure you can call that a car, but okay."

Biting a lip, she dropped her head to the papers clamped to the clipboard. "I'm not enjoying this. Can you please help?"

"Why?" She glanced up and her big, beautiful eyes melted into me. "I haven't seen them this morning. I had a late last night. So—" I shrugged. I saw no reason to mention them having gone to their brother's. I mean, who would help with the harvest?

The ICE agents, in pairs, split up, with two marching our way, leaving Saunders at the sedan, glaring.

"What," I repeated, "are you doing here?" She, again, dropped her head. "Alicia?"

She, pulling the lever on the scaffold, spun the clipboard around.

It was an Internal Revenue Service seizure notice. It stated my father, Jason Alexander Belltower, owed $1.75 million, plus a few hundred and change, in back taxes. They were seizing the entirety of the cellar's contents. There were a few more pages of specifics regarding the inventory. I didn't care. I was too busy attempting to pull the dagger from my back.

"You work for the IRS?"

She nodded, admitted, as if guilty of something greater, "I do."

"But?" There had to be something else, something that'd exonerate her of such betrayal. But she remained silent. And I? I waited to be introduced to the noose.

Austere, bulky vultures, the two agents and their skeletal grins settled around us.

One, a Howitzer with hair, leaned and whispered in Officer Tilden's ear.

"They're not in the house?" she, the first shovel of dirt on the coffin, asked.

"What'd I say?"

"Answer her, you—"

Officer Tilden held a hand to the looming Howitzer.

With easy nonchalance, I, reflected in his glasses, said to myself, "Not that I know of."

"Not much of an answer," the other agent, a bald submarine, replied.

A late afternoon in late September 2006, the sun melting orange and purple on the horizon, found me exiting a ferry from Rhodes to Brindisi and learning a lesson regarding authority, the hard way.

Heading for an exit and the taxi kiosk, a customs officer and his wrinkled, faded blue uniform had asked with a curled forefinger twitching itself in an uninviting invitation, "*Signore, per favore*, may we talk with you?"

"Why?"

"Is it not enough," another officer, taller, slimmer, asked, pushing himself from the salt and sun-bleached tide wall he'd been bored against, "for my partner to have asked?"

"Well, it is, but—"

"You," the tall one declared, tapping my shoulder, sauntering past and toward the opposite end of the dock, "will come with us."

"As much as I'd love to come with you, I've a competition to get to."

Whisked roughly to a cluttered, customs vestibule smelling of cigarettes, toxic aftershave, cheap red, and Bolognese, I knew I'd emphasized the wrong words.

As the cold, lubricated glove, one lump of a knuckle after another slid up and up, the excess gel smearing and slathering my ass, I realized the practicality of acquiescing to authority and that there may be some merit to butt play.

"Yeah," Howitzer agreed, "not much of an answer."

"That's not what your mother said."

Bald Submarine, to Officer Tilden, advised, "Please remind him... On second thought, don't."

They, with an extra elbow or three, muscled past and marched into the house. Another pair moved up the hill to the crushing facility, while the last two circled the house and drifted into the vineyard.

"Are you stupid?" Officer Tilden asked.

"You know I am."

The whir of the van's lift, the shudder of its rolltop door clattering open startled us and killed her reply.

Three broad-shouldered men in blue coveralls stood at the back of the moving van, a fourth scrambled up and passed down a pair of dollies.

"You can't."

"I'm sorry," Officer Tilden said, as the swarming clatter of wheels grew.

At what juncture did Caesar know he'd been betrayed?

Officer Tilden pulled a stapled set of pages from the clipboard and held it up. It was snatched by the first passing mover as they and their dollies stormed into the house.

And at what juncture did Caesar realize he wasn't being deposed but assassinated?

"You can't," I repeated, still inadequate. And, because doing the same thing over and over often, if not always, changed the outcome, I repeated, "You can't."

Officer Tilden, because one dagger wasn't enough, indicated a tally, the outstanding balance, an asterisk beside it.

I followed her finger to the explanatory paragraph: *Much of the authenticity and provenance of the wine is dubious, thus its 'value' is questionable. Therefore, we foresee an outstanding balance of $1.35 million, if not more.*

Not just assassinated, but slaughtered with short, blunt, rusty knives.

Senior year, our first production was *West Side Story*, and I'd been cast as Diesel. As I caught my breath, Professor Magaldi had advised, "Screaming, shouting, that's easy anger. The silent ones are those to fear."

With such advice boiling my blood, I bit my tongue and let the anger pour from my eyes in deep, molten rivers.

"I'm sorry," Officer Tilden admitted, "I'm just doing my job."

"I," I said, biting a bit harder, "believe that's what those goddamn Nazis said."

From the doorway, a mover interrupted our glaring. "Where do you want your station set up?"

Officer Tilden yanked a few sheets from the clipboard, handed them to me. I crumpled them in my fist and she moved into the house. "Here, I'll show you."

"You can't miss it; it's square in my back," I quipped, pumping my thumb at the spot.

I glared at Saunders. He, with a fake smile, that was likely sincere, waved, climbed into the sedan, and drove off. The gravel's clatter was the last few shovels full on the coffin, finishing the mound.

Officer Tilden and her stormtroopers had been on this type of raid before. In less than three hours they'd gutted the cellar. I'd sulked at the kitchen table with a yet opened bottle of Buffalo Trace and one of Dr. M's pills for company. I'd been granted special dispensation to fill the chicken tote bag with what wasn't on her list, bourbon.

The house echoed like a mausoleum, as I'd said to Officer Tilden before she'd slammed the door in my face, "Scrooge and the Grinch would be proud."

"Dixon—"

"Mister Belltower. Thank you very much."

"Dixon, I—"

"Tell it to yourself the next time you look in the mirror. If you can."

She hesitated. Rather than a half-hearted excuse, she nodded and slammed the door.

The barrels of whisky remained tucked in their corner. An official notice was taped to each: *Tampering with this item will constitute a Fed-*

eral offense as defined in Section 15 of the McKenzie Act. Perpetrators will be prosecuted to the full extent of the law, which could be as much as a fine up to $250,000 and/or 5 years in prison.

The ICE agents, as expected, hadn't found the brothers. Howitzer had handed me his business card. "If you see them, you need to contact me. Otherwise, you'll be considered an accomplice and—"

"Held accountable to the full extent of the law?"

"No one likes a smart ass."

"Drizzle honey on it," I advised, "much more palatable that way."

"You know," he threatened, plucking the card from my fingers, "we'll be back."

Waving them away with a middle finger, I marched back in, did my own slamming of the door and howled in throat-scorching werewolf.

After a dozen more, I yanked the cork from the Buffalo, threw myself onto the couch, and, brooding devoutly on Officer Tilden's betrayal, pondered the order I'd be watching every last war movie in.

Having settled on the first seventeen, I tossed a Doctor M pill in and took a long sip off the bottle of Buffalo. Unconcerned with ever forgiving the beautiful Brutus, I hit play on *Kelly's Heroes.*

Just before Kelly and his heroes distribute the gold, another storm of gravel thundered the house and my sinking, little world.

Footsteps, across the gravel and down the walkway, grew closer, until a knock bruised the front door.

I sipped.

The bell groaned and died.

With an ambivalent shrug, what difference if it were yakuza or cartel hit men, I lumbered to my feet, shuffled to the door, and opened it

A slightly chubby, middle-aged man stood smiling, nervous. He had thinning, brown hair with temples embarrassed with gray, excessively white teeth, and wore what most would call "golf club formal."

I sipped.

I knew this stranger or at least his younger self. "Matt? Matt Holmes?"

"Yeah. Hello. Hi. Long time."

"A long time."

He extended his hand, which, after glancing at the big, black, tinted window SUV sitting in the middle of the drive, I shook awkwardly.

"So, why are you here?" But I knew. He'd come to collect on *il bacio della morte*.

However, instead of henchmen spewing from the SUV, a squad of middle-aged, pasty white folk stumbled out and waved.

"What happened to your face?" he asked.

"Besides time?" I asked, waving back to the familiar strangers.

"Yeah."

"Attacked by novitiates, bees, codgers, and my therapist."

"No. Really?

"Yes. Seriously." Indignant, I added, "I mean it. It's the truth."

"Okay. Okay. I hope you gave as good as you got?"

"I did not. Those novitiates were mean bitches."

He laughed.

"So now, why are you here?"

He glanced over his shoulder, "We're out wine tasting and—"

"Yes, please." With an added wave to the others, I declared, "Two minutes."

"You're ready?" Matt, still at the door, was as surprised as the others. They'd yet to make it to the vines.

Back in my standard Seinfeld—jeans, button down, white, dress shirt, the mourning jacket, and tennis shoes—I tottered near normal. With more enthusiasm than expected, I pulled my phone and wallet out. "I am. So, who's this we you speak of?"

"Well, there's," with a forefinger, he found the first two, "Scott and Jennifer Stetson."

"*Quelle surprise*, right?"

"What?"

"Did she get the three kids, the dog, the convertible, and the Mc-Mansion?"

"One kid. Autistic. Three cats. Four-bedroom in Waikiki Heights. And I think a Prius."

"And Scott? The same, except for the Prius?"

"BMW 4-door something."

"Wanted to be—" I didn't know or care, but the dread of needing to perform like a "normal human" was making me anxious.

"Don't know. But he's an optometrist."

"I see. Clearly, he saw—" I fell silent, reminded myself, normal, normal, normal. "And the Norse god? Is that Jennings?" Gregory Jennings transferred from San Bernardino, California, junior year of high school. I didn't particularly know him, distinctly didn't like him. I fingered the pill I'd tucked in a pocket, told myself Naomi's lie—"It's going to be okay."

"Yep. Sporting the new company car around. He's in group insurance, Molokai Mutual."

"So, is that all? Or are there more clowns in the car?"

"No. Though there's another group meeting us there."

"Another?" He hesitated. "Who's in the other group?"

"Besides my husband?"

"Kevin? Is he still at Nike?"

Matt smiled, "He is. He just got promoted."

Gregory called out, waving us to the phallic symbol of his inadequacy, the SUV, "Hey, lovers, let's go."

"Walk and talk, Matty. Walk and talk." We sauntered over as the others clambered inside the behemoth. "Who else do you want to warn me about?"

He delivered the sitrep. "There'd be Gregory's wife, Amanda. She, because they're control freaks, is the other designated driver. Colin and Brenda were last-minute additions. Because no one knows how to say no." Matt seemed oblivious to the humor of his comment, as the two were founding members of The Yes Squad. "And one other, I think. However, that was left to Jen. So?"

"So, let's get this fiasco over with."

"Funny. Kevin said the same thing."

"Smart man. And not just for snagging you. Shall we?"

Inside, besides the stench of new leather, I found everyone wearing the red rouge of drink and smiling like piranhas. They'd been to one if not two, wineries before abducting me.

"What happened to you?" the older Scott Stetson asked.

Having recently delivered my line, I knew it and kept it. "Assaulted by novitiates, bees, codgers, and my therapist."

Perplexed, dogs in space, he and the others stared, what cat had they invited into their capsule?

Gregory, starting the car, piped up, "Are you done making out back there?"

"Only if you're done being an asshole." Through the shocked silence, I snapped my fingers and, in a pompous, aristocratic voice, British of course, directed, "Now, be a good lad and drive on. Mustn't be late to mummy's." Wow, I needed to tone it down. The frustration and annoyance with Officer Tilden, everything, was bubbling through.

Jennifer, up front as copilot, slapped a restraining hand on Gregory's arm, and whispered in his cauliflower ear. Dutifully, though reluctantly, he put the car in gear and did as instructed.

Fingering the pill, I mumbled an apology.

In the awkward aftermath, Jennifer, a shark sensing blood, said, "So, Dixon, it's good to see you." The others mumbled unenthused echoes. "And since we know what everyone here has been up to, maybe you'd like to fill us in on what you've been up to?"

"Honestly, nothing of particular interest."

"Really?" Gregory jabbed, checking traffic, guiding the SUV out onto 99W with a forceful acceleration.

Something in his tone made me believe they knew the shit I'd been in and recently waded through.

Sure, they were out wine tasting, but how much of that was pretense? Let's go to the circus, see the dancing horses and the trapeze artists. You know, they've also the Elephant Man and the Bearded Girl?

"Really," I passed a placating smile around, warm food on a cold plate. On their disappointed suburban mashed potatoes, I splashed some hot sauce. "Unless you count traveling the globe as a hired killer."

They laughed, and I, strapping my Crushed Durden on, delivered dead in their watery eyes, "Google mini-Nazis slaughtered in Paris."

They laughed more.

And, recalling Katrina's final words, "Death to tyrants!" I levelled my Durden, a shotgun, and pulled the trigger, "Do it."

"Jesus, Dixon," Matt soothed, placing a placating hand on my arm, "you need to take a chill pill."

"I did," I admitted. "It just hasn't kicked in yet." And I heard in my head myself say to myself, laughing, "Like the situation, like the shit that's happened."

Looking out the window, the blur of the roadside reminiscent of the situation, the shit, I ignored the echo of Kelsey's stilettos tapping a desperate goodbye and asked, "How long until we—"

Gregory, flicking the turn signal, exiting us off of 99W, judge to a convicted murderer, cut me off with "Not long," and drove up the hill, toward the gallows.

I'd lost my Durden and Jennifer's excitement bubbled over, "You're so going to love this place. It's just like Tuscany. I mean, we've never been, but—"

The others joined the bubbling. "But it's so gorgeous."

"And the views are amazing."

"And the wine is pretty good too."

"What? Are you joking? It's fantastic."

"If you can afford it."

"Oh, come on, you've paid more for one of those stupid cigars of yours."

A cold fear enveloped me and seeped into my blood and bones. We were heading for the monstrosity on the hill. I had no particular beef with opulence, except with those who regaled in it.

The gold, curlicue script emblazoned across the gleaming black, wrought iron archway over the glistening, honey-hued brick drive declared *Saint Pierre Winery*. On the gate, same gleaming wrought iron, same gold lettering, *Tutto è bello, se hai vino*.

I considered mentioning the incongruity of a French-named winery with an Italian catchphrase but felt it would be absurd.

Gregory, over his shoulder, translated, "All is beautiful, if one has wine." He lowered his window and pressed a button on the gate's callbox.

"I love that," Jennifer confessed.

"Because it's true," Matt agreed.

"I know. Right?"

I texted Naomi. "Call me. In hell. Literally. Get me out. Plz."

To my surprise, she texted back. "No." Middle finger.

I lied, "I found the manuscript. Call me."

The gate creaked open, and we wound our way through the immaculate vineyard.

Ignoring the banter about *terroir* and biodynamism, I tried again, lied again. "It's finished. It's great. Call me."

Gregory, in the rearview, asked, "So, Dixon, what do you think?"

Sighing, I placed my head in the noose, "I'm sorry, what?"

"Dundee Hills? Or Burgundy?"

"Oh, goddamn, not big, broad generalizations. Particularly where that slutty, bitch-princess, Pinot Noir is concerned." I could've gone on, but their offended faces suggested I shouldn't. They were my ride back, so I offered a token of forgiveness. "Please?" It smacked of insincerity and hypocrisy. I pointed to my face, "Sorry. That was the novitiates talking."

My panic, seemingly unable to do normal, grew and I texted Alicia. "Where r u? I miss my wine and u." Smiley face. Once I'd sent it, I realized my mistake. Officer Tilden and I were on ill terms, betrayer, betrayed. Worse though, it'd been the truth.

Before I undermined with a JK or LOL, Jennifer, her excitement cooling, used a red-hot poker to poke the bear. "So, what are your thoughts on Oregon champagne?"

Pocketing the phone, resigned to fate and fingering the pill, I started, "The difficulty I have with champagne, or bubbling wine, is—"

Jennifer's phone buzzed and, forefinger keeping me from digging my grave deeper, she stated, "The others have arrived and await us."

Leaning to Matt, I hissed, "Please note, your revenge is complete."

He leaned into me and, hand returned to my thigh, whispered, "Oh, no it's not."

Moments later, we parked in the extensive, paved lot behind the monstrosity on the hill.

No. No. No.

Yes, it resembled Tuscany. If Tuscany were a cheap, Milanese, prostitute chewing pink bubble gum and smoking a hand-rolled cigarette under a streetlight.

No. No. No.

They piled out and stretched dramatically. I, running through escape scenarios, stayed seated.

Jennifer ducked her highlighted head in, "Dixon, did Matthew mention we set you up with someone?"

No. No. No.

Gregory had taken the keys out of the ignition and tucked them in a pocket.

No. No. No.

Salvation, the banquette and bourbon, was three miles, if not four or five, over and through vine-covered hills, a few insolent creeks, a few patches of desultory pine.

No. No. No.

"She's not that ugly, is she?" Scott received a playful punch from Jennifer, a kiss, and a gentle push.

"Ignore him. She's perfectly lovely." Jennifer glared at the others and challenged them to challenge her.

None did.

Gregory, tapping the SUV's hood, called, "Hey, Belltower, let's go," as the others sauntered up the manicured walkway to the imposing teak front doors.

Knowing where hope lay, in the shitter, I followed.

Jennifer drifted back and, with a cold, grip on my wrist, pulled me aside. "Listen, don't listen to them. Meg's had a hard time recently and I'd be grateful if you could try and be a gentleman."

"I'll have you know, I'm known on all seven continents for my gentlemanliness."

"And maybe keep your 'humor' to yourself?" She used air quotes around humor. "Some of us have found it offensive."

"My humor 'offensive'?" I air quoted her back as she turned and followed the others. "What are you talking about?" Where could they have seen my act? I'd only done, maybe, thirty shows, and all were in wee shitey clubs in the UK. "When have you seen my act?"

"Not now, Dixon. Not now. Just be nice. Okay?"

"Okay. But," I whined as we neared the dark, imposing doors, "what about me? Is anyone going to be nice to me?"

Chapter Twenty-Five
AN OUTHOUSE FILLED WITH POSING POSERS

The long, sleek windowed, Frank Lloyd Wright rip-off was as unappealing inside as out. Teak this, glass that. Its smooth, clean lines declared, "We've a heightened sense of the current acceptable trend in architectural design, but no creativity or unique insight. We do not innovate but pander." Though incorporating the natural stream as a feature through its expanse was a nice touch—the lone one.

Unlike Sheppard's, there was a reception desk and large, round, glass tables with comfortable cushioned chairs, and... servers? What the hell was this? This wasn't a winery, but a pared-down restaurant.

The group, led by a tall, angular young man too self-assured to have ever enjoyed life, turned a corner and disappeared.

"Do you have a bar here?" I asked.

The young woman stilled her stylus on the inlaid computer screen. "Sir? A bar?"

"A chin-up bar."

"Sir?"

"I'd like to work out. To vent. To... Oh, *gottverdammt*." I stomped after the others, contemplating snatching a bottle off a table and running for the trees scattered along the ridge.

Everyone, on my arrival, was deep in conversation around the rectangular onyx table in the private glass alcove. All seats, but one, mine, were taken. In front of it, like the others, lay a tasting mat and five glasses each with a meager few ounces.

My seat was to the right of a man in a sky-blue paisley shirt. I assumed Matt's husband, Kevin, as Matt sat on his left. To the right of the chair sat a woman with shoulder-length brown hair, who, even from such an awkward angle, seemed familiar. She was in conversation with a dark-haired woman, Brenda Fuller, Colin's wife. I'd shared a few classes, a few fated high school productions with Brenda.

Across the table sat the other two couples.

Amanda, Gregory's wife, a severe-looking, platinum blond in a dark, shimmering blouse, turned her gray eyes on me.

Sitting, I gave a slight nod and smile of recognition.

Brenda, with her nod, indicated to the woman her "date"—me—had arrived.

The woman turned and extended her hand.

It didn't cross the slight expanse. Her smile, once a bright, frolicking creature, as if struck by lightning, died in an expanse of flame and smoke. "Jesus fuck, not you again."

Through the startled gasps, I, shaking Dr. M's hovering hand, agreed, "Indeed, good doctor, me again," and cackled softly, maniacally.

"You two know one another?" Jennifer asked, incredulous.

"Meant for one another, you mean," Kevin observed with a laugh. "Look at their noses."

"We've met," I clarified. "And, at least to me, it's a funny story."

"Wait, Meg," Brenda said, reinforcing Jennifer's incredulity, "is he the one?"

Doctor Montgomery nodded and continued blinking in confusion at how a villainous monster could be her date.

The self-assured young man who'd led them to the table returned and, in the rarefied silence, with a slight bow, began, "Welcome to Saint Pierre Winery. My name is Rapha, and I'll be your tasting host today." Everyone mumbled a greeting, and he continued. "Before you are five wines which exemplify the quality and dedication Saint Pierre prides itself on."

Rapha prattled about the wines. Their details and descriptions printed beneath each made him unnecessary. My attention had waned at "welcome" and, with the continued silence of my phone, I turned to the nearest provider of hope.

I had the first two glasses finished, an insipid Pinot Gris and a mundane Sauvignon Blanc, before Rapha, along with a few others, attempted to keep me from my goal, the reds.

Past their protestations, Rapha, hands waving for me to stop, decried, "No. No, sir. You—"

"Rapha, please, shut up."

Oddly enough he did. I'd need to return one day and apologize.

The table joined him in stunned silence, when the de facto ruler of the group, Gregory, echoed Rapha's sentiments, "Everything is done sequentially, such that—"

Leveling my hardest Durden glare at him, I picked up the next glass and tossed it back. And the next. And the next. I reached for the doctor's Pinot Gris.

She slapped my hand away.

I administered a cursory apology, "In Europe too long. Metric system and all that." With a palm across my chest, hoping I didn't sound sarcastic, I insisted, "Rapha, please, continue. Though, I see no reason for you to parrot the pandering BS on the tasting mats." I tapped mine. "Assume we can read. And that you're more than a handsome mouthpiece for a mediocre brand. Okay?" Sullenly, he nodded. "Now, rather than regaling us with the superfluous knowledge of malolactic fermentation, the nuanced differences between French and American oak, and how variations of a barrel's toast can affect—we all know it and love it—perhaps you can tell us about the first glass you ever had? And what you want your last glass to be?"

Kevin, like the others, was engrossed in a whispered conversation with their neighbor, I stole his Estate Cuvée Pinot Noir and tossed it back.

Shaken, Rapha mumbled something about "pre-ordered small plates" and exited stage left, immediately.

Standing, ignoring the hissed suggestions not to, I did so and chased.

Yet to reach the fourth glass, lingering over the single bloc Chardonnay, the group's heated whispers died on my return.

Kevin's glass I'd absconded with hadn't been replaced, and I was thankful I'd brought a replacement. Unlike the previous one, this one was full.

Slipping into my seat, I placed the glass in front of him and, with a wink, said, "You're welcome." And, ignoring Matt's insistent attempt to gain my attention, I asked, "So, what'd I miss?"

I waited for the accusations, the questions.

Curiously, there were none. Rather Amanda, with a tilt of her glass, a thimble's amount sparkling the bottom, asked, "So, Dixon, tell me, did you like the Chardonnay?"

"I did not."

"Oh." She, as I'd ignored the first principle of improv, sounded as disappointed as Rapha had, though she'd not be getting an apology, as I'd given the young man.

To Amanda's frown, I added, "I could tell you, with all kinds of wine jargon. But that shouldn't diminish your enjoyment. Like what you like. Ignore what anyone else says."

Art had put it more succinctly, "Love what you love and ravage everyone else." The wizened professor continued, rhetorically, "Do you know why Crushed continues to use frozen pizza boxes to mask the bottles?" Of course, I didn't. He enlightened. "It's a reminder we're all individuals and what's inside that counts. And bags—black, brown, whatever—imply we're all alike. We must appreciate pepperoni and mushrooms as much as the combination and the stuffed crust." He sighed. In Sancho, he'd accepted even those who enjoy chorizo and pineapple were worthy of being loved.

While the others foundered in silence, I added, "And as they say in that wine thing I'm not affiliated with, 'It's just pizza.'"

"And why," Gregory, prince to the rescue, muscled in, "do you think your opinion would affect her, let alone anyone? Are you such an expert?"

Spotting Rapha hesitating at the service entrance, I held a shut-up palm to Gregory. "Yes. Yes, I am." With the other hand, a quick, backhanded, two-fingered, godfather gesture, invited Rapha and his makeshift crew over.

On their arrival, to the group's confusion, they replaced the placemats and tasting glasses with standard Bordeaux and four water pitchers of wine, two white and two red. And, accompanying a dozen tapas plates, there were gray slate slabs covered with cheeses and charcuterie accompanied by baskets of bread.

Gregory and Amanda, indignant, demanded, "What is this?"

"What are they doing?"

"What's going on? Rapha?"

Poor Rapha turned his soulful, dark eyes on me and I turned to the others, "You've all been here before, right?" They nodded as if confessing to a minor misdemeanor. I turned to Colin and Brenda. "So, why do you keep returning?"

Though the indiscretion could be viewed as a felony in The Yes Squad's bylaws, they confessed, "Because it's safe."

"Thank you," I said, standing and shaking Rapha's hand as the others carted the items back to the expansive catering kitchen. "And," I insisted, "make sure you call me. Hell, just stop by. Okay?"

"Okay," he agreed. And, with a quick, awkward hug, a "Thank you," he drifted off toward the reception desk.

Shocked, confused faces stared at me.

I answered, though didn't explain, "Because 'someday,' usually, never comes."

Gregory, annoyed at the ambiguity, red flairs blooming his cheeks, demanded, "What is this? Dick-son?"

Ignoring the provocation and disinclined to explain my heartfelt apology to Rapha or the peace offering of granting the use of two fermenting tanks and enough of the harvest to fill them, I hoisted a pitcher in each hand, queried the table, "White or red?"

After a moment of hesitation and glances of confusion, the orders poured in.

"The only question," I declared, circling the table, pouring, "you need to answer is, do I like it? Ignore everyone, particularly Ashley Armstrong of World Wine News. She's a paid propagandist."

"I've met Ashley. She seems reputable."

"Ashley, and I know this because we regaled in a heated and twisted tryst with a Bollywood actress in Bangalore, is in the pocket of a wine conglomerate." I took a deep breath. "But that's neither here nor there. Secondarily, are you with people worthy of your time and the wine?" Sitting, I finished with Art's standard phrase in such circumstances, "Now, shut up and drink."

Everyone, even Gregory, assisted by an insistent nudge from Amanda, did exactly that. They shut up and drank.

Perplexed faces, they glanced around. The reds and the whites swapped glasses, conferred in hushed whispers.

Colin, over Brenda's back, the doctor's head, was the first to voice his curiosity, "What are these?"

"I know," Jennifer admitted, "They're good, right?"

"Dixon?"

"Gregory," Amanda asked, "is this the cuvee select, vintner's reserve, Valerie Bianchi did in 2019?"

"That was 2018." Gregory leveled his eyes, stuck some severity on his voice. "Dixon, what are these?"

"Does it matter?" Kevin observed, "They're delicious."

"Quite right, good sir." I *tinked* his glass with mine. "It doesn't matter."

All around, glances and shrugs were exchanged. The group commenced pecking at the cheese and charcuterie, speculating, through slurps, on the vintages.

Through the sapling pines granted permission to remain along the constrained stream, a strawberry-blonde woman with regal features and an air of invincibility meandered. Drifting to a table, her dagger smile cut grins and pleasantries off the gathered.

She, I realized as she floated to another table, wasn't a fantasy but a familiar monster who'd killed something of mine once. Oh, wait, it'd been my life.

She wasn't saying hi to friends, but pleasing people with her presence, which meant this fecund hovel was likely her and that *Diablo* St. Fer's collaboration.

Sonoma, my ass. Oh, Art, I'll have choice words for you when next we speak.

Dr. Montgomery listed to my shoulder, "Who, pray tell, is that?"

Staying locked on the monster I pulled the lint-covered pill out, tucked it on my tongue, sipped, swallowed, and replied, "Queen of the Damned."

The doctor, seconds from analyzing such an observation, was cut off by Matt, "Dixon, did you hear?"

"A stake through the heart should kill her?"

He glanced around, "What? No. Trisha Andretti has RSVP'd for the reunion."

"The reunion?" I asked.

The doctor chimed with, "Trisha Andretti?"

Matt nodded. "An old classmate Dixon had a crush on."

"Did he?" the doctor encouraged, "Tell me more."

"Any idea," I interjected, "what she's been up to?"

"I thought she'd started a sheep farm in New Zealand?" Scott offered past a mouthful of salami, brie, and baguette.

"No. No," Jennifer declared shaking her head, "raising reindeer in Norway."

Brenda fondled the stem of her glass and added, "I thought she moved to Reno. Became a dealer."

"Drugs?"

"No, Colin, you dolt, cards."

The shark circled our way. I filled my glass, sipped, and speculated, next time, a little less A-1 and another minute of aeration.

Behind a curious smile, the doctor asked, "You went to school with Matthew and Troy?"

"I did. Mahalo Middle School and Aloha High."

"You're kidding, right?"

"No. Like Greenland, an advertising ploy. Aloha is the greyest, drizzliest city in Oregon though home to Sunshine Pizza, Sunny Lanes Bowling, and Sky Blue Realty."

Encouraged by her broken-nosed, grimaced laugh, I described the convoluted evolution of how our mothers, over *Sex and the City*, had bonded.

"Witches and bitches?"

"It was endearing, though accurate. Particularly for mine."

"Care to expound?"

"Yes, but not here. Not like this." Her eyes quizzed me, but I ignored them. With my glass, I indicated the others and asked, "And how do you know these pretentious twats?"

The doctor's answer, as the shark arrived, droned past my inattentive ears. Warily, I watched it smiling and laughing (almost as if it were human) with Gregory and Amanda.

Draining my glass and pouring more, I insisted, "Anything that happens here doesn't affect our client-therapist relationship or confidentiality, right?"

"We don't have—"

"Excellent. So glad to hear it." Around the doctor's pout, I stood. "Well, if it isn't Elizabeth Anne Pillsbury. How are you, Liza?"

The gathered fell silent, sensed something, something more interesting than wine in water pitchers and charcuterie.

"Dixon?" Through her shocked confusion, Liza played pleasantly surprised well. "Dixon?" She patted Amanda's arm, promised, "We'll talk more," and, gazing upon the doctor, glided to us and asked, "So, this is Katrina?"

I placed a hand on the doctor's shoulder and claimed, "It is. And we're deeply in love. Aren't we, love?"

Everyone leaned, waited, watched.

"So in love," the doctor—Yes Squad worthy—replied placing a hand on mine, "that sometimes I can't believe how happy I am. It almost makes me sick."

"Is that what happened," Liza observed, smelling blood, "to your nose? Sickness? Or, more likely, cosmetic?"

The ladies' eyes locked, grappled Greek style.

The doctor's nails bit my hand as excited whispers ran round the table.

Past the pain, I exhaled, "I'll take the bullet. It's the least I can do for such lovely pills." I pecked her cheek and straightened. "So, Saint Pierre? This is your little sister venture, is it?" Liza, reluctant, extracted herself from the doctor's hold and spun on me. I, oiled and ready to go, did as promised, "And Ro-Ro? How is he? Still dabbling in Bitcoin and other bitches' britches?"

The group's gasp was drowned by Liza's slap, the short, sharp retort of palm on cheek.

In the startled silence, the *smack* echoed off one floor-to-ceiling window after another, after another, after another.

Ignoring the embers of arousal, I sipped, waited for the echo to die, and, briefly, considered apologizing. Instead, "Well, I'll take that as a yes."

Liza, predator to prey, searched for an escape. Prepared to flee, she stilled as a tall, dashing man in a dark suit sans tie swaggered out the employee entrance.

"Ah," I observed, my remorse extinct, "speak of the necrophiliac."

Roland St. Fer, a contented cat, patting shoulders, giving nods and smiles, curled through the room toward us.

I didn't like admitting it, but he looked taller, tanner, more chiseled, healthier, and happier than last I saw him. Though it had been winter, maybe his contentment couldn't be ascribed to Liza or being a multimillionaire with smoldering good looks? I mean, a little Vitamin D could go a long way.

From the edge of their seats the group watched and waited, as I extended my hand, "Monsieur St. Fer, as per usual, your timing is impeccable."

"Is it?" he said, automatically taking my hand, nodding magnanimously to the group, and realizing, "Belltower?"

"Indeed. And note, I have just besmirched your good name and implicated you in cheating on," I indicated Liza with a nod, "your lovely bride with corpses."

Liza and St. Fer shared a strained smile, which likely explained some of the sincerity behind her slap, his looking healthier, happier.

"And," St. Fer, searching for solace, asked, "what do you think of the estate Pinot?"

All verged on disclosure, but I declared, hoisting my glass, "An absolute marvel. Sublime and nuanced. Earthy, though not overwrought. It's impeccable. But with such inspiration so near," I again indicated Liza, "I imagine one must always wish to mirror such perfection?" The silence grew taut, and I plucked at it. "I should think Parker gave it a ninety-five or ninety-six?"

St. Fer leaned and confessed, "A ninety-one, *le petit merde*."

"Much like me, I fear."

He stepped back and, rubbing the glistening shoulder of his chin, appraised my fragile, blue-and-black visage, "*Et pourquoi?*"

I explained not selling the property to RoEl Unlimited.

His unconcerned shrug, his "*C'est la vie*," wasn't enough. Not nearly. I'd been Caesar; for a change, I'd be Brutus. "Parker was generous."

Liza, sensing the escalation, said, "Dixon, don't."

"Eliza?" St. Fer queried glancing furtively between she and me.

Had he not whisked her away, I'd not have met Katrina, aka Kelsey, aka Madame von Klit, and Paris would've remained a city of light and love, rather than fire, pain, and giant genitals.

"Please?"

But, because she could be blamed as much as he, I didn't.

"The estate Pinot is cloying and cautious. It panders, not to," fully engaged in the role, I glanced to the doctor, "ethereal heights, but ignorant insights. You know," I nodded at Liza, "inspiration and all that. At best an eighty-two. At best."

The group, mouths agape, stared bewildered, amused, and confused. Did they berate the verdict or applaud the honest tenacity of the judge?

St. Fer considered a rebuttal, though instead gave a defeated shrug to Liza and, to my consternation, marched off mumbling soft, French epithets.

Liza spun on me, an appraising smile draped like a vampire's cape across her lips.

I didn't have a wooden stake. I sipped and hoped death would be quick and painless.

"Well," she said, going for the jugular, utilizing an ill advised confession I'd drunkenly disclosed one eve, "I hope she can suck your cock like Shannon." She slashed another scimitar smile at the doctor and walked away.

Dismayed, Gregory slumped in his chair, "Do you know who they are?"

"Wait," Jennifer asked, perplexed, "did she say Shannon?"

"Besides pretentious assholes?" Taking a deep breath, I admitted, "I do know who they are. And likely, Gregory, better than you."

"And," Amanda waved a ring-heavy hand around, indicating the fecund hovel of the winery, "do you know we're investors in this?"

It was impossible to discern if she'd meant it as a point of pride or recognition of guilt. It did explain why they kept returning.

"Scott," Jennifer quipped, "your mother's name is Shannon."

"Yes, honey, I'm aware of that."

"But didn't you say it was Matt she'd—"

"No," Scott snapped, glancing a glare at Matt, "he claimed it was a hand job."

"See," Kevin said to Matt, "I told you, you weren't the only one."

"Do you," Matt replied, while Colin and Brenda bit their tongues, "ever keep your mouth shut?"

"Yes. All the time."

"Really?" Matt was dubious.

Emboldened by another sip, Jennifer zinged, "Like when your cock is in his mouth?"

Rather than explain Kevin's mouth would be open to accommodate Matt's cock, Scott piped up, "Sweetheart, that's a bit crude, yeah?"

"This," Matt confessed, unaware of his hypocrisy, "coming from someone who'd bragged about being so deep muff diving you had to 'breathe through your butthole like a dolphin'?"

Jennifer spun on Scott. "Who the hell did you—?" And to the table, "Not once has he eaten me out. Not once."

"It's a friggin' rainforest down there. I'd need a machete to—"

"So who the fuck was she?"

Before he lied, his eyes had disclosed the truth with a glance to Amanda.

"You've got to be shitting me," Gregory decried. "That putz was your Orlando fling?"

"What?" Jennifer shouted.

"Yeah," Gregory, utilizing a finger and a fist for visuals, admitted, "he let her—"

None offered a superlative, so I obliged, "Peg the poop chute?"

After Jennifer asked, "Why is that different than when Matt and I double-teamed you?" the proceedings devolved quickly.

Chairs squeaked and squealed across the marble floor, as everyone stood and shouted accusations at one another.

"So," I asked the doctor, "what's a therapist like you doing in a winery like this?"

She, as the ruckus grew, replied, "Same as you, I suppose. Needing entertainment."

We turned and watched the show.

Amanda pointed accusingly at Jennifer. Jennifer returned the favor with both middle fingers. Scott and Gregory, pushing one another, were involved in an intricate dance of "I dare you." Matt was shouting at Brenda about her telling Gregory what he'd told her in the "strictest of confidence," while Kevin and Colin stared longingly at one another.

"You're not going to stop them?" I asked, appreciative of such restraint.

The doctor shook her head. "Sometimes you have to get through the ugly on your own."

"You sound like every chick's mother."

"Excuse me? Chick? Isn't that.... Oh, like a baby bird?"

"I wonder," I said as Jennifer shoved Gregory out of the way to get to Amanda, "if we'd be more appreciative if we had to fight for it rather than be thrown into it."

Gregory stumbled into Scott, who took offense and pushed back. Gregory collided with Jennifer who ran into Amanda. Matt, exacerbated by Brenda, moved to do some peacekeeping. He was late. Scott was raising a fist, pulling his arm back to punch Gregory. Scott's elbow, however, plowed into Jennifer's nose as she wrestled with Amanda. Jennifer screamed in agony but tightened her headlock on Amanda. Blood, from Jennifer's nose, streamed over both the ladies and slicked the marble more.

Kevin and Colin extended a handful of black bev naps toward the combatants.

Gregory and Scott, blindly swinging fists at one another, attempted to separate the ladies. The ladies, each with a handful of someone's hair, staggered in a tight tornado.

Realizing the danger, I grabbed a pitcher.

Rapha, aware the impending catastrophe, had fled the table he'd been educating and arrived in time to snatch the other three carafes.

Smartly, in unison, we stepped back.

Slipping, sliding in the blood, groping and grabbing one another for leverage and balance, in a giant bundle of flailing limbs, they slammed into the table. The slate slabs, the cheese and charcuterie, the glasses, everything, crashed to the floor.

Limbs entangled, the five sprawled across the floor, grappling and grunting.

Hoisting the carafe in a victory salute, I declared, "I owe you."

Rapha acknowledged, "Yes, you do," and, with a slight bow, exited.

The doctor and I, fleeing the fiasco, serpentined through the other tasters as they gathered, crowded for a view, phones recording the festivities.

Unlike a Crushed event, none, to my disappointment, were placing bets. I may not like her, but I would've put a twenty down on Amanda.

Crossing the stream, we slowed, and I topped our glasses off with the last of the dark mélange. Tucking the carafe behind a fern, I asked, "Dr. Montgomery, may I call you Megan?"

"You may. But with a caveat."

"Go on."

"Don't overuse it."

"May I—"

"Or abuse it."

I *tinked* her glass. "I can indeed agree to that, Megan."

A fist of the back-of-house crew in their stained whites charged from the employee entrance bolted for the knotted mass of flailing limbs.

We slipped through a glass door onto a wide balcony that wrapped around the building.

Shouting, shattering glass erupted.

The door closed, decapitated the cacophony, and we found ourselves in a sudden oasis of silence and fresh air.

We stumbled past the dark, stoutly cushioned couches and chairs, the gas fire pits to the glass railing. Catching our breaths, we, to the subdued *thump, thump* of the unfolding scuffle, fought the urge to turn and took a moment and contemplated the undulating expanse of the valley.

"Have you," I asked, killing the quiet, "ever been to Tuscany?"

"I haven't."

"That's too bad, but," I added, waving a dismissive hand at the hillsides, "let it be known, this looks nothing like it."

Chapter Twenty-Six
SWINGING INTO THE UNEXPECTED

The taxi's abrupt argument with the gravel pushed Megan and I from the quixotic equilibrium we'd established after overindulging at Tapas Picas, a little cantina with cheap beer, excellent *mole*, and better hand-rolled tortillas, and Megan's favorite spot

In the gnarled thunderstorm, we realized the chariot had a destination and our delusion of permanence was exactly that, a delusion. We had a decision to make.

"Shall we keep it professional?" I asked as we slowed to a stop.

She nodded and held out a hand. "I think it best."

From a jacket pocket, I extracted the wrinkled lump of bills and offered it. "I've another thousand or so inside. So very, very professional." She laughed, and I added, "Maybe a slice of deep dish?"

"I hope that's not an innuendo. It's not, is it?"

"No. Though it was made by Troy."

"Troy? You mean," she pointed to her bandaged nose, "this Troy?"

"Yes, that Troy."

Gazing over my shoulder, she took a moment to consider the consequences and, shaking her head, said, "Maybe another time."

"Okay," I tried not sounding as disappointed as I was. Time alone implied time to contemplate everything I didn't want to contemplate.

Pushing the door open, Megan placed a hand on my arm, "I would, but someone's waiting for you."

Mini-Nazis hell-bent on revenge? Vlad's rabid admirers' hell-bent on revenge? Or Kelsey's family, per usual, hell-bent on revenge?

"Who? How do you know?" I craned my neck for a glimpse of the killer, killers.

Parked in front of the walkway sat the innocuous sedan, while the mournful squeak of the porch swing rhythmically scratched the cold night air.

"Do you know who it is?" Megan asked.

"I do."

"And you know," she said, her therapist cap firmly returned, "you don't have to go if you feel threatened or in danger, right?"

"No. I do." I gave her a quick peck on the cheek and added, "Thank you. I had a nice time."

She sounded surprised and agreed, "You know, I did too."

"Well, perhaps another time?"

"Perhaps. Perhaps."

I handed the driver a few bills, told her the standard "keep the change" and climbed out.

The crunch of the taxi's tires died and I, resigned, marched to beautiful Brutus.

Nearing, I glimpsed a curious glint in her hand.

"Belltower," she called out.

"Officer Tilden."

"*Il faut que'on parle.*"

"I believe you meant to say, you need to apologize." She didn't reply, and because it'd been a long-ass day, I sat on the swing, though at the opposite end.

The glint wasn't the 9mm but a bottle of bourbon. Thankful, I asked, "What are you doing here?"

"Drinking." To prove her point, she sipped and tapped the space next to her.

Complying, I scooted and observed, "My bourbon?"

"I got a text about you missing me."

"Oh. Right. Yeah."

"The front door was open. And not having found your ninja or mini-Nazi murdered corpse, I settled for the second-best thing." She sipped.

"Still, it's my bourbon."

"Technically, it's the IRS's."

"It was yakuza and cartel assassins. And—"

"Right. Your bourbon." She nudged me with the bottle, and I accepted it.

Was it prudent to add bourbon atop the day's other libations?

"Really? You're not drinking with me?" Before mentioning Megan, the Tecate and mezcal, or the winery, Officer Tilden added, "It better not be because I'm black."

"No," I scoffed, "It has everything to do with this morning and nothing with your color. Though maybe a little with how much catsup you use."

"Well, good. I apologize."

Sounding like Professor Magaldi, but not caring, I asked, "Now, please, with more sincerity?"

"Belltower, I'm sorry. I meant you no harm or injury." We both hesitated. She added, "But if it wasn't me, it would've been someone else. Better to have it done by someone who likes you, right?"

"Someone should've told that to the Italian border guards."

"What?"

"Nothing. Just... Nothing."

"Maybe," she said, reaching into the shadows beneath the swing, "this will help you forgive me?" She extracted a bottle and handed it to me.

In the thin, yellow light from the bug-browned porch light, I read, "Domaine Romanée-Conti, Romanée-Conti, 1971." Over the skipping of my ecstatic heart, I asked, "Where in the hell did... My father's cellar?"

"Yep. There are some amazing bottles in there."

"Oh, I know. I had the Lafleur. And the Petrus."

"I'm glad." And she meant it. "And they were good?"

Sadness welled in me as I admitted, "They were excellent." Though redacted the important part—they would've been superior with you.

Taking the bottle from me, Alicia returned it to the shadows from whence it came. "Now will you drink with me? Or are you afraid of ending up under a table?"

"For that, I'll do practically anything with you, under, on, or with a table."

Her smile grew mischievous. "You're not placing any limitations on me?"

"I'm less interested in limiting myself and my experiences and more interested in what you ask."

"Really?"

"If the request is genuine and not meant to humiliate. Or degrade. Then absolutely. Yes." She seemed befuddled at my sincerity. As proof, I pounded my chest with my right hand cupped in a C and declared, "I will never use what I know of you against you. This I swear." I pounded my chest twice more, repeated, "This I swear."

She shifted to quizzical mistrust.

I explained the difficulty in the Crushed world of making friends, fearing they'd use some personal insight or knowledge during competition. I repeated my vow, took a sip, and handed the bottle back.

She did the same, though I didn't have the heart to disclose it lacked validity until she'd been initiated as a full-fledged Crusher.

"So," I asked, past another sip, "Howitzer and Bald Submarine, they'll return?"

"Who?"

"The ICE agents."

"Oh, Rodgers and Cavanaugh?" She shook her head and shrugged, "Not likely. Two isn't worth their time. I mean, they were only here on Saunders' request, so—"

"Saunders, what a weasel-faced prick."

She laughed. "You have no idea."

"Probably not, but I know I could drink you under the table."

"But not out of my knickers?"

"You, I imagine, are not a knickers wearer."

She sidled closer and leaned against me. "Oh? And what do you imagine I wear?"

"Alicia, seriously, please, what the hell's going on?"

She snatched the bottle back. "What, you're not attracted to me?"

I snatched it back. "Very much so. It's just—" I held the bottle out of her reach. She kept reaching for it, while I admitted, "Alicia, everyone is attracted to you." I took a quick sip and gave it back, "But few believe they can handle you."

"I work out," she confessed, tapping her sides. "No love handles here."

"You know what I mean."

"I'm not worth the trouble?"

"I'm saying—" I fell silent. She handed me the bottle. I sipped and plowed on. "I'm saying, someone would need to have their shit together, because you seem to."

"Maybe," she scoffed, "Maybe not."

"And if they didn't, you'd intimidate them. Or see through their bullshit. Or something like that." I took another sip and ended with, "But, if it helps, I think you'd be worth the trouble."

"It does." She, a self-defense class maneuver, swung a leg over and straddled me.

"Well, hello, Miss Alicia."

"Hello to you, too, Mr. Dixon." She wiggled, adjusted herself, became more comfortable and me less so. "And hello to?" She smiled and wiggled more. The swing creaked more.

"It is, and shall remain, nameless. Anthropomorphizing such an appendage—"

Her lips crashed headlong into mine; mine into hers. Tongues, sweet and tainted with bourbon, slipped and slid around. Our hands gripped and groped and... And I hesitated, pulled back.

"Is it," Alicia asked, haloed by the sallow yellow porch light, "Dr. Montgomery?"

"No," I said, knowing it wasn't, but unsure exactly what it was. "No."

Alicia rolled off, "Is it because I'm—"

"What? No. No. No. I've been with women of—" Before digging an unnecessary grave for myself, I asked, "What were you going to say?"

"No. Please. After you. What were *you* going to say?"

We swung and the night's crispness, the chill crept in, enhanced the spell of her enticing proximity.

We passed the bottle back and forth, took small sips, and swung.

"Okay. I thought you were going to say something about being black, or African American, or—"

She, shaking her head, laughed.

I took the bottle before she spilled it, or worse, dropped it.

"So, were you going to lay out your rainbow of conquests as proof of... of what?"

"No. I just... I want you to know I don't care about the label, but what's inside the bottle. Beauty is beauty."

She repeated her earlier performance of straddling me.

I juggled the bottle, nearly dropped it.

Once we'd rediscovered our previous equilibrium, she suggested, "Sergeant Firm?"

"What? Oh, you mean?"

She squeezed, smiled, and nodded, "I do."

"No."

"Pepper Grinder?"

"No," I laughed, "No."

She ran a finger over my chest, found a nipple, squeezed it gently, and asked my smiling grimace, "You still have that syrup, right?"

I, without regret, surrendered and confessed, "I do."

"And the jellies and jams?"

"How about, first," I said, to my erection's disappointment and nipples glee, "you tell me what you were going to say?"

"It was nothing." Ignoring her lie, our lips crashed into one another again. This time though, before tongues slipped and slid, she pulled away. "Oh. Oh, fuck. Oh."

To my ear, and disappointment, she didn't sound aroused. She sounded distressed.

As confirmation, she hurriedly wobbled off.

"Alicia? You okay? Alicia?"

She staggered a step. Something, after a sharp tink, shattered. And she, with the loss, dropped her head into a shrub and became sick.

The sublime, delicate, buttery, purple-fruit richness of the Romanée-Conti wafted around us, and, thankfully, overrode what Alicia watered the shrub with.

The bottle's broken glass sparkled in the porch light, while the wine, all that effort and time, languidly seeped into the shadows below the bush.

Promising, nay, vowing to kick fate between the legs someday, I took her hand.

She squeezed tightly and mumbled something else.

I placed my other hand upon her back, comforting, and, because I too had had my head in many a bush, I reassured, "It's going to be okay. It's going to be okay."

Chapter Twenty-Seven
FURY AND FORGIVENESS

First, the brothers and I heard Alicia's cursing. Second, was her clumsy clambering as she stumbled from bed. Accompanied, of course, by more cursing. Third, was the rapid stomping and slamming of a door. Lastly, footsteps pounding down the stairs, down the hall, and into the kitchen.

"Hey, asshole," she called as she steamed in holding a clump of her vomit-fouled hair in a fist, "why didn't you—" Spotting Egan and Julio, she pulled to a quick stop. "Hi."

They raised their steaming mugs of coffee, while I made an introduction, of sorts, "Since you nearly killed them, I believe you know the Brothers Carapaz, Egan and Julio?"

She sported her usual allure and the same clothes, dark jeans and blouse with a white undershirt peaking out, though barefoot.

The brothers and I were seated around the kitchen corner table, stained breakfast plates pushed aside, each with a newly filled mug.

Alicia smiled warily.

I'd warned the brothers about ICE, though I'd kept Alicia's connection and involvement unmentioned.

Nonplussed, they'd nodded sagely.

"It's to be expected."

"Why wouldn't a king enlist a dragon to guard his gold?"

More than a few reasons had come to mind, but I'd understood Julio's point and I'd not recited Cummings' "me up at does."

"Yes," Alicia said, "I do remember them. Hello. And good morning."

They replied in kind, though behind their smiles a peculiar reticence lingered.

After a heartfelt apology, which they accepted, Alicia, walking away, insisted, "Can I talk to you?"

With a shrug to the Carapaz's amused grins, I excused myself and followed.

Egan, playfully, said, "*Comandante*, we shall clean up in here."

"And begin," Julio added, less playful and more sarcastic, "slaving in the vineyard."

I had a few choice retorts, but was joining Alicia in the living room, and cursing the bright morning light.

We retreated to the movie cabinet's darkened corner, and I, hiding my amusement behind the mug, asked, "You wanted to talk?"

"I don't recall much." She frowned and added, "But I know you didn't hold my hair back." Before I could enlighten, she'd extricated her fingers from the tangled messy-mass and waved them around. "Asshole."

I stepped back as she flung the coagulated goop at me. It splattered dull, Rorschachian across my chest and dribbled in wet lumps to the carpet. *Splat. Splat.*

I gazed into Alicia's sleep-deprived, puffy, red eyes. "Do you perhaps recall what I said about being with you?"

"We did not hook up. Did we?"

Believing she wouldn't be receptive to embellishment, regardless how satisfying the tale, I clarified, "The difficulty?"

"Oh, right. That. Yes, I do."

"Of the four women I'm certain that had African heritage, you," I did a slight and soft "Wahoo" with a gentle, festive hand waving, "happen to be the only one to be sick in my presence. I, therefore, reverted to Wanda's advice—"

"That bitch Sykes, again?"

"Not to touch your hair."

"Oh. Well, still—" Alicia stared into her grime glistening palm. Thankfully, Wanda may've been correct.

"Did you look in the bathroom?" She shook her head. A bit of sick splatted to the carpet. "After you do, I'll expect another apology. And then you can join us for—"

"Screw that. I'm starving. Quick rinse. Right back."

While I cleaned the bourbon stenched splotches from my chest and the carpet, the brothers tackled the kitchen.

On my return they were gone. If they were "slaving" I didn't know and didn't like the implication. Regardless, I had the inclination to check messages. All four were of the same nature, my "friends" blaming and berating me for the ruckus at the winery, their subsequent injuries, and expenses.

Alicia, hair glistening, walked in and interrupted my brooding. She pecked my cheek, settled in front of the plate I'd prepared for her, and said, "You're a sweetheart," before she, unapologetically, polluted it with a heavy squirting of hot sauce and catsup.

On her second bite, I asked, "So, what did you want to discuss last night?" She stopped chewing and stared. "I assume there was something more besides getting it on with Max Power?"

"Who?"

With a crooked finger, I indicated the beast lurking beneath the table.

She smiled, sipped at her coffee, sighed, and confessed, "I'm wondering if I can ask a favor?"

"After you broke that Romanée-Conti? I think you owe me."

Agony etched her face, "I did what?"

She was too beautiful, and it was too early, to confront such loss. I redirected, "You stayed. Why?"

She hesitated.

"Because of Saunders?"

"Because of my great-grandfather."

"Okay. Not the reply I expected. Tell me more."

"He competed during Prohibition. He was a street taster. This was before Eugenio... Oh. You know, don't you?"

I nodded. "I do. Eugenio simply formalized it. Made it more palatable to the middle class." As she nodded, I observed, "So, Saunders thought you could exploit that, if your beauty and gentle prodding didn't work?"

"Something like that. Yes."

"Okay. So who was your grandfather?"

"Great-grandfather. Malcolm Freeman. And so Saunders—"

"Wait. Wait." Confused, I interrupted, "Your great-grandfather was Malcolm Freeman?" She nodded. "*The* Malcolm Freeman? The first man of color to win a World Championship? Well, unofficially. I mean... *That* Malcolm Freeman?"

"No. No," she said, shaking her newly rinsed head, "not that one, the other one."

Her deadpan delivery was perfect, "Fine. Fine. Stupid question. But go on."

She explained, Malcolm's last few years were with her and he'd taught her, besides a few tasting tricks, the love of wine. "Though, it being rural Georgia and my ma, her words, 'the best kind of Southern Baptist—sober and austere,' didn't take kindly to the bottle, of any sort."

"Not even baby?" I asked.

"You're funny," she smiled back.

"Well," I admitted, "looks aren't everything." For more comic relief, I added, "And you haven't even seen my penis. Yet." She sighed, disappointed or disgusted, quite likely both. It reminded me of someone I'd been adequately forgetting—Katrina. No, no, Kelsey. Kelsey Anne Conrad of Billings, Montana. Not... Shit, I was going to need a Megan pill, and sooner than expected.

"I'm sorry," I said, disappointed and disgusted with myself, "but I know little about my father and nothing regarding his taxes."

"Oh," she admitted, placing her mug down and returning her fork to the hot sauce and catsup contaminated plate, "I know that now."

"So?"

"So," she said, laden fork hovering, "I'd like to work for you."

I stared, more confused than before. "What do you mean? Work for me?"

"On the vineyard," she admitted after a swallow with a smile, adding, "With Egan and Julio."

"They don't work for me. They—" I trailed off. Oh. "*Comandante.*" They'd worked for my father. My father was dead. I now owned the vineyard. Egan and Julio worked in the vineyard. Therefore, QED, they worked for me. Somehow, as accurate as it was, it sounded incorrect. Past a confused frown, I asked, "You're sure they'll want to work with you?"

"Excuse you? Because I'm black?" Her fork knocked the plate's lip, added an exclamation to her question.

"No, no, no," I said, hands waving away any offense that may've lingered in the air. "No. I mean, you are."

"Obviously."

"But you did try to kill them." Her glare was ringed with sadness. "Ok, I'll stop."

"It would be appreciated." She shot a few hesitant glances as she poked at the eggs.

"No, it's just that they know you work for the government. They're liable to be less than excited."

"Well, I'm not investigating them."

"Hey, you don't have to convince me." She sighed, stabbed the eggs more. "And, honestly, I think they'd appreciate the help." She remained dubious. Tired of watching the torture, I asked, "So you'd leave the agency?"

"Yes."

"Big step?"

"Yes."

I was, of course, curious why she'd be willing to jump here and now. However, rather than confront the obligation of an unspoken expectation, I went with repeating platitudes. "It'll be okay. It'll all work out."

"And," she asked, returning the fork to work, "you believe that?"

"God no. Sentimental tripe."

I turned from her surprise, her gorgeous, earth-brown eyes and spotted Egan and Julio loping up the drive. "Hey, there they are. Why don't you go ask them?"

"What do you mean?"

"I mean, go ask them."

She frowned.

"Ask them if you can work for them." She stared. I explained, "They, if they don't already, will run this place."

The explanation wrinkled her brow. The fork wavered, and I expounded, "Alicia, I'm not inclined to grow anything. I mean—" Was that disappointment at the edges of her lips? I did want to grow something, and more than Max Power. But it was nigh too soon to consider something with her, wasn't it? I veered from insight and declared, "Drink, yes. Grow, no." To the beginning of rebuttal, I held up a firm hand. "I love wine. But it's the mystery I love. I don't need to peek behind the curtain."

She considered arguing, but I shook my head. "Go ask them." My phone had an epileptic fit across the table. "Go. And if they say no, tell the bastards they're fired."

Laughing, she stood and again pecked my cheek.

"Thank you," she said with surprising sincerity, before marching out the back door, calling out to the brothers.

Past the clatter and clang of the door's shutting, the growing apprehension of my heart, I rubbed at my cheek and answered the flailing phone.

I was greeted with... "Hey, Heavy Breather, hello. Glad you called. Have I got news." Past their breathing, I disclosed the news of Mother and Aori marrying and moving to Kauai, the insight into Alicia's great-grandfather, the surprise of Troy and his pizza, and, finally, how I'd been howling with someone, who, I speculated, "It's likely Aori. But I'm not sure. Interesting though, right? Right?"

They heavy-breathed in agreement.

I thanked them, hung up, and peeked out the window.

Alicia had caught the brothers. She said something. They laughed. She said something else. They stepped away, huddled in consultation. After a moment, they started up the slope with an inviting wave. With a clap and skip, Alicia followed.

Because I was being monitored, the phone rang.

Realizing I'd neglected to mention the tragedy of the broken Romanée-Conti, I answered, "Heavy Breather, I forgot to mention—" There was heavy breathing, but this was strained and, though I loathed the word, it was accurate, sorrowful. "Hello?"

"Dixon?"

"Sancho?"

"*Sí.*"

Considering his default demeanor, unconditionally optimistic, one of the many reasons we could never fuck, he sounded sad and forlorn. I ascribed it to the time difference and was struck with inspiration, "You and Art should visit. I know its Pinot Noir land, but there are a few decent wineries here."

There was something more than fatigue in his silence.

I hesitated. Why pet a cat if you knew it would scratch you?

And that was the silence—Mother returned from the vet, watching Tabitha flee from the carrier and into the kitchen for her kibble.

"Mom?" I'd asked to her vacant stare as I patted a thigh with my dog eared copy of *Rosencrantz and Guildenstern are Dead*.

She, as kitty crunched on kibble, yanked a bottle from a splayed, cardboard box and, marching into the kitchen, announced, "She has leukemia. Happy?"

Having learned nothing, I asked, "Sancho, what's wrong?"

Instead of a warning, of providing a cigarette or blindfold, he simply pulled the trigger, "Art's dead."

With Tabitha, we had three months to snuggle and pet and spoil before a final trip to the vet was required. With this, I had nothing, except my frustration. "What? What are you talking about?"

"Art's dead, Dixon. He had a heart attack. He's dead." Sancho cried. His sobs filled the phone and my heart.

Rather than settle on my second favorite stage of the Kubler-Ross grieving model, anger, I skipped to my contribution, Number 6, lying. "It's going to be okay. It's going to be okay."

I'd wanted to believe what I'd told Alicia with her head in the shrub, or at the table moments ago, and now with Sancho, but I didn't. I didn't believe it. And yet I kept saying it. "It's going to be okay. It's going to be okay." As if the repetition would manifest the impossible. "It's going to be okay."

I calibrated the time by the sunlight's angle and discovered it no longer held merit or mattered. Any time was a good time for a drink.

Once Sancho had fallen silent, had cried himself out, and couldn't carry on, I added, "You're not alone in this. Just let me know how I can help and I will. Okay?"

"Okay."

"Okay."

I hung up and stared around the chicken-infested kitchen. It was too soon to understand the magnitude of Art's passing, but I knew it catastrophic. After he'd retired from the circuit, he'd become not just my confidant but my mentor. He was the closest thing, since Josiah, I had had to a father, unless you counted Mother, which many did.

Even with all those stupid chickens staring at me, I knew what I'd do. It was, however, less like doing and more like observing the fire rather than being consumed by it.

First, he placed the phone, a thin, sleek, silver thing, in the sink's disposal. After placing a red, cast iron soup pot over it, he turned the disposal on. The metallic screaming sounded remotely like the pain reverberating within him.

Once the phone had been shredded, the disposal ground to a smoking stop, he descended into the cellar to select the choicest... He stopped. He stared at the racks. Like his heart, they were empty.

He remembered Beautiful Brutus's betrayal, and his sorrow doubled, trebled, as he realized he'd be descending into oblivion, not with layered *grand crus*, but blunt bourbon.

Forlorn and devastated, dragging his sorrow, a long, dark chain, behind him, he returned upstairs where he collected a jacket and scarf off the coat rack. He slunk them on and, with a grimace, hoisted the bourbon-bottle laden tote bag over a shoulder.

On his way through the living room, he grabbed an aquamarine blanket from the couch and, out the French doors, stepped into the day that would be his last.

He selected the approximate center of the vineyard, where the two tractor paths intersected, north-south, east-west. The crossroads was fragranced with the earthy mustiness of damp dirt and grass, wildflowers, and a wilted, old rose bush at the end of a row. The standard bugs, much to his annoyance, flitted here and there.

Snuggling into the thin shell of the blanket, his sobs emptied him, more and more and more.

Determined, he finished the bottle from the other night, no, last night. Regardless, it delivered him to his desired destination—unconsciousness.

Later, he didn't know when, an odd purring, a somnolent growl of a prehistoric tiger, grew closer and closer.

Pulling the blanket back, he squinted into the bright, afternoon sun.

The scene resembled a 1980s Japanese anime interpreting a 1970s Spaghetti western. A scrawny coyote sniffed his ankle, found it too fouled for nibbling, and chose to urinate on it. Two vultures, perched on posts, watched bemused, agreeing with the coyote's decision.

Resigned to accommodating the coyote, the man put a new bottle to his lips.

The vultures, curious, perhaps envious, leaned closer, their eyes blinked in unison. He toasted his reflection and drank again.

Nearing, the growling tiger startled the vultures. They, with furtive, forceful claps of their wings, struggled into the azure sky.

Finished with his toilet, the coyote gave a final, satisfied sniff of the sodden cuff and trotted off.

The growl had grown to such a pitch even he, fatigued and intoxicated, could no longer ignore it.

He suckled on the bottle and rolled over as the ravenous tiger, blocking the sun's angry eye, charged over him.

With the sharp snap of bone, I, so disappointed, slammed screaming back into my broken, abused body.

In quick succession, I threw one bottle, then another. They shattered and stenched the pristine afternoon air with bourbon. They also caused the green beast to chuff to a slow idle.

"¡Dios mio!" Julio exclaimed, horrified, jumping down and staring at the jagged, blood-streaked bone accusing from my leg.

Descending into shock, I fumbled the last bottle from the chicken tote. It's cork fought me, tooth and nail. Before I sobbed, defeated, Julio, pale as a midday moon, snatched it and opened it.

After a long, long suckle, he handed it back.

Having mimicked his suckle and recalled a previous proclamation pertaining to a similar situation, I repeated to the bone and blood, "Well, fuck me."

Julio, taking the bottle back, scrutinizing the circling vultures, replied, "*No, gracias, comandante. No, gracias.*"

Chapter Twenty-Eight
A BIGGER, BRIGHTER, BETTER PITY PARTY

"You're sure you're going to be okay?" Alicia asked, worried and concerned, from the loft's doorway.

"Here, there, any and everywhere," I proclaimed, "'tis the same during such days of want and woe." I'd been blathering poetic since Julio, after his second gulp of bourbon, rolled me, the bottle, and my shattered tibia into the tractor's scoop.

In response to such eloquence, a Darth Vader ringtone doomed from her pocket. With a glance and grimace at the ID, she, turning her back, answered.

The Brothers Carapaz, the major movers in transitioning me from below to above, were tucking the last of the refilled storage boxes in a corner.

"Why and what for dost thou wish to cast me to such barbarous lands?" I'd queried Alicia and the hospital's therapist, Ms. Vanessa York.

"Not necessarily for fear of you harming yourself," Ms. York had insisted.

"But just," I'd countered, indicating the distance with thumb and forefinger, "a wee bit of a little?"

"No. But for ease and convenience of care." She'd turned to Alicia, who, embarrassed, had smiled and explained the dangers of hobbling downstairs or in and out of a claw-footed tub.

The curved, new-age crutches returned their canines to chewing my underarms as I swung from the elevator and discovered my father's loft wasn't as barbarous as imagined.

It was a chic, modern, and Viennese-like penthouse suite, which included a flat-screen HDTV, an Ascaso espresso machine, a California king-size, down comforter covered, mahogany, Swedish-styled bed, and expansive valley views.

Besides incorporating the gravity feed system's elevator, it also had a walk-in shower and sauna.

Alicia remained on the phone as the brothers slipped past, each patting my shoulder, offering their concerns and condolences.

"You brothers are a good pair and I would care, someday soon, to share a glass or two with you."

"*Sí. Sí*," Julio agreed, guilt continuing to stain his words.

"Whatever you need, *comandante*," Egan offered, "we'll bring it to you."

"A gallant offer, though the lass to your left I would be bereft if she did not deliver it herself."

"Eat a dick, asshole," the lass did declare, stabbing the phone with a finger. The brothers and I turned. Frowning, Alicia glared. "What?"

"Forgive me, sweet princess, but didst thou—"

"Oh, just drop it. What do you want?"

"Did not the fair Ms. York—"

"Suggest we humor you?"

"I am rather heavily sedated, though am fairly certain she did say something to such effect." The brothers nodded in agreement.

"Stop that. You weren't even there."

"No, but they're supporting their *comandante*. ¿*Sí*?" The brothers returned to nodding. "So, what's going on?"

"I've got to go back to DC."

"Why?"

"To kick some boys in the balls." Egan and Julio stepped back. "And that weasel-faced prick—" Again, Egan and Julio stepped back. "Stop that."

"Saunders?"

"He's got me on a flight first thing Wednesday morning. Tomorrow morning."

"Maybe, *comandante*, we should—"

"Stop calling him—"

"So, today's Tuesday?" I asked, neither interested in the question nor its answer.

"It is. And... Where are you going?"

"What?" I turned. The three, still at the door, were a few crutch-lurches farther away. "Just getting a head start." They shared a few confused glances. "Egan, because the other two have failed, I believe it's your turn to try and kill me? Shall we say Friday?"

"*¿Que?*"

Alicia leaned to the brothers and whispered something.

The brothers laughed, waved, and, forsaking the tediously slow elevator, clattered down the steel stairway.

Alicia stared, her soft smile wary and melancholy. "If you need anything, text me. Or call."

"Really? Because last I recall...."

She laughed. "Anything. Anytime. Text. Or call."

I might be at 35,000 feet on painkillers, but I was confident in reading the innuendo correctly.

"It's too bad I don't have—"

With a nudge of the chin, she indicated an unboxed, gleaming-white phone on the glass coffee table. "It's all ready to go."

"Great."

"Yeah." Somehow the practical had veered us from the romantic.

"Well," she said, fidgeting with the sedan's key fob, "get some rest."

"And you enjoy DC."

"Not likely."

"Yeah." And somehow the future had undermined the present.

"Well... bye."

"Bye."

She closed the door and, like the brothers, took the stairs. Her footsteps were hollow exclamations on my disappointment.

Damn, we needed to work on our goodbyes, they were horrible.

On the inside of the door hung a red and white metal plaque with a stylized portrait of Gary Oldman. It declared, "Keep Calm and Garry On."

Alicia's clatter died, the metal door clanged shut, and the soft, gravely crunch of footsteps faded into the distance.

Too tired to cry, I stared around, and sincerely asked, "What would Gary do?"

Sitting on the couch, suckling a bottle of Noah's Mill bourbon, I was midway into Episode 12 of Season 3, when the familiar *thump* of the downstairs door interrupted.

In a cupboard crowded with board games I'd opened on my brief quest for something red and winey, I'd discovered a box set of *Sex in the City*.

Revisiting the ladies, particularly with bourbon, I'd lost track of time. Based on x minutes per y episodes equating to z hours, I hypothesized it was likely Friday. And, with the last, wavy vestiges of pinks and oranges consumed by darkness, it was early in the evening.

I pressed pause and, with growing consternation, waited as the lazy bastard took the elevator. Its somnolent hum only trebled my consternation, anxiety, trepidation, and etc.

The elevator sighed reluctantly to a stop. The doors, approximating the same sigh, opened. And, after five quick strides, shoes chirping like chipmunks, the interloper's knocking erupted.

Having rehearsed since the *thump*, I delivered my lines perfectly, with conviction and condemnation. "Goddamn it, go away." They knocked more. "Go away!"

I knew the asshole was no one I wanted to talk with as the brothers, braving the ICE gauntlet, were attending a *quinceañera* and Alicia was in DC.

More knock, knock, knocking. It clattered poor, stern-eyed Gary.

Wobbling to my foot, I scooped up the crutches, hobbled for the door.

The past day or so, thanks to Carrie and her lovely cohorts, I'd been empowered to utilize the new phone, for good.

First, I'd called Naomi.

"So," I'd said, meaning it, "I'm sorry. Very."

Rather than the deserved rebuff, "You're a sniveling wanker and a twat," I'd been greeted with a gruff, "Go on."

And I had. I'd confessed, "*The Yank* was a *roman a clef*. I borrowed, no, sorry, stolen, most, no, sorry, the entire plot and incidents from a flatmate and my Aldi coworkers."

"It did seem a bit rich for such a milksop as you."

"And *The Jerk* is no more than a blur on my debilitated memory."

"Now tell me something I don't know."

"I'm SloPony42?"

"That sounded like a question. You forget the UK is the CCTV kingdom."

I laughed and asked, "And so?"

"Home Office is considering whether to punish or parole."

"Oh."

"Yeah. Assuming you'd like to return to the UK."

"Do I?"

She considered it and asked, "Do you have anything else?"

I'd soldiered on and pitched an anonymous tell-all of the dark underbelly of Crushed.

"And what's that?"

"It's the *Kumite*, the *Fight Club*, the MMA of wine tasting."

"I'm going to need more than that."

"Why?"

"Because it sounds stupid."

Desperate, I rambled into the void. I explained most of the history and some of the nuances of a competition. Ending, "I might know someone who could coauthor with me."

"That annoying reporter?"

"Yeah, Radcliffe." The silence returned. "Naomi?"

"You're a wanker and a twat, and if I don't have a proposal and the first chapter by the end of the month we will never speak again. Ever." It was my turn to linger in silence. Her voice's cold edge meant she meant it. "Is that understood?"

"It is. Yes."

"Good. Now leave me alone." And she hung up.

Emboldened by such success, I'd called Sancho.

"What do you want, Dixon?"

"I want to apologize."

"For what? And why?"

His tone was sharp and jagged, something I'd never heard from him. I hesitated.

"Dixon, what do you want?"

As with Naomi, I'd told him the truth. "It's not going to be okay. Yes, it'll get easier. And you can't help that. And it doesn't mean you care any less. It's just that asshole Time washing the pain into the past. But there'll be moments, for no reason, when shopping for breakfast items, or crossing a sun-dappled stream, or being assaulted by bees, you can't help but feel lonely and alone and helpless and as if you're drowning in despair." I fought the tears and continued. "And that's okay. Everyone does. Everyone. And if someone claims they don't, they're a wanker and a twat."

Past a soft chuckle, he asked, "You don't want anything?" He seemed confused, as I was with his question.

"Well, you to be happy."

"And nothing else?"

Except for Sancho, I knew nothing of Art's family. I could imagine how someone's passing could cause a rift in family relations. Hence, why my father's will was so incongruous—it was so easy. It was one of the few, the very few benefits of being a lone child.

"Dixon?"

"No. That's all. You happy. That'll do. Thank you." It was funny, not because I meant it, but because I'd never considered the same for myself. Odd. Though, considering my parents, maybe not? "Oh," I added as a middle finger to them, "and for you to know, if I can help, you just need to ask. Okay?"

"It's funny you should say that."

His tone implied it wasn't.

I'd gulped a bit more bourbon, slumped onto the maroon leather, Pedro Balducci loveseat, and echoed Naomi, "Go on."

"You're sure?"

From the Balducci, being in the loft's expansive, lone bedroom, I had a direct view of the glass-walled, walk-in shower. Ignoring the various Oedipal, incestuous ramifications of who likely enjoyed it, I declared, "No, but do so anyway."

He sighed a chuckle, and a silence limped in and collapsed between us. "Sancho?"

"People are making accusations."

"Okay." The silence remained, corpse-like. "What kind of accusations?" Over the years Art had related there'd been so many from so many over so many years, it'd become absurd. Literally. "Sancho?"

"That Art was assisting St. Fer."

"In cheating?" I hadn't gasped or shouted "Bullshit!" or... because it was outlandish. Impossible. Inconceivable. And yet.... It didn't matter. Art was dead. St. Fer defeated. And I was something I'd never been— content. "Sancho, just get out of Dodge." I then explained Dodge was a town and not a car, though it was.

"And go where?"

Adopting a quaint Russian accent, I offered, "There is mythical land. Greece. There is caldera view bungalow—" With everything remembered, my voice faltered, failed and, Icarus enflamed, fell. So I just said, "Or come here."

"I'd love to come there."

"Seriously. Think about it."

"Okay. I will."

"And if you need anything else," I added before hanging up, "let me know. Okay?"

"Okay."

After Sancho, before I'd lost momentum and regained my insanity, I'd called Radcliffe.

"What's going on? Why are you calling me?"

Ignoring his perfect parroting echo of me, I explained the basic premise of the proposal for a Crushed tell-all.

"That sounds somewhat similar to what I pitched you a few days ago."

"Is that a yes?"

"Things got messy here. London. Made the mistake of returning. I'll be over soon as I can. We can pound out whatever she wants then. So who's the agent?"

"So, you're saying yes?"

"I am. But I'll need something in writing and signed. Now who is she?"

"Naomi Waters. She's with—"

"Upton Ink & Associates. I know." He sounded impressed. "How'd you end up with her?"

"I'm that good in the sack." He laughed. "No. It's true. No joke." He hung up.

Between Season 2 and 3, the unsettling déjà vu of Mr. Big's disclosure had rattled me and I'd called Bussy.

"What," I'd asked Split, "are you his secretary?"

"Shut up, Yank. What do you want?"

"Uh, to talk to Bussy." I hadn't meant to sound so snotty, it was just natural. Though before I explained, he'd hung up. I called back. And again. And again.

Needing to postpone Mr. Big's and Natasha's wedding, I'd left three messages, each longer than the previous, explaining the situation with Home Office and giving my heartfelt apologies about, well, everything.

Another storm of knocking clattered the door, "Goddamn it, asshole, you're screwing my introspective buzz!"

I'd also had the audacity, aka stupidity, to browse a Crushed community board. A member, MommaMerlot87, had posted links to other sites that wanted my "head on a platter," "balls in a blender," or "fingers, toes, and teeth for a druid necklace."

The lone link I'd clicked, www.v3h.net, whisked me to Vlad's Vulfy Vulf Hounds, a self-ascribed group of Vlad fanatics. Their lone tenet was "bringing justice to the bourgeoisie proletariat pig-dog"—me.

Regardless of sounding like 18th-century French revolutionaries, they, like Vlad's other mourners, in solidarity, smeared their upper lips with peanut butter.

Acquiring my fill of the fringe, I visited the official unofficial Crushed website. I'd hoped for communal support and camaraderie. Instead, Art's passing had ignited a power struggle, and the chat rooms were rife with contention and accusation.

The unrest centered on the confirmation an unnamed production company affiliated with an undisclosed cable network wanted to broadcast competitions.

A group of Crushers, most major factions (Pinot Noirists, the bubble people, Chardonnayists, Merloans, Pinot Grisians, Chiantists, Syrahists, Cabernetists, et cetera), were pro "going mainstream."

My Malbecians had joined the Ameronians, Neuf-du-Papists, Sherries, Porters, and others, in aligning with a coterie of independents adhering to keeping Crushed true to its roots—"clandestine, free from corporate cash, and unsullied by snobs and pretentious posers."

I agreed with the sentiment of adhering to the founders' intentions and ideals, as well as the romantic concept of perpetuating history. However, overt adherence to antiquity, particularly when antiquated, was, so I felt, rather myopic.

Hobbling to the door, I glared at Gary. What crazed and maniacal lunatic lurked beyond? Had Egan taken me seriously regarding assassinating *el comandante*?

Another round of harried knocking startled me.

"I swear," I swore, "I'm going to punch you in the face!"

I fisted up and flung the door open.

Already sporting a broken nose, it'd be redundant to punch the woman, so I asked, "Why are you here?"

Megan moved past and seduced the bottle of Noah's Mill from me. "Please, no existentialism, particularly before you punch me in the face." She sipped from the bottle, fought the swallow with a grimace, then shoved the bottle back. "And it's good to see you too."

"Yeah," I agreed as she glanced around, "you too."

Impressed with the destruction I'd rendered in so short a time, I waved the bottle about and declared to the empty boxes, wrappers, and bottles littering the loft, "I've been self-healing."

"You mean medicating?"

"Do I?" She snatched the Noah's, took a swig, and marched around, while I explained. "English. American. British. Spelled the same, pronounced differently. Tomato. Tomato. Aluminum. Aluminum. Potato. Potato."

"What'd you do?" she asked my leg, handing the bottle back.

Sipping, I repeated, "Why are you here? Besides postponing Charlotte and Trey's wedding?"

She didn't ask, but I handed her the bottle.

She sipped then returned it. "Whose wedding?"

"Charlotte and Trey's." I pointed to the television, the frozen image of the ladies. Each with a bouquet of white roses, Charlotte in her wedding dress, moments before walking down the aisle. "I feel I'm on the verge of some insight regarding... Not important." We stared, confused. It was my turn to worry. "Megan, why are you here? Because you seem too frantic for this to be a booty call."

"It's Troy. He's going to do something crazy. Really crazy."

"Well, that clears things up. Thank you. Quick, to the Batmobile!" I handed her back the bottle and asked, "And really crazy? As opposed to partially?"

She, not sipping, handed the bottle back, "He's threatened to—"

She fell silent, snatched the bottle, sipped, and gave it back, as I finished her sentence, "To do something crazy?"

"Yes."

"Really crazy?"

"Oh," she sighed, "if only I had my mace."

"Would a battle axe do?"

She searched her pockets, and I pointed to the double-headed, two-handed battle axe mounted on the wall above the gas fireplace.

She, rightfully, ignored my victory. "He swore he was going to, and I quote, 'Go full Carrie.'"

Disappointed, I shook my head.

"What?"

"Oh," I declared, before returning the Noah to my lips, "if only I had a dollar for every time I've pulled a Carrie."

Chapter Twenty-Nine
THE BEAST RISES, AGAIN

I'd told myself, five times prior, to ignore the speedometer and keep an eye on the car, the pole, or the tree, Megan would plow us into. Perhaps I could fling myself—Geronimo!—from the wobbly, red Saab convertible before impact and it burst into a bright, beautiful ball of flame.

Shooting past a 25 mph speed limit sign, I glimpsed a four and a six on the Saab's green, digital speedometer. Being pressed against the window as we fishtailed around a roundabout, my tongue remained locked in the well of my mouth.

She straightened the complaining car out and over a slight ridge, I, for the first time in a long time, glimpsed my original arch nemesis— Aloha High School.

It wasn't so much that I'd disliked high school. I'd simply become embroiled, seduced, and Stockholmed into the angst of my fellow students and the general ennui of teachers and administration.

The great, gleaming beast loomed on the horizon and I, having planned never to set eyes upon the ill-omened beast again fell silent and brooded.

Bypassing a congested four-way stop, we sped through a Long John Silver's drive-thru. I gave a smart salute to the pimple-faced cashier, who returned a confused wave as they leaned from the window.

Nearing, massaging a palm, I recalled the first time I'd stepped onto Aloha High's main stage, under the proscenium, for *Our Town* auditions.

"A monologue? No, ma'am," I'd admitted with a coquettish smile.

Professor Magaldi, a beautiful, stern-faced woman with the sparkling, green eyes of a satisfied crocodile framed by black-rimmed glasses, demanded, "Explain."

"I thought it a clever pun. You know, bring the shit, yo." I was already, should my acting career be a bust, working on my stand-up. "A mono-log." I mimed pooing and explained, "A mono-log."

I'd hoped my reputation as a versatile actor, able to shine as Tin Man, Bad Wolf, or Haunted Tree on Mahalo Middle School's portable stage, would've preceded me. Thus affording a pass regarding the rigorous audition criteria Professor Magaldi had devised.

"The Harpy of Aloha," however, was having none of it.

"You do not," she noted, "have to do it well. You simply have to do it."

Mother, after my sour complaint on the iniquities of existence, threw a thin, rosé-hued booklet into my chest. She sipped the Barolo and suggested, "Act Two, Scene 3. Or, perhaps, Act Four, Scene 4."

The following afternoon, loins girded with a monologue, I took the stage and delivered "The Beast" from S. Anthony Haskins' obscure play, *On the Horizon*.

In stunned silence, Professor Magaldi looked up from her clipboard, pencil diligently tapping itself into dullness, "Mr. Belltower, do you know what the piece you've just performed is about?"

"Two minutes and thirty-five seconds or so? Likely shorter, I'm nervous and—" With the few laughs, if nothing else, I was on the right road to stand-up.

"No. Not its length." There was more laughter. Professor Magaldi glared the culprits silent. "Do you perhaps know its subtext?"

I didn't, but being a freshman I could get away with going Dopey. "Hunting and killing a whale?"

"Maybe. Maybe. Do you know the specific type of whale..." She glared at the seniors. "...Moby Dick is?"

I did. I'd done my research. However, as those in the wings waited for my answer, I heard S. Anthony Haskins' lines in a new light. The imagery, likewise, morphed. Captain Ahab's thrusting of his stiff harpoon deeper, deeper into the whale's quivering, virginal, white flesh took on new meaning. And the answer to her question—sperm—caught in my throat.

Less because I was lazy, but more as I suspected Professor Magaldi and the others expected me to have selected another, I returned in the winter for *Sense and Sensibility* with "The Beast." And the spring for

Macbeth. After the first year, well, it was tradition, and I'd spout such spume until the end.

"What are you doing?" Megan asked, as the night's cool wind slapped me in the face.

I'd spun the window down. I leaned out and, pointing a stern forefinger, declared in my best Nantucket, "There, upon the inky horizon, the Leviathan looms! Hand me my javelin, and I shall affix the beast's heart with my rod's wanton stiffness!"

Instead, Megan shot us through a yellow light as it went red. Horns, too close, screamed at us.

Moments later, the Leviathan, Aloha High, bright and brilliant with two Hollywood movie premier searchlights illuminating the underbelly of the fat, puffy clouds overhead, rose before us.

Remaining firm in panic mode and foregoing a spot in the crowded parking lot, Megan burrowed the Saab aslant across a low-lying shrub.

The Saab filled with the stench of hot oil, as she hopped out and bolted for the front doors where a group of reunionists loitered, smoking.

I didn't follow.

Megan had her own crazy going, and I, under the glowing hulk of the beast, pondered how much I'd lost and gained inside something so reminiscent of a prison.

Returned, Megan knocked on the hood. "Hey, Dixon, you okay?"

"No," I admitted, snatching crutches and stumbling from the Saab.

Once out of the shrub, crutching for the smokers, I asked over my shoulder, "Are you coming or not? Because it sure looks like your car has."

Ignoring me and the pooling oil, Megan hobbled up the steps with me, past the middle-aged hoodlums, through the taffeta-choked doors, and into the beast's bowels.

Someone had seen *Back to the Future* many, too many times. As undeniable proof, "Johnny B. Goode" wailed over the PA system. The guilty party had decorated Enchantment Under the Sea appropriately with mermaids, tridents, seashells and fish, floor to ceiling.

Most attendees were also dressed era-appropriate, the 1950s. I, however, was in baggy gray sweatpants with the left leg cut off at the knee, a vintage Grateful Dead Steal Your Face Skull Dancing Bears T-shirt, and, as a last-second addition for respectability, the infamous memorial service suit jacket.

Circumnavigating the registration table, Megan hedged her momentum.

Running into her, I, still in Ahab, declared, "Lass, unless ye want the oar up yer bunghole..." I nudged her hip with a crutch. "...ya best keep thy tack true."

Megan spun, made to comment, but noticed we'd caught the scrutiny of a registrar who'd been nibbling at a paper plate mounded in something red and noodled with two big ears of garlic bread. "You two. There." Hurriedly, the plastic fork stabbed and left erect in the red mass, he wiped his mouth, prepared to interrogate.

Recognizing the power of the crutch, the Nantucket, and the crazy, I cocked a crooked eye upon the lanky lad and, like the sea briny bastard I was, leveled crutch, and commanded, "If ye want ta swallow the hook I be glad ta give it ta ye straight, deep, and in the crook." Even at eighteen, it boggled how I'd not heard such phrasing and innuendo.

"Dixon?"

"Hernandez?"

Miguel was a year behind me, but years advanced. Difficult childhoods did that. He'd found some solace and escape as a stagehand.

We stared at one another, unsure what to do, though he knew what to say, "I see you're still Ahab-ing?"

"It's been a slow transition. Yes. But it's nearly complete." Waving my hands up and down, I indicated my visage and costume. "And you are?"

Mirroring my gesture, he declared, "Artistic director, Caliente Theatre Ensemble."

"Don't know it. Tell me more." Megan's sharp elbow had other designs, like puncturing a lung. "Miguel, apologies, my associate here is afraid of something crazy, really crazy, going down tonight. Like a 'full Carrie.'" Before he asked, I clarified with a smirk, "The horror movie and not Mr. Grant."

"Honestly," Miguel admitted, glancing around, "a little telekinetic revenge would be a welcome distraction. Though if there's anything nefarious and 'corn like,' well, you know where that'd be happening."

The implication of going full Carrie was one thing, going *Children of the Corn* was decidedly different.

Miguel handed me his business card and, after a "See ya sometime," returned to his station to idly stab the red mound and, unenthusiastically, stick it in his mouth.

Moving deeper into the beast, Megan asked, "What'd he mean by 'corn like'?"

"The janitors at the time were creepy. And none knew if it were real or a ploy to be left alone."

"When you say *creepy*? You mean... What?"

"I mean—"

Nearing the gymnasium, just past the illuminated, glass trophy cabinet, bright, flashing, multicolored lights exploded and strobed the walls and lockers through two pair of wide open, double doors.

We slowed and stopped as Prince's "1999" roiled out and drowned us.

Leaning, dropping the Ahab, I shouted into her ear, "I mean, cleaning carts decorated with dolls heads and listening to Rob Zombie and such."

Prince and the lights pounded us and we hesitated, confused about what next to do.

If Troy were going Carrie, it'd be here, in the auditorium. It was, however, a marginal showing and the body count would be minimal as only a handful gyrated center court, while another forty or fifty were knotted and clumped around the room.

"What a pile of shit," Megan observed over my shoulder

Regardless of the statement's accuracy, it was a poor turnout, it was, coming from her, also surprisingly harsh.

Prepared to make apologies for my drunken, dancing alumni, I discovered she'd declared such into her phone.

She faked a smile, and I countered with, "I know, and it's more than that fake smile, there's something you're not telling me. And—" Her lie died in her throat as I implored, "Don't."

The strobing washed over us as we stared, as Prince suggested how we should party.

Prince shifted to Pink's "Get the Party Started," the lights increased their strobing, and I admitted, "And that's fine. It doesn't matter. Trust me, all endeavors are futile. Find joy in the doing, not in the need to accomplish and finish."

Before being accused of appropriating Zen monkhood, I spotted an oasis in the forlorn desert. Taking her hand, I led Megan, past a few initial protestations, through the forest of tables covered in standard white linen with a centerpiece of a faux pineapple candle and a pile of plastic flower leis.

At the end of the defiled buffet, chafing dishes open and steaming like an Icelandic spa, squatted a silver punchbowl surrounded by an array of unfinished cups.

Having been shackled, four days of seven, to the *Oleander Princess*'s Jimmy Buffet Brunch Buffet, I'd learned a few hacks on how to transform a piss-poor punch.

I ladled a plastic cup of mottled greenish-pink concoction and gave it a tentative sniff.

Megan eyeballed me.

I handed her the cup and ladled another for myself.

She hesitated.

I sipped then slurped. "Is that Robitussin or NyQuil on the finish?"

"Very funny."

I chewed on the musky medicinal aftertaste. "Maybe something veterinarial?"

Megan sipped and spat back in the cup. "Vile. No wonder no one's drinking it." Pressing her cup amongst the others, she added, "Though NyQuil would be my guess."

Being a true Crusher, I persevered with another taste. The mouthfeel was viscous with notes of mildewed corduroy, dirty mint, spoiled blood orange, and tired leather with an effervescence reminiscent of Alexi's boubles.

"Don't drink that, you idiot."

Distracted by a tall, tan and chiseled asshole, I raised the glass.

"What'd I say?" she said, taking the cup, and placing it with the others.

The asshole was followed by a strawberry-blonde Medusa.

Aiming a crutch, my Nantucket returned, "Yonder, lurks our prey."

St. Fer and Liza, with furtive glances, slipped through a door behind the DJ table.

"Why are they here?" I queried, Nantucketless. "Neither attended this prison."

I knew the door they'd slipped through led to an expansive storage closet, its metal shelves filled with cleaning fluids, sponges, toilet paper, liquid soap, and paper towels. There was also a set of stairs leading down to the building's small intestines, the furnace, and the janitor's locker and break room.

Insight, a stiff harpoon, struck, "Are you interested in the seedy, though entertaining, underbelly of the wine tasting world?"

"What are you talking about?"

"Follow me and—" I turned to where she stared, horrified.

Our evil doppelgangers, Gregory and Amanda, each with a black eye and a cut lip, glared.

"So, Dick-son," Gregory spat, "how do you like the punch?"

The music slowed to Chris Isaak's "Wicked Game," the lights likewise softened, and I sensed an urge Katrina had claimed to be *yaytso vsmyatku*, "wanting to do wrong to prove someone wasn't right."

Blindly, Durden dead on Gregory, I picked a cup up.

"No," Megan declared taking the cup, "no."

She turned to return the cup, and I snatched one from around her other shoulder.

Tossing the vile concoction down, I grimaced, "I like it right fine." Handing the empty to Megan, I asked, "And what are those two twats doing here?"

Gregory, wearing the Devil's grin like an evening gown, explained, "Liza's my plus one."

Amanda, in hell's high heels, added, "And Roland's mine."

"Bravo," I declared with a few light golf claps as my stomach argued with the cup's contents, "and good for you guys. Master Shibari and Mistress Bukaki are a lot of fun." To add authenticity to my lies, in Japanese, I recited a *jisei*, a death poem, from a 14th-century Zen monk, Kozan Ikkyo. I'd learned it to provide some unnerving gravitas when next I dueled Mochi.

Rather than secure my victory, it only highlighted their ignorance. Thus, I was forced to acquire another glass.

"No." It was Megan, again.

She was late, again, and accepting an empty cup.

"Though make sure," I added, slapping on a Scottish brogue, "you bring extra Valium and lube. And don't be afraid of using an extra finger—if'n ya know what I mean? St. Fer likes it a wee bit deep. Well, we gotta go make a baby. Have a fantastic time. Maybe see ya around the dungeon sometime? *Ciao*."

They floundered, and I hobbled for the supply closet door, tugging Megan along.

Waving a crutch before us, I bellowed at the clinging couples crowding the floor, "Get thee vile corpses from our path."

Partially, they parted and we, squeezing, hobbled through.

Stumbling around DJ Honey Pot's table, I threw a wrinkled tenner to her tattooed arms spinning the sweet vinyl, and requested, "Blutnacht's *Wut die Wut*, please."

"What?" the ponytailed hipster asked, sloughing off a headphone from an ear, "What?"

Releasing Megan's moist palm, I hurried to her ear and repeated, though translated, "Blutnacht's *Rage the Rage*? Can you play it?"

"You mean, *Wut die Wut*, don't you?"

"Damn, right I do," I agreed, slapping another tenner down.

She turned to the sad, sloping couples shuffling lopsided around the floor and, wolf in the fold, smiled. "Yeah, okay, why the hell not?"

She scooped the bills up, and I observed, "You sound like me."

"Well, thank God," she said, strapping the headphones back on the ear, "I don't look like you."

"What is," Megan asked as I passed, hurried for the door, "'Rage the Rage'?"

"Baby making music," I laughed, as my stomach and the elixir escalated their disagreement.

Bursting into the storage closet, I staggered to the basin sink in the corner and, turning on the tap, shouted, "Geronimo," and stuck a tickling forefinger down my throat.

Once the last vestiges of punch had vacated my gut, I greedily slurped at the water's stream and Megan asked, "What was that all about?"

Staring at the slurry gurgling, draining down, I admitted, "That was horse laxative laced punch, some bourbon, a pill or two, and—"

"I know you know what I mean."

"I do."

"And?"

"And that was about many things. Someday, maybe, I may explain."

"But?"

"But we've not the time. And..." I ran my fingers over the cluttered collection of dolls' heads hammered and glued to the red-painted two-by-four framing an old Miller High Life beer mirror above the sink. "... not here, where they can hear us."

Chapter Thirty
DEEP, DEEP INTO THE BELLY OF THE BEAST

Descending the circular, metal stairs into the bowels of Aloha High, Megan, above the clatter, asked, "Why would you think Troy would go Carrie Bradshaw? That's ridiculous."

"But someone using telekinetic powers isn't?"

I'd asked Megan to keep me "distracted," though I'd altered my request to "entertained."

"Why?"

"I fear some of that horse laxative may've—"

"Horse laxative? How do you know that? Are you and Troy accomplices?"

I laughed, "Absolutely not. Because if I'd have concocted that punch it'd be frigging delicious."

"Then how do you know there's horse laxative in there?"

It'd been Art, in Sydney, after the closing ceremonies of the 2014 Duel Down Under, who'd first introduced me to "I Bet You Can't."

His one revenge for knocking him out of the competition had been lacing the final shot with... "What's that last component?" I sipped again. "Chalky, tart with a leathery sweetness." The Jägermeister, Yukon Jack, and pink lemonade had been easy. The last tart bit was a stumper.

Tossing the last of the concoction back, I requested the remainder from the mixing bowl and pondered it more.

Art chuckled, handed me a glass of Shiraz and, to my confusion, a roll of toilet paper, and toasted, "To knowing when to say no."

"I just know. Okay?"

"Okay," she agreed, as we stumbled from the stairs into a dense gloom.

The basement was darker than expected and a place I'd never been.

Readjusting the crutches, I sniffed the oil-heavy air. "And I'll have you know, Carrie B, can go as crazy as anyone." I sniffed again, fear filling my eyes.

Megan's clammy palm gripped my wrist. "What? What is it?"

"The children, they're close."

"What? Who?"

"Those of the corn. You don't smell the hay? The blood? The corn?"

"No. I do. However—"

An agonizing groan of disappointment surged from an undulating orange light at the end of a short, wide hall and stilled Megan's rebuttal.

"Good. Neither do I. So, maybe," I added, tapping the back of her hand, "you berate me for my poor sense of humor later?"

"Like when we're making a baby?"

"Absolutely not."

"Good."

"Definitely after."

She released my wrist and followed as I hobbled off toward the orange glow.

The janitors' break room had been elegantly retrofitted into replicating a candle-lit Tunisian hookah lounge, though *sans* hookahs.

Spectators, twenty or thirty, most incognito in the shadows, sat around on thick, colorful, Persian rugs. A few, in the pools of candlelight, I knew. Squirrel-eyed Sara was here with Nathan, each sipping an insipid rosé, while Ogden and Wheeler, hunched in a corner, grumbled over tumblers of red.

These gatherings popped up at competitions all the time. Those ousted would congregate and tell their tales of woe and loss in a more "civilized" venue. With the world championships in Portland next week, and only an hour away, there were bound to be dozens of these sprouting up all over.

Daniel, retaining his overseer position, ruled over the lone table, a rickety, square card table illuminated by a milky light bulb dangling overhead, a red plastic cup duct taped around it concentrated the light into a focused spot.

To my surprise, Sheppard faced off against Rapha.

Megan and I slipped into a darkened corner at the end of a series of lockers.

She leaned, "What is this? And why is my mother here?"

"It's a 'Sack Down,' a perversion and a ridiculous piece of snobbery, hence the stench of lilac potpourri, the Vivaldi, and... Who's your mother?"

"The woman there with—"

"Sara Squirrel is your mother?"

"What?"

"A pet name."

"She happens to be the mayor of McMinnville."

"And she happens to be a pushover for a Crusher, what's your point?"

"That she—"

Sheppard, cursing, stood from the table. Rapha matched him. The room tensed. Daniel, in true overseer form, quoted from the Crushed book of proverbs, *Clustered Wisdom*, "'One cannot blame the wine for what one did not find.'"

Begrudgingly, the two shook hands.

Sheppard stomped off to complain to Ogden and Wheeler, while Rapha accepted an envelope chubby with cash.

"Let's find Troy," Megan said, "and get out of here."

"Why? The punch was obviously—"

"Couldn't it be a ploy, for something bigger?"

"Bigger?" I recalled Paris, the vagina, the penis, and ass. "Well, maybe. But what?"

Before I repeated myself, Megan whispered, "There she, he, Trisha... they are, is."

It took a moment, but... Troy was presenting himself as Trisha. Besides the highly realistic wig, he wore a shimmering, black chiffon dress with matching diamond earrings, bracelet, and necklace. He looked much more like Carrie Bradshaw than scary Carrie from the horror movie.

Curiously, he was being escorted to the vacated dueling table by none other than that asshole St. Fer.

"I," I admitted, "hate that pompous ass."

"Language," hissed Sara Squirrel at my other elbow. I turned to where she'd been and found Nathan giving me the middle finger.

I blew him a kiss as Megan whispered, "Mother, what are you doing here?"

"Trying to keep things civil with potty mouth here about to—"

"No. This isn't about him. This is about you, here, doing what, exactly?"

The gathered hissed for silence.

Sara, provocatively close, ignored Megan and whispered to me, "Why do you hate him so?"

"You're suggesting," I noted with contempt, "the mousse, the smirk of satisfied condescension, and wearing those turd-hued loafers without socks, isn't enough?"

"Oh, I hated him from when he said sweet Rieslings watered the flowers of hell, but I'm going to need more if I'm going to tell you what I know."

I turned to Sara Montgomery and reconsidered her. Not for the proximity of her ample bosom or watery, squirrel-brown eyes, but for her honesty. Damn, I loved Crushers.

While Daniel, St. Fer, and Troy settled around the table, I, drawing the ladies a few steps back, explained my hate.

After the Bruges incident, which both agreed was enough, I continued. "He's won three of the last four championships and is on the verge of tying Art and Lincoln James's record. Though none can prove it, all know it, he cheats. And I've mentioned the mousse and lack of socks and—"

Megan, a calming hand on my arm, asked, "What is wrong with you?"

Years ago, Naomi, after asking the same, had suggested, during the editing of *The Yank*, "Perhaps you'd benefit from therapy?"

After feigning, "I'm outraged at such an outlandish suggestion," I'd agreed, if for no other reason than to prove Mother wrong—"No, you can't help me."

"I don't think you can call it stealing," I'd replied to the good, though annoying, Doctor Angela Cartwright-Burns, whom I'd hated the moment I'd entered her tweed and leather-bound office.

"Misappropriating others' experiences for your benefit?"

"You've a diagnostic term for such a phenomenon?"

"I think it more a disorder."

"I'll take that," I declared standing and walking out, "as a no."

Tearing at the gold-plated plaque attached to the brick wall of the stout building, I'd sheared off two fingernails.

Sucking bloody digits, I marched down the street cursing the doctor for being correct. I was a thief and, ironically, a soon-to-be-published one.

At the time—poor, heartbroken, and without the camaraderie of my fellow Crushers—the insight hadn't affected me, much.

Then Kenan took his life.

I'd discovered, far too late, that it's impossible to make amends to someone if they're dead. Not to mention if others, Bussy, Naria, and Split, had sworn, on the deceased's grave in the cold November rain, their undying commitment to sweet, sweet revenge.

Megan and Sara continued whispering who should be doing what, while I half-heartedly suggested to myself, "Just walk away. Just walk away."

I'd been delusional regarding the adjusted Kubler-Ross grieving model. I wasn't on six but remained on two. Thus, after Kenan, Katrina, my father, and Art, I needed to vent.

Interrupting a tasting, however, was the epitome of *faux pas* among Crushers.

"Just walk away."

Most of my manners, however, were gleaned from Mother or on the *Oleander Princess* in international waters. And once *Wut die Wut* began thrumming through the ceiling the future was inevitable.

Going full Cockney, I called, "Oy, St. Fer, ya old dental flosser, ya up for a Moriarty?"

Impeccably bored, and with little surprise, St. Fer raised his eyes.

Daniel, recognizing me, seemed intrigued and kept silent, while Troy stammered, "What are you doing here?"

Pressing a forefinger to his burgundy lipsticked lips, I utilized Megan's answer, "No existentialism. Please. Though if you come over and bake another pie, I might tell." I gave him a peck on the cheek and turned to St. Fer. "What say we, Ro-Ro, make dis interesting and throw down some bees and honey?"

"Dixon, besides a new clothier," St. Fer yawned, "what do you want?"

"You to stop being a merchant banker, but that's asking a giraffe to lick its bottle and glass."

Over the smattering of laughter, Liza chimed from the shadows, "Dixon, for god's sake, you mockney, stop. You can't do the rhyme or the accent."

"Listen, Danny Glover, you stop going north and, will ya?" Lest he try something gallant, I placed my lipstick-smeared finger across St. Fer's lips. He turned and wiped, while I reverted to my natural voice. "I can't be that bad, you knew it was Cockney."

Liza, pinched and pissed, arrived.

St. Fer, obligated, gave her a cursory glance, a sad smile, as she hissed a whisper in his ear.

The tasting glasses, unlike the industrial, thick-rimmed, Cold War era glasses used on the circuit, were delicate and elegant Spiegel's. The wines, three of them, were presented in the classical, trite, and typical fashion—light to dark, left to right.

Snatching St. Fer's darkest glass, I swirled, sniffed and sipped. And, scraping claws down Liza's chalkboard, I returned to the Cockney, "Now that there's a right sweet piece of time." Finishing the glass, I returned it to the table and my voice to normal, "Margaux. Marquis de Terme. 1994. Quite lovely, unlike—" I turned to Liza.

"You, Dixon," she cursed, "are an ass."

St. Fer, achieving chivalry late, stood and shouted, "Security!"

Troy gripped my cuff and yanked me to him. "What are you doing?"

"I'm here with Megan to find out what you're doing."

"Megan?" A guilty tremor scrunched his face. He dropped his head slightly. However, at least to me and my trained acting eye, it didn't strike genuine.

Through the whispered excitement the heavy boots of security neared.

"Are you doing anything else, bigger and badder, than the punch?"

"They discovered that?" That seemed genuine, ninety-ten.

"Well, yeah. That shit tasted like shit. But why'd you do it?"

"I've my reasons."

"I'm sure you did. And though you look particularly enchanting to-night, if there's something you're not telling me, I will turn you wicked, forever." It was a line I planned on incorporating in a vaguely imagined amalgamation of *Snow White and the Seven Dwarves* meets *Sex in the City* meets *The Seven Samurai* meets *The Tempest*.

His eyes drifted from Liza to me, and I added, "Is that understood, princess?"

I'd hoped my tone, the "princess," would've riled him to disclose something more if there was more. Instead, it just made me sound like an asshole.

He, cold and sincere, agreed, "It is."

"Good."

This time I was sure Troy was going to kiss me.

I was unsure what I'd do, because as Trisha, he was, they were... A granite palm collapsed upon my shoulder and straightened me.

"*Hola, amigo.¿Que pasa?*" I asked from a remarkably comfortable position—my tiptoes.

Ignacio, the burly server from Tapas Picas, smiled and lowered me, as I reaffirmed the deliciousness of his mother's cooking, "Particularly the *mole poblano.* Is it possible to get the recipe? And those hand-tossed tortillas were—"

St. Fer, after a sharp whisper and nudge from Liza, cut in, "Get him out of here."

Ignacio grimaced with annoyance, as did his muscled cohort. I didn't know his name but was sure I'd seen him at the restaurant.

Sensing their loyalties divided, I attempted a line from *Dead Men Don't Wear Plaid*, "'I'll double it, and we'll beat the shit out of him.'"

Before anything was decided, the soft patter of urgent and providential footsteps echoed down the hall, closer and closer.

All turned as a pear-shaped silhouette filled the doorway. The middle-aged woman wearing a blue pleated, poodle skirt, and white blouse with an old Aloha Warriors letterman's jacket stuttered to a stop and, out of breath, panted, "They're about to make the 'Most Likely' announcements."

"King and queen and all that shit?" someone asked from a candlelit corner.

"Yes. All that shit. And the write-ins too."

None cared and yet all were curious. Particularly with the write-ins, anyone could be nominated for anything. The prospect was simultaneously unnerving and titillating.

A murmuring gobble-gobble of speculation pecked the crowd.

"You see, St. Fer," I winked, placed a palm on Trisha's shoulder, and scanned the crowd for his accomplice, "you won't have to cheat, because no one cares."

"I do not need to cheat, Dixon."

"Tell that," I said, struggling a high-five desirous palm into the air from under Ignacio's grip, "to Liza here. Oh, ouch. Zinger." I waggled my palm. "St. Fer, you're going to leave me hanging? Really?"

The exodus of spectators, intrigued at the sudden escalation of the situation, slowed, stilled, and stopped. Shoulders were tapped, whispers ran ahead, and most returned.

It'd been too long since I'd performed in front of an audience, appreciative or not.

Slipping on my devil's grin, I asked, "So, Ro-Ro, you wanna go?"

Ignacio, a playful sparkle in his eyes, relaxed his grip.

Troy took a glass, golden like a California Chardonnay, sat back, and sipped.

Encouraged, I, lest those at the foot of the circular stairs be confused, repeated louder, "Duel."

St. Fer shook his head. "No."

"Duel."

"No."

"Daniel?"

"Sir?" Realizing his role in the farce, he exchanged the amused spectator cap for the overseer's tight helm. "What?"

"Duel. How long to cobble an official one together?"

"Maybe," Daniel admitted, "ten minutes. Maybe."

"That," St. Fer said, "is too long, is—"

"Not what Liza said the other night." I winked and waggled my high-five hand. It remained neglected.

"And," St. Fer added to his excuse, "we'll miss the king and queen shit."

"Oh, you pervert, you like watching that nasty stuff, don't you? But that's why you got Liza, right?" This time she gave it a go, though found my cheek instead.

The bright skin scream silenced the residual whispers tickling the room.

"Mmmm," I observed, noting St. Fer's flinch, "like old times. Except, without your butt plug, right?" The second brought a bit of blood and seasoned my mouth as I finished the scene. "But I suppose that's why you've got St. Fer?"

Liza brought her arm back. At its apex, the fingers curled into a fist. Zeus on high aimed his righteous lightning bolt.

Everyone waited, anticipated.

A few prayed.

A few, the guilty, ran for cover.

There was something beautiful about the destruction of something so ugly, regardless if it was deserved or not.

From the shadows, a silhouette shot out, grabbed Liza's arm, "How about you don't?"

"Oh, Katrina, if you were only worth my time." Liza snatched her arm away and stalked out.

I caught Megan's sleeve as she attempted to follow. I shook my head and said to St. Fer, "How about we settle this—" I hesitated. I knew now wasn't the time, though what alternative had I?

Daniel, the overseer cap snug as ever, suggested, "IPNC Sunday?"

There was an enthusiastic smattering of excitement at his suggestion.

I didn't know what IPNC was. I doubted it was that two-week rash I'd developed after Mai-Li's hand job. Regardless, Sunday I was familiar with. And, thanks to my improv training, and those assholes Pavlov and Skinner, I agreed, "Yes."

St. Fer shook his head, "*Pas possible*. That's three days before the world championships. No."

"And," I taunted, as I'd not vented nearly enough, "a day after I ravage your mother like a Tijuana hooker."

"My mother is dead."

"Like I said, a day after I—"

To my mild surprise, St. Fer lunged. He got a few good swings in, but I'd remembered the night at Sheppard's and blocked most.

Ignacio, late enough I'd likely need to tip him, pulled me away, but not before I landed a swift foot between St. Fer's legs.

St. Fer, gripping his groin, coughed, once, twice, and crumpled to the floor.

Before I could revel in victory, Ignacio apologized, "I'm sorry," and slammed two quick blows into my belly. He'd pulled them, but they still sent me to my knees.

Reconsidering tipping him, I gasped for air, as St. Fer spat at me, "*Putain*."

"Screw that Russian, dictator asshole."

"No. Not Putin. *Putain*."

"And I hate that gravy-smothered potato-cheese shit more."

"No. Not poutine."

"Jesus, Ro-Ro, I know. I'm being clever, dumbass." Past the remaining spectators' chuckles, I was struck with inspiration. "I'll wager the vineyard." The chuckles turned to gasps.

St. Fer raised his head and wiped the spittle from his lips.

I did the same.

"And what would you have me wager?"

There were many options, but I, the clown, said, "Your mother."

Chapter Thirty-One
DOUBLE, DOUBLE TOIL AND TROUBLE

On a paint-splattered, brown plastic chair in the makeshift catering kitchen in the science lab, the caterer's not having been granted use of the school's facilities, I again found myself with my head tilted back with wads of toilet paper filling my nostrils.

Norris, a second-year med student and part-time caterer, had proclaimed on a curt examination, "Congratulations, you're the proud father of a broken nose."

After St. Fer had headbutted me, Ignacio, reluctantly, separated us.

Past the blood and outrage, we'd spun on Daniel, "When and where?"

Less enthusiastic, he again suggested, "IPNC this Sunday?"

"Fine. Five, six million?"

"Seven. And your father's vineyard?"

"Fine. And fuck you."

"And fuck you back."

"And fuck you back and forth until Tuesday."

"And—" St. Fer gave a guttural, frustrated howl and marched off as my laughter hounded him until he clattered up the stairs.

Yes, the seven million wasn't what the Enrights' had attempted to entice me to sell for. The three million discrepancy wouldn't matter if I won. I'd have the winery and money to pay everyone off, Boonen and the IRS. Maybe give each a few hundred thousand as a "Fuck you." There was, however, a single word jitterbugging on the blade between Heaven and Hell—if.

Megan, like Troy, had disappeared after the scuffle. I didn't care if they'd gone off together, in opposite directions, or to fix the Saab. It was the fact Megan was my ride home that annoyed me.

After another sip of medicinal Merlot, I, around a grimace, pressed the cone-shaped wads deeper and dug through my pockets, questing for a pill. Not for my nose, but for the residual melancholy, the impending Doom soon to destroy me and my future.

Distracted with my finger's quest, Kris, the young woman I'd finally recalled from my father's memorial and Norris's coworker, went unnoticed until she demanded, "You, Mr. Broken Nose, where's Norris?"

Sharpening a clever on a rough, blood-stained stone, I stated, "I don't know. I suppose off catering to someone somewhere."

"Was that supposed to be funny?"

"No."

"Good. Because it wasn't."

I raised my head, squeaked a swollen eye open, and stared at the mouse-limbed, chicken-bodied young woman.

She hesitated.

It was enough for us to know who ruled this ridiculous roost.

Losing some attitude, though reinforcing IT tech support people were the truest of assholes, she added, "Tell him, or better, tell Shasta, the school's server is down. I set up a hot spot and... Screw it. I printed the king and queen shit out. It's in there."

Squeezing the second eye open, I asked, "You mean the 'Most Likely' survey?"

"Yeah. Whatever you want to call it." A manila envelope sat aslant a crumpled box of tea crackers. "Anyway, some French dude offered me a thousand for something 'civilized,' so—" She shrugged and went to work. "Civilized? I mean, what the hell, food is just poop in a tuxedo for Christ's sake."

She slapped together a healthy helping of appetizers, scattering them across a stained doily covered silver tray, tossed back the remaining remnants from a bottle of Pinot Gris, and charged off.

After another sip of the insipid Merlot, I heaved a sigh and picked up the envelope, pulled the printed sheets out.

The first page spouted the standard BS from high school. King and queen, as before, were Christopher Starr and Courtney Sullivan. Most likely to succeed: Brian Morton. Most likely to have another abortion: Valerie Osmond.

The other two pages, the most interesting, were the "write-ins."

Most likely to go bankrupt investing in mail order beekeeping kits: Simon Anderson.

Most likely to be attacked by chipmunks at a national park: Carla Roseburg.

Most likely to fall overboard on a cruise ship: Melinda Lakewood.

The fourth and final page was a statistical page by category, though inverted from fewest votes to most.

The king (nine votes) and queen (seven votes) were second and third, behind Most likely to be sainted (no votes).

Four of the top six categories—Most likely to Remake *The Crying Game*,

...to Perform in *M. Butterfly*, ... to Star in *Victor, Victoria*, and ...to Have a Las Vegas gay cabaret—all had a transparent connection, while also having the same "winner," Trisha Andretti.

For me, these were reasons warranting the horse laxative, if not going full horror movie Carrie. However, I was perplexed at how the administration could allow such overt hostility. Of course, much of the previous administration had passed and this activity wasn't necessarily monitored by the school's current wardens. If anyone had the authority to curtail such behavior it would be the organizers, the alumni, and my fellow students.

Finding the lint-furred pill, hoping to stem the welling rage, I gobbled it with the last of the Merlot.

Standing, needing a little pain for clarity, I pulled the bloodied toilet paper cones from my nose. I dropped the sodden, red boogers in a nearby garbage can—*thup thup*—and began pacing as best the cast and crutches allowed.

Living insulated and secluded in suburban cul-de-sacs, frequenting Christ-filled drive-thrus, and believing the Harlequin romance propaganda was all well and good. However, to say shit anonymously, unaffected by the consequences, was cheap and easy bullshit.

Hobbling around the catering-laden science tables, a thick mélange of anger and frustration had come to a rapid boil.

Considering the top vote-getter had nearly double our graduating class, the process was highly dubious. Regardless, I still heard the magnificent voice of Don Pardo announce in my head, "And, with 943 votes, the Man most likely to have a Russian porn star for a fiancée? Dixon James Belltower! Let's hear it for Dixon! Dixon, come on down because you're the next contestant on Life's a Big Pile of Shitty Shit."

In third place with 303 votes, Most Likely to Decapitate His Fiancée's Lover-Dog. Well, I'd won, again. Wahoo.

Softly cackling Joker-esque, I glanced around as a plan poisoned my pill and Merlot-adled mind.

Norris and his catering cohorts had smartly emptied the cups crowding around the punchbowl back in, which, back to nearly full, sat on a silver cart neglected in a corner.

Tottering over, I dunked a forefinger in the tepid liquid, placed it in my mouth and sucked.

Norris, under the weight of a chafing dish, peeked in. "Hey, have you seen Kris? She was supposed to—"

He fell silent as I, shaking my head, popped my finger from my mouth—*pop*—and grew a ghoulish grin.

"Why are you grimacing like that?"

Digging into the coat pocket, pulling the last, wrinkled wad of winnings out, I asked, "I wonder, Norris, can I ask a favor of you?"

Chapter Thirty-Two
HIGH SCHOOL POOP PARTY

Should Heaven exist, it would be similar to what I woke to. A muted, yellow light diffused a sullenly quiet room. The sheets I curled in were soft and sumptuous and were scented with lilac. There was also the right amount of wondrous and whimsical birdsong.

I was dressed in the softest, most comfortable pair of pajamas I'd ever known. They were periwinkle blue and had a leg sliced up the side to accommodate the cast.

My skin tingled and had the glistening sheen of an Italian sports car. And my hair? It was light, luxurious, and billowed from my scalp like an insistent kite.

Though refreshed like I'd not been in weeks, my nose retained the expected stuffy swollenness of it being broken. After a few antihistamines, I'd be ready to go for Sunday. Since the TOD wasn't until six, there was plenty of time for attuning my palate.

Other than the vagaries of the TOD, I recalled nothing more from the night before. I had, however, had the foresight to make preparations for waking. On the nightstand were two white pills (aspirin, I assumed) and one of Dr. M's. There was also a snifter with a copious amount of a copper-colored liquid, which, on a sip, I confirmed to be more Martell's. My secondary brain—my phone—sat beside it.

Perplexed, and impressed, at how I could've been so planful, I tossed the pills down with a nice swallow of brandy.

Luxuriating, waiting for the next wave of heaven, I attempted to recall how I'd returned to the devil's den, my father's loft.

My mind was a *tabula rasa* and there were no obvious clues to begin an inquiry, so I turned my attention to the phone.

The first two messages, though not Heavy Breather, were of someone breathing heavily and, eventually, hanging up. The third was something else, entirely. A man, in frenzied, berserk tones and foul-mouthed expletives ranted, raved, and raged on how he was going to take pieces of me and feed them into a woodchipper. He hadn't left a name or number.

After another, longer sip of Martell's, I deleted the message and listened to the next. Again, it was a death threat. The next nine were the same—death threats. None, however, held any insight into how I'd returned.

Could Megan have driven me back? Maybe Alejandro in the ambulance? Maybe Troy and these were his pajamas? Maybe... Annoyed, I swung out of bed and reached for the crutches on the other side of the nightstand. A sneaker wave of nausea slammed across the beach of my brain. It flung me face-first into the nearby armoire.

Crumpled on the floor, I rubbed the swelling over my eye and checked my palm for blood. Though it was pale and accusing as ever, I discovered a loosened recollection.

Norris, practical and upstanding (it explained my underlying dislike of him), had declined to assist me with the punchbowl. Kris, however, after I'd assured her, "Yes, the entire wrinkled wad," had agreed.

With the help of a hand blender, a few egg whites, confectioners' sugar, red food coloring, and a few other odds and ends, I'd perked up the punch.

Kris had tucked five or six sleeves of plastic cups on the cart's lower shelf and we'd wheeled the punchbowl out.

The gymnasium, giddy with anticipation for the disclosure of the Most Likely awards, had slumped into silence. The overhead lights were on, though the disco lights continued flashing and sparkling the empty dance floor.

The unsuspecting masses mingled and, verging on a road less traveled, we hesitated.

Kris filled a cup and sipped. "Hey, Broken Nose, this isn't so bad."

"Yes, Chicken Girl, I know. I've magic taste buds."

"So," she asked, taking another sip, "what else is magical about your mouth?"

A hollow, metallic shout, the downstairs door slamming shut, echoed up the stairwell and threw me into the dark well of the present.

A foreboding cacophony of footsteps clanged and clattered on the steel stairs.

Kris was a nice enough, young woman. And there was the rub. She (so I estimated) was under what I, and a vast majority of the global populace, felt an acceptable age difference would be. Not to mention also having the Siren's sinister sparkle in her pale brown eyes.

Naomi had once explained about her ex, Rachel Densmore, "It's alluring, the energy, the *l'appel du vide*, but want some consistency, a bit of normalcy, then you're a conniving bitch that's only interested in—" Naomi smiled, calmed, and quoted, "'*Be wary the Siren's call, for she shall love you all the more in your fall*.'"

The metallic *clank* of each step grew closer, closer, closer.

If Kris and I had accomplished the diabolical and improbable scheme and escaped for celebratory drinks, perhaps, drunk on elation and grain alcohol, we'd done something truly stupid—had sex.

Hadn't I considered a meteor fling so bright it'd burn the past from me?

Hobbling from the bedroom, unprepared to greet her and explain the tragedy of our mistake, I'd take the back stairs and escape.

Hurried whispers, however, hissed from the living room.

If Hell existed, it would initially manifest itself as Heaven, making the descent more poignant, more devastating.

With the snifter empty, I had no choice, unto the breach I went.

Egan and Julio, each with a plump, military green duffle bag, searched for escape.

"What," I demanded as they spun at my thump, thumping, "are you guys doing?"

"Sleeping Beauty," Egan observed, "has woken."

A key rattled in the door.

They dove for cover, while I wondered what else I'd given Kris besides keys to the apartment.

The door bolted open, "Aori?"

Egan and Julio peeked from behind the couch.

She flung a pink, hard shell suitcase into a corner, and I asked, "What are you doing here?"

"Your goddamn mother is a nutbag. That's what I'm doing here."

"Well, yeah, I know that. But why are you—" I glanced at the brothers as they stepped back, kept the couch between them and her.

"Why didn't you tell me? Warn me? Fuck." She kicked the couch and the brothers jumped back a few steps. She stalked to the expansive, two-door, brushed silver refrigerator. "Fuck!" she screamed, throwing it open. "Fuck!"

Egan, like his brother and their duffels, slipped for the open door.

"No. No. No. No. No," I whispered, waving a frantic hand, and cutting them off.

"Dixon," Aori cried, "she tried to kill me."

Aori, forlorn, stared into the refrigerator and I implored, "Please?"

"On our goddamn intimacy retreat."

"Please?" The brothers hesitated, huddled, and conferred in hurried whispers.

The refrigerator's door slammed shut, "Shit-pineapple-hell!"

The brothers broke apart, Julio declared, "You help us. We help you."

I didn't know why it'd taken so long to arrive at such an obvious solution. "Yes. Yes. Of course. Obviously."

Regardless the verbal agreement, none knew who was contractually obligated to do what when.

Aori, clutching a two-thirds full bottle of Sauvignon Blanc, slumped to the couch, crying. She yanked the cork out with her teeth and spat it toward her suitcase. After a long slug, she asked, "Who the hell was watching *Sex and the City*?"

The brothers admitted they'd started the other night, but at my behest.

"Initially," Egan admitted, "we were disappointed."

"*Sí. Sí.*"

"We expected—"

"*Mucho mas*—" Julio made a fist and gave a few quick jabs to the air.

"*Sí. Sí. Mucho mas.*" Egan also jabbed the air.

Aori snatched the remote, kicked the DVD player and, turning the television off, declared, "Well, we're not watching it."

"Yes, but Carrie and Mister Big are—" Egan fell silent as I shook my head.

"His mother?" Julio asked.

"Yep," Aori confirmed, "his stupid, stupid mother."

Settled on the balcony, gathered around a wobbly, wrought iron table and under its sun-bleached pea-green umbrella, we'd cobbled together a brunch, of sorts.

"After the sunset intimacy ceremony," Aori stated, "she'd been all butterfly kisses and cuddles." She took a quick sip, continued. "And then, in the middle of the night, without provocation..." She took another sip and crossed her heart, "...she attacked me."

As few enjoy insight given in hindsight, I didn't share my *il bacio della morte* hypothesis.

Taking another slug of the accursed Sauvignon Blanc, she finished, "And so I slammed a lamp over her head and left." She shrugged and took another slug. "So, why're you all up here?"

Silence answered; so she turned to me.

I turned to Egan and Julio.

They, as I topped up their glasses, accepted the invitation.

"All was *muy tranquilo*—" Julio admitted.

"*Muy tranquilo*," Egan echoed.

"And then *ayer*, yesterday," Julio shrugged and sipped.

"The ICE assholes," Egan explained, "returned and, *lo siento*, we hid here."

"Don't worry about it," Aori said, waving a dismissive hand. "I understand. Too well." Rather than expound, she, along with the brothers, turned to me.

I added my shrug to the pile, "No particular reason." I lifted my leg, showed off the boot wrapped around my shattered ankle. I knocked it with a knuckle and noted, "Julio here tried killing me with the tractor."

He was too incredulous at the accusation to comment, so I continued, "And I'm just here recovering. These two incompetent assassins know that."

A strange, unnerving silence gripped the group.

It seemed they expected something else, something besides the truth. I was confused.

"No, Dixon," Aori said with something approximating concern, "why are you *still* here?"

Oh, I heard the emphasis and asked, "What do you mean, 'still here'? Where else would I be?"

"Maybe hiding?"

"Hiding? Why?"

The brothers nodded in agreement, "*Sí. Sí.* Hiding."

Frowning, I took a stabilizing slug of brandy and admitted the sad, confounding truth, "Honestly, I don't recall anything." To their disbelieving stares, I explained, "I had the same reaction the previous time I ingested horse laxative. So—"

Aori gasped and, rather than ask about the horse laxative, said, "Then you don't know?"

"Know what?"

She and the brothers shared glances.

"Okay," I said, as my annoyance gained traction, "so what happened?"

Julio, biting a smile, poured the last of the brandy.

"Is there," I asked, eyeballing the inadequate level of the elixir in my glass, "any point in lying about whatever happened?"

They shook their heads in perfect synchronicity.

Shivering with cold horror, I asked after a quick sip, "Because you know?"

Remaining synchronized, they nodded.

I chewed a lip and, knowing where the truth lay, said, "Okay, go on—show me."

They, much too jubilant and excited for my liking, yanked their phones out and fingered them.

Egan won and turned his to me. The other assassins hit pause, clattered their chairs around me, locking me in.

Of course, I recognized the battlefield—Aloha High's gymnasium.

A phone's table-high view, near the balloon-infested, double doors. Beneath the blue, gold, and green Warrior mural stood a man. The man, a beaten boxer, face black-and-blue wore a bloodied, Grateful Dead T-shirt under a black jacket, baggy gray sweatpants, while his left ankle was encased in a gray-plastic medical boot.

Could there be another soul so unfortunate? There had to be. Didn't there? Didn't there?! And yet, as he swayed, tapping his fingers against his thigh in time to the music, I knew—it was me. The only one to be so lucky to be so unfortunate was me.

I wanted to turn away. I wanted to find a cave and live hermit-style, in denial. I wanted to pretend the new me remained the old me. But I couldn't. And I realized, if you couldn't stop the trains from colliding, shouldn't you watch and be a reliable eyewitness to the tragedy, the horror? A true Crusher would.

Egan, too caring and concerned to be a successful assassin, lowered his phone.

I, true Crusher to the end, slipped a hand under it and, to everyone's surprise, raised it.

The video showed me, having acquired a microphone, hobbling alongside the catering cart with its punchbowl. Kris handed out cups of punch, while I expounded on "the virtues of community," "the coming together to celebrate not just who we once were, but who we've become," and "giving the middle finger to time and expectation."

I knew I could bullshit with the best, but this was extraordinary. I was two things I rarely was—eloquent and sincere. And, knowing where the trains were headed, it was frightening.

What was more frightening, and confounding, Kris and I were a remarkable team. If my Glengarry Glen Rossing didn't sell them, her Sullivan Nod and admission did.

The cinematographer accepted a glass and asked, "This is different right?"

"Different?" Kris replied taking a sip from her glass, "It's the best."

Propping their phone against a pineapple candle, they asked, "You're sure?"

The screen filled with our torsos, the punchbowl, and the cinematographer's hand with the infamous cup of punch.

Above my blathering in the background, Kris's reply was sharp and succinct, "Of course I am. You can trust me."

The screen went dark and Egan, with a nervous grin, stopped the video.

I sipped as Julio and Aori huddled over their phones, quickly consulted one another. We shifted and scooted around Aori's phone.

Her pencil-thin forefinger stabbed the screen and the next video in the train wreck commenced.

The shot, directly across from The Yes Squad's table, showed Colin and Brenda, a few other members. Even Miguel was there. Kris and I, having finished circulating through the crowd, were on stage, waving and giving enthusiastic thumbs up.

Colin, finishing the indoctrination ceremony, making everyone an honorary member of the squad, lifted his cup and proclaimed, "Welcome to the squad! Yes! Yes! Yes!" He handed the mic to Brenda who recited the Nine Vows of Yes. All reciting along and finishing with, "Thus I do solemnly swear to accept yes as the bedrock of my life, my existence, my world. Yes! Yes! Yes!"

Everyone raised their glass and erupted in a boisterous echo, "Yes! Yes! Yes!" Everyone, even those who'd been reticent, drank their cups dry. On finishing, most glanced around, surprised at the flavor and quality of the concoction, quite a few wandered to the cart for a refill.

Aori killed the video and turned her dark, intense eyes on Julio.

Egan and I joined her.

Julio gulped and adjusted his phone.

We scooted. We scrunched. And he punched play.

Unlike the previous two videos, firm and steady, this was a shaky, wobbly view from the plate end of the buffet line. The gymnasium had collapsed into a turbulent sea of activity. The cinematographer, in stuttered stops and starts, panned around and showed the masses moaning under intestinal distress. Handfuls staggered toward the exits.

An angry knot of the stricken accosted The Yes Squad's table. The stricken, however, were repulsed by the squad's enthusiasm and conviction at embracing the yes of the impending shitty apocalypse.

Over the frenzy, a woman's voice, panic-stricken, moaned, "Roger, oh, my god, the emergency lines are busy. It's just a recording."

The cinematographer, Roger, spun the phone and refocused on a pear-shaped woman in a poodle skirt and letterman's jacket.

Curled on the floor, a phone to her ear and a spilled basket of butter rolls for a halo, she swore, "Roger, if you're recording me, I will—" Gripped by a painful contraction, she groaned, curled tighter into a fetal ball.

Roger, moaning, fighting his contractions, gallantly placed his phone against a chafing dish and tottered into a stack of plates.

In the aftermath of the shattering, from the floor, he wheezed, "Oh, sweet Jesus, take us. Take us now. Please."

A tide of panic surged through the auditorium as the first of the afflicted soiled themself. Hysteria, as the inevitability of their plight became apparent, engulfed the room and, en masse, people fled for the exits.

Over the chaos, the squelching of chairs, the crack and crunch of plastic cups being trampled, I, mic returned, calmly claimed, "Don't run. It accelerates the absorption, undermines the experience. Accept the shit. Accept it. Yes. Yes. Yes."

Unable to exit in time, most staggered a few steps, stopped, and, gripping the back of a chair, a neighbor's hand, resigned to their fate, shat themselves.

Julio, with a sigh, pressed pause.

The soft, spring breeze blew, the birds chirped, time slipped quickly by, and I, into the snifter, asked, "Is that all?"

"I think so," Aori answered.

"*Un momento*," Egan admitted, "I found—"

Again, we shuffled ourselves around and returned to his phone.

Though the crime scene had shifted, it was one I knew—Wash-A-Kari, a self-serve carwash, replete with three washing stalls, two vacuum stations, and a vending machine protected by a padlocked, metal grate.

Under the bright halogen lamps, two people, naked, a man and a woman, were using a high-pressure hose on themselves. Around an ankle, the man had a trash bag duct taped around it. They, erotically, were cleaning themselves, every crack, cranny, and crevice. This likely explained the Italian sports car glow, the waxy sheen of my skin, and my buoyant head of hair.

Egan hit pause.

The frozen image showed Kris straddling me in the last stall. She held the nozzle overhead, its spray, cut through by the lamps' bright light, sparkled with diamonds and rainbows.

I placed the snifter to my lips and suckled at its teat. Being empty, I discovered only disappointment.

"Four videos?" I commented, hopeful. "That's not so bad, right?" The last one, "Sexy Wash-n-Wax a GO-GO-GO!" had the most views with seventy-five. So things could've been... With more glee than I thought necessary, the three scrolled through nearly two hundred offerings of the Aloha High poop party, aka the Poo-ocalypse.

Aori, in a strange competition with the brothers, found a video that showed me on stage, helping Kris escape being dragged down by three irate women, their legs, socks, and shoes marred with brown smears.

Behind us, gesticulating wildly and screaming, were Megan and her mother, Sara.

I turned to Kris and asked her something. Giggling, Kris pointed to Megan. Megan promptly slapped me and, with a middle finger held high, stormed off with Sara in tow.

The image panned back to Kris and me. We, uh-oh, were kissing. A barrage of butter rolls forced us to flee. However, in the background, Liza and Troy, still in that amazing dress, were also kissing deeply, passionately.

With an empty glass, I couldn't continue. I, confused, stood, stumbled into the loft, and asked over a shoulder, "What episode are you guys on?"

Aori, following, declared, "No. No. No. As your stepmother, I cannot condone watching such filth."

The brothers joined us as the low growl of gravel scratched at the afternoon air.

We turned and Julio stated the obvious, "A car."

"Who?" I asked, though knew none of us knew.

The car skidded to a stop. Its door opened and slammed shut. Someone ran across the gravel—*crunch, crunch, crunch*—and flung the downstairs door open.

Perhaps a crazed, shit-stained classmate or Five-o here to arrest Aori for Mother's murder? Kris was pregnant and... The door clattered shut.

Egan and Julio hoisted their duffle bags and started for the door.

I held out a crutch as footsteps pounded up the metal stairs.

Hobbling to the nearest corner from the front door, I dropped a crutch, took a defensive position, and suggested, "Take the back stairs."

"*Comandante*, what are you doing?" Julio asked.

"Getting my revenge," I explained, steadying myself, gripping the crutch like a bat. Oh, I was going to clock Howitzer or Bald Submarine. I didn't believe I was lucky enough for it to be Saunders.

Embroiled in the Paris tragedy, with Home Office, and the reunion poop party fiasco, another misstep shouldn't matter much. Thus invigorated with saving my comrades from the unjust arms of The Man, I gripped the crutch tighter, tighter.

"Oh, this is going to be good," Aori observed, drinking from her bottle.

The Carapazes each made the sign of the cross.

I pressed myself against the wall, pulled the crutch farther back, and yelled over a shoulder, "Take Halen. Go! Go! Go!"

The marauder pounded onto the landing.

They, deer in headlights, gazed stunned and dumb.

"Go!"

The loft's front door exploded open, footsteps pounded down the short hall, and, as I swung, a voice shouted, "No one move, federal—"

Before I asked why they'd stayed, the body *thudded* to the floor.

I stared at the corpse, confused. There were plenty of places to dispose of it; it was whether any of us could dismember someone so beautiful.

"Alicia," I stammered, "why did you... What are you doing back?"

She snatched the bag of ice and applied it to, she couldn't decide. Her forehead sported a rosy red splotch the dimensions of the crutch, while the back of her head, a blip of blood peeking through the scalp, had grown a significant lump.

Egan handed her another bag.

Placing one fore, the other aft, she thanked him and, with a sigh, accused, "I can't believe you were going to dismember me."

We, the guilty, broke into a fervent though short-lived, blame game. It erupted, quieted, erupted, and died.

"So," Alicia turned to Aori, "it didn't work out?" Aori shook her head. "And you two? You didn't run?"

With a nudge from Julio, Egan explained, "We hope to stay." Julio whispered something to Egan. "*Sí*. Here in Oregon."

"Favor for favor?" I reaffirmed to their nodding.

"A permanent address. And job. A sponsor."

"An affidavit of support."

"*Sí*. It would go a long way."

"Getting visas."

"Yeah, about that," I grimaced, "there are some complications." I explained the situation, the back taxes, the bet, the taste-off, and, ending on a positive note, added, "But we've a day to plan. A day for the nasal congestion to dissipate. A day to—"

Egan and Julio shook their heads.

Aori, from her rehearsal corner, attempting to replicate Alicia's crutch collapse, slapped her cheeks and froze in a gasp of horror, Edvard Munch's *The Scream* or that stupid kid from *Home Alone*.

Alicia stood, walked to the kitchen, and dropped the bags in the sink, *splat, splat*. She picked up the last bottle of bourbon, and, after a long slug, echoed, "Yeah, about that."

Chapter Thirty-Three
TIME, THOUGH ART A HUNGRY, HUNGRY MONSTER

"Sunday? No. No. No," I declared, hoping my fervent denial could turn time back, or, at minimum, stop it. "It can't be. No. No. No."

The bitches and bastards of my apocalypse, Alicia, Aori, Julio, and Egan, as I hobbled around the loft, held their phones toward me. Each indicated the day to be Sunday.

"No. No. No. No. No. No."

Worse, they showed the hour, 3:48.

"In the afternoon?" The bitches and bastards nodded. "No. No. No. No. No. No."

My hobbling grew more frantic. There wasn't enough space or time. I slid both balconies' doors open. I hobbled back and forth, from one railing, through the loft, to the other railing.

The clear, clean, spring air and the sunlight, helped, some.

Back and forth I hobbled.

The four retreated to the kitchen, huddled around the bistro table. Wary and fearful, they watched.

With my underarms chafing and blistering, I slowed and transitioned from panic to problem-solving. Realizing it was problems, plural, I recommenced my pacing.

First and foremost, I needed to get to the taste-off. Easy enough, we had three cars at our disposal and Linfield College was but ten miles away.

Second, and most important, I needed to win.

And there lay the bare bodkin. My palate had been befouled by bourbon and the contaminating concoctions of brunch—marinated asparagus, sweet, Southern coleslaw, graham crackers, lemon-infused sardines, and more.

After such malevolent munchies, my broken and clogged sinuses were a forest fire of inflammation.

And as much as I loved the meds, they played a slow, summer afternoon game of checkers with my palate. The world, my senses, everything, lacked nuance. All was a smooth, flat, and placid conformity.

I didn't need fine, I needed edges, something to grasp and grapple with.

Lastly, there was my arch nemesis lurking in the wings. No, not St. Fer, but the self-inflicted ghost, performance anxiety. Incorporating a bit of ritual, like the park bench, I'd been able to circumvent much of my apprehension. But at that moment?

I stopped mid-loft and turned.

The four broke from their huddle and stared.

Were they horsemen or comrades?

Staring at my lone functioning foot, tottering on its toes, I dropped my heel, waved, and smiled.

They, after Aori's elbow prodded, did the same.

During my acting career, unlike many of my Aloha High cohorts, I'd not been infected with the directorial bug. I'd always felt, Mother decrying "more emotion" and "make me feel it," directing was analogous to dog ownership. And, like owning a dog, it gave one the misconception one was in charge. In charge, not just their minute sphere of influence, but the entirety of their existence. It was a fool's charade.

One fateful evening, forty minutes before curtain, such an assumption was given manifest proof of its accuracy.

Returning from another final pee, I'd made the mistake of picking up Kermit, the green room's green phone. It was Brenda, for our current production, *West Side Story*, she was the assistant director, choreographer, costume designer, stage manager, and prompt person.

"Hey, Bren, you guys are—"

"Late. Yes, Dixon, I know. Thank you for stating the obvious."

In the background, Professor Magaldi screamed, "The show must go on!"

"Where are you guys?"

"That doesn't matter." I wanted to disagree, but Bren marched headlong into the musket fire and declared, "You're directing. You are to—"

CRUSHED

She didn't give me time to explain how I couldn't. She did, however, in a frantic five minutes, give a basic overview of all her responsibilities, though without insight into how to accomplish any of it.

"But Bren, I—"

"Break a leg," she commanded, it sounding more curse than encouragement.

Before she hung up, Professor Magaldi repeated the same old platitude, "The show must go on!"

It did, even after the entire cast and crew, the concessionaires, Wendy and Robin, and three surly, smoking janitors declined my pleas to accept the directorial mantle and a case of Wrong Way Red.

The performance, therefore, had been a catastrophe, complete and utter.

Like accusing the guillotine of the execution, none placed blame directly on me.

Shelley Constantine, the Warrior Bugle's intrepid senior theatre critic, had in her review put it succinctly enough. "There are not enough derogatory superlatives in all the languages in all the lands to describe the dumpster fire that engulfed our humble stage the other evening. Suffice it to say, whether audience member, cast, or crew, none had left unscathed from third-degree burns covering the entirety of their soul. As one patron declared on exiting, 'Heaven shall be all the sweeter for we've survived hell.'"

Shelley had graciously granted me an excuse, "How was Mr. Belltower, the poor, impromptu director, to know the bucket marked 'water' contained gasoline?"

The next day, Professor Magaldi listened, quietly, attentively, to the tear-laden confessions of cast and crew. She, constantly nodding sagely, would offer a heartfelt, "I understand" and "You've been heard. Thank you."

Once everyone had shed their grievances, she'd asked, "Did anyone die or lose a limb?" We grumbled a desultory denial, as she, waving her bandaged and pinky-less hand, dramatically declared, "Well, I did. I did."

It'd become our battle cry for the remaining performances—"Well, I did. I did."

I stilled my waving hands.

It eased the troupe's tension, allowed them to take a few furtive sips and me to glance around, check for an elderly Schnauzer hell-bent on devouring a pinky before it visited the vet a final time.

If they were going to believe in themselves, horsemen or comrades, they needed to believe in me, didn't they? But, did I believe in me?

I'd never been lead in any production. And, no, the Tin Man wasn't a lead, but, as Mother had put it, which I agree with, "Is an annoying and winey sidekick."

Channeling Patton, Churchill, Anakin Skywalker, and Wade Wilson, I adopted a firm, husky voice, though with a playful *joie de vivre*, and directed, "Aori, I need a bottle of the best red you've got. You bring me anything white and I will—"

She bolted into the kitchen and rummaged through cupboards.

I turned to the brothers, "Egan, Julio, I need you two to decide which of you will drive interference and who'll be the blocker."

They stared slightly less confused than Alicia.

Aori, clattering drawers open and closed, asked, "A blocker? What are you talking about, *comandante*?"

One weekend, when a grandmother had died, I never learned which, Mother had sequestered me with Mister J, and TCM had a Burt Reynolds marathon. For a week after, I'd adopted a wee southern twang and a laugh like a pony on nitrous oxide, until Mother declared, "You continue playing it Reynolds and I'll deliver you to the bottom of a river."

"¿*Comandante?*"

"I think it was *Cannonball Run* or maybe *Gator*? Doesn't matter. The first car gets any police to chase. The last car, the blocker, keeps any from catching the prey."

Aori, at another cupboard, again popped up, "Prey? What, *comandante*, are you talking about?"

"Like church?" Julio asked.

"No. The prey, me, with you two driving interference and blocking, will drift in unscathed and pummel that Camembert-sucking bastard St. Fer."

The brothers echoed, "*Sí, sí, sí,*" shot me thumbs ups, and huddled, planning.

"Alicia," I declared to her amused, appreciative beauty, "I need you to get on the horn and see if you can get eyes on Linfield's Oak Grove. I need a sitrep on the tasting arena ASAP. Anything your sources can tell us, we want it." And establishing authority and authenticity, I added, "Understood? Ten-four?"

She smiled and fired off a smart salute, "Yes, captain."

"*Comandante*," the other three corrected.

With everyone assigned a task, I calmed. But to have a chance, I needed to thaw my congealed sinuses. Therefore, questing, I hobbled to the bathroom.

The Balinese-styled, wood medicine cabinet held only an array of medical gauzes, likely for Aori's *butoh*.

On my return, the brothers were comparing routes on their phones, Alicia, to my surprise, was on hers, while Aori was missing.

I called out, "Aori, where art thou? I need to add coffee to your quest."

"Coffee?" she asked, ducking out from behind a refrigerator door.

"Yes. Beans. Ground or whole. Anything to neutralize this abused appendage." I waved my palm at the black-and-blue, swollen, oozing volcano I'd once called nose.

"I got this, *comandante*," Aori declared, throwing, with speed and accuracy, a small, dark bundle.

I extended a hand for the catch. It thumped into my chest and fell to the floor.

It was a bag of coffee.

I picked it up and stared at the stylized golden kitty sniffing a mug of coffee. The rising steam declared it to be Nine Lives of Nirvana, a brand of *kopi luwak* and roasted by Sweet Butt Roasters out of Binji, Sumatra.

"Will that do?"

"It will indeed." Opening the bag, I peered in. Being not a pretentious twat, I'd never had civet cat pooped coffee, but more importantly, "What's the word on wine?"

Aori, hand cupped to her mouth, swaying from the fridge's door as if on the deck of a befouled ship, called out, "Got some something, *comandante*. But no red. No red."

"Well, it best not be that Sauvignon Blanc shit."

"Nay, *comandante*, it be tainted like with blood." She hoisted a half-empty bottle of something pink and horrific, White Zinfandel.

"Bring me the harpy's piss. It'll need do."

Aori arrived with the bottle and the brothers, agreeing on a route, echoed one another, "*Sí. Sí. Sí*," while Alicia, hanging up, swore, "What a weasel-faced prick."

"Saunders?"

She nodded, though expounded no further.

I began to ask, but Aori arrived, handed me the half-bottle of harpy's piss, and, taking Alicia's hand, pulled her away, saying, "Let's talk."

Grimacing a sigh to the ladies' backs, I observed, "'Tis better than accursed water."

As Aori had previously, I tore the cork free with my teeth and spat it into the corner.

Taking a big swig, I swished and gargled with the floral, jam and cran sweetness.

I swallowed and, so condemned, lowered the congealed mass of my nose into the bag of *kopi luwak*.

I inhaled.

I pictured the bench.

I enveloped myself in the solitude, the tranquility *sans* novitiates.

I gathered my focus, collected it, centered it, and concentrated it.

I inhaled again.

I pictured the dueling table and the presented glasses.

I reveled in the raging music clawing my ears raw.

I bathed fully, completely in the vultures' ravenous rending of buffalo's carcass.

I rejoiced in the stench of rotten Roquefort and moldy meat.

I envisioned my triumph.

I manifested the outcome, its magnificence—me victorious, an f-ing Caesar, Buddha, or... The pristine spring afternoon was shattered by "*Ride of the Valkyries*" raging the air.

Yanking my nose from the cat poop coffee, I declared to the vindictive heavens, "For my sins the avenging angels did descend."

Ignoring my phone vibrating across the coffee table, I joined the troupe rushing to the western balcony's railing,

A party bus, confetti, balloons, and a champagne bottle oozing bubbles stenciled on its side, wheezed to a stop in the lower parking lot.

"Okay," I declared, panic staining my voice as the American version of mini-Nazis (less leather and more swastikas) poured from the bus, "new plan."

The diminutive marauders, as if they'd done reconnaissance, were coordinated. The vanguard beelined for the house, burst through the front door, and poured in. A second squad descended on the Carapaz's El Camino, puncturing its tires with red-handled screwdrivers.

"*Dios mío*," Egan cried, shaking his head, as Julio placed a comforting hand on his shoulder, "poor Pablo."

"Come get some, you unholy bastards!" Aori screamed, shaking her sparrow fist. "Come get some!"

Once done with poor Pablo, they raged into the house.

I repeated, "New plan."

Everyone stared, as a splinter group surged up the hill, fell upon Alicia's sedan,

"Uh, new plan?"

Cringing at each *pop* and *hiss* of a tire, Alicia asked, "Are you asking or telling? Because—" "*Ride of the Valkyries*" died and the day collapsed into a grave of silence. "Because we're waiting for you to lead us."

Shouting exploded from below and we spun back to the railing.

The marauding horde from the house, having found it empty, joined those charging up the hill.

We turned to one another, each echoing the other, "New plan," as the first few exploded through the downstairs door, and clattered up the stairs.

Chapter Thirty-Four
NOOKIE ON THE SIDE

The John Deere, my foot aching against its pedal, was topped out at 35 mph. Highway, 99W was crowded with Sunday traffic. Alicia and I, of course, were the root cause of most of it. And plenty were passing, eyes bulging, fists and phones directed our way, letting us know it.

Aori and the brothers, fleeing in Halen, had distracted the mini-Nazi horde.

Alicia and I, on the infamous tractor, escaped through the vineyard, plowing through the thick patch of shrub, dodging a few pines, some more successfully than others, and swerving out onto the highway.

Across the median, headed in the opposite direction, the party bus, mini-Nazis dangling out the windows screaming over the Wagner, pursued Halen.

Based on our superlatively poor mathematical skills, we had roughly seven miles, or twelve minutes, before our arrival on the outskirts of McMinnville. No matter how long or short it actually took—"Hey, you idiots, get that piece of shit off the road!"—it was going to be an annoying ride.

Alicia pressed herself closer and asked past the wind, the hum of the tires, the honking, and heckling, "What are the Crushed rules about being late?"

"Regardless what you call it—forfeit, disqualified—I lose. Late is late."

"Not even a five-minute window or something?"

"Crushed prides itself on discipline. Giacomo Salvatore, a two-time world champion, was fond of saying, 'Lateness is being slovenly with god's gift—Time.'"

"Shit," she sighed, "the bastard sounds like my father."

The next few minutes were spent in relative silence. Well, we were silent, the rest of the world, however, was a cacophony of curses, honks, and humming.

The tractor's gentle rocking, the steering wheel rubbing my thighs, and Alicia's proximity had created an awkward and unwanted stiffness, as a distraction, I asked, "So, why'd you return?"

"To warn you."

"About?"

"About everyone knowing your location after high school poop party' went viral. That's—pun intended—some funny shit."

"It is. And thank you for the warning."

"I should also warn you, this tractor ride is making me horny."

"You too?"

"What?"

"What do you mean?"

"What do you mean, what do I mean?"

"Horny."

"Oh, right. My first boyfriend of any consequence worked on a farm. And, well—" She slid a hand further around my waist and, scooting back, dropped the other between us and her legs.

"What are you doing?" I asked even though it was obvious what she had in mind and her hand. "Alicia now is—"

"The perfect time to repay me."

"Oh, under the table?"

"Broken bottle doesn't mean broken promise, does it?" She squeezed. I bit my lip. And my phone rang.

From a pajama pocket, I struggled it free, and informed, "I'm going to answer this."

"Go ahead. Just don't mind me." She, moaning softly, continued her manipulations.

I'd lost Naomi's first, few sentences, but had caught up as she confessed, "They've agreed. I've got the contract up on the screen now."

"Naomi, I'm sorry. I can't—"

Alicia's lips returned to my ear. "Is Naomi cute?"

"What?" I asked, bewildered, though mostly aroused.

"They've agreed to three months for a first draft."

"Didn't I tell you? There isn't a manuscript. There's nothing."

"I disagree," Alicia squeezed, "that's something. Sort of." She squeezed more.

"You did," Naomi agreed, "but the Crushed tell-all? They want that."

"And I want," Alicia ran her tongue around an ear, nibbled the lobe, and gripped me tighter, "us three entangled and entwined."

"Now is not—"

"Where are you? Was that a woman's voice?"

"Just send the contract. Send whatever."

"Dixon?"

"Just send it. Okay?" I hung up, lifted my aching foot off the pedal, and, ignoring my unfinished sentiments regarding time, steered the Deere into the overgrown shrubbery along the highway's shoulder.

We only lost a few minutes, but they were precious minutes, both in satisfying our desires and in making it to the TOD.

Alicia and I continued pulling, plucking twigs, briars, and grass from our hair and clothes, when the Valkyries returned.

"Please, don't tell me—"

"Yep," Alicia confirmed, "party bus."

Trying to pound more speed from the Deere, I stomped the pedal. The epileptic needle jitterbugged more, but the tractor didn't dance any faster.

Behind us horns blared, closer and closer.

A briar bit a hip and in my panic I, again, answered. "What do you want?"

Radcliffe, foregoing his standard, went off script, "Dixon, you Crusher, where are you?"

Ignoring the camaraderie, the slur to his words, I countered, "Where are you?"

"I, my friend, am at that damn tasting thing, where you're not. And need to be."

"Well—" I glanced over my shoulder.

Alicia gave me a peck on the cheek.

Aori had taken Halen's helm. Laying heavily on the horn, OM bellowing like a foghorn, she glided through the confused knot of traffic.

The party bus was only four or five car lengths behind. A few min-Nazis, the most enraged, remained *Mad Max* style, swaying from windows. Most, however, were amassed around the driver, waving middle fingers and feigning slitting their own throats.

"Give me that," a gruff voice cut in. "Belltower, you need to get that skinny ass of yours here. Now."

"Sheppard? What are you doing with Radcliffe?"

"He was nosing around the winery and... Just get your ass here. We're verging on a Cockfosters."

"A Cockfosters?" My fear didn't diminish with the repetition.

"Yes, please," Alicia sighed into an ear, returning her hand to my fore.

"St. Fer's rallied the mainstreamers to his cause and is assigning board positions right and left. A few of your hot-headed Malbecians are ready for a revolution, so, well, yeah, the fate of Crushed depends on you getting here."

"So, I don't have to win?" I asked, hopeful. And there'd be solace knowing I'd saved the competition, even if I lost the vineyard.

"Damn, son, are you dense? Of course, you gotta win."

"No, see, I thought—"

"Dixon?" Alicia pulled her hand from my fore and tapped the speedometer. It'd dropped below 25.

I pressed my foot down; the Deere gained speed, slowly, begrudgingly. "Belltower?"

"Five, six minutes," I swore, as we lumbered past the Welcome to McMinnville sign, "and if not—"

Over the Valkyries, the sirens screaming, Sheppard answered for me, "You best keep driving until you find a deep, dark hole to hide in."

Aori, with the party bus pulling alongside, kept Halen's course true and the brothers prepared to be boarded.

The bus, however, followed Alicia and me as we sped in a gentle curve off the highway through traffic and into a quaint residential section of town. Behind us, the party bus plowed through the snarl of honking, skidding, crashing and crunching.

What the tractor lacked in speed, it made up for in agility, at least compared to the party bus and the squad cars caught in its wake. After the first few corners, I, more than Alicia, comfortable with the screaming of metal, had stopped glancing at the destruction amassing behind us.

Exiting through a backyard fence, freeing three white, miniature poodles, and a Pomeranian, and dragging a length of chain-link, Alicia shouted something.

"What?" I yelled over the dogs' yapping. "What?"

Her words were lost beneath a metal *screech* as the tractor's bucket gouged a crevice from a green Subaru.

"What?" I repeated as the chain-link wrapped around a stop sign, was torn loose. "What?"

Somehow we'd lost the bus and the poodles, though the Pomeranian, angrier than ever, remained. In the relative silence, Alicia asked, "Are you laughing?"

A block in front of us a squad car, lights flaring, sirens blaring, turned a corner. I made a hard right, lumbered us onto a set of railroad tracks.

I, a bobble-headed doll, tears streaming down my cheeks, replied, "A-a-and c-c-crying."

"C-c-crying?"

"Y-y-yes."

"W-w-why?"

The tracks crossed a roadway, became less severe, and, over the honking, the curdled cry of the Pomeranian, my reply was audible, "Because this is the most fun I've had in a long time I just don't want it to end, but I know—"

We returned to the tracks, the bouncing and thundering.

Not wanting to wallow in the sentiment of my statement, I turned to the practical, "D-d-do y-y-you s-s-see t-t-the u-u-university?"

Alicia stood, gripped the roll bar, and searched for the university as we bounced along. "N-n-no, n-not ye-ye... W-w-wait." She tapped my shoulder and pointed toward a brick building with a gleaming white cupola. "The-the-there."

We turned off the tracks and aimed for the building. The vision of racing through campus *Animal House*-style on a tractor with a beautiful woman had me garnering another erection.

Alicia, however, seeing the gleam and glee, directed with a forefinger, "Park it there."

"But, Alicia, we can—"

"Park it."

Dutifully, and disappointed, I parked the Deere behind a pair of industrial-sized, dark green dumpsters.

"I wasn't going to run anyone over," I pouted as we dismounted. Yanking the crutches from the bucket where they'd been weighted down with an old tire, I added, "At least not on purpose."

Linfield was a small, private university of venerable, red brick buildings on 189 park-like acres with nearly two thousand students. Besides the wine industry, the university was the town's brightest jewel in its crown. Once a year it would host the International Pinot Noir Celebration, aka IPNC, which, behind the UFO Festival, was second in civic celebrations.

Alicia raced and I hobbled around a corner and into a shadowy service alley between two lecture halls. We stumbled to an immediate stop. Blocking the alley was a bowling team huddled and hunched together as if in prayer.They all wore black, short-sleeved bowling shirts with red and orange piping. Over two crossed, flaming pins, in Russian red, Cyrillic lettering, was written Vlad's Pack.

They were actually dipping fingers into a jar and... "Goddamn it, Mort, chunky? Seriously?"

"Stan, that's all they had. Kids must love the smooth shit, because—"

In unison, they turned.

Beneath peanut butter mustaches, they sported white plastic, vampire fangs. They growled and snapped viciously.

I waved, and Alicia, already spinning and running, grabbed my arm and tugged me along as handfuls of peanut butter splattered the walls behind us.

The pack howled and chased.

Leg flaring with pain, I hobbled faster.

They neared and I, over a shoulder, threatened a crutch at the pack. They howled and gnashed their teeth more.

Turning back, Alicia had inexplicably stopped.

I plowed into her, and we tumbled into a pile at the feet of the six young men who'd stepped from the shadows.

They, like Vlad's Pack, were also in uniform. Theirs, however, was more somber and austere. Black practical shoes, slacks, belt and short sleeve, button-down shirts with a white Hospitaller cross emblazoned on the pocket.

Looming over us, they scared me more than the pack, which growled on arrival as the Hospitallers surged protectively around Alicia and me.

The stoutest of the six, a short Thor, commanded, "Brother Quentin, take them. Go."

A tall, skinny brother extended a sweaty palm, "I am Brother Quentin. Please, come with me. I shall lead you to the tasting."

Stan, with a great, blood-curdling howl, charged headlong into the brothers. The others, howling, joined the fray.

Following Brother Quentin, we dashed up a short set of stairs into a building.

"Sister Kelsey," he explained over the hollow echoing of our footsteps, "strayed. She'd been seduced by dark forces to do questionable things for much money."

"Isn't that how the world—" Alicia punched my shoulder. I fell quiet.

Bolting from the building, we hurried down a flower-lined path and into another brick building. We took a quick left and Brother Quentin pointed toward a set of sun-brightened doors, "It's just beyond—"

The doors were flung open.

We skidded to a stop as mini-Nazis poured in, and the hallway filled with the ungodly sound of Wagner.

"Belltower!" they screamed. "Belltower!"

I'd relieved myself in the briars after tangling with Alicia, so what ran down my leg was negligible.

Alicia confessed, "I just peed myself."

Before I could commiserate, Brother Quentin urged, "This way."

We turned a corner and found more pouring in through another set of doors.

We backed away as a voice slithered along the hall's walls, "Belltower, come out and play-ay."

I turned to Alicia. "You don't have your gun, do you?"

"You frisked me pretty good in the bushes, you'd know if I did."

"I did, didn't I?" She smiled. Sunlight from the mini-Nazi choked doors glinted, sparkled through her hair, and highlighted her lips and eyes.

"Goddamn," I confessed, "you're beautiful."

The horde, as Alicia and I gazed at one another, took up the eerie challenge. "Belltower, come out and play-ay. Belltower, come out and play-ay."

I'd call 9-1-1, but I'd lost the phone, or so I assumed, during the frolicking.

"You ready to do this?" I asked, handing Alicia one of the crutches.

"I am," Brother Quentin replied, doing a flurry of karate moves. They'd been done with such conviction I believed he believed he knew karate.

I did know standing next to such inspiration (Alicia, not Brother Quentin) I was prepared to fight for the possibility of frolicking with her again.

Gripping the crutch, I took a few practice swings. "Oh, yeah," I admitted, grinning and giving Alicia a wink, "this feels good. Real good."

She and Brother Quentin, as the mini-Nazis neared, backed away.

Channeling my most magnificent Aori, I screamed, swinging the crutch, beginning to spin on the boot, "Come get some, you unholy bastards! Come get some!"

The horde hesitated.

I twirled and twirled. "Come get some! Come get some!"

They didn't.

Growing dizzy, my spinning wobbled, tottered. Soon, with a shout of warning from Alicia, I staggered face-first into a wall.

Brother Quentin flashed more karate at the horde, though his exclamations, "Karate! Karate! Karate!" undermined my previous conviction.

Alicia, while I jabbed the crutch at the encroaching horde, pulled me to a corner and admitted, "I've always wanted to do an Alamo."

Before I countered why "doing an Alamo" was a horrible idea, shadows sprung from a derelict archway as a brisk volley—*pop pop pop pop pop*—of corks crackled the hallway.

Mini-Nazis collapsed to the floor, writhed, and groaned in pain, as the stench of champagne filled the air.

Stunned, the world fell quiet and still.

Another volley of corks rang out—*pop pop pop pop*.

More mini-Nazis collapsed and joined their comrades in writhing and groaning.

A grizzled, old man stepped into the light, "Will you get your asses moving? Please?"

"Sheppard?" Alicia and I stuttered as the other codgers—Ogden, Bennett, Fulton, and Wheeler—joined him, along with... "Radcliffe?"

"Hey, mate. Bloody good times, yeah?" Synchronized and in unison, they fired—*pop pop pop pop*—another volley. "Bloody good times."

An ominous, peanut-buttered howl joined the Valkyries.

I spun on Alicia, "Don't say it. Don't."

But she did. "Alamo."

Chapter Thirty-Five
ONCE MORE, IDIOTS, INTO THE BREACH

Nearing the Oak Grove, hounded by Vlad's Pack and the mini-Nazis, Sheppard encouraged, "Keep shaking, people. Keep shaking."

Two of Brother Quentin's brothers, Brother Samuel and Brother Neil, had joined us. They'd even ransacked an Argyle winery booth, resupplying us with three cases of bubbles. However, their vows forbade them from using weapons, so they were relegated to shaking and removing the foil and cage on the bottles.

Aghast and confused, I stared. The Oak Grove wasn't another ironically named dingy, dive bar or seedy night club, but exactly that, an oak grove.

It was disconcerting.

I slowed as the wolf of my anxiety knocked on the door of my straw house.

"What's the problem, Belltower? Keep moving." Sheppard gave his bottle a few quick shakes, pointed it around, and scanned the crowd.

Our escort, covered in champagne and peanut butter, took up defensive positions at a nearby table. The brothers prepared bottles, while Ogden gave a few pack members a Morpheus hand invitation to come get some.

They growled, bared and gnashed their teeth.

Alicia, after taking out another over-eager pup, accepted a primed bottle, her thumb straining against the cork, "Dixon, what's wrong?"

The other brothers had arrived, and she'd been denied her Alamo. Though... "Dixon?"

"No. No," I swore, "This is insanity."

But it wasn't. It was a pleasant grove of old oaks casting dappled shadows across a grassy meadow. And the meadow had been transformed into a wine tasters paradise. Forty or so round banquet tables were scattered about, each crowded with tasters. Encircling them were three dozen vintners offering their most select vintages.

Though, as the outraged and surprised faces attested to, our arrival had compromised their paradise.

At the heart of the tranquil scene, at a silver bistro table, sat the handsomely moussed and sockless asshole, St. Fer. He chatted with three preeminent Crushers, Reginald Octavius Thorndike, Mallory Wise, and Sebastian Moncrieff, all were part of the "mainstream movement."

I'd only competed against Moncrieff, once. He'd edged me in a quarterfinal at the 2017 Dubai Scalding Sands Classic, 22-20.

"No," I declared, shaking my head. "No."

Where was the German death metal? Where are the videos of fornicating wildlife? What of burning baklava? This, particularly the Wisteria-laden air, was repellent and unacceptable.

Sheppard's scruffy cheek scraped mine, making the memory of Alicia's all the sweeter. "Belltower, what's the problem?"

"What," I asked, my heart Taiko drumming my ears, "is everyone doing here?"

"Word got out about the duel between you and Frenchie. So—" He shrugged.

Losing at a competition was ignominious enough. And, if an early round, a solitary endeavor, only disappointing yourself or those foolish enough to have bet on you. This? This was too much. Much too much depended on too little—me.

Everyone was here.

Liza and Troy in matching dark jeans and a white dress shirt held hands at a table. I understood Liza leaving St. Fer, but why had Troy visited me?

Megan and Sara, with Nathan and the Enrights, shared a table and bottles of something light and white. Megan, repeating her act from Poop Party, gave me the middle finger.

The high school assholes, Gregory and Amanda, Jennifer and Scott, and a few others, crowded two tables scrunched together. They were angrily miming slashing throats and shooting me.

Matt and Kevin, I was happy to see, were at The Yes Squad's table. And there was Alicia.

"No," I declared. I'd find a cave, likely in Greece. I'd become a hermit. I'd... Alicia, champagne bottle cocked on a hip, smiled, winked, and mouthed, "Blackberries."

I smiled wanly and recalled her and the brambles along the side of 99W.

Going *Glengarry Glen Ross*, Colin shouted, "Always be closing, Belltower! ABC! ABC!"

But I wasn't closing, I was losing. Losing my nerve, which meant I'd lose the TOD and the vineyard and, subsequently, Alicia, who'd run off with that weasel face prick Saunders.

In the background, backlit by emergency lights, a stern-faced Officer Jenkins, spearheading a cadre of state troopers, forced the handcuffed Aori and brothers Carapaz through the crowd.

Hanson Smythe and his I-LOBers scrambled from their table, armed themselves with champagne bottles, and marched for Jenkins.

The codgers, bottles in hand, followed by a case carrying Brother Quentin, joined the I-LOBers.

"Mr. Belltower," Moncrieff called out, "we're waiting."

"Bloody brilliant," Radcliffe declared, vigorously shaking his bottle, following Sheppard.

Alicia, suddenly at my side, nudged me in the ribs with her bottle, "You okay?"

"No."

"Mr. Belltower, are you forfeiting?"

St. Fer straightened from his feigned slouch of ambivalence.

Silence engulfed the grove, everyone leaned forward and waited.

I'd never been cast as a villain, regardless of how many times I'd auditioned for such.

Mother had explained, as my rant on the shortcomings of my physique ended, "You've a soft, feminine visage, Dixon. Embrace it." She handed me a glass.

After I'd surmised, "Rioja Reserva," she added, "Accept your limitations and exult in everything else. Otherwise—" She'd shrugged and poured more.

"Dixon?"

"He," I declared, having decided on something, spat into my palms, and slicked back my hair, "is going to bring the ugly and give everyone *il bacio della morte*." And before Alicia asked, I explained.

She, a mischievous smile dancing on her lips, agreed, "Okay, let's bring the ugly."

"Mr. Belltower?" Moncrieff insisted.

Alicia flicked her thumb. The cork exploded from the bottle, screamed off an oak, and, at the end of its trajectory, died in a few awkward, hops at Moncrieff's feet.

To the delight of all, Alicia emptied the bottle over me, kissed me quickly, slapped me hard, and walked away, decrying, "You might like it in the ass, but you, ass, can't treat me like one."

Bubbling rivulets of golden foam fell from my chin and sparkled down me and the ground around. The briar scratches burned, and the soaked pajamas gripped my groin.

Ever observant of such humiliation, Scott called, "Dixon's gone commando!"

I tugged and, after a few quick yanks, the turtle's head returned to its shell.

My doom imminent and more apparent, a few others had gathered to ingratiate themselves upon St. Fer.

Professor Magaldi, during improv exercises, would advise, "If you've not gone too far, you've not gone far enough." After Sue Morgan dropped drawers and, using her tampon, scrawled in blood on a wall, "Jesus is God," the professor had placed a few caveats on her statement.

Regardless, I tore at the pajama's breast pocket and exposed the hairy nipple undulating behind it. Thanks to a thorn's tear, I yanked at it and exposed the other.

"So, Ro-Ro," I observed, walking to him, swaying hips, pinching nipples, and licking lips, "I see you still got the toadies licking your sugar-sweet britches."

Moncrieff, amused, shooed the toadies away, as I squeezed harder and added, "Isn't that right, Liza?"

An "Ooooohhhhh" rose from the crowd, and I mimed lapping water from a bowl.

The pack howled and Troy started from his chair. Liza caught him and coerced him back into it.

Thanks to Alicia, the string quartet broke from Brahms into an inspired, thrumming version of Blutnacht's *Die Neunte*.

Blocking the sun with a hand, Moncrieff appraised, "Are you, Mr. Belltower, able to compete in such a state?"

Aloha High, sophomore year, our first production was *The Importance of Being Earnest*. Professor Magaldi had magnanimously granted me Merriman on the two Sunday matinees, while Brandon Fisher, a senior, held the other performances.

Wednesday morning, off to school, under Mister J's door, I'd slipped a ticket for Sunday's show.

Dress rehearsal had been that afternoon and returning I'd discovered my old overnight bag on his "Nice Underwear" doormat. I was sure all our old oldies had been buried, so... There wasn't money stapled to a strap. There was, however, a bottle in the bag. Taped to it was a note, which, inadequate, read: *Save the bottle for when you need it most. And we'll have new neighbors soon. Grandma Bubba has exited stage left. Also, we'll need more Wrong Way for next week's Sex. Thank you. —Mother*

My Merriman portrayal was sober and desert-dry. Professor Magaldi had observed, "If you would've done that earlier you'd have had the role for the entire run."

The witches and bitches, each partaking of a glass or two more than their usual, claimed the Wrong Way was my best batch yet. And Shannon had providentially proclaimed, "This is what I want after giving a blowjob."

The secret was I'd seasoned the Wrong Way with tears. And, because Mister J would've approved, I'd incorporated the needed bottle, a Coppola Claret.

I suggested to the abandoned St. Fer, "If the toadies have given up, I got a few hounds out there that'd love giving you a go."

Vlad's Pack, flinging peanut butter, barked and howled.

Pointing a crutch at them, I raised a leg, mimed pissing on all their stupid peanut butter-slathered faces.

Stalking through the nervous crowd, snatching glasses, and chugging them dry, they barked and howled more.

The mini-Nazis, rhythmically bobbing heads, snaked around tables, and gravitated to the quartet.

Sheppard and Smythe had come to an understanding with Officer Jenkins and returned to their guarding table.

"Mr. Belltower..." Moncrieff sighed. "...I ask again—for the final time—are you able to compete in such a state?"

Squeezing my nipples, I screamed at the azure sky, "I am Crushed!"

In the startled silence, I sat, crossed my legs, and flicked a nipple. "Thank you, sir, for your concern, but my state shall enhance the legend of my victory. I am Crushed."

"Very well," he sighed again, resigned, "it's your funeral."

Staring dead Durden into St. Fer, I laughed, tugged a nipple, and declared, "No, sir. It's ours. This shall be a mass grave."

Chapter Thirty-Six
A WINE BY ANY OTHER LABEL

My statement, dourer than intended, had set the grove, already simmering, on a gentle boil. The pack and the mini-Nazis continued roaming the tables, with the occasional skirmish breaking out. Alicia had joined Sheppard and the codgers at their table, while the string quartet riffed on a series of Metallica classics.

Moncrieff, with a wary eye on the growing chaos, explained, "With Mr. Sinclair's untimely passing, for your TOD, we've decided to utilize the wines he'd selected for the final round of the world championships. A fitting tribute, don't you think?" He glanced between St. Fer and me. "That is, if you're amenable?"

Ignoring the dark, smoldering hole of sadness in my heart, I squeezed a nipple and refocused my Durden.

St. Fer just nodded.

"Excellent," Moncrieff exclaimed waving to two servers, who, each carrying a tray with three tasting glasses, marched our way.

On their arrival, unsure of the significance of recognizing them, I de-Durdened, "Kris, Norris, you two get around, don't ya?"

Kris, with a wink, licked her lips, "Hey, lover, how you doin'?"

Moncrieff, perplexed, asked, "You know these two?"

"Vaguely," I admitted.

Kris countered, "Only in the biblical sense."

Norris, disgusted, shook his head, while Kris, leaning, whispered, "Don't worry, Romeo, you and your weak, wet rope are safe with me."

"You mean... We didn't?" I asked, still unable to recall what we'd done or hadn't.

"Right," she said, smiling and shrugging, "No pokey, pokey. It happens."

Moncrieff, eyeing the seething crowd, sighed, "Very well. Let's begin."

Sitting up, getting into character, I glared, "A variant of thirty-seven."

Moncrieff gave Kris and Norris a look. They hesitated. St. Fer continued ignoring the world and frowning at his ankles.

"You know, Ro-Ro," I said, commencing my homage to Art, "I've always wanted to—"

St. Fer glanced from his ankles, stared forlorn with uncertainty.

I'd been there, so many times, and not just after getting fingered by an Italian border guard. I glanced at Liza and Troy and understood a portion of it. So, rather than continue about his mother's mouth and butthole, I fell silent.

St. Fer though, needing a bag to punch, demanded, "Always wanted to what, Dixon?"

"It's nothing, Ro-Ro, let it go." And suddenly desiring to get started on my sad, shitty future, I added, "Now, let's get this fiasco over with."

Moncrieff nodded and Kris and Norris stepped forward, while St. Fer, a latent beam of insight sparking his eyes, asked, "It was about my mother, wasn't it?"

"No," I lied, a mischievous smirk undulating my lips.

Lunging, St. Fer screamed, "*Mort á tyrants!*"

Thanks to the other night, I anticipated such. Jumping from my chair, I dodged his swings and blindly kicked. Again, the boot chimed his groin's bell.

He collapsed, rolled, and groaned on the ground, while Moncrieff, shoving me away, swore, "Goddamn it, you animals. Goddamn it."

Kris and Norris tried scrambling out of the way, but stumbled into one another, spilling their trays.

Moncrieff cursed more, and I hobbled to a nearby oak. I pressed my back against its rough, aged bark, as my heart and breathing escalated uncontrollably.

Thanks to our antics, the grove, highlighted by the sharp popping of champagne corks, resounded with hooting, hollering and howling.

Concentrating on the stringed, German death metal, I closed my eyes and attempted to calm myself. Instead, I realized Sheppard was correct. The grove tottered on a monumental Cockfosters, which meant I was that much closer to losing everything.

The rubbing wasn't helping. My heart and lungs kept climbing and climbing.

Above the din, a voice asked, "You okay?"

"No. No, I'm not," I admitted to Alicia, opening my eyes. "I think I'm having a panic attack."

"Dixon," she said with a firm smile, "I thought you claimed to be a Crusher?"

"I am."

"Well then, say it like you mean it."

"I'm a goddamn Crusher."

"Yeah, you are. Now, what are you doing on your toes?"

"Oh, right." I dropped my heels and explained, "A bad habit."

"How about," she said, stepping closer, "you make kissing me a habit?"

I smiled, we kissed, and she joined me against the tree.

Moncrieff had rallied his troops and, with an insistent hand, called, "Mr. Belltower, if you will?" He indicated the table, the wines prudently poured and placed, and where a standing St. Fer glowered.

"Kick his ass," Alicia advised.

"Kick it?" I said, my Durden returned, "I'm gonna eat it."

"You, Crusher, can do whatever you want with it." She pecked me on the cheek and hiked back to the codgers.

The quartet transitioned to classic Wolfsmond. The mini-Nazis formed a mosh pit between the mini-burger food cart and the betting kiosk. And the pack, resupplied with peanut butter (creamy), slathered themselves more and feigned fornicating in their preapproved style—doggy.

"Mr. Belltower?"

The mini-Nazis sang, the pack howled, peanut butter splatted, Alicia smiled, and resigned I hobbled to the firing squad.

Moncrieff, as I arrived, was explaining to St. Fer's scowl, "You're quite correct, *monsieur*. Two of the wines were replaced."

"Why?" St. Fer asked.

"It won't be a problem, will it?" Moncrieff sounded worried, but I wouldn't know about what.

"No," St. Fer replied, shaking his head, "No. Of course not. It's just—"

St. Fer fell into a pensive silence, and Moncrieff, around an accusing glare at Kris and Norris, explained, "The remaining ounces in those bottles was..." He waggled angry air quotes. "...'lost.'"

"Lost," I taunted, elbowing my Durden back to life, "is what Ro-Ro's gonna be when I'm done with him."

"Don't," Moncrieff swore to St. Fer before he could counter. "I'm also invoking an Ice-Nine. So sit and be civil."

An Ice-Nine, the term garnered from Kurt Vonnegut's seminal work, *Cat's Cradle*, was a clause in the competition bylaws that an overseer invoked if a Crusher should disrupt the proceedings or commit other egregious offenses. Punishments varied, though could be as severe as a lifetime ban. It was an effective way of ensuring civility during competitions.

"Gentlemen, you understand the implications?" We nodded. "Then take your seats. Now."

Done Durdening, St. Fer and I did, and the grove quieted, some.

Moncrieff, without further ceremony, placed the timing clock at our elbows, pressed the red button, and declared, "You've five minutes."

Singing softly—*"Küsse gab sie uns und Reben, Einen Freund, geprüft im Tod"*—I squeezed a nipple and reached for the first glass.

My mind, my palate, regardless the exposed nipples, the peanut butter and champagne-rarefied air, switched into taste mode. The long hours of conditioning and training on that poor, scarred bench, in Art's oasis would reap... nothing. I tasted nothing.

How could such effort lead to such agony?

I sipped again. And, again, there was nothing.

Not even an elongated, aggressive slurp elicited the remotest hint of dry grass, peppercorn, baking spice, or surly, dark chocolate.

The barbarous snacks, particularly the wasabi tainted trail mix, the White Zinfandel, the tractor exhaust, the blackberry brambles and scratches, and my coagulated nose, had me and my palate discombobulated.

And though I knew the man who'd selected the wines, I also knew he could be a conniving bastard. For the world championship, Art would've been all the more conniving and bastard-like. I loved and missed him the more for it.

Wine one remained unresponsive and, with remorse, I betrayed it for number two. I sipped, slurped, swallowed. Ah, yes, there was... perhaps a hint of dark cherry?

Abandoning two, I turned to three. It was a medium gold that sparkled like sunshine through honey. And on the nose... Maybe citrus peel, apricot or honeydew?

I, rookie in a preliminary seeding round, glanced at the timer. Sure I'd learned I'd lost a minute thirty-five, but it'd enflamed my apprehension. Rookie. Rookie. Rookie.

Having exchanged her champagne bottle for a glass of something medium purple, Alicia encouraged with a thumbs up. Mouthed, "You got this."

Shaking my head, I placed the barrel of a forefinger to my temple, and pulled the trigger.

The mini-Nazis sang, the pack howled, and my high school assholes applauded, shouting, "Bravo! Bravo! Encore! Encore!"

Desperate to ignore so many assholes, I returned to the wines. This time though, to attune my palate, I ventured past the bench, the park, and sweet kitty to my roots—speculating in Rorschach non sequiturs.

In a rising mantra, I whispered "Pigs riding a dung beetle. Pigs riding a dung beetle."

St. Fer, though he'd been scribbling steadily on the answer sheet, seemed tentative and unsure.

I added another. "Santa bears playing patty cakes."

He leaned back, perplexed.

I explained, sort of, "My first taste of love, Rutherford Valley."

"Over-oaked cabs," he muttered, "typical."

I laughed, "One doesn't choose a first love it chooses you." St. Fer, shaking his head, returned to frowning at his scorecard, and I added another, "Dominatrix ballerina bat."

Turning to the one I needed to love now—wine one—I whispered, "Please, Sugar, dance for me."

It was medium purple and reminiscent of something from the Northern Rhône, likely near Tain-l'Hermitage.

The shadow interrupting me, however, made me question everything as it declared, "Goddamn, Belltower, you're beautiful."

Before I thanked her, Alicia straddled me and shoved her tongue in my mouth.

Our tongues tangoed across a frozen dance floor, slipping and sliding around and around.

Over the hooting, the hollering, something in me, an Antarctic ice shelf, cracked and broke free. I gripped her, pulled her closer, and kissed her deeply, desperately.

She did the same.

Before we'd lost all propriety, Moncrieff admonished, "Ma'am, Mr. Belltower, I cannot have you—"

We broke apart, gasping.

She dismounted and declared, "Win or lose, Belltower, I'll be in your bed."

"Ma'am, please?" Moncrieff shot a stiff arm and finger toward the "exit."

Before I noted I'd not have a bed, a house, or much else if I lost, she'd returned to Sheppard's table.

To my forlorn pout, Moncrieff observed, "You've two minutes, Mr. Belltower."

Desperate, I sighed, "Pippi Longstocking clones bumping butts," and, to my annoyed chagrin, once more entered the breech.

The wines remained uncooperative, but my palate, thanks to Alicia, had been aroused from its dormancy.

I'd never gone head-to-head with St. Fer. Sure, I'd seen him compete plenty of times, but this was the first time sitting across the table from him. And there was something odd about him, about his tasting demeanor.

Yes, he remained sockless, but he seemed, as he tapped his scorecard, less self-assured. He tapped it a few more times and, with a disgruntled sigh, placed the pen down.

Moncrieff, the dirty executioner, announced, "One minute! One! Minute!"

That minute, an eon of drowning in cold amber, was slow, arduous torture.

Regardless my desperation and desire, my frantic sipping and slurping only elicited the vaguest of clues to the wines' identities. And, to my great disappointment, the glasses held only so much. Too quickly, they were empty.

Resigned, I scribbled a few problematic assumptions when the alarm, dull and final, chimed.

Over the crowd's raucous clamor, Moncrieff admonished, "Mr. Belltower, you know better." With slow determination, he pulled the scorecard from under the pen. It, a blind razor, left a jagged blue fault line across the cream colored paper until it pecked the table.

St. Fer, smirking, handed his card to Moncrieff, "Merci, monsieur."

Holding the scorecards aloft, Moncrieff shouted, "The fates of men rest within."

A thunderous round of howling and barking, accompanied by the wet splatter of peanut butter, resounded throughout the grove.

Dodging around the brown splatters, Moncrieff marched to the judges' pavilion, a white plastic table hastily relocated under a hastily erected silver tarp behind a taco cart.

"If you lose," Alicia noted, returning to my lap, "you won't have a bed."

"No," I admitted, finally letting go the instrument of my demise, the pen, "I won't."

St. Fer stared at the white stripes of his bare ankles, while the grove had descended into a precarious World War I Christmas truce. It only meant, as the captains sipped Kirschwasser and fabricated stories about their loves back home, the privates were digging deeper trenches and sharpening bayonets.

The quartet, in preparation for the inevitable, transitioned to Dagger Patrol's acid jazz classic *Klagelied für die Dinosaurier*.

Moncrieff, the grove hushing and shushing, returned with the sealed scorecards.

Alicia, *tinking* my glass, pecked a cheek. "We don't need a bed, we've always the bushes."

Howls and wolf whistles accompanied her back to Sheppard.

Moncrieff, wearing a compressed smile, brandished the envelopes overhead.

The grove stilled.

The strumming softened.

"Mr. Belltower, your score—" Moncrieff tore the envelope open and pulled the red pen corrected scorecard out. Past a smirk and a condescending shake of the head, he declared, "Nine!"

It was a sorry, shitty score. The crowd, at least the few rooting for me, groaned with disappointment. It was one thing to lose a duel getting out tasted, quite another to crumble under the pressure.

With a gleeful flurry, he opened St. Fer's.

Empty envelope waving overhead, the grove on its tiptoes, he announced, "And Monsieur St. Fer's—" Moncrieff's brows, as he chewed back a gasp, bunched and furrowed. Confused, he turned to the judges.

The grove did the same.

The judges, stern and stalwart, though embarrassed, a king to an executioner, nodded.

St. Fer's newly rediscovered smugness withered.

A deep, perplexed whisper, curious serpents, ran through the grove.

"Your score, Monsieur St. Fer..." Moncrieff took a deep breath, stepped back, and sighed. "...nine."

The grove, expecting, wanting, needing resolution, exploded in shock and disbelief. The pack howled as champagne corks singed the peanut butter-laden air. The quartet, caught in a masochistic loop, thrummed, angrier and angrier, until the cellist, eyes rolling back into his head, collapsed.

Moncrieff, sensing the tenuous nature of the grove's seething, hastily withered back to the judges to convene.

More than relieved, I was perplexed. I'd plenty of excuses, plenty, but St. Fer? Had my foot dislodged that much?

A few of St. Fer's allies shouted encouragement. His glare, regardless of his appreciative wave, spoke of sour brooding.

Alicia, back on my lap, our tongues cha-cha-ing, asked, "So, what happens now?"

"Well, usually—" I started, but Moncrieff, a Baptist preacher, arms raised and waving, cut me off, "Silence everyone! Silence!"

The bubbling grove returned, reluctantly, to some semblance of silence.

The cellist, finishing a second cup of water, regained his seat,

The last jars of peanut butter were opened, while champagne bottles were defoiled and shaken.

Moncrieff, as Alicia stood, started her exit, cried, "As per addendum seventeen of the official, international Crushed rules concerning tied TODs, we move to an A.U."

Most the grove, like Alicia, needed an explanation.

In all my competitions, I'd never participated in an Angry Unicorn. Though, of course, I'd witnessed a few. They were a basic TOD but with a preselected bottle for the winner-take-all battle.

"That's it?" Alicia asked, disappointed.

Rather than get into the intricacies of bottle selection and the adherence to statistical randomness of the allotted stockpile, I observed, "You sound disappointed?"

"Well," she shrugged, "it's not quite overtime game seven, is it?" I started a rebuttal, but she cut me off, "Just kick his ass, you can explain your outrage afterward." She gave St. Fer a quick, hard smile, kissed me, and, to more howls and wolf whistles, returned to Sheppard and the champagne-shaking codgers.

Having dismissed Kris and Norris, a glass in each hand, Moncrieff, a Lipizzan stallion, strode to us.

Fatigued at feigning indifference, St. Fer and I sat up.

A reverent hush curled itself into the grove's nervous lap.

Moncrieff placed the glasses before us. They, like Art's championship trophies, were ancient gladiatorial drinking glasses, with brass knuckles incorporated into the stem. Though rather than handblown, these were heavy, stamped things. Each filled with a wine dark as death.

The grove closed in, edged closer, closer.

A surly crow squawked its discontent.

It exploded in a cloud of obsidian feathers.

Ogden sucked briefly on the frothing bottle, tossed it over his shoulder, and called for a replacement.

In the feathered aftermath, without more pomp, Moncrieff declared, "You've three minutes. You may..." He pressed the red button. "...begin."

Sliding my fingers into the brass knuckles of the glass, I held it to my nose. This time, I discerned hints of actual aromas, sweet red fruit, tar, and spices. Hoping to be taken to the answers I didn't know I knew, I inhaled deeper.

Before I sipped, St. Fer had tossed back the entirety of his glass and, with a cursory slurp, scribbled his answers.

The grove inhaled a gasp, exhaled in surprise and appreciation for such panache. Trees swayed, limbs shivered, and a slight flurry of excited leaves peppered the air.

Such surety and confidence confounded me. And, given his performance on the previous wines, it was unexpected. Was it a ploy? Was he playing it Dopey, stealing my role? Or something more nefarious?

I pulled the glass back.

Twice in my career, I'd done the same—feigned surety. And only because at the initial sniff and slurp I knew I didn't know. Such quick assessment was false bravado, a ploy, luring the other into misguided assumptions and fatal errors. Neither opponent had made such errors. And each time I'd been beaten and humiliated.

However, with St. Fer, there was something I never had.

He smiled. Indeed, there was bravado, but also a deep sense of... there was no other word for it... surety.

Most knew St. Fer cheated, but just because you know who the murderer is doesn't mean you don't need to prove it.

Ignoring the boiling grove, I pulled my eyes from the *petite merde* and tried concentrating on the wine and not my imminent demise. It was red. It was... I looked back at St. Fer. He was good, but not that good. This wine was confused. It wanted to be something it wasn't and could never be. It strove for magnificence but would remain pedestrian, inferior. And yet that did not mean it should be dismissed so expediently, as St. Fer had, particularly with so much at stake.

The quartet, choosing a less frantic rhythm, though keeping with Dagger Patrol, transitioned into their metal ballad, *Süße aus der Hölle*.

Vlad's Pack flung, howled, and humped more, while, to my disappointment, in an eerie *déjà vu*, Moncrieff announced, "Two minutes. Two. Minutes."

Automatically, eyes closed, as Alicia resettled on my lap, I cha-cha-ed with her sweet... Her tongue had been poisoned, with Pinot Gris.

"Sweetheart," I gasped, "I appreciate—"

"Mother," an outraged voice screamed as Sara, wiping her mouth, patted my cheek and, smiling coquettishly, whispered, "You're welcome."

Megan twisted Sara off me. Perplexingly, she plunged her mouth upon mine. Her tongue was tainted with a caustic Sauvignon Blanc.

"Megan," Sara swore, "I'm neutralizing his palate. Though—" She winked and nodded toward my groin's soldier slowly standing to attention.

"My palate—" I stammered, as Sara's lips returned to mine. Her hands held firm my head as my eyes searched for help.

Alicia raised her glass, mouthed, "I'm so jealous," and feigned wiping tears away.

Megan, again, flung Sara aside. She leaned but was yanked away by... "Liza?" St. Fer and I echoed.

The ladies glared.

"Catfight!" a pack member yelled, as howls, mad and maniacal, erupted.

Alicia, as Sheppard refilled her glass, continued wiping away nonexistent tears.

Megan glanced at Alicia, and Liza shoved her into Sara and planted a sloppy kiss on me. I stammered protests, as Liza planted a hand between my legs, and fondled and squeezed. "Oh, how I remember where you used to stick this."

Megan, pushed back by Sara, grabbed Liza, who firmly gripped me.

Anchored as she was, Liza didn't go gently but took me too. Nearly vertical, Liza released. I collapsed into my seat as the ladies grappled as if in a judo competition.

"Catfight!" the pack yelled. "Cat fight!" The quartet strummed and the mini-Nazis moshed, while gobs of peanut butter splattered around.

St. Fer stared at his ankles and chewed a lip.

This time the tongue was tainted with a sublime Barolo, likely a Gaja. I'd need more to distinguish vintage or if it were Conteisa or Sperss. Regardless of such curiosity, I pressed the culprit away, "Not now, Troy. Not now."

"So," he said, sipping deeply from his glass, "you're saying sometime?"

"What I mean—"

Troy's mouth returned and I, as we separated, discerned Conteisa, 2015.

Moncrieff, amused, declared, "One minute, Mr. Belltower. One minute."

"Either way," Troy declared, standing, "we'll always have Petrus, Petrus, Petrus."

Before I asked for clarification (had I recalled the night incorrectly?), a shriek shattered chaotic cacophony.

For an instant everyone, everything froze.

Kris, through the crowd, wine-stained and peanut butter slathered, ran shrieking—"He's mine! Mine! All mine!"

The gathered parted like a commanded sea.

I turned to Alicia.

She hoisted her glass and smiled.

The codgers, along with Sheppard and Radcliffe, luridly and lewdly thrust hips.

"He's mine! Mine! All mine!" She screamed and, flying squirrel style, launched herself onto Sara.

Sara, joining in with her banshee wail, backpedaled as Kris, extending her tentacles, grabbed Liza and Troy—"Mine! All mine!"

Megan, confounded by the spectacle, undecided whether to assist or flee, was mowed over. She, with the others, writhed in a congealed clump of gooey limbs on the ground.

Moncrieff, as the crowd's blood lust rose, held out a hand and kept St. Fer from joining the fray.

I clamped a palm over my glass, as a brown blob crapped across St. Fer's knee. He turned a disgusted eye to Moncrieff.

Moncrieff dunked a forefinger in, licked it. Over a few crisp, crunching chews, he declared, "Extra chunky Skippy," and then observed, "Thirty seconds, Mr. Belltower. Thirty. Seconds."

My nose, blood diverted to my groin, had cleared and the wiggling parade of tongues had rejuvenated my palate. And the grove's seething, though not quite animals fornicating or a bloated carcass being devoured by carrion, was chaos enough to work with.

I sipped and slurped. The soft, subtle wine rode the blind merry-go-round of my mouth, round and round. It was the most enigmatic wine I'd ever tasted.

"Twenty seconds, Mr. Belltower. Twenty. Seconds."

The grove had descended into a primordial Cockfosters and I, *diablo*, loved it.

"Fifteen seconds, Mr. Belltower. Fifteen. Seconds."

I took the last mouthful and slurped. Beyond the dark cherry and ripe plum, it was missing the tannic tartness of a young wine, although...

"Ten seconds."

...it had structure yet lacked layers.

"Nine."

Tragically, it reminded me of someone.

"Eight."

Fighting my tears, furiously writing, I answered.

"Seven."

I answered and remembered.

"Six."

A pencil tucked behind an ear, smiling up from a crossword.

"Five."

His crisp laugh at learning he'd have none of my holes.

"Four."

I wiped my eyes, placed the pen down, and swore, "We are Crushed."

With the grove frozen in anticipation, Moncrieff counted the final seconds, "Three. Two. One." He collected the scorecards and, before marching for the judges, took a moment and scanned them.

The grove buzzed with excitement.

Glancing between St. Fer and me, Moncrieff held them aloft.

The grove gasped, held its breath.

"The competition," Moncrieff announced, "is completed."

The grove, realizing a verdict hadn't been announced, stormed forward, clamoring for resolution.

The codgers and I-LOBers fired off a series of warning corks into the turf. Spraying bubbles like riot hoses, they established a precarious perimeter, and, bottles at the ready, Sheppard *et al* escorted Moncrieff to the judges' table.

Radcliffe, spraying a few pack members back, swore, "Bloody brilliant this is, mate. Bloody brilliant."

A convoluted frown twisted St. Fer's lips as he asked his ankles, "Who is that British twat?"

I smiled and realized I no longer blamed him for destroying the life I'd wanted with Liza. He was the nearest prince inclined to save the damsel from the ogre. Besides, considering the Alicia-gleaming future, I'd likely need to thank him.

Regardless, if Liza and Troy hadn't, my destroying him and his world would hurt him more than him destroying mine. And for that, I tried not to rejoice, too much.

"Belltower," he asked, "that smirk? *Pourquoi*?"

"Just know I'm sorry."

"And," he glared, "you should know, I don't care."

Maybe, when I too was a multi-millionaire, I'd join him in not caring. As it was, I needed some self-comforting. I wandered fingers to a nipple and caressed the hairy nub. And, hoping he never discovered how fate had ravaged him, I squeezed.

Alicia, Radcliff, Sheppard and the codgers, coupled with the Hospitaller brothers and the I-LOBers, held a precarious defensive perimeter. The grove, under such vigilant surveillance of loaded champagne bottles, had quieted and quelled into a simmering stew.

At Mort's insistence, the quartet had returned to *Klagelied für die Dinosaurier*, though a much-sedated rendition.

The contorted knot of Kris, Sara, Megan, Liza and Troy, since they'd not descended into an orgy or bloody brawl, had been separated. Each, a stranded starfish, lay sprawled across the champagne-saturated grass, gasping for breath.

The betting kiosk, already inundated by the confusion caused by the first-round tie, became overwhelmed and the three blokes operating it fled in fear. A squad of outraged punters chased.

Kris, snarling at her fellow starfish, crawled toward me, sniffing the ground like a hunting hound. Licking her peanut butter-slathered lips, she crunched nuts and neared.

The grove—what form of entertainment was this?—deepened its quelled quiet.

St. Fer, wolfish grin grown on his broad lips, lifted his eyes from his naked ankles and asked, "Belltower, why are all your bitches crazy?"

Alicia, not hearing St. Fer's comment, just sipped, smiled, and waved.

Confused at St. Fer's American-toned vernacular, I sat up to ask, but Kris swayed to her feet, stumbled to me and stage whispered, "Oh, sweet Dixon, if only—" She pressed a peanut butter, grass-covered finger to my lips, kept me from protest. "No, don't. Don't. Just know we'll always have Wash-A-Kari." Removing her finger, she kissed me with a surprising amount of tenderness and walked away, "Aloha, sweet Dixon, Aloha."

She spun back. "And don't tell anyone, Norris and I put Molly and acid in the water." She winked and placed her slathered forefinger aslant across her lips. "Shush. Shush."

Well, that explained most the chaos consuming the grove. People were high and not on the heady optimism of good wine.

Kris, a drunken, giggling sprite, skipped off to Liza and Troy, hugging a tree and groping it and one another. Squirrels excitedly chattered overhead.

Alicia, with another mocking toast, mouthed, "Thank you," and sipped.

Déjà vu gripped me as Megan, trailing a sincere middle finger behind her, pressed Sara and Nelson through the crowd.

The judges' deliberations, rather than a quick few minutes, had lingered past the ten-minute mark and Sheppard and company's perimeter was becoming untenable.

An elevated electric whisper buzzed the grove as Moncrieff, a perplexed look percolating his face, walked from the judges' table. He slapped the envelopes against a thigh. He stopped and, to the grove's consternation, returned to the judges.

I didn't know the judges; neither had I seen them on the circuit. Each, dark-haired, dark-eyed, wore, besides an official, lemon-yellow, Crushed judge's blazer, a stern Derden. Likely they were hired guns to keep this TOD as honest as possible. Perhaps that explained St. Fer's constipated grimace, odd, inconsistent accent, and poor first-round score?

The electric whisper returned as Moncrieff abandoned the judges. Weaving through the champagne-wielding border guards, he called out, "Silence! Please! Silence!"

He didn't get it.

He tapped Sheppard's shoulder.

After a series of well-aimed corks, a showering of bubbles, he got most of it, begrudgingly.

"And," Moncrieff added, "for God's sake, have some decorum. Please?"

Ogden took out another crow, while Wheeler, through the haze of dazzling dark feathers, pinged a cork off Stan's thrusting buttocks as he feigned dogging Mort.

The grove, a volcano's gurgling caldera caught beneath a blizzard, gradually, quelled.

"As is custom," Moncrieff noted, eyes blazing for someone to challenge him, "we will proceed in reverse order. Therefore," he nodded to St. Fer, "you, monsieur, are first."

"*Oui. Oui. Bien sûr*," St. Fer acknowledged, annoyed, "Go ahead."

"Monsieur St. Fer," Moncrieff announced, opening the envelope and removing the scorecard, though not looking at it, "your score is two."

Everyone, even the quartet, asked, "What?"

"Talk about," someone, me, observed, "dropping a deuce, that's a shit score."

Shedding the initial shock, St. Fer jumped to his feet and grabbed Moncrieff by the cravat, "This is an outrage! A conspiracy!" The hand not gripping Moncrieff flailed at the judges, "That's a Mouton. A Mouton Rothschild! A 1985!"

"Monsieur St. Fer," Moncrieff sighed, shaking his head, pulling his cravat from St. Fer's fist, "I'm sorry, but it's not."

"*Putain*." St. Fer swore, circling in a tight circle, "*Putain. Putain. Putain.* It is. It is. It is. Can they not read? Or maybe you—" He caught himself. His circling slowed, though he kept with, "*Putain. Putain. Putain.*"

Had he seen the bottle? But when? It would've been masked before arriving at the grove or had someone informed him before its masking?

Regardless of the nuances of the deceit, he knew his error.

"*Oui, monsieur*," Moncrieff agreed, "the bottle is a Mouton Rothschild, 1985." St. Fer stopped as the grove fell silent. "Though what is in it is not."

Confused, like all, St. Fer stammered, "What? How? I mean—"

Placing a hand on St. Fer's shoulder, Moncrieff declared, "*Je suis desolé, monsieur, mais*... Ice-Nine. I'm sorry, truly, but Ice-Nine."

The grove gasped and returned to its previous howling, peanut butter throwing, and mosh pit ways.

St. Fer, however, with a defeated nod, slumped into his chair and stared between his sockless ankles at the growing puddle of spent champagne.

"Therefore," Moncrieff continued, turning to me, "with great pleasure, I can announce Mr. Belltower the winner."

The sharp *pop pop pop pop* of champagne corks filled the air as the wet slap of peanut butter resounded all around and the quartet sang, "*Alles ist in Ordnung mitten in der Nacht, wenn die Wolken kommen, um den Mond zu töten.*"

I'd planned, lest the universe deemed retribution be swift and severe, on refraining from celebrating. But, after the past week, I couldn't.

Pinching nipples, I jumped to my foot, kicked the air a few times (karate-style) and screamed, "Take that, Fate, you snivelling twat!" I then hopped around, hugging people and drinking everything offered.

Slathered and lathered in peanut butter and bubbles, I fell into Alicia's arms.

"Damn," she said, handing me a glass of a giddy, little Lambrusco, "is that a banana in your jammies or are you just happy to see me?"

"Both," I replied as we collapsed against an oak and kissed. "Both."

Chapter Thirty-Seven
A DANGLING, LITTLE EPILOGUE

Having woken alone and made the usual pot of cat poop coffee, it was another existential morning. I was out on the loft's eastern balcony with my first cup, contemplating the vines languishing in the morning sun, when Naomi called.

Every few days, her day done, sipping something insipid—Pinot Grigio or IPA—she, incredulous, would call wanting the truth to another sordid incident.

"She beat her up and then married her?" Considering Aori's perspective, I wanted to invert the statement. Regardless, somehow, after all the evidence, Naomi, like me, remained incredulous.

"How could the captain condone such behavior?"

"Seriously, a blowjob from a friend's mother?"

"You got sick in your father's urn?"

Considering *The Yank*, of course she had suspicions. Ironically, this time, what seemed fiction was fact.

After I'd posted bail, Radcliffe, before returning to the UK, had spent a week, ten, twelve hours a day, interviewing me. The Baskerville bastard had quickly discovered my kryptonite—deep dish and red wine.

Therefore, where I'd considered obfuscating or simply lying, I hadn't. Instead, I'd told more truth than expected.

Like Naomi, Radcliffe would call to confirm facts and ask for specifics, and more detail.

"Mallorca was 2016 and Milan 2012?"

"The Italian border guards? Brindisi? 2006? What were their names?"

Thanks to my babbling, especially when reveling in a *grande crus*, Radcliffe, hamster on a wheel, was churning pages out.

Lidia and Ganymede, regardless the impracticality, had wanted *Crushed* in stores before the world championships, hence Radcliffe's hamster impersonation.

However, they'd been rescheduled for some time after harvest, late October or November. The Ice Winers and the other late harvest lot complained, to no avail. None were listening, as all were arguing over the location. There was also the issue of ensuring another "St. Fer Fiasco" didn't recur. Needless to say, the entire organization and community was consumed with distrust and accusations.

The first Tuesday of July had found me mildly lamenting the silence of the vineyard and I'd gone looking for community in the Crushed forums. The website's welcome page, however, had been revamped. Rather than random metal music playing while snippets of obscure films and documentaries flashed, a still and silent bottle graveyard loomed.

Bottles of various shapes were buried upside down, leaving only a portion of their label exposed. The foremost bottle, a standard cabernet, had a message on it: *Due to the lack of coherent governance and proper oversight, we the undersigned, with much regret, though with greater hope, have negotiated with Empty C Productions for the exclusive worldwide rights to administer Crushed. From hence on they are fully responsible for all and everything regarding Crushed, not limited to licensing, broadcasting, competitions, et cetera, et cetera.*

I'd bypassed the legalese and found the undersigned. They were four dozen of the world's most vaunted, respected, and preeminent Crushers.

The note ended: *We hope you, the Crushed community, understand.*

A few did; most didn't.

Some, I'm sure, like me, wondered why they hadn't been asked to sign. Regardless, the message boards and forums exploded. Everyone wanted a piece of the money pie and many claimed authority to sign papers and or be the spokesperson or something.

That night the website went dark, Error 404 dark.

Nearly two months later Crushed remained offline, both as a website and as a competition. It was sad but not unexpected. And if one adhered to the concept of three, I'd lost a girlfriend, a father, and so why not Crushed?

I'd mentioned the Crushed dysfunction to Naomi, and, like me, she wasn't surprised. And Lidia has yet to mention anything to Radcliffe, which, when she asked, I supported with vindictive glee.

"So, Ms. Waters," I asked, standing out of the glare and returning inside, "what needs confirming today?"

"Oddly, nothing. Just a hello."

"Really?" I scoffed.

"Well," she admitted, "Lidia is curious how your homework's coming."

In preparation for the recalibrated spring release, I'd been instructed to "increase my online footprint and social media presence."

I declared, "I'm diligently and dutifully contacting the most noted wine professionals around the globe."

She laughed. "I'll come up with a better lie. But nice attempt. So, how's Alicia?"

"She returns next week, Thursday."

"And," Naomi asked with a curious curl to her question, "where will she be staying?"

I hesitated.

A day after my sentencing, Alicia had returned to DC to ostensibly "teach a weasel-faced prick a new trick or two."

The time apart granted us the opportunity to talk. We'd agreed, as we floundered for discussion worthy subjects, we preferred frolicking.

"Currently," I answered, "we're leaving that TBD."

"And the Kelsey thing? That's not weird?"

"It is. And it isn't."

Alicia one night, on one of our regular weekly calls, each sloshy from drink and desire, had asked, "You were going to propose to her?"

"At Chez Shea."

"*Gesundheit.*"

After the requisite, "Thank you," I'd tumbled into a convoluted metaphor regarding the multiverse and walking through a transitional doorway, from one me to the next, finishing with, "It's not the time involved, but the distance, the dimensions."

She'd then said the three best words I'd ever heard: "Forget the past."

Oh, how I wanted to, though Moncrieff might have other plans.

He, using the envelope containing my scorecard, had tapped my shoulder as Alicia and I separated from our kiss. Past an unctuous smile, he'd observed, "You know, Mr. Belltower, your score was interesting. Very interesting." His smile grew and, laughing, he turned and walked away.

The conniving bastard disappeared into the chaos bubbling the oak grove and Alicia had observed, "You're not going to tell me what he meant, are you?"

"I can't, because I don't know."

"But you could speculate."

"I could, but it'd do us no good."

"Okay. So what do you have in mind instead? To do us good?"

I'd taken her hand, led her through the throng (snatching Mort's jar of peanut butter along the way), and, breaking into a vacant dorm room, placed her upon the bed and said, "Here, let me show you."

I topped off my mug of *kopi luwak* and rubbed where the monitor had chaffed my healed, though atrophied ankle, raspberry red.

For "reckless endangerment with a motorized vehicle" coupled with a few other various violations, Judge Stapleton granted me six months of house arrest. I'd also been shackled initially with a three-month sobriety ruling.

"That, Madame," I'd proclaimed, "is excessive and—"

"Make it four," she'd announced with a solid *thwack* of the gavel. "Would you, Mr. Belltower, like to make it five or six? An entire year perhaps?"

Recalling the snap of a rubber glove, the sloppy, wet kiss of cold lubricant, I acquiesced, "No, judge, I would not."

I exited the loft as Naomi asked, "Okay, what's wrong?"

"Nothing." I seemed as surprised as she at the word and added, "And that's what's wrong."

"Well, that makes sense."

"And that's what's weird. I'm not worried. About anything. I'm actually excited. About everything."

Yes, I was apprehensive regarding harvest, as the Brothers Carapaz were currently in a holding cell somewhere, but Maria Hernandez, Miguel's sister, an immigration lawyer and business associate of the Enrights, assured me, after filing the affidavits of support, and a few other documents, "The brothers will be released soon enough."

"Excited? About everything?" Naomi asked, rightfully dubious. "Even the ugly f-word?"

We each hated the future but for distinctly different reasons.

"Short term, yes," I pressed the button and the elevator's door sighed open.

"Good. About time, right?" I laughed and agreed, and she added, "Now, get establishing that online presence. Okay?"

"Yes, ma'am," I grumbled, placing the mug in and pressing down.

"You better. Otherwise, I tell Boonen and all the others where you are."

The moment we'd finalized the contract she'd threatened such disclosure. And without equivocation, she'd assured me she was serious. I believed her.

The thing was, the winnings from spanking St. Fer had bolstered my bank account to breaking and I'd paid Boonen off, ASAP.

The man, in my estimation, had been oddly downcast on receiving the funds. "Boonen is glad for you. Less so for Katrina." I'd considered asking a few thousand questions, but knew I'd likely dislike the answers. So, again ignoring the future, I'd said, "Thank you. And if ever I need something, I'll think of you."

"Boonen," he sighed breathlessly, "would like that. He's happy to give you anything."

After such a curious, heartfelt admission, I'd mumbled a more awkward thanks and hung up.

As intimidating as Boonen was, it was the other competitors (Mochi, Sangria Bob, Helga Gotlieb, et al.) rounded up in the raid I was worried about. I unsure they'd believe I hadn't conspired with the gendarmes. They could, should competitions resume, make my life a marble in a blender. Therefore, remaining incognito seemed prudent.

"Now, off you go. And we'll chat later." Naomi hung up, and I found myself wrestling a familiar opponent—silence.

Tucking the phone in a pocket, me and my atrophied foot limped down the stairs.

The issue with Naomi's amorphous assignment, "establishing an online presence," meant being online. And, honestly, I didn't feel like adding to the Internet's existential cesspool. I'd send an email to a wine blogger or book reviewer, but would invariably, transition to watching cats riding turtles and autonomous vacuums.

Collecting the mug from the elevator, I turned and confronted the facility, its deep, somber hollowness, the stage and chairs, and their dire expectancy.

Aori, having kicked two officers in the groin, wouldn't be fulfilling such an obligation soon. She'd received six months in the local, minimum-security prison. Her incarceration had afforded her and Mother the opportunity for reconciliation.

On a video chat, Mother, amusingly, had admitted the same of Aori—she trying to kill her. They, a bit too long and sincere for my comfort, had laughed. Though in the end, each had agreed the fasting, the seaweed enema, and, particularly, the ayahuasca, had facilitated their paranoia, the visions of murder and human sacrifice.

Each echoed the other, "We'll be stronger for it."

They'd been so convincing, I feared they'd rehearsed it. Regardless, to my chagrin, I'd agreed to attend their rescheduled wedding.

"Winter solstice?" Mother had suggested, while Aori chimed in, clapping, "Oh, my goddess, that would be amazing. Yes. Yes. Yes."

They'd broken into planning and I, not needing to be entangled in their dysfunctional vortex, had queried a wedge, "And father's ashes?"

"Mixed it with poi," Mother had confessed, "fed it to a pig, slaughtered and barbecued said pig for the luau."

"The big ass party," I whispered.

"Yep. It was so delicious everyone wanted the recipe." She laughed and added, "Jesus, Dixon, of course, we didn't. We'll do it when you get here, as a family."

"The poi and the pig? Or?"

"I'll leave that up to you," she laughed more and, blowing kisses, disconnected.

"Aori?" I asked, confused.

She'd waved a dismissive hand, "Oh no, son, I agree with your other mother, it's your choice," and she too disconnected.

Mother remained in Kauai, preparing the retreat for Aori's return. Thus, I'd found myself alone, making cat poop coffee in the mornings, baking pizzas for dinner, and sipping wine until it was howling time.

Speaking of howling, from the sullen, cool shadows, where a few empty barrels lingered and I'd set up a little bed, a strident *meow* resounded.

Besides making coffee, one of my morning tasks was feeding the newly arrived queen, Claudette.

On the third call and the promise to never visit their store again Beren had let me speak with Hakim. He'd agreed to the task. With the help of a few thousand Euros, and, to my surprise, Beren's assistance, they'd been able to work magic. And, after a few visits to the vet, they'd, with a gleaming blue passport, had shipped her over.

She, stretching, yawning, sauntered out and looked around.

"Hey, sweetheart, how you doin'?"

I'd tried hosting her in the loft. The height and relative opulence, however, had befuddled her, so she'd accepted the facility's cool expanse and obliged me with the use of the stage.

Settling on its down left corner, I reached under, extracted the bag of kibble and a small, silver bowl. I shook the bag. Blinking and wobbly with jetlag, little kitty scampered over.

She nudged an ankle and I apologized, again. "Sweetie, I know it's not ham or butter, but this is healthier. I think." I shook some kibble into the bowl and placed it on the floor, before Her Majesty.

After a sharp look of consternation, she got to nibbling.

I tucked the bag back under the stage and groped the shadows for the bottle I'd opened the night before, a Sokol Blosser Pinot Noir. With the other palm, I petted Claudette and whispered, "It's going to be okay, sweetie. It's going to be okay."

Thanks to the Italian border guards, Fabio and Lorenzo, I'd been introduced, post finger prodding, to *caffè corretto*. Rather than air-plane-fuel grappa as they'd glugged in, I topped off the coffee with a quick pour of Pinot.

The Feds, as they'd returned the cellar's contents, hadn't been apprised of my sobriety ruling. Or, as Alicia had pointed out, "They had, they just didn't care about you or the local authorities."

I sipped and poured a bit more.

Even though I didn't understand *butoh*, I'd felt guilty about dismantling a space where sacred work had occurred. And, after a cathartic howling session with a bottle of luscious Rafanelli Zinfandel, I'd begun cobbling together a new stand-up routine, titled "To-i-Let."

Standing, shaking my arms, rolling my head around, warming up, I walked around the stage and its inverted noose.

Claudette eyed me and returned to her kibble.

Naomi, as expected, had been supportive, "I think it healthy and proactive. Take advantage of the buzz and exploit it while you can."

However, having won millions on a poorly blended wine I'd created long ago, hence Moncrieff's insinuation, I felt it inappropriate to mention I'd become less invested in *Crushed* and was considering a sockless life of lethargy.

How Art had acquired the Mouton and why he'd incorporated it in the championship and at such a pivotal point, I didn't know. And likely never would.

The sadness, thanks to Kelsey, I knew would dissipate. And thanks to Alicia and little Claudette kitty, I'd realized one can find hope. Ignorance, well, that would linger. Such knowledge didn't help.

Topping the ignorance list was the Paris installations. Yes, videos of the Eiffel Penis, the hairy Arc de Vagina continued circulating, but stories regarding probable culprits, like 12M, had ceased. Even the French right-wingers had moved on to complain (again) about the price (too low) of Spanish wines.

The initial hysteria had been undermined as the penis and the asshole had been dismantled. The Arc, however, had become a rallying point for a women's movement demanding the vagina (in the French language) be designated feminine, thus *la vagina* and not as it was *le vagin*, masculine.

Not unexpectedly, Saunders has been silent regarding the French and their outrage. Alicia had promised to return with a full sitrep.

And Bussy? I'd called, but the woman's sultry, prerecorded voice had only noted the number was no longer in service and nothing more.

And the UK terrorist accusations? Naomi assured me Anderson at Home Office had assured her as long as SloPony42 didn't resurface the investigation needn't go further. I was past the melancholy of losing another alter ego and so mildly pleased.

St. Fer's lawyer, Dominic Stroud, a hard man with a soft face, had insisted on meeting in person. Unlike the Enrights, he'd only brought himself and a compact, silver, military-grade computer slung over his shoulder. The similarities to Saunders were unsettling.

Settled into a chair at the coffee table, I on the couch, he vigorously punched my bank account information in, and I'd asked, "So, where's Ro-Ro crying baby-style?"

Concentrating on his task, Stroud said, "I'm not at liberty to say."

"But you don't deny he's crying baby-style?" Stroud leveled his stern blue eyes and pressed a button. I added, as my account blossomed with a seven followed by half a dozen zeros, "Well, let him know, I'm happy to kick his ass any time he wants. I think he likes it."

With a curt nod and playful smirk, Stroud replied, "I'll indeed do that."

I'd also, because it was likely a nail keeping St. Fer on his cross, asked about Liza, Troy and Kris. They'd, if memory served, had followed Alicia and me through the throng, into the building, and a dorm room down the hall.

"Vanished," Stroud claimed, snapping the computer shut and standing.

"Vanished?" I asked, suddenly staring at the bulbous lump of his groin.

"Would you like me to repeat myself? Or can I leave?"

Smiling, I joined him in the vertical, and said, "Both."

Our eyes, angrily, tangoed and he, adjusting the computer over a shoulder, declared, "They've vanished," and marched off. The loft's door shuttered shut and, after a moment, his Audi churned gravel on its escape.

The most infuriating item of my ignorance was Heavy Breather. There were suspects, but none particularly plausible nor with a particular motive. Therefore, the mystery lingered. And only once had I considered it Death, predictably breathing down my neck, though too lazy to do so in person. Such an asshole.

And thanks to the quiet solitude afforded by incarceration, I'd had time to reflect, more than I'd desired.

During a saunter through the vines, I'd recalled something Kelsey claimed her grandfather, Anton, had said, "A smart dog knows when to ignore a bone."

I though, not the brightest mutt in the kennel, had been gnawing the "What If" bone. It was a hard, fecund piece of frustration and my gnashing wasn't making it softer or smaller but causing it to lodge deeper in gums and throat.

What if I hadn't had that third espresso? What if I'd ordered the *feuilleté au jambons* first and not the *jambon beurre*? What if I'd stayed at Art's wine shop?

The sharpest shard was what if when Kelsey had yelled, "Dixon, wait," I had?

"Dixon, wait."

If I had, everything would've been different. Everything.

What if. What if. What if.

Finished with her meal, Claudette hopped onstage, nestled at a corner, and began cleaning herself. She'd started losing the sharp lines of the street and understood the guilt I was struggling to ignore.

Settling next to her, I gave her a few rubs between the ears, and said, "I know, sweetie. What if. What if."

"Dixon, wait."

I hadn't, and everything remained "different."

Worse, better, it was difficult to say, though likely not for Kelsey, Vlad, the mini-Nazis, or for little kitty here.

It did and didn't make sense.

And I had no choice but to accept that.

Therefore, keeping my heart from wallowing, drowning in melancholy, I found myself with an inclination to return to the stage.

Taking a last sip of the wine-flavored, cat-poop coffee, I set down the mug and stood.

The cold, reverential silence and Claudette's confused eye caused me to reconsider.

Perhaps, rather than fill the void with futile screams, if it were possible, I should try and enjoy it, the silence?

With a sigh, I resettled next to little kitty.

She returned to her cleaning and I, rather than another sip of the mug, melted across the stage. Splayed across the murder and magnificent hanging tree, I stared into the rafters, synchronized my breathing with the cobwebs.

Unlike Claudette, I preferred being myopic, particularly regarding my father.

I inhaled-exhaled with the cobwebs, idly petted little kitty, sighed and admitted, "Dad, I'm sorry, but—" My voice sounded sharp and strained in the stillness. I hesitated.

Kitty, ears twitching, held her head in expectation.

I hated it but admitted it, regardless. "Mom was right. Leaving you was the best thing. If only you'd been abducted by a vampire lord's coven and used as a blood slave. Instead—"

Kitty snuggled into the crook of my arm and doused my burgeoning tirade.

Turning back to the cobwebs, I petted her for a few minutes more, until all that was left was a whisper, "I'm glad I didn't know you better."

Claudette swiveled her eye on me, "Not you, sweetie, my, well, let's call him dad."

Her eye glinted with knowledge and she snuggled back into my arm as I agreed, "Yep, the poi and pig can have him."

Sadly, in the hurt of the admission, I felt better.

I sighed.

The cobwebs undulated.

Claudette curled tighter, purred a little harder, and time, as usual, ate slowly into the future.

A firm series of knocks hollowed through the facility and startled me from fully falling asleep.

Lightly cursing the loss of our reverie, though expecting it, Claudette and I raised our heads.

I scratched her ear as the facility's door yawned open.

She and I exchanged a glance as a shout echoed, "Hello? Mr. Belltower? Hello?"

Claudette stretched, prepared to bolt for the shadows, but, patting her, I reassured, "Don't worry, sweetie, it's neither Death nor novitiates. Just Rapha and a few friends."

The four, silhouettes backlit by the day streaming through the door, slunk into the facility, excitedly whispered and pointed at the equipment cluttering the shadows.

Standing, I waved and, adopting Sheppard's drawl, declared, "About time, you tea drinkers, I've been needing distraction."

They, continuing their whispering and pointing, waved back.

Patting a thigh, I stepped off the stage and encouraged, "Come on, sweetie. Let's go meet our new brothers and sisters."

Claudette wasn't having it. She was locked in on annoyed and suspicious.

"Sweetie?"

She turned, slunk off past the noose, over the murder, when the sharp, electric crackle of a bag ignited the air.

Eye wide with excited expectation, she turned to me.

Through a smile, I fought back a laugh and asked over a shoulder, "Rapha, you brought the kryptonite?"

"I did, sir. Yes."

"Shut it with the 'sir' and crackle bag. Though be prepared for—"

Again the electric crackle ignited the air.

Claudette, tail flagpole firm, bounded off the stage and scampered past to the foursome. Kneeling, they greeted her as Rapha extended a butter-slathered hunk of ham, which she gleefully accepted.

They huddled around her, petting and praising, while, to my surprise, tears crowded my eyes.

I drifted back to the stage, wiped my cheeks and sat.

I stretched out and pulled the mug to me. As it warmed my palms, I stared puzzled at the intimate play being performed before me, realizing I'd finally found home.

Acknowledgements

First and foremost, to Tim and Tammy: No words, likely nothing, will ever be enough to thank you for the support and sanctuary you provided when I needed it. Damn, how I love that beach house. And you guys. ☺   Thank you. Eternally.

To my father, at a family function, handing me a glass, and not understanding the ramifications on asking the most innocuous of questions—"So, what wine is this?" Regardless the Wonderland hole I've gone down, thank you.

To Bobo kitty, jumping from that tree and adopting us was a leap of faith I shall always honor, uphold, and be thankful for. So, my little buddy, thank you.

To Trooper/Trouper/Tru, our little, stray sweetie—far too short, but all too meaningful. We love you. And are far better for it. Thank you.

To family, friends, and various other tiers of acquaintances (likely wondering why I put two cats above them, one of which (such audacity from the little minx) is deceased): You shaped, molded, guided and helped me into me. Somehow, for the moment, the experiment seems to be providing positive results. So, Thank You. Thank You. Thank You.

To my fellows at Powell's Books (Cedar Hills) and the Multnomah Arts Center, we were prematurely separated (two bike accidents will do that), but you've stayed (a bright lighthouse) in my heart ever since. Thank you.

To everyone in the medical and emergency professions, more specifically to those that assisted me on the scenes, at the hospitals, and through my recoveries—THANK YOU!!!

To Francis and the team at 100covers, you were professional, precise and friendly. One could ask for nothing more. Thank you.

To Kayleen at Booyah Creative, you had the insight and creativity to interpret my mushy idea into something magnificent and beautiful. Thank you.

To Rob at Inventing Reality Editing Services, your insights made me realize (and I paraphrase)—It's not about finding the imperfections but shining shit. Thank you.

To the UK border patrol officer that denied my entry, thank you. You hastened a decision that likely would've remained unfulfilled for far too long. Again, thank you.

And to my sweet Lana, after all this, "Will you marry me?" Oh, wait... ☺

And, lastly, to myself I say—"Good job, Cooper. You hopeful idiot, you finally did it. Good for you."

UPCOMING RELEASES FROM EMPTY C PRESS AND M. THOMAS COOPER

Fermented: The sequel to *Crushed*. Belltower, returned to France, is forced to assist the French police in investigating the world's most nefarious wine counterfeiters.

Contemporary Wine-Centric RomCom

42: The reissuing of the underground, cult classic. A man attempts to reunite with his family after they disappear forty-two days after his forty-second birthday.

Psychological Thriller

Harvest: A bad boy chef, hailed as a savior for the survival of an alien species, must save Earth from the impending harvest.

Adult Science Fiction

A Dagger in the Shadows: A theatre loving orc, enslaved to a band of cutthroats and thieves questing for a dragon's legendary treasure, must escape to save his beloved.

Young Adult-Adult Fantasy

Bobo's Revenge: A stray cat returns to an isolated chateau to free his friends imprisoned and experimented on by a mad scientist.

Young Adult-Adult Graphic Novel

Curious? Want to know more?

Visit www.CooperTheWriter.com or www.EmptyCPublishing.com.

www.ingramcontent.com/pod-product-compliance
Lightning Source LLC
Chambersburg PA
CBHW050017120726
47903CB00006B/1803